# By Gretchen Craig

## NOVELS

*Always & Forever: A Saga of Slavery and Deliverance*
(The Plantation Series, Book I)

*Ever My Love: A Saga of Slavery and Deliverance*
(The Plantation Series, Book II)

*Evermore: A Saga of Slavery and Deliverance*
(The Plantation Series, Book III)

*The Bargain*
*Crimson Sky*
*Theena's Landing*

## SHORT STORY COLLECTIONS

*The Color of the Rose*
*Bayou Stories: Tales of Troubled Souls*
*Lookin' for Luv: Five Short Stories*

# *Tansy*

# Gretchen Craig

Pendleton Press

Published by Pendleton Press.
Copyright © 2015 by Gretchen Craig
**www.GretchenCraig.com**

All rights reserved.

Kindle e-book edition available from Amazon.com.

ISBN-13: 978-0692366448

ISBN-10: 069236644X

# Tansy

## Chapter One

For weeks, before she slept, Tansy Bouvier imagined herself dancing with an elegant, handsome man whose gaze promised love and forbidden pleasures — only to waken later in a tangle of sweaty sheets, shaken by dreams of laughing men and women whirling around her, herself in an over-lit circle, alone, isolated, and unwanted.

But this was not a dream. The dreaded moment was upon her, the moment she had prepared for all her life, and she must smile. Maman gave her elbow a pinch, a final warning to sparkle. Tansy raised her chin and followed her into the famous Blue Ribbon Ballroom.

Droplets of fear trickled down her spine as she fought both the dread and the foolish romanticizing of what was essentially an evening of business. A beginning, not an end, she whispered to herself. Time to forget girlhood dreams, time to forget Christophe Desmarais. This night, she entered the world of plaçage in which a woman's *raison d'être* was to please a man, a very wealthy man. In return, she gained everything — riches, security, status.

In spite of the fluttering in her stomach, she found herself captivated by the glamour of the ballroom. Gas lamps glowed like yellow moons between the French doors, and crystal teardrops in the chandeliers sparkled like ice in sunshine. And the music. Tansy's chest lifted at the power and fire of a full orchestra, strings and reeds and percussion propelling the dancers around the floor.

Maman chose a prominent, imminently visible position near the upper curve of the ball room to display Tansy and her charms. Tansy's task tonight was to make a splash, to outshine every other girl who'd entered the game earlier in the season. No, she thought. Not a game. Tonight, Tansy would meet her fate: luxury or destitution, security or whoredom.

What if none of the gentlemen wanted her? What if none of them even noticed her? What then?

"Smile," Maman hissed from the corner of her mouth.

"I am smiling," Tansy replied through wooden lips.

"That is not a smile. Look like you're glad to be here. Watch the dancers."

White men in stiff collars wove intricate steps and turns through the line of women, every one of whom wore a festive tignon over her hair. Tansy squinted her eyes so as to make the dancers and the chandeliers a blur of lights and swirling colors. Such a grand, beautiful sight, as if the most renowned ballroom in New Orleans were not the scene of business and barter.

She had imagined the men as leering and brash. Instead they seemed aloof and slightly bored. The young women, though, were as she expected. They wore masks with bright smiles and welcoming, deceiving eyes that promised gaiety and delight. She was meant to do the same.

"Loosen your grip on that fan," Maman whispered. "It is not a sword to be brandished at the enemy."

Tansy swallowed and opened the fan with cold, stiff fingers. She spied her friend Martine on the dance floor, vibrant in a red velvet gown. How splendid she looked in the red tignon wrapped in intricate folds around her head. She laughed, her eyes sparkling as her partner leaned in to speak into her ear. Martine had already been to several balls and had regaled Tansy with tales of handsome gentlemen who whispered love and promises as they twirled her around the ballroom. She was having a grand time waiting for the right protector to offer for her, but Martine had a boldness, a carelessness, Tansy could not match. And Martine had never been kissed by Christophe Desmarais.

Tansy glanced again at her own yellow silk, the neckline cut so deep she felt indecent. If Martine was a vibrant scarlet tanager, she felt herself to be a mere mockingbird masquerading as a canary. She touched her matching tignon, terrified it might slip on her head. "I'm too conspicuous in this dress," she whispered to her mother.

"Nonsense. No other girl here can wear yellow like you can."

A Creole gentleman, dark haired, dark eyed, no doubt very charming, bowed to Maman. "Madame Bouvier."

Tansy breathed out in relief. She might feel conspicuous, but at least she was not invisible. The gentleman was tall and handsome, his nose straight and long, his brow rather noble. For a moment, she let herself believe this handsome man would fall in love with her, and she with him, and they would dance and laugh and feel drunk with love, together, forever. She wanted to believe it.

Tansy's foolish moment passed. Maman knew every gentleman in New Orleans and the status of his bank account. If the suitor were wealthy enough, he would be encouraged.

After the merest glance at Tansy, the gentleman murmured something polite to Maman, who nodded her approval.

He bowed to Tansy. "May I have the honor of this dance, Mademoiselle?"

With a curious feeling of detachment, she accepted his arm and followed him onto the dance floor. It was only a dance. She liked to dance. She'd let the music carry her.

The gentleman wore an expertly tailored coat of deep maroon paired with gray satin knee breeches. He did look very fine, but more to the point, very prosperous. He smiled at her. "Lovely evening."

*I mean you no harm* she interpreted. *See how nicely I smile? See how I have not once gazed at your plunging neckline, eyeing the wares?*

"Yes," she managed to say. "Lovely weather."

The dance led them near the orchestra's platform. Tansy darted a glance at Christophe, sitting among the violinists. Oh God, he was watching her. Her stomach dropped and heat rushed to her face. For the rest of the dance, she focused a frozen gaze on her partner's ear, and if he said anything else, she did not note it.

At the end of the set, the gentleman returned her to Maman, tossed a bow at her and went in search of more pleasing company. Maman scowled. "If you don't stop acting like a dry stick, I will take you home this instant."

Like the puppet she felt herself to be, she loosened her shoulders, unclenched her teeth, and obeyed. No dry sticks allowed. She would be a willow branch, graceful, pliable. Yes, that was her. Pliant Tansy Marie Bouvier, a willow to be bent to fit her destiny.

Tansy had a moment to collect herself as another Creole gentleman bent over Maman's hand and made the customary flattering remarks. He seemed pleasant, not inclined to devour young women at their first balls. He smiled. No, no fangs, no sharpened canines.

"Monsieur Valcourt, my daughter, Tansy Marie."

He was of medium height, medium build, medium dark hair and medium brown eyes. Not handsome, not ugly. Maman raised an eyebrow. Such a wealth of information in that eyebrow: this man is rich, this man is a catch, and if you know what's good for you, you'll make him fall in love with you.

"Mademoiselle, will you dance?"

Squaring her shoulders, she followed him onto the dance floor.

Tansy's resolve to ignore Christophe faltered and her eyes found him again. His focus was on the music, his brow creased in concentration. She knew men didn't set so much store in a kiss as women, but she would never forget it. She gave herself a mental shake. It was because of that kiss that her mother had dragged her here, two weeks before her seventeenth birthday, to ensure they both understood that Christophe, a mere fiddler, could not afford a beautiful canary like Tansy Marie Bouvier.

Monsieur Valcourt's attention seemed to be on the music, his gaze primarily directed over her shoulder as he moved her through the steps. He danced well. She liked the fact that he didn't try to charm her, nor did he seem to expect her to dazzle him.

They joined hands as they moved into a turn. Her cold fingers warmed in his palm, and his assumption of connection, of ease in their touch loosened her reserve. A comfortable man, this Monsieur Valcourt.

An older gentleman circled through the line to partner Tansy with a turn through the dance. He leered at her décolletage, yellow teeth on display, and he held his mouth slightly open with the tip of his tongue visible. The thought of his tobacco stained fingers in intimate contact with her skin sent a shiver of revulsion through her.

Or else, she remembered her mother's threat. Find a protector, or else face a life of penury, a few years in a brothel until your looks fade, and then what, eh?

The dance moved on and Monsieur Valcourt reappeared at her side. When he took her hand with no leer, no meaningful squeeze of her fingers, she breathed in freely for the first time all evening. The music ended. He bestowed on her an open, guileless smile that warmed his brown eyes.

*Tansy*

Yes, she could live with this man. She didn't need to survey, and be surveyed by, a dozen or two other gentlemen. And if Maman was right, that her looks would assure her any man she chose, then she would as soon choose this one and have it done with. He seemed nice. They would likely have a family together. They would be happy enough.

She allowed herself one last glimpse of Christophe among the violinists. He met her gaze over his bow, and for a moment her vision tunneled so that all around him was hazy darkness, Christophe himself bathed in light. She closed her eyes and turned away.

Perhaps no woman could choose her own fate, but she would take control of what she could. She would be the placée of Monsieur Valere Valcourt.

Tansy opened her eyes and bestowed on Monsieur Valcourt her most dazzling smile.

## Chapter Two
### Five years later

Tansy danced with Annabelle's Monsieur Duval, he of the yellow teeth and dandruff-dusted shoulders. Her friend had skin two shades darker than her own and her wide nose reflected her African heritage, so of course Annabelle had not been able to attract the most desirable of protectors. Even so, she reported her patron kept her in comfort, never beat her, and came to her bed no more than once a week. He'd given her two wonderful children of whom he seemed fond, and she found her life reasonably happy. For that, Tansy smiled at him as he led her around the dance floor.

The new placées-to-be danced all around her, dewy-eyed, round-chinned, and thrilled to be attended to by handsome, wealthy gentlemen. She spied one, however, who was as tense as Tansy had been at her first ball. And now, Tansy was at ease here in the Blue Ribbon ballroom, a woman more than twenty, a woman with a child.

The orchestra took a break. Monsieur Duval returned to Annabelle, and Tansy joined Christophe where he leaned against a column, the picture of languid ease. He dressed as all the musicians did, but on him the black jacket and white linen looked dangerous, the light in his roving black eyes distinctly carnal. She'd noticed more than one young woman eyeing him from behind their fans. But of course, as a man of color, however light, he was admitted here only as a musician.

Christophe handed her his glass of punch and nodded toward her dance partner. "You've made that old coot a happy man tonight."

"Maurice? He is an old coot, but a nice one." She finished his punch and handed him the glass, accidentally touching his fingers. Her breath hitched. They never touched, not since the night before her come-out in this very room. Trying to appear unfazed, she slowly fanned away the warmth in her face.

She eyed Christophe's scraped knuckles. "I see you've been brawling again."

He grinned. "Me? A shining example of virtue for all my students?"

She shook her head. "If they knew you were a brawler, they'd worship your very shadow."

"Don't tell, though. Their mamans and papas would not be well pleased. Have you noticed the Russians?"

"Is that what they are? I'd love to hear them speak."

He gestured for her to precede him. "Then allow me to introduce you."

"You've met them?"

"My legendary fame as a poker player has earned me an invitation to their table after the ball."

"I suppose you will show them no mercy."

With a wicked glint in his eye, he gave her a malicious smirk. "I will not."

They strolled toward the Russian delegation, Christophe's hands behind his back, a foot or more of space between them. She was well aware he took pains not to touch her. It was right that he do so. She belonged to Valere, after all.

"And where is your beloved paramour tonight?" he said.

Tansy stiffened at the slight curl in Christophe's lip. It was a game he played, trying to goad her into defending Valere, but she'd recently begun experimenting with goading remarks of her own.

"He's at the society ball across the alleyway, of course, with his cousins and friends. With the other *gentlemen*." She gave him a withering glance from head to toe to indicate how far he was from the status of gentleman.

Christophe chuckled. "Well done. You'll overcome your regrettable affliction yet."

She was indeed afflicted with an intransigent case of niceness, as Christophe called it. What he meant, she supposed, was that she was dull.

They split to walk around a cluster of people drinking punch. When they rejoined, Tansy fanned her face and looked about with an air of disinterest. "Valere courts a Miss Abigail, I believe."

"Miss Windsor? My fiddle and I played at her birthday ball in January. Pretty girl."

Tansy tilted her chin and looked down her nose at him.

"Forgive me. I have erred. I meant to report that the girl has buck teeth, a flat chest, and mousy hair."

"Indeed you should." Tansy drew her fan briskly through her left hand, in the age-old language of fans an indication that she detested him with all her heart.

Christophe threw his head back in a laugh. He nodded toward the arched doorway. "And here is the gentleman in question."

The slight ache of tension behind her eyes eased as Valere Valcourt leisurely made his way around the dancers, the hundreds of candles in the overhead chandeliers casting a gentle glow on his wavy brown hair. Descended from a disgraced French nobleman who'd been exiled to the wilds of Louisiana a century ago, Valere represented the quintessential Creole, privileged, entitled, at ease in his world.

Christophe slipped away. He had, as far as Tansy could remember, never actually been in Valere's presence.

Valere stopped to talk to Monsieur DuMaine, a man whom Tansy knew to be searching for his fourth placée, having tired of the others. Though he must be very rich indeed to have paid the penalties for breaking three contracts, he epitomized the most dangerous sort of protector in the world of plaçage. There could be no security in an alliance with a man of his reputation.

Martine, clad in her signature red, strolled past the two men, gently fluttering her fan in signal to Monsieur DuMaine. So Martine vied to be number four in this man's serial harem? Tansy did not like the idea of her friend allying herself with such a man. Tansy was no green girl, and the man was handsome, but really — didn't she understand he'd gone through three women in only five years?

Tansy watched Martine's little drama, worried at her friend's lack of judgment, but she was amused, too. Du Maine's eyes tracked Martine as she rolled her hips, touched a hand to her elaborate tignon to call attention to her slender neck, then made her way around the dancers toward the balcony. A scarlet tanager among wrens, she turned at the exit, raised her fan in her right hand to cover the lower part of her face, and flashed dark eyes at DuMaine. Mouth slightly open, he nodded vaguely toward Valere and strode away in pursuit. Tansy nearly laughed aloud at the man's haste.

Valere caught her eye across the room and smiled as he came to her. She put away her nagging jealousy over Miss Abigail Windsor. She had always known he would marry. He needed heirs, legitimate sons. His marriage didn't mean he would abandon her and their son. Valere's own father had raised his legitimate family with his very proper white wife, and yet had remained attached to the same placée for twenty years. She and Valere and Alain were a family now, regardless of when he married.

"Here you are," he said.

"Good evening, Valere." She smiled for him. She always smiled for him.

He stood at ease by her side, surveying the ball room, his glance falling on the group of large, bearish men in their rather rustic fashions.

"Do you see we have Russians here tonight?" she asked. "I would love to hear them speak, wouldn't you? And don't you suppose those heavy beards are hot? I don't imagine they're accustomed to our humidity."

"Russians, are they?"

And that was as much interest in Russians as she could elicit from him. So many other things she would like to talk about. Did the Society ladies dance until they glowed with perspiration? Had Valere danced all evening with Miss Abigail? But of course she could not speak of his other life.

"Shall we dance?" he said.

As Valere guided her around the dance floor, she yielded herself to the music, her mind adrift in the flowing colors of the violin, the oboe, the bassoon.

At the end of the number, Valere whispered in her ear. "Let's go home."

Tansy's lingering anxiety vanished. At least for tonight, Valere desired her, not the pale-faced Abigail Windsor.

Tansy reached for the blanket and pulled it over Valere's bare chest. In an hour or two, he'd get up to dress, then he'd leave her for his townhouse. In the morning, Alain would not even know his father had been there unless she told him. Valere took their son for granted, as he did so much in his life, but he was a good man.

Tansy lay a light kiss on his jaw and got up. She lit a candle, wrapped herself in her robe, and settled into the overstuffed chair with her book. This one was about Spaniards discovering the new world. How she would like to have been there when Columbus first made landfall, thinking he was in India. And found all those Indians! She stifled the laugh burbling up at the linguistic absurdity. She was just getting to the part where Cortés discovered the great city cut through with canals.

"Come back to bed and keep me warm." Valere's voice was muffled in his pillow. She blew out her candle and slid in beside him. "Cold feet! Woman, what have you been doing?"

She stuck one cold foot between his shins. "Reading. Did you know the Aztecs built a city very much like Venice? Canals through and around. And like New Orleans, the water table was so high, they practically lived in the marsh. I suppose it's even hotter in Mexico, though."

Valere tossed an arm over her belly. "Why is that?" he mumbled.

She moved her head to see his face on the pillow, but it was too dark to decide if he were teasing her. She suspected he was not. "It is so very much further south, you see."

"Is it?" He shifted to get comfortable. "Go to sleep, Tansy."

## Chapter Three

Tansy helped Alain tie his shoes, took his hand, and set out for the Academy. She tried to do all her errands early in the day when she was sure Valere still lay abed in his townhouse and so wouldn't call while she was out. Her first task this morning, to return Christophe's History of the Americas.

She and Alain climbed the schoolhouse steps. Too early for the students yet, morning breezes wafted cool air into Christophe's schoolroom. Alain dashed for the resident cat who allowed herself to be caught and petted.

Christophe raised his head and in that one unguarded moment, revealed a depth of pleasure at seeing her that flashed through her with far too much warmth. "Good morning," he said.

"Finished the book."

He reached for it with his large, capable hand. That hand had once pressed her body against his. She'd been trimming the jasmine vine that threatened to cover the French doors and he'd stepped into the courtyard. With a gleam in his eye, a glance over his shoulder to check her mother was out of sight, he'd pulled her under the green canopy.

"What are you doing?" she'd whispered.

He caught her in his arms and dared her with his eyes. She could have backed away, like a good girl. But she'd let him pull her close. Let him lean down, the smell of jasmine and Christophe's own scent filling her head. She sighed. He kissed her. His hand traced her backbone till it rested at her waist, and then he pulled her in to his body. When he touched her tongue with his own, her breath caught. When he parted her legs with his knee and deepened the kiss, she completely lost herself in him, in the searing heat of his hand through the back of her dress.

Then Maman had stepped into the courtyard and shrieked as if a tiger mauled her only child.

Tansy jumped back, guilty and ashamed. But Christophe, all the while Maman scolded and railed, ran his thumbnail up her spine and then cupped her bottom and squeezed.

The next night, Maman had presented her at the Blue Ribbon Ball.

Tansy swallowed. She had no business remembering that stolen moment. She belonged to Valere. She was a mother. And Christophe was a respected man, a teacher, a musician. And yes, a gambler who sometimes showed up with a bruise on his chin and a busted knuckle. The two of them were no longer love sick adolescents.

"What did you think of it?" he asked.

"Very sad, the Aztecs losing everything to the Spanish, and then they died from those dreadful plagues." Did Christophe allow himself to think of that kiss? She didn't, she really didn't. She was settled now, and one long-ago kiss didn't mean so very much anyway.

"Not a happy story, no."

"Now I want a book about plagues."

Christophe laughed. "Aren't you the morbid one? Alas, my library is sorely limited." He swiveled his chair and ran his finger along the books shelved behind him. "How about this one?"

She looked at the spine. "*Candide.* What's it about?"

"Where would be the fun if I told you?" Christophe held his arm out. "Alain, come show me your letters."

Alain abandoned the tabby cat and climbed into Christophe's lap. When Alain glanced at her, a secretive smile on his face, Tansy raised her brows in collusion.

He picked up a chalk and laboriously drew an A on Christophe's slate. With his forehead scrunched in concentration, his tongue between his lips, Tansy thought him the most intelligent, handsome boy in New Orleans. He'd practiced his letters for weeks now and was about to astound his friend by writing his entire name.

"ALAIN?" Christophe exclaimed. "You wrote your name! *Tres bien!*"

Christophe hugged him and turned him around on his lap so he could look him in the eye. "You, Alain, are a great scholar."

"*Merci.*" Alain slid off Christophe's lap to pursue the cat.

Tansy sat at a student table and opened *Candide*. Christophe had given her her first book, too. In her last month of pregnancy with Alain, she had lumbered across the Quarter with Maman to visit Christophe's mother. By chance, Christophe had dropped in, a book under his arm. She'd not exchanged a single word with him since that day under the jasmine, but there was no distance between them. They talked and laughed and drank his maman's punch. When he rose to leave, he handed Frankenstein, the Modern Prometheus to her and said, "Keep it." And so Tansy read her first book, staying up late into the night, frightened and fascinated.

Christophe came around his desk and sat on a corner to lean over her.

"This one is fiction."

"Is it a love story?"

When she glanced up, Christophe's eyes were on her. Sometimes he focused on her as if she were a puzzle he'd like to solve. Sometimes, like now, she felt he would lift her to her feet and take her across the desk. He wouldn't though. Christophe had never deliberately touched her since their first, their only kiss.

She couldn't meet his eyes when he forgot himself like that. It unsettled her, it hurt her. In another time, another place ... Well. She was spoken for. She was so very fortunate to have a kind, generous patron like Valere. And really, Christophe had no interest in her any more. Just now and then she let herself think he did.

Christophe removed himself to sit behind his desk again, and she breathed more easily. "Not a romance, not like you mean," he said. "But it's fun. It'll make you laugh."

"You don't need it for your students?"

"Those rascals? They're not ready for satire, the little brutes. We're reading a story about a boy and his dog at the moment."

"I want a dog!" Alain said.

"I thought you wanted a cat," Tansy said.

"Maman, I want a dog and a cat."

"We'll ask your father. Perhaps he will allow a kitten."

Alain engrossed himself in the chalk nubs he found on the desks. Christophe's lowered voice barely suppressed his impatience. "Why would Valcourt object to Alain having a pet? Surely that is of no interest to a man who is seldom in the house when Alain is awake?"

When Alain was awake? Tansy's face heated and her shoulders stiffened. She busied herself putting the book in her shopping bag. "He doesn't like surprises, that's all."

She yanked the drawstring on her bag and knotted it too tightly. Christophe thought she was a fool, a childish fool, for deferring to her patron. How could he think that of her when his own mother had been a placée at one time. And yet he made her feel she led a lamentable life. She did not need his disapproval. Maman supplied enough of that for a dozen daughters.

"Alain." She held her hand out. "It's time to go."

"Tansy." She turned toward Christophe, but she still did not look at him. "I beg your pardon."

Now she raised her eyes to his and saw only a mask, rather cold, certainly closed off. "It's nothing. *Adieu*, Christophe. I'll return your book next week."

Christophe sat, elbows on his desk, his eyes closed behind his steepled fingers. Regret scorched him. He'd upset her, again. Her visits every week to borrow a book were too important to him to risk frightening her off, and he'd hurt her. When would he learn to keep his mouth shut? He should know better than to even mention Valcourt. She almost never did.

He rubbed his face. This was an old hurt. He simply had to accept the life she'd chosen. No, that wasn't right, he thought, the bitterness edging back into his mind. She had not chosen. Her mother had done that for her. Tansy had been too young, too immersed in the plaçage culture to see other possibilities for herself.

Estelle had molded her daughter into what every white man seemed to want, a biddable woman. Christophe remembered that day at the lake when they were children. His mother and Tansy's had taken them for an outing and he and Tansy had run wild, darting in and out among the tall pines, shrieking and shouting with abandon. That Tansy had been free and bold and unafraid. She had been herself.

But Estelle suppressed all that joy and used Tansy's inherent sweetness to turn her into a nice girl, a biddable girl. Except that one afternoon when he'd caught her under the jasmine vines and kissed her. Tansy had not been sweet or biddable then. She had seized that moment, seized him in a kiss that seared him to his toes.

Christophe ran a hand through his hair. Was she that hot when Valere took her to bed? He shook his head. He had no business thinking of that. Even if Estelle's steady hand propelled her, Tansy had entered into this life with her eyes open.

What added to the bitterness, though, was that he could have supported her from the time he was twenty, a year or so after she'd been taken to the Blue Ribbon. He had already begun investing his poker winnings by then and he'd quickly become a man of property with a growing bank account. He'd never be as rich as Valcourt, but he could keep her and Alain in comfort with his pay as a musician, his salary as a teacher, and his income from the houses he owned in the Vieux Carré.

He squeezed his eyes shut. If he'd only had a little more time, been a little older when Estelle sealed Tansy's fate.

He opened his eyes to stare across the room, trying to find the resignation that sustained him. When he'd met her at his mother's that day, her belly full and round, it had been nearly two years since he'd been in the same room with her. Tansy had been radiant. But weren't all women in her condition radiant? Or had she glowed with love for her protector? He hadn't known. And now? She had her fine clothes, her own cottage, a generous allowance. All she need do in return was pretend to adore some fatuous rich man who deluded himself he could buy affection. The muscles in Christophe's jaw bunched. Valere Valcourt was empty, vain, and idle, yet he possessed Tansy Marie Bouvier.

Did she live a lie, pretending to love that ass? Or had she actually developed an affection for him? Christophe hadn't made it out, and it gnawed at him.

The thunder of feet in the hallway announced his pupils had arrived, ready to have their heads stuffed with numbers and letters and facts. He breathed in deeply. When the rascals stormed into the room, he welcomed them with a smile he didn't feel.

# Chapter Four

As the afternoon shadows deepened, Tansy listened to Valere's breathing quieten until she was sure he slept. Then she slipped out from under his arm, dressed quietly, and wrapped her headdress into a simple tignon.

She meant to persuade Valere to eat supper with them when he woke. He was always in such a rush to go on to the next thing, but it was time he spent an hour with Alain. She lit a fire and put a chicken on to stew with capers, peppers, and rice.

At the gate between her courtyard and Martine's she whistled for Alain to come home. Martine came out behind him dressed in a silk caftan of the same vibrant print as her tignon. Even at home, Martine looked elegant. She sauntered over and breathed in the smells from Tansy's cook pot. "I believe I will invite myself for supper."

"Ah, *désolé*. Valere is eating with us tonight."

"Ooh la la." Martine raised her brows in mock admiration. "The gentleman dines with his shadows."

Tansy's smiled vanished.

"Ah, *chère*. I don't mean to quarrel. Enjoy your company. I'll bring a bottle of wine over later and eat your leftovers."

Tansy put her hands on her hips. "Valere is not 'company,' Martine."

Martine held her palms out. "Heavens, I've annoyed you twice in one minute. Alain, run get the pineapple off the table for your maman."

When he'd scampered off, Tansy met Martine's skewering look, her chin up. They'd had this quarrel before.

"This is important to you, feeding your gentleman."

"Of course it's important. Why wouldn't it be? He is Alain's father."

"*Chère*, I only worry for your heart. Valere is good to you, but you are not his life. You would do well to remember that." She threw her hands up again at Tansy's scowl. "All right," she said over her shoulder. "Enjoy your evening."

Her teeth clamped together, Tansy turned her back on Martine and went to her chopping block where she mangled a loaf of bread. When Alain brought her the pineapple, she stabbed into it. Martine the cynic. She had no notion of loving her protectors, whichever one she happened to be enjoying at the moment. She had no tenderness in her. She and Alain were not shadows, not superfluous satellites to Valere's sun, as Martine had once uncharitably described them. They were a family.

She rinsed the pineapple off her hands and dried them on her apron. Anger never got anyone into heaven or even into happiness. With a deep cleansing breath, she recited her mantra: There is only now, and now is very good. Martine was a good soul, a dear friend, as true as a sister. She shouldn't let her skepticism get to her. Martine simply didn't understand love.

She had Alain help her set the table. "Non, *cher*. Remember? Like this." She used her bent thumb to measure the distance from the table's edge to the plate's edge. The wine glass had to be just so to the right of the plate, the forks, knives, and spoons precisely arranged on either side. Once Alain had placed the last spoon, she stood back to admire his work. "See? It you take care, it will all be perfect. Now play quietly, Alain. I'm going to wake your father."

Valere had rolled to his stomach and lay sprawled across the bed. She sat beside him and ran her hand over his bare back. When he didn't stir, she leaned over and whispered in his ear. "*Bien-aimé.*"

"Hmm."

"Get dressed, beloved. I've made your supper. And Alain has something to show you." She got up from the bed. "Valere?"

"All right. Give me a minute."

He still didn't move. "Would you like me to prepare a bath?"

He sighed heavily. "Takes too long. Just a basin."

Fireflies flickered in the courtyard when Valere came to the table. "I can't stay long. Have an engagement tonight."

"Of course. But it's early yet. Sit down, eat. Relax with Alain."

She served him a bowl of hearty stew, fragrant with spice. Valere had little to say, still logy from sleeping too long in the hot afternoon.

"Shall I tell you something funny from this book I'm reading?"

He spooned gumbo into his mouth and shrugged.

"There's a hero named Candide and this fool named Pangloss who, no matter what misfortune befalls, believes all is for the best. The port of Lisbon — in Portugal?" She looked at him to see if he knew where Lisbon was. She got no reaction. "Well, just as Candide arrives, a terrible storm tosses his ship about and a man is thrown overboard. In a moment of great bravery, Candide is about to jump after him, to save him, but his friend Pangloss holds him back."

She felt a little desperate. Valere was in an ill temper. He all but ignored her. She went on, hoping to at least divert him.

"Well, says Pangloss, there is no need to rescue the man. Why?" Valere did not even look up for the punch line. She could only finish the story. "Because the Bay of Lisbon was made for this very purpose, for this man to be drowned in it. And so, in this best of all possible worlds, the man's drowning is the best of all possible events."

She gave a little laugh. It had seemed funny to her when she read it, but now. Valere put his bread down and looked at her. "You read too much. This is mere silliness."

She suddenly felt very small. Very dull. "Yes, Valere. I suppose it is."

She placed the pineapple spears on the table, sprigs of mint at the edges making a pretty plate. Valere stabbed a chunk directly from the plate and put it in his mouth. Tansy glanced at Alain, hoping he wouldn't emulate his father's bad manners.

"Are you finished, Alain? You may bring your slate to the table." She looked at him conspiratorially. He'd waited all week to show his father that he could write his name.

Alain returned with chalk and slate. "Look, Papa."

Valere wiped his mouth with his napkin. "All right." He pulled Alain on to his lap. "Let's see what you've learned."

Proudly, Alain began forming his letters. Valere speared another piece of pineapple and gestured with it toward Tansy.

"By the way, I won't see you in the coming week. Maybe not the next either. Getting married tomorrow." The blood rushed through Tansy's ears, nearly drowning out his next words. "I'll have to spend some time with the bride, all that."

She'd had no idea the date had been set. She would not even have known he was betrothed if Martine hadn't told her. She'd thought he'd marry in the autumn, maybe not even till Christmas.

She smoothed her napkin on the table. Folded it, smoothed it. Folded it again. "I see."

Valere shook his head. "I don't know how I'm to endure five days shut up in the bedroom with Abigail. We can't go out, no one can come in. Her mother insists on it. Where did such a custom come from? I'm certain my brothers never had to do it." He shook his head again. "Insane."

She agreed it was a stressful way for two people, strangers, really, to begin a life together. But did he really expect her to sympathize with him?

"A, L, A ... you're writing your name? Well done, young man. Hop down, now. I have to be off."

He tousled Alain's hair. He stooped and gave Tansy a quick kiss. "Thank you for supper. Wonderful gumbo."

He crossed to the mahogany humidor Tansy kept for him and plucked out a cigar. He tucked it in his pocket, found his hat and cane, and he was gone.

Tansy washed the dishes, unable to settle herself over Valere's marriage. Tomorrow! She hadn't had time to prepare herself. She pressed the back of her hand against her nose. Stop it, she told herself. The past is past. The future may never come. She wiped her face on her apron. There is only now. And now is not so bad.

An hour later, Tansy heard Martine come through the gate. She quickly splashed cool water on her face and applied a light dusting of powder. She'd stay out of the candle light and Martine would never know she'd been crying.

Martine was teasing Alain. "Did you save me some supper?"

Tansy glided into the room with a smile. "We did. But, alas, our greedy papa ate all your pineapple, didn't he, Alain?"

"May it burn his stomach!"

"Martine!"

"Oh, I don't mean it. Where's the corkscrew?"

Alain participated in removing the cork, twisting the screw until Martine pronounced it enough. She held the bottle and he pulled, the cork flying out with a satisfying pop.

Once Martine had eaten and Alain been put to bed, they put their feet up on the low table and poured themselves a second glass of wine.

"I hope you and Alain had a good evening with your Valere."

"Of course."

Martine wiped at a drop of wine on her glass. "I only ask because it looks to me as if your lovely eyes are swollen."

"Oh, it's nothing." Tansy waved her glass to show how inconsequential the news. "Valere is marrying Abigail Windsor tomorrow. I suppose I was a little maudlin about it."

"Hmm. I don't suppose you received an invitation."

Tansy shot her a mean look.

"It doesn't have to change anything, you know," Martine said.

"I know. He'd have told me if he wanted to ..."

"Cancel the contract. It's such a cold, bloodless phrase, isn't it? But one gets over it. As long as you have a break-away clause to protect you. And knowing Madame Estelle, you do."

Martine had endured the end of two arrangements. The first, the gentleman had had the bad taste to actually fall in love with his new wife and terminated the contract. With a generous settlement, of course. The second time, Martine had made a point of engaging with an elderly gentleman, always looking to the future. He died six months ago, leaving her a modest though respectable sum. She now trolled the quadroon balls for a new protector, not because she needed the money, but because she was bored, she said. Lonely, Tansy thought.

They lay their heads back, lost in their thoughts. Then Martine asked, "Do you ever dream, Tansy?"

"Of course I dream."

"No. I mean wide-awake dreams. Do you not ever wish for more? For, I don't know, adventure, romance, snow-capped mountains, a carriage with matching gray horses?"

The muscles in Tansy's neck tightened. Martine, always prodding, always poking. "I have everything I need. I'm content. No need for matching gray horses."

"Ah. I see."

"What do you dream about?"

Martine waved her hand in the air. "Oh, the usual. A handsome stranger, tall, of course. Wealthy, preferably. He'll waltz divinely. He'll come into my life like a windstorm, sweeping me up, adoring me. Claiming me. He'll make love like a stallion." She thought a moment. "And we'll make each other laugh."

Tansy smiled. "A fairy tale, Martine. But I wish you your prince with the endurance of a champion, a shining aura over his head, and a bouquet of red roses to throw at your feet. I'll dream of that for you."

"You'd do that for me?"

"Am I not your best friend?"

They poured themselves another glass of wine and settled back. "I saw her a couple of weeks ago, on Canal Street," Tansy said.

"Miss Abigail? Dare we hope she's short, fat, has a big nose with warts — or no — no nose, thin lips, and ... let's see ... she's near-sighted and has only three teeth in her head?"

"Alas, none of those. She's blonde, blue-eyed, petite. Very pretty." Would she make Valere happy? Tansy knew just when to touch, how to touch, where to touch to bring Valere to ecstatic climax. She rubbed her finger around the rim of her wine glass. "But I doubt Miss Abigail's convent education included instruction in how to please a man." Did she read? Not that Valere would care if she were as ignorant as ... as he.

Martine snorted. "You know, the reason the wedding distresses you is because, deep down, you're convinced that if you make love with a man then you must love him. Or worse, that he must love you."

Tansy closed her eyes. Did she believe that? Of course not. She was not a child. But making love could grow into love. And it had. She and Valere loved each other.

"You think I'm cynical," Martine said, "but your head is full of romance. If you would only realize that what you have with Valere is perhaps more than simply business, but not much more. He has not and will not give you his heart."

Temper flashed heat over Tansy's face. "You know nothing about Valere's heart."

"I know men. And yes, I also know of placées whose patrons kept them for the rest of their lives. Maybe that was love. Or maybe simply habit. But for most of us? Ask yourself this, what would Valere do if you died?"

Tansy tightened her fingers on the lace at her bodice. "What a dreadful thing to say."

"Tansy. Think. How long would it be before he found himself a new honey to keep here in this very cottage?"

"He'd be lonely."

"He'd be horny."

"You are the most atrocious crapehanger." She should just go to bed. Martine did not understand. She and Valere had been lovers for more than five years now. How could there not be love?

"I see you twisting that lace. I'll go. But just one more question. The weeks before Alain was born and he had to abstain from sex, with you at any rate, how often did Valere come around? Two questions, sorry. And how old was Alain when he first saw his son?"

"That's enough." Tansy stood. "I'm going to bed."

"Wait, Tansy." Martine put her wine glass down. She kissed Tansy's cheek. "Don't go to bed mad at me. I only want you to take care of your heart."

"I do. Valere does."

Tansy put the wine glasses in a basin of water so the mice wouldn't lick themselves giddy on the drops at the bottom. She rinsed out the bottle to discourage the palmetto bugs from doing the same. Then she blew out the candles.

As she undressed in the ray of moonlight, she remembered Martine had been in love once. They had both been nineteen, Alain a baby, and Martine's first patron had just abandoned her for his bride. A handsome Creole, the handsomest man either of them had ever seen, had waltzed Martine through the evening. They met again at the next ball, and the next. Renault, his name was, a cane planter. He called on Martine's mother to propose a contract. Tansy and she had hovered on the other side of the parlor door while Madame Dubois and Monsieur Renault discussed terms. Martine's eyes had been full of stars, her heart pulsing for this man.

The contract papers laid out on the desk, Madame Dubois picked up a quill to hand to Monsieur Renault.

The door squeaked open. "Madame?" Maggie, the cook, peered into the room. "Please forgive me, but ... a man at the back door says I didn't pay him for the last box of coal, and I know I did."

"I'll deal with him shortly, Maggie."

Maggie cleared her throat. She widened her eyes and raised her brows. "He's very insistent. Perhaps you should come right now."

Even hiding behind the other door, Tansy had heard the urgency in Maggie's voice. Martine's mother had excused herself, taking the quill with her, and followed Maggie to the kitchen. Maggie had heard from the Duvall's cook who'd heard from Monsieur Renault's valet that the gentleman had twice undergone treatment for the pox.

Madame Dubois had sent him away. Martine had cried. And cried. She'd grown pale and lost weight. Her mother kept her home from the balls until she recovered her looks, then insisted that Martine don her best gown, rouge her cheeks, and reenter the fray. That led to her second protector, whom she accepted with a cold eye on his mortality. By then, Martine had lost faith in love. She developed a shell around her heart that only Alain and she were allowed to penetrate.

Tansy did not discount Martine's disappointment, but her starry-eyed state over that Monsieur Renault had been mere infatuation. Martine knew nothing of the kind of love she and Valere had, the kind that grew into comfort and ease with one another.

Martine was right, though, about the weeks before Alain arrived. Valere had excused himself, saying he had a new race horse he was running this season and simply could not find the time to come by. She had thought she would die of boredom. She ached all over and she wished he'd come and rub her back or help her pass the waiting. And the day after Alain was born? Christophe showed up, with his mother, to see the new baby. He had immediately gone to the crib and, without a moment's hesitation, picked Alain up and cradled him in his big, sure hands. How long was it before Valere came to see his son? She remembered exactly. It had been three weeks, long enough for her to have healed. And then he had refused to handle his son, afraid of how tiny he was.

But that was four years ago. Valere had been merely twenty-four. He'd grown up since then. And wasn't this the best of all possible worlds?

## Chapter Five

The morning of Valere's wedding, a fine day of blue skies and balmy breezes, Tansy picked up *Candide* and put it down. She tatted lace a while, and lost interest in that. What if she strolled over to Jackson Square, just by chance happening to be there when Valere and the new Mrs. Valcourt emerged from the cathedral? But if he should see her, she would die of mortification. He'd ignore her, and that would hurt. Worse, she might embarrass him.

Determined to shake off her gloomy mood, she enlisted Alain in a thorough housecleaning. First they rescued toys from under the bed. Alain had a tendency to toss the blocks all together in the toy box, and that wouldn't do. She helped him sort them so that the red blocks were with the red, the blue with the blue. Then she refolded all of his clothes, arranged his shoes so they were precisely placed side by side, each heel the same distance from the edge of the shelf.

Next they gathered sheets and filled the washtub with water from the cistern. The two of them were up to their elbows in suds when Maman Estelle dropped in.

It did not surprise her that her mother should come this particular morning. Fierce as a hawk in protecting Tansy as she'd negotiated her way through the plaçage market, she nevertheless was ever ready to twist whatever thorns she could find embedded. And the marriage of one's patron was indeed a thorn.

"I find you in quite good cheer." Estelle peeled off her lace gloves and tossed them on the table.

"And why not, Maman?"

Estelle eyed her knowingly. "Why not indeed?" Absently she licked her thumb and wiped at a smudge on Alain's cheek. "So. You mean to hide here instead of positioning yourself outside the cathedral in self-pity?"

"As you so often point out, what Valere does when he is not with me is none of my affair."

"I have taught that, but whether you absorbed it I've always had my doubts. You are entirely too attached to him."

Faced with her mother's nagging criticisms and her habit of shredding tender feelings, Tansy often found herself sounding very much like Martine. "Isn't that what he buys when he provides me with this house, an allowance, a child with his name? My attachment?"

"A seeming attachment would be sufficient." She narrowed her eyes. "And why are you doing your own sheets? Have you not received your allowance?"

Tansy considered her mother. Estelle's face was still unlined, her figure trim, her hair black, though that might be the result of dye judiciously applied. She had had three patrons in her day, and might yet find herself an old gentleman who'd enjoy the comforts of a mature woman. Had she cared for any of those three men, including Tansy's father?

"My allowance is fine. Marie comes on Tuesdays. I wanted them clean today."

Acerbic, even mean, Maman was no fool. Tansy might as well acknowledge Valere's wedding hurt her. She stilled the laundry paddle and looked her mother in the eye. "I'm not like you, Maman."

"More's the pity. Hurt feelings where your gentleman are concerned are entirely pointless. Bring your comb, Alain. Your hair is a mess."

Tansy stirred the wash pot, the lye-scented steam wafting into her face.

"Look at you. You'll spoil your complexion in that heat."

Tansy bristled at yet another well-worn admonishment. Don't sit in the sun. Don't get your hands dirty. Don't slouch. Don't ever, ever show your displeasure. Except for a tightening around the mouth, Tansy obeyed that last stricture.

"I have fruit and bread and cheese if you'll stay for lunch, Maman."

Estelle waved her hand. "I have an engagement."

Valere habitually dropped in several times a week, sometimes in the afternoon, sometimes in the evening. Tansy kept herself ready. Sweet-smelling, sweet-tempered, available. With no expectation of his coming this first week of his marriage, she realized how much of her life she spent waiting for his unannounced visits. After her first day of discontent, she found the certainty that he would not call liberating. She and Alain had the entire day to do as they pleased.

She packed a picnic and set out for the park, the two of them swinging hands and enjoying the day. Midway up the block, she tightened her grip on Alain's hand. Colette Augustine lounged in the doorway ahead, idly smoking a cheroot. She wore red velvet though it was still morning, and she allowed long tendrils of silky black hair to escape her tignon.

Colette's mother had once been a placée, but her brother Nicolas had decided their fortunes lay outside of plaçage. He became a procurer of young girls for the brothels, and when Colette reached fifteen, he'd introduced her to the life.

Tansy, when she too reached fifteen, had caught his eye. She'd wandered away from Maman in the market and he'd approached her. A handsome devil, tall, broad-shouldered, he'd had the voice of an angel, whispering to her of freedom and choices, of affection and pleasure. He'd stroked a finger down her arm and promised to love her and protect her, and God help her, Tansy had thrilled at his touch, at his warm breath on her cheek.

Maman had appeared and raked him across the face with the spiny top of a pineapple. "You speak to my daughter again, I will have you arrested. No, I will have you beaten and thrown in the river."

Nicolas, blood beading on his chin, had managed a cocky smirk and eased away into the crowded market. That was not the end of it, though, for Estelle grabbed Tansy's arm and marched her down Levee Street to the same brothel where Augustine's sister Colette made her life. Without knocking, she barged into a red and gold parlor, empty in the early morning. The lavish furnishings spoke of elegance and prosperity. Maman thrust the curtains back for the sun to reveal the tawdry cheap gilt, the worn spots on the velvet, the dust and the grime.

"Take a good look, Tansy Marie," Maman had demanded. Then she'd dragged Tansy upstairs where four doors opened on to the hall. She threw the first door open to reveal a small, bare room that reeked of a musky scent Tansy did not recognize. The sheets were twisted, thin, and stained.

Maman had thrown open the next door and disturbed a woman sleeping in an identical shabby room. The woman had squinted at them from an unwashed face, her yellow hair greasy and uncombed. "Who the hell are you?"

Tansy had wanted to flee, but Maman gripped her wrist. "Take a good look, Tansy. This is what Nicolas Augustine offers."

"Get the hell out of my room!"

The woman's snarl revealed two missing teeth. A pink scar marked her cheek. She smelled of sweat and that same musky sourness that lingered in the other room.

"How old does she look to you? Thirty? Forty? I promise you, she is no more than twenty."

Tansy tugged at her mother. "Come away, Maman."

"How many times do you suppose she's had the pox? How many times has she dared the knife to rid herself of yet another unwanted brat?"

"Maman!"

Maman turned on the whore. "How many men did you fuck last night?"

The whore cackled like a demented hen. "Scared for your little chick, are you? Think a colored girl like her can do better?" She laughed again.

Tansy had twisted free of Maman's grip and run from the house.

She'd been sick when she got home, and she'd never forgotten Maman's point. Without a patron's protection, she would be the prey of men like Nicolas Augustine. All these years later, Tansy's stomach still roiled remembering the smell in this very brothel. Swiftly she crossed the street, watching Colette from the corner of her eye. Colette tilted her chin up and blew smoke, then raised the cheroot in salute with a sneer on her face.

Alain tugged at her hand. "Maman, there's the hurdy gurdy man. Come on."

She let Alain listen and give the man a coin, then they went on to the park. She settled under a sycamore with a book while Alain ran off with a friend from Mrs. O'Hare's who babysat for neighborhood youngsters. They chased each other and rolled in the grass and found every small patch of mud in the park. Tansy reminded herself little boys were supposed to get dirty and messy, and really, they had the whole day to themselves. Valere would not come to her this day, would not know she'd let herself become sweaty and sun-kissed.

In the heat of the afternoon, she persuaded Alain to cool off in the shade for a while. Certainly against his intention, he drifted off. When she too grew drowsy, she leaned back and closed her eyes, unconcerned for once if her skin should darken in the sun. The lightness of a quadroon's skin was part of her fortune, and unlike the delicate ladies of society, she could not shield her face under a broad-brimmed bonnet. A tignon wrapped around her head offered no shade at all. But today she didn't care. Valere would not notice whether her skin had darkened or not.

She woke to a tap on the bottom of her shoe. Christophe stood over her, grinning, and gave her boot another little kick.

"Just like in the old stories," she said lazily, "the devil has come aknockin."

He laughed, his face alight with fun. "Tired out your little man, have you? Seems an excellent place for a snooze." He stretched out on the grass next to Alain, sharing their shade. Sometimes he quite shocked her, his ease with himself, at the ball, anywhere. She admired the length of his legs, the slim hips, the tightness of his sleeve above the elbow when he leaned his head on his hand. Unbidden, an image of the slight paunch Valere was developing came to mind.

"Through with school for the day?" she asked.

"Yes, and with money scorching my pockets. I played three parties last weekend, and you know what I do with my fiddle money."

"Books!"

"You want to go with me? My favorite bookseller keeps a stall on the levee."

It was one thing to visit Christophe at the school where Madame Rosa was just in the next room. She went there, after all, to borrow books, not to meet with him. But, old friend or not, he was a young man. Who had once kissed her. Whom she had kissed. "Fie, Christophe. What would Maman say if I were seen walking with you?"

"She would say, That hussy, Tansy Marie Bouvier. I shall have to give her a piece of my mind!"

His imitation spot-on, Tansy laughed.

"Come on. No doubt your maman is sitting in someone's parlor drinking coffee. I'll let you choose a book."

"Really? My choice?"

Christophe carried Alain who woke from his nap cross and groggy. They walked up Esplanade to the levee where hundreds of people worked and shopped and strolled. Stevedores carried goods over gangplanks, and ox-drawn carts squeaked up to the loading docks. The smell of the river strong here, they threaded their way through the throng to a stall where a wizened man in faded black stood among piles of used books.

"Monsieur Desmarais, *bonjour*! You have a son!"

Tansy darted a look at Christophe. Would he be embarrassed?

Christophe still carried Alain on one arm, the boy's arms around his neck. He pressed a hand against Alain's back in contradiction to the answer he gave. "No, Monsieur, he is not mine." He shifted toward Tansy. "May I present his mother, Madame Bouvier?"

"*Enchanté*, Madame. You have a fine boy."

They spent a pleasant quarter of an hour perusing the books laid out on a plank table. Alain sat on the ground with a book of *Aesop's Fables* open on his lap. Christophe had a dog-eared volume of essays by Montesquieu under his arm.

"Tansy," Christophe said. "I would not hurry you for the world, for the stars, for the very heavens, but — " He nodded toward the sky where dark clouds were piling into impressive masses.

"Oh, but I can't decide." Tansy held up a copy of *Pamela* and another of *Tom Jones*. "Which one?"

She could see Christophe about to speak, fun in his eyes, and then abruptly the sparkle disappeared and he turned away. "You must make your own decisions."

Tansy swallowed and blinked. She handed the bookseller one of the books, she didn't notice which one. Christophe paid the man and the three of them strolled back up the levee.

She tried to pretend she had imagined the sudden coldness in Christophe, but she couldn't manage it. There was that disapproval again, that impatience as if she were a recalcitrant child who continually disappointed him. It made her feel unbalanced and unsure, as if her life were not all it should be. Should be? Who was Christophe Desmarais to decide what her life should be? Her life was wonderful and he was a pompous prig.

Having worked herself from hurt to angry, she felt much better. Then, as always, she found she could not hold on to the anger. It always seemed to slip away, like water through her fingers. Christophe was right. She was nice. Well, so be it.

The wind blowing upriver from the Gulf picked up. Rain began to plop down in huge drops. They held hands, Alain in the middle, and ran for it. By the time, they reached Tansy's door, their hats and shoulders and shoes were soaked. Laughing, Tansy pulled Alain in with her and then stood aside for Christophe to enter. Instead of coming in, he took a step backward, and then another. Surely he would come in — it was pouring. No one could fault a man for seeking shelter in a downpour like this.

"Christophe?" Water streamed off his hat brim, curtaining his dark eyes, but she read the tautness of his mouth, his unwavering gaze on her face. "Christophe," she demanded. "Come in."

He shook his head and stepped further away. Abruptly, he turned and strode off into the rain.

She watched him until he turned the corner, then slowly closed the door. After a supper of hot soup and bread, she put Alain to bed, then curled up on the sofa. Rain still pattered on the courtyard bricks. Wind rattled the shutters. Her new book lay in her lap unopened. They'd had a wonderful day, she and Alain. Such ease, free of anticipation, of waiting. Talk and laughter with Christophe. Yet she'd never felt so alone.

In the morning, a March wind chilled the cottage, but sunshine lit the banana tree in the courtyard. Later she and Alain could walk along the levee and watch the paddle-wheeled steam ships. They could have another day of freedom ... she stopped herself. Freedom? She missed Valere, of course she did, missed expecting him to knock on her door.

When a knock did come, Alain jumped down from his chair and ran. "Christophe!" he called out. Pain pinched at Tansy's chest. He never ran for the door when he thought his father had arrived.

Alain pulled the door open, then stared at the young man on the stoop. "Madame Bouvier?" The boy, perhaps fourteen, handed her a note. "I'm to wait for your answer, Ma'am."

Tansy unfolded the paper. "Tansy — Rosa is sick. Desperate here. Can you take the eight year olds for the day?" Christophe.

"Oh," she breathed. He wanted her to take a class? Her, Tansy Marie Bouvier, to be a teacher for the day? She pressed her hand over her heart.

"Ma'am?"

"Yes! Tell him yes. Quick as I can get there."

She bundled Alain and together they marched down Decatur and up Decatur to Madame Rosa LeFevre's Academy for Boys. Tansy had yearned to go to school when she was a girl, but Maman had hired tutors, dancing masters, and voice teachers so that her childhood lessons had been learned in solitude. And now to be in a school, as a teacher? She couldn't stop smiling.

Monsieur Fournier met her in the hallway, his white hair showing the effects of running his hands through it in frustration. "Madame Bouvier. Thank heavens you're here. I simply cannot teach quadratic equations while the eight year olds babble about dogs and toys. Come this way."

He hustled down the hallway to the last door on the right. Tansy followed him into a scene of pandemonium. Eight little boys climbed over and crawled under tables, chased each other, giggled, and crowed at the top of their voices.

"Gentlemen!" Monsieur Fournier clapped his hands together loudly. One child seemed to hear and faltered in his wild scramble over chairs, then regained his momentum and kept going. The aging master found a ruler and pounded it on the desk, again to little effect.

Tansy looked down at Alain and winked. She walked to the center of the room, raised Alain to the top of desk, and began to sing.

*Alouette, gentille Alouette*

*Alouette, je te plumerai. Je te plumerai la tête.*

*Je te plumerai la tête,* Alain chimed in.

*Et la tête*

*Et la tête,* Alain repeated.

*Alouette*

*Alouette,* Alain sang.

*O-o-o-oh* ... Tansy drew it out dramatically, waiting for the boys to join in.

*Alouette, gentille Alouette*

The last of the rapscallions gathered round her, Tansy waved at Mr. Fournier as he gratefully retreated to his own classroom.

No one came to advise her what to do with a room of eight year old boys, so Tansy improvised. They sang all the verses of Alouette from plucking the poor skylark's head all the way to its tail. Then Frère Jacques and half a dozen other folk songs every child learned in the nursery.

By then, Tansy had arranged the boys in a circle on the floor around her. The boys displayed skin tones from deep brown to nearly white, every one of them the child of gens de coulour libre, the free blacks who were an integral part of New Orleans.

"Now what shall we do? Numbers? Letters?"

"Stories!" a dusky child cried out.

"Very well." Tansy began the tale of The Lost Children. As she described the brother and sister wandering lost in the forest, their eyes grew big. When she came to the part when Jeanette fooled the devil by cutting off a rat's tail instead of Jean's finger, they giggled. But when she described how the children slew the evil one in order to escape, they clapped their hands over their mouths, horrified, though they must have each heard the story a dozen times.

Tansy reminded them that they must practice their letters or surely Madame Rosa would be disappointed when she returned. When everyone had his slate, she said, "What is the first letter of Jean?" Everyone called out "J" and then made the letter on their slates.

At the end of the day, Tansy left Alain with Christophe and went upstairs to see Rosa. The room was dark and stifling. Tansy glanced at the window, wishing she could open it for some light and air, but she knew any doctor would insist it remain closed.

"Rosa?"

Rosa pulled the blanket from over her face. "Who is it?"

"Tansy. I've come to see how you are."

"Ah, Tansy. I'll either be just fine, someday, or else I'm never getting out of this bed again."

"Well. I'm expecting the first. You're not too hot?"

"I could use a fire, in fact."

Tansy bustled around the small apartment building a fire and making tea. She told Rosa all about her day with the children.

"Can you finish the week for me?" Rosa asked.

Valere wouldn't come see her for a week or more, that's what he'd said. She could do as she pleased. "I can. You don't need to worry about a thing. The boys and I will do very well together."

Friday afternoon, Monsieur Fournier presented her with an envelope. Her pay. For having worked, for having had a wonderful time teaching her boys. She didn't open it. She didn't care how much money she'd earned, only that she had earned it. All her life she had admired teachers, tutors, masters. When Christophe had become a teacher, she'd been so proud of him. A poor boy of color whose white father had died bankrupt, he had worked hard and made himself into a distinguished professional. And she, Tansy, a mere placée, had had a taste of that profession. She hugged that newly won pride to her as she strode home with Alain.

At bedtime, stretching and yawning, Tansy hung her dress up and arranged her shoes precisely in the bottom of her armoire. She pulled the mosquito netting aside and paused. The bed was rumpled, the pillows awry. Valere had been here? She'd missed Valere! A smudge of dirt from his boots marred the foot of the satin coverlet.

Heavily, she sat down on the edge of the bed. He'd come and she wasn't home. In all of their five years together, she had almost never been out when he came, hardly ever. She ran her hand over the coverlet. He'd waited for her, here on the bed. Maybe he even took a nap.

She pressed a hand to her chest. Had he been angry? He'd never been angry with her before. She'd never given him cause to be angry before. She lay down and curled into herself. "It'll be all right," she whispered. Valere was even-tempered and sweet-natured.

A hint of his familiar scent lingered on her pillow. Her bones began to loosen, her body sinking into the mattress. She closed her eyes. Why was Valere here and not with his wife? Had things not gone well with Miss Abigail? Probably he had simply missed her and Alain. She smiled and drifted into sleep.

After a quiet weekend, no Valere, no responsibilities, Tansy sipped coffee as Alain gobbled buns, bacon, and orange juice, all the while kicking his feet, thumping them against the chair legs.

"Alain." Tansy raised her brows at him. He stopped kicking. In a few minutes, biting into his second bun, his feet swung again. "Alain?"

He stuck a slice of bacon in his mouth and let it hang out like a tongue, a deadpan expression on his face.

She laughed. Plenty of time yet for a four year old to learn not to swing his legs. He wiped his fingers on his shirt as he climbed down from the chair. "I'm finished, Maman. Let's go."

She looked at him over her coffee cup. "Go where?"

"School!"

"Alain, we aren't going to school. Madame Rosa is well now."

"Maman, we have to go to school. My friends are waiting for me."

Tansy's forehead creased. She had thought he understood. "Sweetheart, we aren't going to school. We only went to help Madame Rosa, and she's well now."

Alain stood very still. His lip trembled. "They'll miss me if I don't come."

She folded him into her arms as great hiccupping sobs shook his little body. "Oh, darling." She rocked him and wondered why not? Valere had never come before early afternoon. While Rosa taught the other boys, she could work with René. He was behind the others. He needed help.

"Alain." She held him back so she could see his face. "What if we make a deal, you and I?"

"What kind of deal?"

"You don't wipe your hands on your shirt ..." She hoped for a grin. She got a hopeful look. "And we'll stop by the school. Just for an hour. That's all. And when it's time to go, you don't fuss about it."

"That's a good deal, Maman."

Tansy let herself and Alain into the school, the building quietly ahum with voices from the classrooms down the central hall. She paused at Christophe's open door, meaning to let him know she was there. He paused mid-sentence when he saw her, his eyes wide with surprise. She smiled and raised her hand to him, then walked Alain to Rosa's classroom.

Rosa stood at the front of the room, her eight charges at their desks in front of her. She looked pale, but her voice was strong. "What does 'broom' start with?"

*Tansy*

"P!"

"D!"

Alain, still holding Tansy's hand, looked up at her and whispered "B."

"Madame Bouvier. Come in. Look who's come to see you, boys."

"*Bonjour.*" Tansy beamed on them, so glad to see them once again. There was Pierre, his missing front tooth the only flaw that kept him from being utterly beautiful. Sidney, his eyes gray, his skin light. And Marcel, as dark as you ever saw among the free gens de colour.

Alain marched in as if this were where he belonged. He chose to sit with Marcel, who scooted over to share his desk.

Tansy tilted her head toward the door. Rosa came to her and showed the class her back to afford them a moment of privacy.

"Could you use a little help, say for an hour in the mornings? I could work with René, or Sidney, to bring them up to where the other boys are."

Rosa squeezed her arm. "You are a blessing."

Tansy sat in the back with René, their slates on their laps. He did not yet recognize all the letters or know what their sounds were, so it was easy to know what to teach him. She saw though that his attention was captured by the chalk he held tightly in his left hand. He simply could not find the right grip, nor could he draw a smooth, straight line. René was smaller than the other boys. Perhaps he simply had not yet grown enough to use his hands deftly.

"Let's try this." With the chalk held sideways, she covered his slate with a light layer of chalk. "Now use only your finger. This finger. Draw me an A."

"I would get chalk on my finger."

Tansy drew in a breath. "Yes, you would. But see here, it wipes right off." She rubbed the chalk in her palm and then wiped it off with René's eraser cloth. "See?"

He sighed deeply. With the cloth gripped in one hand, at the ready, he glanced at the A on her slate, then made his own with strange gaps on either side of the crossbar. But the lines were straight and smooth.

Tansy squeezed his hand. "Excellent."

She glanced up to see that Alain was behaving. He sat elbow to elbow with Marcel, his legs swinging, his eyes on Madame Rosa.

When Tansy thought to check the time, she realized it had been well over an hour. She hugged René and sent him back to his desk. Quietly she motioned to Alain. He scowled, but she held up one finger, her brows raised. He cleared the grimace off his face and slid down from the chair.

Rosa waved at Tansy as she took Alain's hand and left the room.

Christophe stepped out of his classroom. "I heard your steps in the hall." He placed his palm on top of Alain's head, but his eyes were on her.

Tansy straightened with pride. "I'm going to help Rosa for an hour every morning. Teaching."

He tilted his head, considering. "You like to teach."

She smiled. "I'm good at it, Christophe. Who would have guessed?"

His mouth curved into a faint smile. "I would have."

She drew in a breath. "Really?"

His smile was gone. His eyes bored into hers. "Really."

She gave an embarrassed laugh. "You never told me it's fun."

The smile returned. "Sometimes they're little hellions, then it's not so much fun."

"They're only hellions because they know that underneath that demon scowl you try to scare them with, you're just a big six foot baby doll."

"Ow! Better a demon than a baby doll." He moved a step to look at her back. "Ah yes. Wings. I thought so."

Alain's eyes grew wide and he twisted around to look at his maman's wings. Christophe laughed and caught him up. "You think your maman's an angel, do you? Maybe you're right."

She was about to tell him better an angel than a baby doll when she got caught in his gaze. Sometimes she felt he looked so deep into her eyes that she had no secrets, no private thoughts that he could not see. But she did have private thoughts, so secret she seldom let herself acknowledge them. She broke away from that penetrating gaze.

"So you're coming tomorrow?" he said. His voice had lost its teasing lightness.

She nodded. "An hour or so in the mornings. Just to help."

"Good."

Sunday she and Alain and Martine went to Mass and spent the rest of the morning together gossiping. Alain entertained himself with a length of chain with hooks on either end. Tansy tatted a row of lace in ecru thread, and Martine ignored the embroidery in her lap.

"Maman said you disgraced yourself at the ball, dancing every dance with your Monsieur DuMaine."

Martine's mouth quirked. "Disgraced myself? I believe I did." Her face broke into a brilliant grin. "Tansy, I think he's going to make an offer."

"Who will negotiate for you?"

"Ah, you'll never guess. Madame Estelle Bouvier. Who better?"

"Maman?" Tansy narrowed her eyes. "I suppose she will charge you a fee?"

"Of course. Your maman is quite shrewd, but no one ever mentioned that she is charitable."

"But for you, I wish — "

"Don't think of it. It's business, that's all. I have no idea how to handle all those figures."

"I bet you'd do very well."

Martine smirked. "Well, yes. I could do it. But it leaves a taste in the mouth of the gentleman to see his placée behaving as if she had a brain — and an avaricious streak."

"Both of which you have!"

"Of course. But Monsieur need never know."

Tansy put her tatting shuttle down. She'd been uneasy all afternoon. She'd made no arrangements with Mrs. O'Hare to keep Alain today. "I hate to change the subject, Martine, but if Valere comes — "

Martine waved a hand. "Send Alain to me. And if I decide to visit Annabelle, I'll take him with me."

Tansy sighed. "I don't know what I'd do without you."

"What everyone else does. Set the child down in the next room and cower him into behaving." Martine frowned. "As my mother did. I don't want Alain hearing all those noises in the other room, wondering if his mother is being hurt, feeling left out and alone."

"My father never came until after I was asleep."

Martine brought her needlework close, squinting at a stitch. "So you never saw him. And he never saw you."

She shrugged. "He gave me presents on my birthday. And Christmas and New Year's Day. He seemed fond of me."

"Tell me, Tansy. If it's not the money that interests you, what makes you the perfect, docile placée?"

Again with the goads! Impatience quickened her tongue. "Why do you not see it could be love? He is Alain's father!"

"Fah. I know your Monsieur Valcourt. I've danced with him at the Blue Ribbon, I've seen him with Alain. He is not a man of deep feeling, Tansy. I can't believe he inspires it in anyone else, either."

Tansy's mouth tightened. "We are not going to have this conversation again."

Martine held up her hands. "All right." She tapped her mouth with two fingers. "Consider my lips sealed."

In the early evening, Valere did arrive. He looked very fine in his royal blue frock coat and buff trousers, his side burns neatly trimmed, his upper lip smoothly shaved.

Smiling, always smiling, she welcomed him with a kiss. "Alain, come say hello to your father."

Dutifully Alain left his wooden train and said hello to Valere.

"How do you do, Alain?" Valere patted him on the head and then raised his eyebrows at Tansy and tilted his head toward the bedroom.

She stifled a sigh that he had nothing else to say to his son. "I believe Martine has been baking, Alain. Do you smell it?"

He tilted his nose into the air and closed his eyes. "Gingerbread!"

"Off with you then," she laughed.

Alain hardly out the back door, Valere took her shoulders and began walking her backwards into the bedroom. He maneuvered her to press her against the wall, ground a kiss onto her mouth, and scrunched up her skirts until it was around her waist. "I missed you," he murmured against her lips. He cupped her and she startled. She wasn't ready.

"I missed you, too," she breathed. She stalled him a moment, working at the buttons of his stiffened vest, easing the tightness over his belly. He arranged his arms for her to pull his coat and vest off, then playfully pushed her till the backs of her knees hit the bed. He ran his hands down to her derrière, stroking and squeezing. Giving herself a moment to bring her mind to lovemaking, she slowly untied his cravat, pulled at his shirttail and rolled his trousers off him. Then she tantalized him by undressing herself, slowly. Once she was nude, he grabbed her down to the bed and plunged himself into her. She gripped his shoulders and held on. That was all she could do and all he wanted.

Valere was not usually so abrupt. He was not a bad lover. She didn't think. She'd never lain with anyone else, but he often brought her with him to that shuddering release. He liked it when she panted out his name, when she groaned with need. He didn't have the patience for that today. She wondered about his marriage bed that he was so feverishly eager so soon after his wedding. Of course, he would not speak of his wife, nor would she ask.

When he lay on his back, content, relaxed, she snuggled against his chest. "I'm sorry I wasn't here when you came by Friday."

"I only had a few minutes anyway."

Didn't he wonder where she'd been? In all their time together, she had been here, in this house, when he wanted her. Did he have no curiosity about her life? She'd love to know all about his, what his sisters did, what his mother thought of his wife, whether his wife was in love with him. Probably not, she considered. Most of the marriages in Valere's circle were about alliances and property.

She opened her mouth to tell him she had been at the school, it had been such fun, Alain had loved it, she'd felt so useful. She swallowed the words. He would not understand what it had meant to her. And he was not interested.

It hurt, a little, that he didn't ask. It shouldn't, of course. Her mother had crabbed at her a hundred times about falling in love with her protector. Had she fallen in love with Valere? She waited for him. She kept the cottage neat, herself bathed and fresh for him. But in the mornings, when she knew he would not come, there was a certain freedom in those hours which, she realized with some surprise, she enjoyed.

With the arm that lay across his chest, she squeezed him a little. Wasn't she always glad to see him? He was in her bed, his arm around her. They belonged together. They had a child.

He let out a regretful sigh and untangled himself from her legs. "Have to go. Dinner with the in-laws, you know."

She handed him his stockings and shirt. As she tied his cravat, she stopped a moment to touch his cheek. "It's wonderful to be with someone you love."

Valere frowned. He took her hand from his cheek. "I'm married, Tansy."

A tight cold knot twisted in her chest. What had she been thinking? In a corner of her mind, she could see Maman sneering at her.

"Of course. I understand." She finished with his cravat and helped him on with his coat.

In the front room, he picked up his hat, turned to give her a quick kiss, and left her to lead his "real" life.

# Chapter Six

Monday morning, Christophe sat at his desk with an open book, but he read with little attention. He listened for Tansy's footsteps in the hallway. When she arrived, he could hear Alain peppering her with questions. Something about how could dogs walk with four feet without getting tangled up because he only had two feet and he sometimes got tangled up. Christophe smiled. Such a bright little boy.

He strode into the hallway purposefully as if he had an urgent task ahead of him. With raised eyebrows to feign surprise, he called "Tansy!" Perhaps he overplayed it. He covered it by bending over Alain, who wrapped himself around one of Christophe's legs. God, he loved this child. He didn't know when it had happened. When he first saw him, he supposed. The man Valcourt seemed to feel little attachment to his son, as if his own efforts had little to do with his being born. How could Tansy forgive him for that?

Until that day when he'd found Tansy and Estelle visiting his mother, he'd thought he was over her. After all, he'd been just a boy when he'd lusted after Tansy Marie. He'd had a woman he saw regularly, a woman he was fond of. Still was fond of. But when Tansy had smiled at him in that familiar way, her whole being open and radiant, something inside him cracked open. A woman's smile, no longer a girl's.

He'd seen her at the balls, of course, him in the orchestra, her on the dance floor. But he had determinedly made no eye contact and pretended he didn't even know she was in the room. He knew, though, and he had watched. That day at his mother's, Tansy in advanced pregnancy, she seemed gloriously happy. Because of the man who kept her? He'd corrected himself. Because of the man with whom she'd been placed. But, he'd thought, didn't all expectant mothers glow like this? Maybe she only tolerated her Monsieur Valcourt. Yes, he'd known the man's name. He'd known where he lived and where his estates were. He'd even known with whom he spoke at balls and how he led with his left foot when he danced with Tansy. He'd simply chosen to pretend the man had been consigned to Hades.

And now she was back in his life. He often debated with himself whether that was a good thing, to allow this yearning for his first love. His love. And then Tansy would look up at him with guileless affection, as she did now, and his heart fluttered in his chest.

Tansy raised her basket. "I've brought coffee."

He peered into the basket and frowned, dramatically disappointed. "No beignets?"

Tansy tilted her head and scowled. "Do you deserve beignets?"

"I do. Yes, I do. We both do, don't we, Alain?"

Monsieur Fortier popped his white-haired head out his door. "Did I hear someone say beignets?"

Sadly, Christophe crushed the man. "She doesn't think we deserve beignets."

Tansy rolled her eyes. "All right, next time."

Christophe grinned at Alain. "I think we won that one, don't you?" he whispered.

"I heard that," she sang softly.

Christophe moved his books and papers so Tansy could pour. He handed Alain a large piece of chalk and gestured toward the big black board behind the desk. He'd never known a child who didn't crave to draw on that board.

The three of them talked about the students, who needed a nudge, who was racing ahead of the others. And through it all, Christophe watched Tansy. She had the same avid expression she showed when she wanted to talk about the book she'd just read. Her eyes were bright, her lips slightly parted. This was good for her. She needed a wider world than the cottage on Ursaline Avenue, than the dull man who kept — with whom she was placed.

The outer door opened and a stampede of boys rushed in. Christophe swallowed the last of the coffee and quirked a smile at Tansy. "And so the fun begins."


Tansy worked with René all week. He fretted about the size of his chalk or a speck of dirt on his trousers, and his slate had to be exactly squared with the surface of his desk. He still tuned her out if a bird twittered outside the window or a boy behind him coughed. But he tried, and he learned. He knew half the alphabet now, in only one week. He was a bright child, and now that he was catching up, he smiled more and seemed to sit less stiffly in his chair.

Tansy smiled more, too. She'd had no idea how much she would love this. What had she done with her days before she spent two hours every morning at the school? She felt as if there were a drab before and now this bright and shining now. She knew she was good at this. Her lace tatting was mediocre, her cooking unremarkable. But she could reach these children.

During the short morning break on Friday morning, Rosa took her down the hallway to the small dark office. Christophe sat in a straight-back chair, his ankle crossed over his knee. He had a mild smile on his face when she came in. She sat next to him, curious why Rosa called her here. Then it occurred to her, Rosa didn't want her help anymore. She would be asked not to return.

She swallowed hard and clasped her hands together. They always trembled when she was upset or frightened. And if Rosa sent her away, she would be upset. She tightened the muscles in her face. She would smile, she would be light and gay. She didn't have to be here, after all. She had a life in her cottage with Alain and Valere.

Rosa squeezed herself between her desk and the wall to sit down. She put her clasped hands on the blotter and cleared her throat. Tansy clamped her teeth. Why did Rosa need to clear her throat if she were not going to say something bad?

"I spend hours every week looking at numbers," Rosa said. "We need lamp oil, we need custodians, brooms, books, paper, ink, chalk, slates, window washers. All of which must be ordered, inventoried, paid for."

Tansy nodded. She had no idea why Rosa thought she needed to know this.

"I could spend two hours a day just running this place." Rosa glanced at Christophe and back to Tansy. "If you would accept the job, as a paid teacher, we would like to hire you to take over the eight year olds' class, two hours each morning."

Tansy's eyes widened. "A job?"

Christophe grinned at her. Rosa smiled. "You and I would plan the next day's lessons, you'd teach, you'd do what you have been doing, but for all eight of them at the same time."

Tansy felt like bells were ringing in her head. She couldn't speak for the clamor. Christophe's eyes were shining. He looked ... he looked like he was proud of her. Tears pricked at her eyes, but she blinked them back.

"What do you say?" Christophe asked.

"Yes!" A laugh burbled up. "Yes."

Rosa opened a drawer and drew out a paper-wrapped bundle. She shoved it across the desk. "Open it."

Tansy untied the twine, opened the paper, and unfolded a heavy, burgundy apron like the one Rosa wore. Across the bib, the initials RLAB. Rosa LeFevre's Academy for Boys.

This time she could not blink away the tears. Christophe leaned over and wiped at her cheek with his thumb. "I take it you like the apron?" he said softly.

She laughed, but she wanted to cry, to sing, to shout. She was a teacher!

Rosa slapped her hands on the desk. "Right. We need to get to class, Christophe. Tansy, we'll see you Monday morning." She wrested herself from behind the desk and bustled into the hallway.

Christophe stood and held a polite hand out for her. She ignored his hand and jumped up, her arms around his neck. "This is the best day!"

He stroked her back and patted while she clung to him. When she let go, she looked into his face and the glee drained right out of her. His eyes were too dark, too somber. He ran a thumb over her mouth. Then he stepped back.

"I have to get to class."

Tansy pressed her hand to her lips where he'd touched her and closed her eyes. Abruptly, she blinked. These silly tears. How foolish she was. She wiped her face and went to find Alain.

## Chapter Seven

His fiddle under his chin, Christophe played the second set when Martine arrived at the ball. He'd heard she was after a new protector. From his perch on the orchestra's platform, he enjoyed watching the courtship rituals as gentlemen admired and ladies flirted, the fans in the room fluttering like butterflies in clover. This time it would be Martine casting the net as if she were the hunter and her chosen one the hapless butterfly.

He could only smile at Martine in her signature red, her bodice threatening to slip below what was decent even here. He'd always liked Martine, the hauteur on her face unable to conceal the mischief in her eyes. She looked good in that red dress, especially with so little of it to cover her.

Martine entered the dance with a young man whose blond curls spilled over his collar. He could be no more than sixteen, his limbs lanky and awkward. No doubt the boy's father or his older brother had brought him to introduce him to the delights of a quadroon ball, but he would not be getting into bed with any of these women tonight. If he wanted immediate gratification, he would have to visit one of the rougher ballrooms where short-term transactions, sometimes lasting a mere half an hour, were quickly made and consummated. For now, though, the boy was entranced by Martine's décolletage.

When Martine waltzed by, she shared a feline smile with him that said she knew exactly what was on her partner's mind. She leaned a little closer than was quite right, displaying her rather magnificent chest. The boy would soon be so hot he might be unable to remember his dignity. Christophe quirked a wry smile at her as he bowed his fiddle.

He turned his attention to the music, fingers flying over his violin, the bow an extension of his arm and his heart. If he hadn't found his calling with Rosa, he'd have happily played out his life in ballrooms and private chambers. As the orchestra gave a rousing finish to the waltz, he glanced over the dancers and again lit on the tanager red of Martine's gown. The pup she danced with spoke while he held her hand, but Martine's eyes were on the gentleman behind him. Eyes wide, lips parted, she seemed to forget the golden haired boy. DuMaine approached, a commanding, confident air clearing his path.

Even from where Christophe sat, he could see her glow. This was not good. He knew very well how ill-advised it was for a young woman to become enamored of a gentleman at the balls. Her role in life was to effect his infatuation, not the other way around. In the world of plaçage, stories abounded of foolish girls who gave their hearts away only to be crushed by the realities of their status. Surely Martine was too smart for that.

Ignoring the boy, DuMaine held his hand out for Martine. As the music resumed, Martine gazed into his face, only a hint of smile on her face. She seemed entranced. Christophe hoped it was mere flirtation, but he feared he saw genuine captivation. He'd hate to see her hurt, but there was nothing he could do about it. Unless he put a word in his mother's ear, who might put a word in Tansy's mother's ear, who might take the trouble to speak to Martine. It was a bitter thing, for a man to be so marginalized in his own world.

Tansy and her mother Estelle entered the ballroom, and all of Christophe's attention focused on Tansy as he played an old familiar piece. She wore a diaphanous gown of pale gray cut to expose her shoulders and reveal a modest hint of cleavage. As ever unaware how lovely she was, her eyes roved to see if her Monsieur Valcourt were in the room. When she saw she had arrived first, he saw her shoulders relax.

Was that the sign of a woman in love, for her to be more at ease out of the man's presence than in it? He allowed himself to wonder what Tansy's shoulders might signal at his own presence.

A corpulent older gentleman claimed Tansy's first dance. His face glowed with pleasure to have her hand in his. Tansy, gracious as always, smiled at him even though he set a pace unfortunately a little faster than the music. When the gentleman whirled her just under the platform where Christophe played, she caught his eye, her expression part pain, part amusement. He grinned at her. She danced away, he played on.

The next time Christophe saw her, she was in the arms of Valcourt. They danced well together, he admitted, but he saw no signs of enchantment. None of Martine's starry-eyed gaze, nor Monsieur DuMaine's hot-eyed look. They seemed merely pleasant together. Well, they'd been together five years now. Five years and three months.

Tansy, smiling, looked up at Valcourt, listening to him. He supposed she needed him. A patron, after all, was called a protector for a reason. A beautiful woman of color faced uncommon pressures. She had little power to resist if a white man chose to exploit her, misuse her, abandon her. At least plaçage minimized those threats.

Teeth clamped, Christophe pressed his chin into his violin. Why was he not used to this? He and Tansy had shared a kiss when they were just kids. Years ago. He should be over that by now. Perhaps he needed to play with a different orchestra, at a ball Tansy and her paramour did not frequent. Why do this to himself?

Tansy loved to dance. Surefooted and graceful, Valere led her round and round the ballroom, dance after dance. He seemed particularly attentive tonight, handing her champagne, gently fingering an escaped curl over her ear. When they danced the gavotte, they moved faster and faster, laughing at the insanely quick pace.

Breathless, he seated her next to her mother and kissed her hand. "I'll come to you later," he murmured. She watched him saunter through the crowd toward the curtained doorway. He would walk through the long, discreet corridor between the buildings to the other ballroom, to finish the evening with his bride. The new Mrs. Valcourt no doubt believed the fiction that her husband's interlude away from her was spent in the exclusively masculine, smoky gambling chamber off the ballroom.

Estelle was in a mood, her lips pursued. "Madame Landry is making a fool of herself."

Tansy sought out the lady. She danced with a nice-looking gentleman, his hair graying, but his posture erect. "What do you mean?"

"That's the third dance she has allowed him. He'll see no allure if she gives herself so freely."

"She's enjoying herself, Maman. Every dance partner doesn't have to be a suitor."

"A suitor," Estelle snorted. "Wouldn't she like that, at her age."

Tansy looked at her mother. Such a mean streak she had. Still attractive, still sought after on the dance floor, but in unguarded moments like this, sour. Madame Landry was her friend, for goodness' sake, and still she pecked.

"And Martine! Look at her. He'll think she's in love with him and then how I am to negotiate a profitable contract?"

"He may enjoy having her look at him like he's a prince, Maman. They look happy, both of them."

"She may allow herself to look interested and fond, but besotted? Three placées in five years? DuMaine is a hard man. She's just making difficulties for herself. And for me."

"I'm sure you're a match for Monsieur DuMaine, Maman."

Estelle's lips suddenly parted in a dazzling smile. "Monsieur Girard," she said.

Tansy knew Monsieur Girard from many balls past. She'd often danced with him herself, enjoying his courtly manner. He was growing stout, his hair thinning, but he was a kindly, gentle man. Tansy smiled at him.

"Mademoiselle Tansy, how do you do?"

"*Bien*, Monsieur. You're looking very well."

He patted his girth. "I am perhaps a little over-indulged, but well, yes." He turned to Estelle. "Madame, might I entice you to dance?"

Gracefully, Estelle rose and accepted his arm. Tansy rather hoped for Monsieur Girard's sake that he did not develop an affection for her mother. He would be much more comfortable with a kindlier soul.

Tansy turned in her chair to watch Christophe play. She saw he was now first violin. He'd never said! So young, and the best violinist in the orchestra. Tomorrow she would congratulate him. Did his mother know? Or Rosa? Neither came to the balls anymore.

Tansy felt a secret collusion with him tonight. They would both have circles under their eyes when they reported to school at eight o'clock after a late night. She herself would be very late indeed getting to sleep since Valere was coming over. A stray vision popped into her head of Christophe bedding a woman after the ball. She blinked. Heat flooded her face. She lowered her eyes, embarrassed at her own imagining, ashamed of herself for intruding on his privacy, as if she'd peeked into his window.

Determined to put Christophe from her mind, she turned her back to the orchestra and watched her mother twirling across the floor with Monsieur Girard. Maman would be furious if she knew Tansy went to Rosa LeFevre's Academy for Boys every morning. Maman wasn't likely to find out, however. She and Alain would be home by ten thirty every morning. That was still early in her mother's mind.

Tansy retrieved Alain from Mrs. O'Hare's where he slept on a palette among several other children. He didn't wake as she hoisted him to her shoulder and walked three doors down to her cottage. Large oil lamps suspended over every corner lit her way, only cats on the prowl through the quiet street.

She freshened herself and changed into the finely-painted silk kimono Valere enjoyed. He liked stroking and nipping her through the silk, opening it only enough to thrust his body into hers.

He knocked softly at the door and she let him in. He undressed by candlelight. She placed his shoes squarely, precisely, at the foot of the bed. She draped his coat, his vest and shirt, cravat and trousers over the walnut valet, careful to smooth any wrinkles. He lay on her bed, nude, ready, welcoming.

Tonight he was in no hurry. He made love to her slowly, even with finesse, so that she was breathless with wanting by the time he entered her. Ah, how she loved it when her body was ready for him, when he drove himself into her, his breath and hers heavy and urgent.

The big four poster shook, even scooted on the cypress boards until Valere cried out and collapsed on top of her. He gasped for breath, then rolled over onto his back. She shifted to her side, her hand on his sweaty chest. In moments, he was asleep.

Tansy pulled the covers over them, lay back, and closed her eyes. The best of all possible worlds, she remembered. It didn't have to be ironic. It could be true. Or close to it. Nothing was perfect, after all, and, really, there was only now, wasn't there? And now was good.

A mockingbird woke her. Pale gray light seeped in through the window shutters. Valere still slept beside her. She bolted upright. He shouldn't be here. His wife would wonder where he'd been all night. She shook his shoulder. "Valere. Wake up. You've overslept."

He half opened his eyes and rolled over.

"Valere." She lit a candle to see the clock on her dresser. Six-thirty! She and Alain had to leave in just over an hour to get to school on time. She was not a mere volunteer who could come and go as she pleased. She had a job.

She shook Valere's shoulder again. "Valere!"

He shrugged her hand off and burrowed into his pillow.

She strode quickly toward the kitchen and started a pot of coffee. He had to leave. Now.

In the bedroom, she opened the shutters and hoped the mockingbird would shrill until Valere was too irritated to sleep. She bustled around the room, opening drawers, closing drawers, dropping a book, then a shoe.

"Good morning, my darling," she called. She thought he was half-awake.

Alain, bright-eyed and curious, popped his head in the door. "Papa's here?"

She hustled Alain from the room. "Remember what we said about school?" she whispered. "It's a secret, isn't it? Grand-mère and Papa are not to know."

"I remember."

She hated secrets. Hated lies even more. But there was no need of telling either of them about school. It had nothing to do with them.

"I'm going to pour your father a cup of coffee. See if you can wake him up."

Alain skipped into the room and climbed on the bed. "Papa!"

Valere turned his head to skewer him with a look.

"Papa, wake up."

"Why?"

Alain threw himself over Valere's body. "So you can have coffee with me."

Valere sighed hugely. "What time is it?" Then he frowned. "Can you tell time?"

"I know when it's twelve o'clock."

He heaved another sigh.

Tansy bustled in with a cup of coffee. "Good morning," she trilled.

Scowling, he flopped a pillow over his face.

*Tansy*

She put her hands on her hips. How was she to get him out of here?

"Valere," she said sweetly. "I don't want you to have trouble. You need to get home."

"Already in trouble if it's daylight."

"You don't want to worry your new wife, darling."

She thought for a moment he was not going to answer. "Let me sleep, Tansy." His breathing deepened. The arm over the pillow relaxed.

She stared at him, his bare chest gently rising and falling. What was she to do?

The idea of waiting here for Valere to wake up left her feeling hollow under her breastbone. She would let Rosa and the children down. Let herself down. But if she and Alain went to school, he'd wake up and she'd be gone.

She put her fingers to her mouth. Impossible to leave him here. Impossible not to.

Alain looked up at her from the bed with big eyes, a sober expression on his face. He was only four, but he seemed to understand exactly what was going through her mind. Choose, she told herself. Just because she'd had so little occasion to make decisions of any importance didn't mean she couldn't.

"Alain," she whispered. "Can you dress yourself this morning?"

He gave her an indignant look. "Maman. I'm four."

She managed not to smile. "Of course." She lifted him from the bed and put him on his feet. "I'll be with you in a few minutes."

Tansy fished a piece of stationary out of her writing desk and dipped her quill in the ink pot.

"Valere, my love. Alain and I have gone to the market. When you wake up, I'll give you a long, leisurely breakfast." He would not want a long, leisurely breakfast. He'd rather stop at the Market and talk to his friends over beignets and coffee, so that should bestir him. Then a wicked thought came to her, no doubt from a tiny vicious streak she'd inherited from Maman. She added, "While you eat, I'll read to you, and then you can read to Alain. All my love, Tansy."

She hesitated. It still smarted, what he'd said to her when she had mentioned love: I'm married now, Tansy. Her mouth tight, she drew a bold, heavy stroke under the word "love." Smiling grimly, she propped the note against his body so he'd see it as soon as he woke. No doubt in her mind that he would be gone when she got back.

She dressed quickly, tied Alain's shoes, collected her shopping basket, and quietly closed the door behind them.

It was a fine spring morning. A cardinal flitted ahead of them, a brilliant streak of red among the green leaves. She'd made a decision. She'd made a choice. She did have a niggling twinge of conscience for the manipulative note she'd written, but she chose to ignore it. See, Christophe? I'm not so nice after all.

She squeezed Alain's hand. "Do you think you and Christophe deserve beignets this morning?"

## Chapter Eight

When she'd taught her two hours, Tansy hurried Alain toward the market. She needed something in her shopping bag to show where she'd been. She half feared and half hoped Valere would still be there when she got home. Maybe he was still abed, maybe even still sleeping. She could quietly take the note back and have his coffee ready for him when he got up. As if she had been patiently waiting for him to rise. But what if he'd wakened and waited for her, long enough for her to have gone to the market and back, and still she hadn't come?

Acid roiled in her stomach. Could she lie to him? I saw a friend at the market, she could say. I lost track of the time. Maybe she should simply tell him where she'd been and what she'd been doing. Maybe he'd even be proud of her. That seemed unlikely, though. The most she could hope for was indulgence.

When she entered the house, she paused at the threshold, listening. She didn't hear him, and the tightness in her chest eased. "Change your clothes, Alain, and I'll cut an orange for you."

Tansy jolted at the figure of Estelle silhouetted in the door to the courtyard. "Maman, you gave me such a start."

Estelle stepped into the room, her arms crossed over her chest. "Where have you been all morning?"

Tansy held up her shopping bag. "To the market."

One carefully groomed brow quirked up. "For nearly two hours? For that is how long I have waited here."

Tansy attempted a laugh. "Why ever would you wait so long, Maman?" She set her bag on the table. "Would you like an orange? Or I could make coffee."

"I've already had coffee. With Monsieur Valcourt."

Tansy hesitated perhaps a moment too long. "Oh, then he's awake?"

"Awake and gone."

Tansy busied herself with unloading her bag. "That's too bad. I promised him a big breakfast."

Keeping her back to Estelle, she busied herself filling the fruit bowl, wrapping the bread in brown paper and putting it in the tin safe. The silence between them seemed to grow in size and weight like some black cloud taking monstrous shape behind her.

"What can you be thinking? Valcourt here, and you gone?"

Tansy touched the base of her breastbone where a knot twisted. She turned to her mother with a shrug. "Valere was sleeping soundly, and I had things to do."

Estelle took a step toward her, her mouth contorted into an ugly square. "You have nothing, nothing else you have to do when your protector is in your bed. You want to throw away everything? You want him to leave you simply because you had things to do?"

Tansy leaned back at the viciousness in her mother's face. Estelle closed the distance between them, took a pinch of flesh on Tansy's upper arm and twisted. "Where were you!"

She slapped her mother's hand away, pain and anger searing through her. She straightened her spine and looked directly into her mother's eyes. "Do not presume to touch me that way again."

Estelle's head snapped back. "What did you say to me?"

"I am not a child. You may not treat me as one."

"You're not a child?" Estelle snorted. "And yet you leave Valere in your bed while you go — you have not been at the market all this time."

"It does not concern you where I have been. I'd like you to go now, Maman."

Estelle's eyes narrowed. "You've taken a lover."

Tansy laughed. "You think I would leave Valere in my bed and go to a lover at seven in the morning?"

Alain skipped into the room and settled himself at the table. "*Bonjour*, Grand-mère. I'm going to have an orange."

Estelle ignored him. She glowered at Tansy, the furrows around her mouth deepening. "Is it Christophe?"

Tansy felt heat flush over her face. "Don't be ridiculous. I do not have a lover."

Estelle snatched her purse off the table. "If you betray Valere, the contract is voided. You know where you'll end up, and you needn't come crying to me to save you from Nicolas Augustine and his brothel." She marched out, slamming the door behind her.

Tansy's hands trembled. Alain's legs swung back and forth. The little house swelled with silence.

Always Nicolas Augustine, as if he were a red-eyed bogeyman. Such an ugly threat. Yet she'd stood up to her mother! What had come over her? She watched Alain roll an orange across the table from left hand to right hand to left. Tansy wiped her hands on her skirt. She breathed in, breathed out, calming her heart, easing her chest. You know what? she said to herself. I feel good. I feel tall.

With a light heart, she said, "Here, Alain. Let me peel it."

"I can pull the segments apart by myself."

"I know you can. You can do many things." Tansy dug into the rind with her thumbnail, the sharp scent of orange rind bursting out.

"Grand-mère was mad. But not at me."

"No, darling. Not at you. Don't worry about it."

At least Maman's outburst had put things into perspective. Teaching at the school was nothing compared to Maman's accusation. Why should Valere object if she were gone in the mornings? He had only come to her before noon perhaps twice in the last five years. She would simply tell him. He could still sleep in of a morning if he wanted to. When her two hours were up at school, she'd come right back. If he wanted to wait for her, she would happily climb back into bed with him.

It was nothing. Valere truly could not care what she did in the mornings. She stole a segment of orange from Alain and savored the sweet, tart juice on her tongue.

Martine rushed in. "Tansy!"

"Whatever is the matter?"

"Nothing is the matter! Look at this." Martine held out a dozen red roses wrapped in green paper.

"How truly beautiful, Martine." She looked at her friend's excited face. "They're from him? Monsieur DuMaine?"

Heedless of thorns, Martine pressed the roses to her breast. She held a card out. "Read this."

*For my beautiful Martine. DuMaine.*

"He says 'my Martine.' You see that?"

Martine's black eyes shone, her cheeks were pink. Tansy had not seen her like this since she'd been a girl in the clutch of infatuation all those years ago.

"Has he spoken to Maman?"

"I don't know. But he will, won't he?"

"I can't imagine that he won't." Tansy filled a vase from the water jug and offered it to Martine. Then she sat at the table and pulled Alain into her lap. He reached for the vase of flowers and began twisting the vase in his hands.

Martine reclaimed them with a laugh. "Alain, *mon cher*, I love you, but you may not have my roses."

He gave Martine the smile of an imp and let her move them to her side of the table. Tansy kissed the top of his head. "Why don't you bring your soldiers in here to play with while we talk? I see the leg of this table is actually the very tall door into a very tall castle."

When Alain had slid off her lap, Tansy reached across the table for Martine's hand. "I believe you are in love, my friend."

A definite flush moved from Martine's neck up through her cheeks. "Love. Fah, I am not such a green girl as that."

"Then what are you? In very great like?"

Martine laughed. "Yes, I am in very great like. Who would not be? Frederick is handsome, charming, attentive. And when he holds me in his arms ... " Martine gazed over Tansy's shoulder, a far-away look in her eyes.

"Yes, I can see this is great like."

Marine turned a sober gaze back on Tansy. "I ... I want him to touch me. I want him in my bed."

Tansy's brows shot high on her forehead. "Martine!"

Martine shrugged. "If you and I cannot say such things ..."

"You haven't already — "

Martine flipped her wrist at Tansy. "No, of course not. At least, not much."

"Martine?"

"Just a kiss or two. Behind the palms." Her eyes twinkled. "And perhaps a touch. Or two."

"I never thought I'd be saying this to you. Are you thinking at all?"

"Of course I am. Have I not already engaged your mother to speak for me?"

"Even knowing how he is? What, sixteen lovers in three years?"

Martine laughed. "Three in five years. You know that." Her eyes took on that dreamy cast again. "Perhaps I shall be his last."

Tansy shook her head. "I don't know what to think. You, of all people. In *like*."

"He's picking me up in his carriage tonight. To take me dancing."

"That means he'll be bringing you home." Tansy tilted her head at Martine with a suspicious look in her eye.

Martine grinned. "Yes, it does."

"Martine, you cannot let him come in. Not before Maman has made arrangements."

Martine didn't answer. She simply stared into the distance.

"Martine."

Martine huffed out a breath. "Of course not. I am not a fool. I know how it's done."

So many times Martine had scoffed at Tansy for being emotional and sentimental, but Tansy doubted Martine's coolheaded resolve this time. The moon glow on her gentleman and the stars in her own eyes blinded her to common sense.

When Martine left, Tansy wrote a quick note to her mother. For all her mother's harshness, she had protected Tansy and kept her safe until she'd agreed Tansy could have Valere. Martine had no family left, but she had Estelle. If for no other reason, Maman would not want to see Martine enter into a liaison without the proper documents, and thus the proper commission to herself. She would know exactly how to keep Martine from any foolish, rash behavior.

She folded the letter and hesitated. It had been so long since she'd seen Martine sparkling and happy. Maman's shrewish, caustic, pitiless tongue would lash and rip at her. She would twist Martine's feelings into something tawdry.

Tansy tore the letter in two. She would not see Martine scathed and humiliated. She would take care of this herself.

At ten o'clock, she sat at her front window watching the street. An elegant black carriage rolled up in front of Martine's cottage. DuMaine emerged looking debonair, handsome, and assured. In a moment, he returned and handed Martine into his carriage.

Tansy gathered a book, a shawl, and a bread roll into her shopping bag. It would be hours before Martine returned, and she'd be starving long before the ball was over. Alain lay on his back, arms and legs splayed out. She took him into her arms without waking him and walked through the adjoining courtyards to Martine's back door. She keyed it open and entered.

The street lamp on the corner seeped in enough to show her the way to Martine's bed. She lay Alain down, then returned to the parlor where she lit an oil lamp and settled in to read. By the time she heard carriage wheels, she'd fallen asleep on the sofa and developed a crick in her neck.

She roused herself and ran her hands over her face. She must look a fright. No matter. She pressed her hand against her stomach in anxiety. Tansy had no experience in denying gentlemen, and DuMaine was a rich man, accustomed to doing as he pleased and having what he wanted. His response to being gainsaid might be quite unpleasant. Nevertheless, DuMaine would not enter Martine's bedroom tonight.

The door opened. Martine entered, leading DuMaine by the hand, her back to Tansy. The gentleman's eyelids were heavy, his gaze ardent. He closed the door with his foot and pulled Martine into his arms, bending her back in a fevered kiss. He'd quickly pushed her gown completely off one shoulder when Tansy said, "Good evening."

His head jerked up, the surprise on his face comical.

Martine twisted in his arms. "Tansy?"

"Good evening," she said again.

DuMaine released Martine, his expression stern and glowering. Tansy took a fortifying breath. "Did you have a lovely time at the ball?" And in the carriage coming home, she might have added. Martine's tignon was askew, her lips swollen and pink.

Martine put her hands on her hips and scowled at her.

"How kind of you to bring Martine home in your carriage, Monsieur."

Tansy understood the man's appeal. He oozed power and masculinity.

"Madame ... Tansy, is it?" His raised brows asked her what the devil she was about. He knew Martine lived alone. She could almost see his mind working. Would she be persuaded to absent herself? He touched his breast pocket, and she knew he considered offering her a ... token ... to leave them.

"Madame," DuMaine began, steel under the smooth, urbane tone. The man did not mean to be thwarted.

Tansy held her hand up, wondering where she got the nerve. "Monsieur, perhaps you don't realize that my friend is alone in the world. No father, brother, mother, uncle, no one to protect her."

"Tansy!" Martine said, that one word full of warning.

Tansy looked Martine full in the face. "But she has me." She turned her gaze back to DuMaine. "Perhaps, Monsieur, you might call on Madame Bouvier on Rampart St. She is experienced in these matters and will discuss the terms of your alliance with my friend."

DuMaine's jaw muscle flexed. His eyes bore into hers and she swore she could see fire in their depths. She lifted her chin and crossed her arms. And as suddenly as the sun peeking through a patch of cloud, his expression brightened. A glint of humor lit his eyes and he granted her a very slight smile.

He took Martine's hand and kissed it with an ungentlemanly warmth, bowed to both of them, and left without another word.

"Tansy." Martine's voice wavered with frustrated yearning. "You had no business — "

"Yes, Martine. I did have business keeping you from ruining your chances with him. You need a contract."

"I have enough income. I don't need a contract."

"Yes. You do. There is a distinct line between having a formal alliance and simply taking a man to your bed. And you know it."

Martine glowered, too annoyed to keep the vinegar out of her voice. "You're so sure that if he had come to my bed, he would not have offered a contract?"

Tansy raised her palms. "Perhaps he would have. Perhaps not. But you will not be thought of easy virtue. You will not stain your name."

Martine's mouth took on that stubborn look. She was truly angry.

"Look at you," Tansy said. "Can you honestly say you were thinking straight tonight? If it had been I bringing home a man I was besotted with, what would you have done?"

Martine tightened her mouth with stubbornness, but she looked aside. Tansy walked to her and kissed her cheek. "I'll get Alain and go home."

Tansy was half way out of the room when Martine said, "No. Stay." She exhaled a heavy sigh. "Have a glass of wine with me."

Side by side on the sofa, their feet on the coffee table, Martine tossed her tignon aside and shook out her hair. "Christophe was there, in the orchestra."

"That means another book or two, no doubt."

"Is that what he does with his money? Buy books? How unimaginative."

"I think it's quite imaginative." She shook her head. "You and Valere don't know what you're missing. There's a whole world in every book you open. I could loan you one — I think you'd like *Candide*."

Martine leaned her head against the sofa back. "Maybe." With a glint in her eye, she nudged Tansy. "He has a woman over on St. Ann. Did you know?"

Tansy sipped her wine. She hadn't known. Why would she?

"Did you?" Martine asked again.

"I hadn't thought about it." But she had, once or twice, wondered ... well, it was none of her business.

"I don't think they're in love. Not according to Alexandra. She lives next door to this Musette Vipont. A widow. No children."

It was on the tip of Tansy's tongue to ask how old the woman was, but she stopped herself.

"Alexandra thinks they are merely comfortable — convenient — together."

Truly, not her business. "The sun's up." Tansy motioned toward the gray bands of early light at the shuttered window.

"Poor Tansy. Alain will be waking up full of energy and you've been up all night."

"I slept a while."

Martine rolled her head to the side and looked at her. "You were quite fierce with Frederick. Who knew you had a tiger in you?"

Tansy laughed. "Was I fierce? I thought I was simply firm."

Martine took her hand. "Thank you."

"You'd have done the same for me."

"Yes, I would have."

Tansy put her feet on the floor. "I hear Alain stirring. I'm taking him home and then I'm going to make a huge pot of coffee."

Martine opened the courtyard door for her. As Tansy passed with Alain on her shoulder, Martine said, quietly, "On St. Ann, one house below Dauphine. The one with the blue shutters."

Tansy didn't have to ask what she meant. But really, Christophe was entitled to his own life.

Tansy paused at the corner of Rue Dauphine. She had plenty of time before she and Alain had to be at school. Why shouldn't she satisfy her curiosity? Christophe knew everything about her life.

She turned down St. Ann and scanned the block ahead. One house down from Dauphine, Martine had said. On this side of the street were a parfumerie and a leather shop. It had to be the house on the opposite sidewalk, a typical Vieux Carré cottage with double French doors and a cypress stoop. Beside the door, a wooden plaque. Dressmaker, painted in gold script.

The dressmaker's door opened, and a stately woman stepped out with a shopping basket. She wore a fashionably cut green dress with a matching, intricately-tied tignon. She must be a decade older than Christophe, but this had to be her. Blue shutters, one down from Dauphine. Christophe's lover.

The woman locked the front door. She turned up St. Ann and strode ahead of Tansy. Tall as a man, the woman was no beauty, but Tansy admired her proud bearing, her long, purposeful strides. This was the woman Christophe bedded, the woman he had chosen. A dressmaker. A woman who made her own way in the world, who'd mastered a profession, who'd created her own life. What had Tansy ever done? Inadequacy bloomed in her chest like a poisonous flower. She depended on Valere for everything — clothing, shoes, fuel, even the food she and Alain ate. When had she ever controlled her own life?

The woman paused at the corner to wait for a hay wagon to pass. Tansy got a better look at her in profile. No, not beautiful, her skin too dark, her face too plain to be a placée. She'd had to learn a trade. Tansy had been born with a pleasing face, a pleasing shape, and a pleasing skin. Why should she apologize for that? What woman wouldn't take advantage of God's gifts?

Yet the poisonous flower shriveled her pride. Christophe had chosen a woman as different from Tansy as she could be.

## Chapter Nine

Tansy held her arms out and slowly turned for Martine's appreciation of her new ball gown. She'd had Madame Odette copy the cut from the latest Paris fashion magazine with the skirt beginning a little lower than just below the bust line, as the classic Empire gowns had done. No longer quite as amorphous and soft an outline, the skirt draped in a slightly conical shape, the bottom twelve inches adorned with bands of embroidery.

"It looks good on you. And your fan, the tignon — " Marine touched her thumb and fingers together. "Perfect. Who would have thought to use turquoise with coral?"

"I would," Tansy laughed. Her headdress was a swirl of silk fastened with a broach of tiny turquoise chips.

"Alain, how do you like Maman's new dress?" Martine said.

Alain glanced up from his line of soldiers. "*Bonne.*" He returned to the task of knocking over the dead and dying British line which Napoleon's soldiers had just decimated.

"Hmm," Martine said. "I'm afraid you are not raising *un homme gallant*. Alain, a courteous gentleman, when asked to comment on a lady's appearance, must say '*Ah, trés belle.*' Or if she looks especially splendid, '*Merveilleuse!*' "

With a flick of his finger, he felled the British general. "*Merveilleuse*, Maman." The blue-coated officer marched over to the fallen red-coat and jumped on him. "*Vlan! Pan!*"

Tansy grinned at Martine's exaggerated sigh. "You better get dressed before Monsieur DuMaine arrives." Enclosed carriages being notorious opportunities for seduction, Tansy had insisted on acting chaperone to and from the ball.

"You can entertain him while I tantalize him with anticipation."

That would do very well, Tansy thought. She meant to have a private word with the gentleman.

Tansy delivered Alain to Mrs. O'Hare, then let herself into Martine's cottage just a moment before DuMaine's handsome carriage rolled up. Tansy opened the door to a vision of masculine beauty. His waistcoat, cravat and tall collar gleamed white against the black cut-away coat. The fashionable long breeches showed off his long legs. His dark hair rose in a pomaded wave over his brow. He smiled knowingly as he took Tansy's hand and raised it to his lips. "Ah, *trés belle*."

Tansy smiled, in part because she was as knowing as he about his intentions, her intentions, and Martine's intentions. And in part because his compliment emerged in the exact tone Martine had used when she coached Alain.

She offered him a glass of wine while they waited for Martine to emerge in her finery. While they sat companionably in Martine's elegant little parlor, Tansy considered how best to approach a delicate subject. Though she was not accustomed to making assertions or giving ultimatums, that's what she meant to do. She might lack the sophistication to address the issue with finesse, but she would have the man understand he could not misuse her friend.

"I understand, Monsieur DuMaine, that neither you nor your man of business has called on Madame Bouvier."

DuMaine shifted in his chair. He drank from his glass. He touched his starched collar.

"Perhaps you have been otherwise occupied these last days?"

"Yes, yes I have been. Business concerns."

Tansy waited, expecting a declaration of his intent to open negotiations for Martine at the earliest possible moment. He merely sipped his wine.

Deliberately, she allowed impatience to sharpen her voice. "Monsieur, I assure you. Tonight will be the last time you may see Martine until you have made arrangements with Madame Bouvier."

He leaned back in his chair, a smile on his handsome face. "And is it you, Tansy — may I call you Tansy?"

"Madame Bouvier."

"Ah, I had not realized. You are — ?"

"Estelle Bouvier's daughter."

"I see." His smile broadened. "And is it you, Madame Bouvier, who will stand between Martine and me? What does Martine say about your ..." His eyes hardened. "Your interference."

Tansy leaned forward in her chair, her eyes very steady on his. "She will complain. She will rail at me. And she will not see you again."

She took a breath and straightened. She was not certain of the last part of her statement, but he need not know that. Tansy set her wineglass aside. "Monsieur DuMaine, you are well-acquainted with plaçage. You understand that a woman like Martine leads a precarious life without a patron. Her color robs her of those safeguards a lady of your class may expect. Her beauty and her upbringing have made her unsuitable for marriage with all but the very few, too few, men of color with her education. Monsieur, without the strictures of plaçage, without the protection of a man like you, she would be subjected to unpleasant, even dangerous choices in this life."

She knew she did not have to explain more fully. Women in her sphere of life sometimes transformed themselves into successful businesswomen with the backing of their first protectors. More often, however, a woman like Martine, or herself, who had no protector, ended up in poverty, worn down by worry and menial work. Far too often they fell into the clutches of men like Nicolas Augustine and the life-shortening perils of prostitution.

"You must not expect Martine to give herself to you without the safety and security plaçage offers her. You see that, do you not?"

He leaned over his knees, his gaze on the floor. At this moment, he did not seem so arrogant nor hard as she had thought. But whatever his feelings, or his reasons for hanging back, he could not have her friend without assuring her of his protection.

His smile was rather rueful when he looked up at her. "You are a shrewd woman, Madame."

She laughed. "No one has ever thought me shrewd. But I believe I am complimented, regardless of your intent."

The man straightened his perfect cravat and found the pattern of the rug fascinating. Was he so shy of commitment? "You are a lucky man, Monsieur, if you should win an alliance with my friend. Not every man has the good fortune to protect a woman who is enamored of him."

His smile only raised one side of his mouth. "Is she enamored?"

"I'm sure you know she is."

His expression sobered. He looked at her a long time before he spoke. "Madame, you know my reputation. Not entirely undeserved."

"You refer, I presume, to your inability to attach yourself for, what do the *Américains* say, the long haul?"

DuMaine set his glass aside with the air of a man who'd decided to explain himself. "My first paramour was very young, as was I. We had a happy year together, at least I thought we were happy. And then I discovered she was unfaithful. Rather hurt, I must admit, I extricated myself from our alliance. For my second placée, I chose a more mature, more settled woman. She was also excruciatingly boring. I don't wish to be indelicate, Madame, but you are a woman of the world. I think you will understand the significance when I say I was not entertained either in the bedchamber nor out of it."

"And the third?"

Tansy believed the man actually looked pained. His voice was hoarse when he spoke again. "I could not please her." He darted a look at Tansy. "I do not mean in the bedroom." He actually blushed, and Tansy liked him the better for it. "The first weeks I thought we would suit, but gradually, and more insistently, every word or gesture from me seemed to irritate her."

He picked up his wine glass but merely dangled it from his fingers, his gaze rather sorrowful. "I don't know why."

He glanced at her, embarrassed. "At any rate, Tansy — now I have revealed myself to you, you must let me call you Tansy. Perhaps you can understand my caution."

She tilted her head to look at him, considering. If she had not seen the tightened flesh around his eyes when he spoke of his third paramour, she would have faulted him for simply making excuses for himself. But his explanation was more than that. She saw it as an admission of regret, of disappointment and unhappiness.

"And now," she said quietly, "you are afraid Martine will hurt you."

DuMaine would not look at her. It could not be easy for a man to admit to vulnerability.

"You do not know her. This ... " Tansy sought the right word. "This enthusiasm she shows for you. It is not like her. She is as vulnerable as you, Monsieur. And I fear you will hurt her."

His head snapped up. "I will not."

"Martine wants love. She's never had it. Can you give her that?"

She thought his eyes misted for a moment. Softly, she added, "There are no certainties in life, Monsieur."

He breathed a shaky laugh. "Death and taxes, Tansy. Those are certain."

"Would you like another glass of wine?"

"She will be yet another age?"

She answered his smile. "She might."

As Tansy poured, Martine made her entrance. DuMaine's eyes warmed, his face brightened.

Martine posed a moment in her flame red gown, her shoulders bare, her arms uncovered between long gloves and very short sleeves. A single scarlet feather adorned her elaborate black silk tignon. A black velvet ribbon emphasized her slender neck.

DuMaine strode two steps to take her hand and raise it to his lips. He murmured something Tansy was not meant to hear, and Martine glowed.

"Ladies," he said. "The ball awaits."

Tansy nearly always arrived at the balls before Valere because he had to make his bows at the society ball before he came to her. Tonight, however, she saw he was looking for her. He spotted her immediately and strode around the perimeter of the ballroom to meet her.

"A new gown? Very pretty." Without another word he led her into the dance. Normally he would release her after a set or two to dance with other women. He didn't mind that she also would dance with others. It was customary. She was his, everyone at the ball knew that, and nearly everyone circulated and traded partners and had a wonderful time. It was a small world, that of the subscription quadroon ball. The season tickets Valere bought for her and himself were priced so that only those gentlemen who took their placées, or their future placées, seriously were admitted to dance with the crème of quadroon society.

After they had danced more than hour, Valere still did not leave her side. He led her to the refreshments and sat with her as she drank lemonade and he champagne. She opened her turquoise fan and fluttered it, no message intended, simply a cooling expedient. Valere relaxed into his chair and threw an arm across the back of hers. He tapped his foot as the orchestra played a quadrille. Tansy imagined that he would leave her in a moment to return to his wife. That was what he usually did, dance a while, drink a glass of wine with her, and then say goodnight and whisper in her ear if he meant to come by after the ball. Tonight, when she had finished her drink, he drained his and led her back onto the dance floor.

When they danced by the orchestral platform, Tansy tried to catch Christophe's eye, but he scowled at the music on his stand. She knew he didn't need to read the sheet music as many times as he'd played these tunes. She shrugged, determined to ignore him if that's what he wanted.

She redirected her attention to Valere. She loved dancing with him, but she had to wonder why he was not at the other ballroom with his wife. It had occurred to her that if he was unhappy with Miss Abigail, it would make her own position more secure. See, she said to herself once again, I'm not so very nice after all, Christophe. Then in the next moment, she disproved her own statement. She felt terrible for wishing unhappiness on Valere and his wife. At any rate, Valere's unusual attention soothed her worries. He did not intend to abandon her for the new Madame Valcourt.

Valere led her onto the balcony to cool off. Not so many flowers in February, but a few late-blooming orange trees sweetened the air. Monsieur DuMaine and Martine stood in the shadows, their heads close together, but DuMaine's hands were behind him and Martine's played with her fan. Behaving themselves, she thought, and smiled to herself.

Valere threaded her arm through his and leaned his elbows on the railing to watch a mangy dog sniffing along the gutter below.

"Thank you for staying with me tonight, Valere. I've loved it." He patted her hand. "I was worried you were annoyed with me for not being there when you woke up the other morning."

"Your mother made a fresh pot of coffee for me."

If he asked her, she would tell him where she'd gone. Wouldn't she? Why shouldn't she? He didn't ask. His thoughts were elsewhere, his gaze on the dog as it discovered a rat and gave chase into an alleyway.

She tightened her fingers on his forearm and tried to keep the timidity out of her voice. "Did you wonder where I was?"

He glanced at her. He patted his pocket. "Do you mind if I smoke?"

So he had no curiosity about where she'd been. No real interest in her life. She supposed she should not be hurt. It was not a surprise, and it had nothing to do with whether he were pleased with her. She swallowed the feeling of being of little consequence to him when he and Alain were the center of her life.

Tonight was lovely, she thought determinedly. Here on the balcony, the faint scent of orange blossoms in the breeze, this moment was lovely.

He bit off the end of the cigar, lit the match, and sucked air through the cigar until the tip glowed. He tossed the match into the street and leaned against the railing. "I suppose I will have to return. But first I need to develop the disgusting reek that is expected of me."

"Someone expects you to smell disgusting?" Tansy laughed.

"My wife. She assumes I am smoking in the card room and expects me to reek of tobacco. Which she claims is revolting." His tone strove for lightness, but Tansy heard a note of bewildered hurt. "And the list goes on. She despises the odor of onions, garlic, sage, lilies, roses, my cologne. Me."

Tansy ran her hand over his arm. "I'm sorry, Valere."

He shrugged. "At least she doesn't stare at me. Her older sister stares at me." He gave a mock shiver.

"You're handsome." She touched his starched shirt front. "She's probably infatuated with you."

"No. She is not. I believe she would give a toad the exact same regard." Valere drew deeply on his cigar, waved it in front of himself and exhaled over his shirtfront. "That should do it." He tossed it into the street, its tip arching red through the night. He squeezed her hand. "One more dance."

It was a waltz. She gave herself to the music, her eyes half-closed, Valere guiding her round and round. Too soon, the music stopped. He escorted her to sit beside her mother, Monsieur Girard at her side.

Monsieur sat rather too close, Tansy thought, and wondered that her mother allowed it. Perhaps her mother encouraged him with an eye to the future. Tansy marveled, admiring her mother's mastery of the fan, of flirtation, of instilling a rosy glow on an old man's face.

To her mother, Valere said, "Madame Bouvier, I am happy to see you looking so well. Girard, how do you do?

On Estelle's other side, Martine sat exuding happiness. She might have been a girl, the way her eyes shone with excitement when she grinned at Tansy. Valere bowed to her. He'd known her for years, of course, and even though Martine did not admire him, he thankfully did not seem to know it.

Valere kissed Tansy's hand and said good night. She watched him approach the corridor leading back to his new family with a reluctant tread and felt a pang of tenderness for him. She imagined he was surprised that his bride, and her sister, did not seem to like him. Valere was not a discerning man. He might easily have seen Miss Abigail's eagerness to be wed and not realized it didn't mean she was eager to be wed to him in particular.

And he was now forever bound to a woman who did not care for him, poor man. She would try to make it up to him. He would need her kindness as much as her love-making as he adjusted to his new life.

The handsome dark figure of Monsieur DuMaine blocked her view of Valere's retreating back. He had two glasses of ruby-red sangria in his hands, both of which he handed to Martine. He winked at her, then bowed to Tansy. "May I have this dance?"

He took her hand and held her close enough to talk to her without the entire room over hearing him. "You will be pleased to know that I have an appointment with Madame Bouvier tomorrow at four o'clock."

She stepped back so she could look into his face. He was grinning at her, a mischievous glint in his eye. "You see what terror you struck into my heart, Madame. The notion of your baring your teeth at me if I should approach Martine again had me all atremble."

A quick surge of pride lightened her steps. Niceness did not define her. She had been bold. She had been assertive. And she had convinced this strong man to do what she wanted. She laughed with him and relaxed into his arms.

## Chapter Ten

DuMaine drove the ladies home in his coach, handing each of them out onto the pavement at Martine's front door. He brushed his lips across the back of Tansy's hand. He pressed his lips to the back of Martine's.

"Good evening, ladies."

Martine let them in and floated across the room trailing her shawl behind her like a train. She twirled slowly and gracefully into a chair, then smiled at Tansy as if she were a cat who'd just licked up all the cream.

It was impossible not to smile back at her. "Well."

Martine grinned at her. "Well." She unwound her tignon and tossed the black silk into the air to watch it cascade to the floor.

Tansy sat down. "Martine, listen to me."

"Oh-so-suddenly-wise one, to what profound words shall I listen?"

Tansy rolled her eyes. "Only this. But perhaps you already know it. Monsieur DuMaine is not the hard-hearted rake he appears. Yes, he has a past with women. He's devilishly handsome, and he knows it. But he can be hurt, just as anyone can. He is looking for more than entertainment, Martine."

Martine clasped her hands together. "Oh, I hope so. I do hope so. I want to give him so much more than , well, sensual pleasures."

Tansy couldn't take her eyes from Martine's face. Naked yearning, fervency, vulnerability. And she had hid it under a hard shell of cynicism all these years. She reached out to cover Martine's fists with her hand. "Then you will do very well together."

"Will you have a glass of wine with me?"

"Valere is coming. I'll go home."

A large figure appeared at the courtyard door. Valere tapped on the glass with his cane.

"What on earth!" Martine said.

Tansy was equally surprised. Why had he not simply lit a lamp and waited? She picked up her reticule and strode toward the door.

"I'll get Alain from Mrs. O'Hare's," Martine called after her. "He can sleep with me tonight."

Tansy opened the door and stepped into the frosty courtyard. "Is something wrong?"

"You weren't home."

"No, but I was on my way."

He stood there like an awkward child. She took his hand and led him to her cottage. Sometimes when Valere came to her, he was so hot for her that she feared he would disrobe her in one urgent tear. But he had not reached for her in the courtyard and he stood idly while she lit the lamp.

She blew out the match and turned to him. No fevered gaze, no lips parted in desire. He seemed distracted.

"Do you have anything to eat?" he said at last.

"I'll make us some breakfast. Will you light the fire? I don't want to cook in this dress."

She undressed quickly but carefully arranged her coral gown on a satin-padded hanger and set her shoes in the bottom of the armoire. She unwrapped her tignon, folded it exactly so before she put it in the drawer, and shook out her hair. She donned a comfortable cotton wrapper and was stepping away when she decided the left shoe was at a slight angle and leaned over to straighten it. Then she was ready to stir up an omelet.

She cut peppers and onions into hot bacon fat, the sizzle and aroma filling her little kitchen. She had feared he would lose interest in her once he was married. She had feared he would count on a houseful of children and forget Alain. Yet here he was. She glanced at him as she whipped half a dozen eggs with a dollop of cream. He was a handsome man, but too much good food had created the suggestion of a second chin under his jaw. She didn't mind if he had three chins, but she wondered what his wife would think.

He brooded his way through breakfast.

"Would you like more coffee?"

He dug the heels of his hands into his eyes and rubbed his hands over his face. Suddenly, he gasped. His shoulders shook. He sobbed into his hands.

Shocked, Tansy jumped up from her chair and wrapped her arms around him. She smoothed the hair from his forehead and kissed the top of his head. He buried his face against her breasts until his shaking stopped.

"Tansy, I've made a cock of it."

"Of what, my darling?"

He breathed a deep shuddering breath. He pulled back from her. "I should never have married that woman. I didn't see what I was getting into."

A tingle rose from the back of Tansy's neck and over her scalp. Anger, true and abiding anger tightened her face. How dare that woman hurt him. Didn't she see she'd married a lamb? Valere had never hurt anyone on purpose in his life.

She palmed his face towards her. "What did she do to you?" she demanded.

He looked away from her. He did not deserve whatever meanness that woman had inflicted on him, but he wouldn't speak of it. Her urge to march across town and slap the new Madame Valcourt subsided. She knew what Valere needed now. She stood and took his hand. "Come to bed, Valere."

She made love to him slowly, gently, soothingly. When he climaxed, he clasped her to him in an urgent, fervent embrace. When she rolled off him, he encompassed her in his arms, hugging her close to his side.

The mantle clock chimed six before Valere fell asleep. Again she didn't know what to do. It was a school day. She had perhaps an hour and a half before she needed to have bathed and changed.

But Valere needed her. She couldn't leave him this morning. Or maybe she could. She had to. But he might be disappointed to find himself alone when he woke. She made a tangle with her fingers in her hair. What should she do?

He stirred. He had not slept twenty minutes. "You're getting up?" she said.

He stepped into his drawers. "Early morning races at Metairie."

Relieved, she propped herself on her elbow and watched him dress.

"I have a horse in the third. Paid too much for him, of course — " He had his dancing shoes in his hand and looked around the room. "Didn't I leave a pair of boots here for days like this?"

She retrieved them from the back of her armoire. "Paid too much for him," he resumed as he pulled his boots on, "but he could win it all back in one race."

So he was fine now. You would never know Valere had any deeper thought than what would happen with his race horse. She mentally shook her head. Maybe his thinking wasn't deep, but early this morning, she had seen in him a capacity to be hurt, to need. Just because he was complacent — he hadn't read an entire book ever in his life, he'd boasted to her once — didn't mean he had no depth to his feelings.

She would not embarrass him by alluding to last night. She kissed him good bye, closed the door behind him, and breathed a sigh of relief. Then she dashed to get herself ready for school.

She'd had no sleep at all. She was glad to be with the boys, glad to read them a story, but her own voice sounded fuzzy and indistinct. When Marcel made a joke, she'd stared at him blankly for a moment before she got it. She couldn't do this without sleep.

At the break when normally Rosa and she had a few minutes to confer about the lessons of the day, she actually yawned right in her face. "Oh, Rosa." She flushed with embarrassment. "I'm so sorry."

Rosa looked at her for a long moment. Tansy wondered if she looked as bad as she felt.

"Your nights are not your own, are they?"

Tansy felt the blood rush to her face, which was absurd. Rosa knew she was a placée. And Tansy was not ashamed of it. But she did not want to explain that Valere had taken to sleeping in at her place, eating into her morning. Lack of sleep from the ball was a good enough excuse.

"Rosa, what if I came in at noon instead of at eight?" She smiled, winningly, she hoped, and waited to see if Rosa scowled.

Instead Rosa cocked her head to one side and, at last, nodded. "I think that's an excellent idea. Monday, then, at noon."

As she left with Alain in hand, she passed Christophe's classroom and gave him a quick wave. He looked at her strangely before he raised his hand. She must look like yesterday's cold porridge.

She took Alain home, fed him, took him to her bedroom and closed the door. She set him down with his toys and said, "Do not leave this room."

Alain nodded and lined up Napoleon's soldiers. Tansy sprawled across the bed. She was asleep in under a minute.

That night, Christophe lay with his hands behind his head. Tansy had been pale that morning, and she'd had dark circles under her eyes. Her tignon, usually intricate and precise, had been loose and lop-sided. She'd smiled at him when she waved goodbye, though, and her step had been firm. She didn't seem ill.

She'd probably had less sleep than the four hours he'd grabbed. He tightened his jaw so he wouldn't grind his teeth. If her protector had kept her up the rest of the night and into the morning, that was his prerogative, wasn't it? That's what he paid for. Did he know Tansy had taken a job? An actual job, requiring skill, knowledge, discipline, patience. Intelligence. Sleep. Probably not. He couldn't imagine many men allowing their placées to work. Other than to work for him, on him, under him.

"Christophe, you're grinding your teeth." Musette ran her hand over his bare chest. "What on earth are you thinking about?"

He draped his arm over her. "Nothing. School."

"Tell me what you taught the boys today."

"Sums. French. Latin. Geography."

"Tell me some geography. Where?"

He traced circles on her dark skin. "Chile."

"What do they do in Chile?"

"Climb up and down a lot of mountains. Grow chilies?"

She goosed him.

"Surely they grow chilies." He shifted so he could see her face, grinning at her. "They definitely have a lot of mountains to climb."

"I'd like to see a mountain."

"So would I." He kissed her shoulder. "I better go."

"Can't stay the night?"

"Early violin lesson in the morning. I'd probably wake you up. Early."

Musette fingered the patch of hair over his breastbone. "How early?"

He tightened his arm around her. "You could get up, oh, at five. Light the fire. Get the bacon and eggs going. Biscuits. Coffee." He thought a moment. "Orange juice."

Musette laughed. "Get out of here, Christophe."

He kissed her on the nose and got up. "Where did you hide my pants?"

"You mean the ones on the chair, the ones with two legs?"

"The very ones. What would I do without you?"

By the time he was dressed, Musette's eyes were closed. He snuffed the candles and let himself out.

The night was clear, not a wisp of cloud, the stars bright in the cold air as he walked home to his cottage. It was small, but it was his, paid for with his own hard-earned money. He had gone to work at the age of eleven at whatever he could find, emptying rat traps, shining shoes, loading ships down at the docks. Then he'd discovered the taverns where Kaintucks, who'd spent months moving goods down the Mississippi on a flat boat, gambled a year's wages in one throw of the dice. Some of them even won.

In those hell-holes, Christophe got himself roaring drunk and indulged himself with women in soiled red dresses. One memorable night — no, not so very memorable, a lot of it was a blur — he too had tried his luck. He'd gambled a month's earnings in a game of blackjack. He'd had two tens! He should have won. But he didn't. That was the last time he ever got skunked at the gaming table, though not the last time he got skunked. Nor the last time he gambled. Determined to recoup his losses, he'd made a science of playing poker, and he made one drink last all evening as he raked in the coins from his less sober opponents. And thus had begun his growing bank account.

His dark house was quiet and empty. He lit a single candle in the bedroom, pulled off his shirt and tossed it in the corner with his other dirty clothes. He'd have to take them to the Chinese laundryman tomorrow or mama mice would start making their nests in them.

He sat down on the edge of the bed to take his boots off. His feet bare, a boot dangling in his fingers, he listened to the whispers of the empty house. A shutter shifted on its hinge. A squirrel scampered across the roof. Here he was, a prosperous man, all alone. He chose to be alone, he reminded himself. He could marry.

He owned several properties in the Vieux Carré. He had his pay from the Academy. He earned even more from playing at balls and private parties. More than enough income for a wife and children.

Not enough, never enough, to tempt Tansy from Valere Valcourt. "Fuck it." He pulled his boots back on, dressed, and went in search of a gambling hell where tensions simmered and he could expect a good brawl to break out. He meant to participate fully.

Christophe dismissed his nine and ten year olds for lunch. They filed out in a bouncing, touching, boisterous line to the common room where Mrs. Thatcher would oversee them for a half hour. Christophe strolled to the teachers' inner sanctum, a small room upstairs overlooking the courtyard. Rosa poured watered wine for Monsieur Fournier, then handed Christophe a glass.

Right on time, Pete from the café next door knocked on the jamb. Christophe enjoyed the mild mystery of lunch time. They never knew what Pete's father would send over. Sometimes rice balls and pulled pork, sometimes meat pies, sometimes a slab of ham between two slices of hot buttered bread.

"What did you bring us, Pete?"

"Boiled eggs. Apple tarts. Cheese sticks. And — " Pete grinned and made a grand flourish with his hand. "I snuck in three pecan rolls."

"Well done, Pete! Your papa's pecan rolls more than make up for eating boiled eggs."

And then the day got better. Tansy waltzed in. Well-rested, he was glad to see. Radiant, in fact. As always, he felt the room lighten, his skin awaken, his blood course through his veins a little faster because she was near.

"*Bonjour!*"

Denis Fournier pulled out a chair and patted it for her to sit next to him. "You look lovely today, Madame Bouvier."

"Oh, please," she said, placing her hand on his arm. "Call me Tansy."

Denis beamed. She'd made his day, just by smiling at him and touching his coat sleeve. Ever the charmer. She came by it naturally, Christophe supposed. She genuinely liked people. Genuinely wanted to please. He couldn't remember her every doing anything just to please herself, however. He tilted his head to look at her as she unwrapped the lunch she'd brought. But she was changing. She made time to read and to talk about what she'd read. She even allowed herself two hours a day to teach little boys. Maybe, he hoped, she might eventually see herself as more than a rich man's plaything.

He reached over to Tansy's lunch and snagged a pickle. She didn't pause as she talked to Rosa, and that unconscious, total acceptance of his theft made his heart beat steadier and stronger. They shared more than a love of books and a long friendship. They were connected.

Tansy finished her bread and cheese, dusted the crumbs off her hands, and pointedly cut her eyes down and to the side, eyeing Christophe's pecan roll. Then she raised a brow, her lips in a half smile, and looked at Christophe sideways.

He was tempted to pop the whole thing in his mouth and grin at her. She'd laugh, but she'd probably bruise him too. He pulled the roll into two very uneven pieces. "Hmmm. Now we have a dilemma. I am honor bound to give you the larger half. But, logic is not to be denied. I am bigger than you."

She turned to face him with narrowed eyes. "It seems to me, Christophe Desmarais, gallantry trumps logic."

He frowned, staring at the pecans on top, glistening with syrup. "Are you sure?"

Tansy appealed to their table mates. "Do you not agree? Courtesy should prevail in every instance, even when one stands to lose the larger piece of a sticky bun."

"Of course you are right, Tansy," Denis declared gallantly, beaming at her. "The lady is always right."

"You are not a fair judge, Denis. You've already eaten yours, and you'd agree with Tansy even if she said the Mississippi flowed north. That leaves you, Madame," he said, looking at Rosa.

You might never know it looking at Rosa's smooth, imperturbable face, but Christophe knew she didn't miss much. She had known his every naughty impulse when he was a lad in her class, knew it before he tried to execute it. She no doubt knew exactly how he felt about Tansy.

Rosa rubbed her hands together. "So I am the judge. I do so love power." She stared at the large and the small pieces and then she scowled at Christophe. "You know exactly what your mother would have said. Tansy gets the whole thing!"

Christophe effected a stab to the heart. Tansy clapped her hands. She opened her mouth wide as it would go and crammed in the too-big piece. Hmmmmmmm!" She licked her fingers, smacked her lips. Then she eyed the remainder. "It certainly was good, Christophe."

He watched her to see what she would do with the smaller piece Rosa had decreed must also be hers. Tansy the people pleaser. She no doubt would slide the bun back to him, sharing, wanting to make him happy with a piece of pecan roll.

She tilted her head at it, miming a hungry woman at war with herself. Then, her eyes alight, she grabbed it and stuffed it in her mouth.

Christophe threw back his head and laughed. She grinned, very pleased with herself. He reached over and thumbed at a smear of sugar on her chin, and her grin lost its light. He'd embarrassed her. Damn it.

She knew what he wanted. How could she not? Two years ago, he'd all but declared himself. He'd told her, as if in passing, that he'd just bought an eighth property in the old quarter. She knew he won at the gaming tables, that he had income from teaching and playing. She had to know he was telling her he could support her and Alain. But she'd made some remark about admiring entrepreneurs and changed the subject. Always gently, always nicely, she always deflected him. She didn't seem to see any alternatives to the life she was stuck in, didn't seem to believe in new beginnings, new choices. That she was truly happy, as happy as she was capable of being, he did not believe for a moment. He did not believe she came alight with Valcourt the way she did with him when she'd jammed that bun in her mouth. She was simply mired in what is instead allowing herself to consider what could be.

As they cleared away their lunch, Christophe mentioned casually, "Ophelia had seven kittens over the weekend."

Would she take a kitten without having the blessing of Alain's father? Had her emerging sense of self advanced that far? He didn't think she missed the challenge in his eye.

"Seven!" she said. "She'll be a busy mama."

That's all she said. But it would be six weeks before the kittens could be taken from their mother. Maybe, in six weeks, she'd make a decision. On her own.

# Chapter Eleven

Tansy cast her eye over her students. Sidney was a good child, but inclined to daydream and stare out the window. He wouldn't do. René had so many problems of his own that he could not be expected to help another child. Louis never stopped talking and would not be alert to how sensitive David was. Giles. He was quiet, but not too quiet. Sure of himself, but not cocky. Maybe he'd be grown up enough to befriend a sad little boy. Without comment, she sent her new student to sit with Giles and share his table.

She distributed a handful of pinto beans to each boy and had them draw circles on their slates. Inside their circles, they placed two beans. And then two more. How many beans was that? Everyone but David shouted out four. Did he not know it was four, or was he just too timid to speak up?

Tansy put addition problems on the board and told them to use their beans to figure out the answers. David stared at the board and at his beans, his hands in his lap. Tansy pulled up a chair next to him. "How many beans do you have, David?"

"I don't know," he murmured, his chin on his chest.

"Can you count them?"

David glanced at the beans. He began to rock slightly forward and back. "Fourteen."

"So you did know? *Très bien.*"

He shook his head. "I didn't know, but I do now."

He had glanced at the beans and counted to fourteen? Tansy saw he was protecting his pride, poor lad.

"What if I gave you one more bean? How many would that be?" She'd never seen anyone rock like that, back and forth, back and forth in an odd sort of rhythm.

"Fifteen."

"And if I gave you two more?"

"Seventeen."

"So you know your numbers."

*Tansy*

"I like numbers," he said, so softly she barely heard him. "Especially eleven."

"You like the number eleven?"

"And 233. I like that one, too."

Tansy sat back in her chair. She'd be willing to bet not another boy in the room had even imagined a number that big. "Can you add numbers that high?"

David flicked a quick look at her and then lowered his gaze again. "Yes."

"What's eleven plus eleven?"

"Twenty-two."

She quizzed him all the way up 99 plus eleven. He never hesitated. "What about 856 and 449?"

His answer was immediate. "One thousand three hundred and five."

Tansy wished she could talk to Christophe or Rosa. How unusual was it to have a nine year old so fluent with numbers? "Can you show Giles how you did that?"

He hung his head. "I don't know how I do it."

Giles had been doing the sums with his beans, his tongue between his teeth. He had heard every word though. "What's six thousand eight hundred ninety-three plus fifty thousand eleven hundred," he said.

Tansy was quite sure Giles had no idea how to even write such numbers much less compute their sums. She was about to intervene to save David's feelings when he muttered, "Fifty-seven thousand nine hundred ninety-three. If you mean fifty thousand eleven hundred is fifty-one thousand one hundred."

Tansy's jaw dropped. Could he be right? She tried to compute it in her head, messed up, tried again, and decided 57,993 must be about right.

"What an amazing mind, you have, David." He wouldn't look at her. Giles shrugged and went back to counting out beans to get eight plus nine.

In the second hour, Tansy read to the boys and then asked them to draw a picture of something in the story. She walked around the room and saw a stick figure climbing a beanstalk into the clouds, an extremely long-necked goose, a giant with hairy arms. David drew a perfect oval in a corner of his slate.

"Is that the goose egg?" Tansy asked.

David gave her a quick look, then lowered his head again.

"Is it an egg?" Giles said. "A golden egg?"

David nodded his head.

"It's good." Giles went back to drawing leaves on his beanstalk. Tansy could have kissed him for speaking to David as if he were, well, normal.

"How many eggs do you think that goose laid?" Tansy asked.

"Six." He picked up his chalk and began drawing egg number two.

She moved on to sit beside René and assured him that it was okay if his giant's eyes were not exactly the same size. "In fact, he's a monster, isn't he? I bet monsters have crazy eyes, one huge and one tiny. What do you think?"

"But they wouldn't match," René said, his voice rising with anxiety.

"No, they wouldn't! Wouldn't that be fun?"

He wiggled in his seat. He bit at a fingernail. Then in one quick swoop, he erased the eyes and painstakingly drew one tiny eyeball and one huge one, so huge it was too big for the face.

Marcus leaned over from his desk. "Look at René's monster," he called. Three other boys crowded round, making René shrink in his seat. Tansy held her breath. This was a lot of attention for René. She hoped he wouldn't tense up and decide it was all too much for him.

Louis suggested he add streaks so the eyes looked bloodshot. René's left knee jiggled. His fingers gripped the chalk till his knuckles were white. And he added streaks!

The boys made enthusiastic ugh sounds and went back to their desks. René stared at the gruesome monster face. Suddenly, he turned a smile on her. The first smile she'd seen! Was this the first time he had let go of perfection and tried something new? She knew how exhilarating that could be. Coming to school every day was the first new thing she'd done in ... such a long time. Since she read that first book Christophe had given her.

There never seemed to be enough time, Tansy thought. At Rosa's invitation, she had joined the Women of Color Society, a group who took food baskets to families in need, and two mornings a week, if Valere had not stayed overnight, she took her

*Tansy*

turn in the little storeroom off the Ursuline Convent stocking the charity baskets. Add to that, Valere now visited her almost every evening. She had no chance to talk with Christophe about books, and she missed it.

Before she left school Friday afternoon, she stopped at Christophe's classroom. He held a taut length of string stretched in a triangle between his hands to show the boys how he could manipulate the angles by shifting his fingers. A man of many parts, Christophe. Here in the classroom, he focused totally on his boys and you might think teaching was his life. In the orchestra, the fiddle seemed a part of him, and surely music was his life. But those fine hands shuffled cards with great finesse, and rolled a cigarette with equal surety.

His hands still held up to show the boys his triangle, he stepped over to the door and raised a questioning eyebrow.

"Will you come for a picnic with Alain and me? Tomorrow?"

For a moment, he looked comical with his triangle hands suspended in the air, his face turned to the side looking at her as if she'd spoken Greek. "You know. A picnic. Food, grass, trees. I'll make your favorite strawberry tarts."

She tilted her head to look at him. Such a strange blank expression on his face.

"All right," he said.

"Tomorrow, then. One o'clock."

That night Valere came to her early enough to spend a few minutes with Alain who again had his soldiers arrayed in straight lines facing each other. "This is the battle of Waterloo, Papa," he explained.

"Waterloo, eh? That's where old Boney beat back the British, you know."

"Maman?" Alain called her to come from the kitchen. "You had it wrong, Maman. Papa says Boney beat the British at Waterloo."

Tansy glanced at Valere who looked very pleased with himself to have produced this nugget of information. She pursed her lips. She could explain it to Alain later. "Is that right?"

"Surely you did not think the British ever beat Napoleon," Valere said.

"I suppose not." Did Valere think then that Napoleon still ruled France? Had never been sent to St. Helena? "Put your soldiers away, sweetheart. Time for bed."

83

Once Alain fell asleep, Tansy took Valere to bed. They made love. Valere fell asleep. She lit a candle and curled up on the settee in her bedroom with a book about the French Revolution. *Liberté, égalité, fraternité* were stirring words, but Paris was not New Orleans. Her own world was one of slavery and caste. No wonder free young men of color escaped to Paris, to study, to make a life in a world without Louisiana's obsession with skin color.

Christophe might have done just that if his father had held on to his wealth. So many sons of placées studied at the Sorbonne or at the Université de Montpellier medical school in the south of France. But Christophe had done very well on his own. She wondered whether he had dreamed of becoming a lawyer or a physician. And she wondered if, now Napoleon was gone, the newly restored monarchy remembered *liberté, égalité, fraternité*. She would talk to Christophe about it tomorrow.

Valere rolled over, his arm reaching across the empty bed for her. He raised his head and blinked at the candle light.

"What are you doing?"

"Only reading."

He seemed to think about that a moment. "Don't do that. I want you with me."

She swallowed a sigh. She wasn't sleepy. She placed the ribbon in her book, blew out the candle, and climbed back into bed.

In the morning, Valere was insatiable. She indulged him, of course, then tried to get up — she heard Alain stirring in the next room — but he pulled her back and took her again. He didn't expect her to pretend to climax, for which she was grateful. And also resentful, she realized. Did it not occur to him that she might not want sex again so soon? She tamped it down. Maybe all men were like this. Probably they were. She was fortunate that Valere often did want to pleasure her as well as himself.

It occurred to her as he labored over her the second time that morning that Valere visited her more often now than he had before his marriage. He made love with more vigor than he had since their first weeks together. Perhaps making love was the source of trouble with his new wife. He had likely not taken the trouble to initiate her into sex, to help her relax and accept what his body and hers could be together. A white society belle, she certainly would not have been prepared as Tansy had been. Maman's lessons had been embarrassingly explicit, humiliatingly personal. Tansy had already understood a man's arousal, and her own, before Valere had taken her virginity.

He climaxed in a desperate, straining groan, then collapsed on her, pressing her into the mattress. Tansy stroked his back, his hair. She loved it when he erupted so fully. Though they had no bond before the Church, she felt an ownership of him, a union with him.

Finally, she whispered, "Valere, I can't breathe." He rolled off her and closed his eyes. She slipped on her negligée and went to see if Alain were awake. He was in his bed, *Aesop's Fables* open before him, telling himself the story of Fox and Grapes. She leaned on his door jamb. "*Bonjour*, Alain."

"Shall I read to you, Maman?"

She climbed on the bed with him. "Yes, please."

He turned back to the first page of the story where there was a drawing of a very sour looking fox walking away from a luscious cluster of grapes. "On a hot summer's day," Alain said. He traced his finger along the line of print for all the world as if he were reading.

When he'd finished, he handed her the book. "Now it's your turn."

They spent a happy half hour with Aesop, then Tansy got him washed and dressed. She made coffee and sliced oranges, waiting for Valere to waken. She'd feed him and he'd be off. She didn't keep up with the horse races, but no doubt there would be one somewhere on a Saturday morning.

He padded barefoot into the little kitchen area where she sipped coffee and wrapped his arms around her from behind.

"*Bonjour, mon fils*," he said to Alain who was spreading jam on his bread.

"*Bonjour, mon père.*"

Tansy squeezed Valere's wrist, pleased he'd called Alain "son." He had never ever denied Alain, but he seldom bothered to acknowledge him either.

He pulled out his chair and frowned slightly. He picked up the book on the seat and tossed it in a corner where it skidded across the floor. Tansy drew a shocked breath, as if Valere had thrown a fragile Chinese vase, or a kitten, or a baby. Of course that was silly, but she picked the book up carefully, with both hands, as if it were bruised. Gently, she placed it on the parlor shelf.

He sipped at the steaming cup of Cuban coffee she poured him and sighed over the rich aroma. "Why don't you come with me to the races this morning?"

"Horse races? In Metairie?"

"It's perfectly acceptable for a man to take his placée to the races. Wives never come. Or rarely. Mine certainly will not."

"But." She couldn't think what to say next. But she had planned a picnic in the park with another man? Of course there was nothing improper about it. Christophe was an old friend, a colleague. But she didn't say it.

"But what?" He reached a hand across the table. "You don't have to be anywhere else." It was a statement, not a question.

"Of course not," she said. Sweat broke out on her upper lip. She felt slightly queasy. She'd drunk too much coffee on an empty stomach. She should eat something.

She withdrew her hand from Valere's and gripped her other in her lap. Christophe would be waiting for her and Alain in the park. She'd promised him strawberry tarts.

"Don't you have a new tignon?" Valere asked.

"I do. The bronze silk."

"Wear that. I'll fetch my carriage while you dress."

As soon as she'd helped him with his cravat and seen him out the door, she stepped quickly across the connected courtyards to tap on Martine's back door. And tap again. At last Martine emerged from the bedroom in her negligée, her hair mussed and her feet bare.

"The house better be on fire," she said when she opened the door. She peered at Tansy with squinted eyes. "What's wrong?"

"I need a favor."

That arranged, Tansy sent Alain to Martine and dressed herself. It had been ages since Valere had taken her anywhere. Even at the balls, she got herself to and from. Not long ago, she would have been thrilled to go to the races with him. Not that she cared two figs whose horse ran the fastest, but she would have been on his arm, doing something together besides rutting in the bed. She put her fingers over her lips. What an unlovely way to put it. She shook her head and buckled her shoes.

Christophe claimed a patch of shade under a catalpa tree and sat back against the trunk. Fresh spring leaves and a balmy breeze — a perfect day for a picnic. When he spotted Alain skipping along, he rose to his feet. He squinted. That was not Tansy with him.

"*Bonjour*," Martine called.

Alain ran for him. Christophe caught him under the arms and lifted him high in the air. When he put him down, he kept one hand on Alain's shoulder and looked at Martine, waiting for an explanation. She merely smiled at him, teasing him. She made him say it. "Where is Tansy?"

She set her basket down and spread out a blanket. "Unexpected event," she said. "But she sent you your strawberry tarts."

"She's not coming?"

"No, Christophe," she said gently. "Sit down. Let's have our picnic."

He opened the two bottles of ginger beer he'd brought, and a bottle of limeade for Alain. Acid bubbles burned his stomach. Where the hell was she? Her own goddamn picnic. She'd asked him, he hadn't asked for a goddamn thing.

Martine tucked a napkin into Alain's collar and unpacked her basket. She paused, her hand on a linen wrapped bundle. "Christophe," she said, looking at him. "Can we not have a nice time?"

He schooled his features into what he meant to be a pleasant expression. "Of course." He raised his bottle. "*Bon appétit.*"

They talked of people they knew, the balls, the news. And about Tansy's new role as teacher. "She has a natural talent," Christophe said. "She makes work feel like play for a whole room full of wiggly boys."

"I never thought she'd step out of Valere's orbit. I don't think she expected to either, but she loves teaching. You did a fine thing, opening that door for her."

He scratched at the ginger beer's label with his thumbnail. "She walked through it on her own."

They watched Alain play with another boy. They chased the child's dog, the mutt bouncing and running just out of reach. If he got too far ahead, the clever dog slowed down or doubled back. The boys' shrieks shattered the peace, and Christophe grinned. Nothing like a child's glee to brighten a mood. He wrapped his arms around his knees. "So, Martine. You and your Monsieur DuMaine?"

Martine laughed. "Tansy hasn't scared him off yet. But she may have scared him. He is to sign the contract with Madame Bouvier Monday morning. And then he will be mine."

He sipped his ginger beer. No, he thought. You will be his, Martine. "You're very pleased with yourself."

"I am more than pleased. I'm ... " She searched for the right word.

"Ecstatic?"

She laughed again. Martine had a lovely laugh. He was glad to see her happy. She had looked increasingly hard the last year or two. Now her face had softened, and she looked younger. She looked ... ecstatic.

They were quiet a moment. Without looking at Martine, he said, "Where is she?"

He didn't know why he asked. He knew where she was. With Valcourt.

"He took her to the races at Metairie."

He nodded, his eyes on the dog running circles around the boys. Martine began packing the picnic basket, slowly, quietly.

"It seems harder for you now than it did five years ago."

Five years ago he'd believed he'd get over losing her. "Of course not. Come on, I'll buy you an ice on the levee."

Alain and his friend collapsed on the grass, writhing and giggling as the dog licked first one face and then the other. Christophe hated to break up the fun, but he could not sit here any longer with Martine's damned sympathy.

The three of them strolled toward the river, Alain holding hands between them. To anyone who didn't know them, they'd look like a family. Prosperous *gens de colour libre*. The beautiful woman, the beautiful child, and the school teacher. He swallowed the bitterness, tried to ignore the hollowness in his chest. He had everything. His music. The school. Musette. Why couldn't that be enough?

# Chapter Twelve

The ground shook. Six horses thundered by in a blur, throwing up dust and clods and the scent of earth.

Tansy stood on tip toe craning to see over the shouting crowd. "Did I win?"

Valere shook his head. "Yours came in dead last." Then he grinned at her. "But mine won."

Tansy clapped her hands. "Then we can bet again!"

"Not if you insist on basing your pick on whether you like the jockey's colors."

"I did no such thing."

She pressed a hand to her midriff. Christophe and Martine and Alain would be eating her strawberry tarts now. Alain probably leaned on Christophe's knee and smeared sticky fingers on his trousers. Christophe wouldn't mind. He'd probably laugh. He wouldn't be angry with her. He would understand, surely he would. Besides, Christophe liked Martine. And Alain would be with him. He wouldn't mind that she hadn't come, not really.

"On what, then, did you base your misguided belief that Number 5 would win?"

"Did you not notice Number 5 had a particularly beautiful tail and mane?" she asked.

Valere taped her forehead, smiling. "By that logic, the next winner should be the ugliest horse on the track."

He took her arm to guide her to the betting booth, threading through the crowd of well-dressed gentlemen interspersed with a rougher looking element. Five or six women, most of them wearing the tignon as Tansy did, stood out like bright flowers in a hedge. Valere was right. Neither his wife nor her friends would be comfortable here.

"Valcourt!" A man clamped a hand on Valere's shoulder.

"Windsor. How do you do?" Valere glanced at Tansy. She could read the dilemma on his face. Did one introduce one's placée to one's friends in a public place?

Windsor ran a frankly admiring gaze over her. It was not the first time a finely dressed gentleman had taken the liberty of ogling her. Too many Americans, which this man with his light hair and blue eyes appeared to be, made false assumptions about women like her, quadroon, better-looking than most, well-dressed. Several times such a man had approached her with inappropriate, insulting propositions.

"Who is this?" Windsor said, his gaze taking the measure of her waist, her hips.

Valere pressed her arm tightly to his side. "Madame Bouvier. My brother-in-law, Mr. Windsor."

A roguish smile spread over Windsor's ruddy face. He raised a finger and wagged it at Valere. "You sly dog. No wonder Abigail is in a snit all the time." When Valere said nothing, he leaned forward at the waist, leering at Tansy. She tightened her fingers on Valere's sleeve.

"Don't keep him too long, dear. His in-laws expect him and his bride at four."

Tansy saw Valere's Adam's apple bob, saw his face go pale.

Windsor laughed. "I see you had forgotten. Would that I could as well. However, I for one will not risk Mother's wrath by being late to her Saturday supper." He touched his hat to Tansy. "Good day, Madame. Valcourt."

Valere remained still, her hand pressed against his side, the crowd breaking to pass around them. He blushed when he looked down at her. "I must take you back."

"Of course," she murmured, wondering at Valere's blush. If he'd forgotten his wife, his in-laws, his obligations for a few hours, she had not.

Tansy tried to entertain Valere on the long drive back, exclaiming over the race, over his win, over what a splendid time he'd shown her. He responded very little, once patting her hand, once muttering something she couldn't make out.

Poor Valere. The line between his brows showed a man in dread of the evening to come. She stroked his hand, sorry for him. When they arrived, Tansy kissed him on the cheek. "Thank you, Valere. I loved being together today."

He looked like a child who'd lost his puppy. "So did I, Tansy."

Tansy crossed the back courtyard to Martine's house and stuck her head in the door. "Hello?"

Alain came running and she swept him into a hug.

"Come in," Martine called from the parlor.

Tansy found her on the floor, a set of blocks she kept for Alain spread around her. "We're building a fort."

Tansy sank to the floor. Alain added another block to his tower.

"How were the races?"

"Great fun! I lost twice, but Valere won three times, so he came out ahead." She pulled her tignon off and let her hair down. "Have you heard from Maman? DuMaine has agreed to terms?"

Martine's smile could have pierced the darkest night. "Signatures Monday morning, ten o'clock."

"I can see you are displeased."

"Monday evening, he'll come to me. Oh, Tansy, I want everything to be perfect. The bedroom, my hair." She raised her eyebrow and looked sassy. "My new négligée."

Tansy waved the idea away. "It will be a waste of effort. That man will have it off of you as soon as he's in the door."

"I hope so," Martine laughed. "But perhaps he will take a very brief moment to admire it first."

How rare, this thrilling expectation of rapture. Tansy smiled, happy Martine was getting the man of her dreams, but behind the smile she hid the green haze of envy. She felt gray and stale next to Martine's glow. She touched her brow. Such an ungenerous thought. She must be over tired.

Martine examined her nails. "You're not going to ask about the picnic?"

Tansy wanted very much to know about the picnic, but she didn't want Martine making uncomfortable inferences. Mistaken inferences. Martine was in love and so she saw love and desire everywhere. She glanced at Martine over Alain's head with a show of indifference. "How was the picnic?"

Martine poked Alain. "Tell Maman. Did we have a nice time with Christophe?"

"I played with a dog, Maman." Alain's eyes were bright remembering the fun. "He chased us and chased us. And then we chased him. And he licked me all over my face."

"What kind of dog?" Tansy quizzed Alain for a few minutes, enjoying him. Then she let him build his fort.

"So you're not going to ask about Christophe. I'll tell you anyway. He had to struggle just to be polite when he realized you were not coming. He managed it in the end, but the man was disappointed."

A heaviness settled in Tansy's chest. It hurt, that Christophe was hurt. Irritation scratched at her, too. Would she have made a fuss if he'd been suddenly called to school, or if he'd felt he must accept a last-minute engagement with his fiddle? Of course not. They were adults. They had obligations.

"He knows Valere has to come first. He shouldn't be surprised if I can't come at the last minute." Tansy preferred not to look at Martine. Her friend had a rude habit of looking through your eyes to the core of your being.

"He does indeed know that, "Martine said, her voice flat.

Tansy rubbed her forehead. Why couldn't she have a friend? Valere certainly had another life, he even slept with another woman. She just wanted to talk to Christophe. About books, about school, about David. About everything. He wasn't like Valere. He read, he analyzed, he thought, he listened to her. He was … interesting. When she was with him, she felt she was interesting, too.

"You're going to make it up to him?"

Tansy shook her head. How could she?

Alain spread his arms wide. "Da da ta da da !" His fort was finished.

Tansy and Martine admired the towers, the moat, the crenellated walls. Then Alain backed off, took a running start, and careened into his masterpiece, sending blocks flying to every corner of the room.

With laughter and a little indulgent scolding, Tansy and Martine helped him put the blocks away. Then Tansy took him home. She would have liked to lie down and put her feet up, but Alain refused to settle down for a rest. She sighed. She put a pot of coffee on to percolate.

How could she make it up to Christophe? In the bedroom, she fished in the hidden drawer of the armoire for two purses. The blue velvet one held the household money from Valere. She chose the one of green satin, the one holding her earnings from Rosa

LeFevre's School for Boys. She splashed the coins on the bed, the pieces of silver clinking together like music.

Valere's allowance was generous, more than enough for running the house, for clothing, for extras like coffee from Cuba and silk from China. But this money was uniquely hers. She ran her fingers through the coins, so very pleased she had earned this money herself. She picked up three silver dollars, more than enough to take to the book store on Decatur. What did Christophe love more than books?

She drank down her coffee and marched out of the house, Alain in tow. At Madame Odette's Sweet Shoppe, she bought them each a praline. On Decatur, they entered the bookshop, a little bell ringing when the door opened. The air was musty, full of the scents of leather and paper and glue. And perhaps a hint of mouse. A lazy cat sprawled in a patch of sun in the front window, one eye open to appraise the new customers. When Alain tried to pet her, she hissed at him and he wisely did not try again.

A very old, very stooped man sat on a low stool, stacks of books all around him. He scowled at them, annoyed at being interrupted in his sorting and shelving. He forced a grimacing sort of smile. "*Bonjour.*"

"May we look around?"

The proprietor considered so long, Tansy thought he might say no. "Very well."

She stepped toward a corridor between tall shelves groaning under hundreds of books, but Alain dropped her hand and squatted next to the old man.

"What are you doing?" Alain said.

The man's cloud of white hair did not make him look angelic. He scowled. "What does it look like I'm doing?"

"It looks like you're stacking books."

"Alain, monsieur is busy."

He conveniently did not see her outstretched hand. "I have books. Three of them."

"Alain."

The old man waved her off as if she were an annoying gnat. His eyes bore into Alain's. "What are the names of these books?"

Alain held up his three fingers and counted them off. "*Aesop's Fables, Tales of Mother Goose,* and *Cock Robin.*"

"And can you read these books by yourself?"

"Yes, I can."

"Alain," Tansy said.

The old man glared at her. "Go amuse yourself. This young man and I are going to read together."

Tansy hesitated. The man was more than grumpy. But he did not, after all, eat little boys. She stepped into the stacks, ran her finger over the first row of titles, and listened to the man and her son.

"Let's say this is a copy of *Aesop's Fables*. Read me a story."

She could hear Alain turning pages. "There are no pictures."

"No matter. Just read."

"It was a hot summer's day," Alain began.

Tansy smiled. He knew that one by heart, and most of the others, too.

She pulled a dusty volume bound in blue leather off the shelf. The Tudors. She traced the gold lettering stamped into the leather. She would hand Christophe this beautiful book with a big smile and remind him she had after all sent him strawberry tarts. He would laugh, and they'd be friends, like always.

She rounded the corner to collect Alain and came to a full stop. Alain was on his knees leaning on the old man's thigh, entranced by the volume from which the man read to him. His voice was a little raspy, from disuse, she thought, but he read with such evident pleasure he had captivated Alain. Then she realized that what he read was not a fable or children's story. She laughed to herself. It was an account of the Treaty of Paris from the last century.

She leaned on the bookcase, unwilling to interrupt. Alain looked like a little man, his face so serious. One would never guess this four year old did not understand every word of the intricate political arguments in the text. He was so sweet, so beautiful. And so smart.

The old man caught her smile and slammed the book shut angrily.

"You have a shelf of children's books, Monsieur?"

"Your boy likes this one."

"About politics? Government?" He must be senile, poor man.

"Yes, about politics," he snapped. "What's wrong with a boy liking politics?"

"Well, perhaps we'll look at children's books another day. I will buy this one, however."

The man shifted Alain's weight off his leg and struggled to his feet. He tottered over to the desk and with creaking joints lowered himself into the chair. He gestured rudely to Tansy to show him the book, then wet the tip of his pencil with his tongue and wrote the title in his ledger.

Tansy paid the man, then took Alain's hand. "Ready?"

"Boy." The old man pointed a bony finger at the book he'd left on the stool. "Take your book."

Alain's smile announced he'd just been granted ice cream and cake and kittens all at once. He ran to the stool and grabbed the book to his breast.

"Monsieur, that is very kind. But that is too much book for a little boy. I thank you just the same."

His eyes gleamed under his bushy white eyebrows. "I'm not giving it to you."

Alain clutched it tightly and looked an entreaty at her. "It's a very good book, Maman."

"Yes, it is," the old man said. "And when you have finished that one, come back and I will give you another."

Tansy nodded her head graciously and then said to Alain, "What do you say when you receive a gift?"

Alain walked around the desk and looked earnestly into the man's face. With deep sincerity, he said, "Thank you for my book, Monsieur."

After supper, Alain wanted her to read his new book, so she began at the beginning. "The participants in the Treaty of Paris spanned the mighty width of the Atlantic Ocean. On its western shores, water lapped the beaches of the newly formed United States of America, on the east, the varied coasts of Britain, France, Spain, and the Dutch Republic."

Tansy glanced at Alain. Surely he did not want to hear this very dry, dense tome, but when she hesitated, he said, "What else does it say?"

"You wouldn't rather read *Cock Robin*?"

"No, I want my grown-up book."

With a sigh, she began page two. Thank heavens he fell asleep somewhere in the middle of page three.

## Chapter Thirteen

The Windsor family were from Philadelphia, but they had adopted the Creole custom of suppers that lasted for hours. And hours. Valere was himself Creole, but his mother's table had always been graced with cousins and aunts and uncles, all of whom had something interesting to say about the theater or the opera or the races. The Windsor's conversation was sporadic, and it was all excruciatingly dull.

Mr. Windsor spoke of business. "The bank has arranged to mediate loans of considerable importance between ...The collateral, of course, is central to the deal moving for ... cotton, so many promised bales ... difficulties, for instance, too much rain, or not enough, or perhaps a hurricane ..." Valere fought to keep his eyes open.

"... considerable capital tied up in slaves. A perfectly sound investment." Mr. Windsor beamed at his wife and son and even shed some of the rays of his success on his two daughters. Valere noticed he did not include him in his expectations of appreciation, and that was fine.

He drained his wine glass, which the "servant" immediately refilled. Abigail's mother did not like to hear her people called "slaves." Valere snorted to himself. Whatever she called them, her "servants" were as bound to the Windsors as his own were to him.

He tried to think through the wine-fog in his brain. What did the Valcourts say when they wished to refer to a slave? Bess, he thought. Or Calvin. Marie Louise. Mandy. Charles. Why would you need anything but the name?

"Mr. Valcourt," Abigail said, her tone waspish enough that he knew this must not be the first time she'd called his name. "Father is speaking to you."

Valere shifted in his chair abruptly to face Mr. Windsor. "Yes, sir?"

"I said — " Clearly the man's irritation was easily aroused. "What does your father expect of the coming season? He follows the signs? The meteorological signs?"

Valere studied his father-in-law. What the hell was the man talking about?

"I understand," Mr. Windsor said with forced patience, "that men of the soil, planters, if you will, are conversant with certain signs that foretell the likelihood of a wet summer."

"Ah." He'd had too much sun at the races with Tansy all morning, and the sickly-sweet scent of gardenias wafted from the vase straight into his brain. He swallowed and blinked. "Yes. Of course. My father has a 'servant,'" he granted Mrs. Windsor a slight nod of acknowledgment, "who watches for those things. A talented man, knows when the calves will drop, when the cane is at its peak, most any kind of foretelling of the natural world."

"And does this man," Abigail's elder sister Lucille asked, "purport to have supernatural abilities or merely a deeper knowledge than even your father?" Her thin lips smirked. "Or yourself?"

Valere truly despised that woman. Lucille was a shriveled old maid at twenty and five. Her mousy hair, pulled back from her face so tightly her eyebrows slanted upwards, was always a little less than clean, her shoulders often dusted with dandruff. Her nose was sharp, her chin even sharper. And she seemed to have made it her mission since his marriage to Abigail to make him uncomfortable at every opportunity.

He looked at her little mud-colored eyes. "Many of my father's *servants*" — this time he emphasized the word meanly — "have both skill and knowledge. Because a man is a slave does not make him an empty-headed fool."

Abigail's brother sat across the table. He shifted his body and gave Valere a slight shake of the head.

Valere dropped his eyes. He'd been about to make a cock of it, quarreling at the table. "But of course you know that," he mumbled, hoping the matter would be dropped and he could retreat beneath the Windsor notice.

"Of course we know there are all kinds of slaves, Mr. Valcourt. Kitchen, wash house, smithy, stables. And even some whose services are quite personal," Lucille said, her eyes determinedly fastened on her dessert.

The table might have become populated by statues. The silence spread through the room like fog. Surely to God the woman did not refer to sexual things at table, in front of her mother, her father, her brother? He stared at her, the blood rising from his collar to his hairline.

"Valets and the like," she finished and took a bite of custard as if she'd had no notion of implying anything otherwise.

Did Lucille know about Tansy? How could she know? Evan Windsor would not have told her he'd seen Tansy, he was sure of it. What man would speak of such a thing to his sister?

Valere stole a glance at his wife. She was as pink as he'd ever seen her. She'd clearly taken her sister's meaning to be salacious. Then she knew? He felt his heart drop low in his chest. He would not have her know for any treasure in the world.

Abigail was so pretty. Her hair a pale honey, her eyes big and blue. She had a tiny waist and sweet little hands, so white, so soft. But she didn't like him to touch her. She didn't even like him to talk to her. He put a hand to the throbbing vein at his temple. It was Lucille's fault, the poisonous bitch.

"Lucille, dearest," Mrs. Windsor said, "if you're finished, let's leave the gentlemen to their cigars."

The three ladies rose and wafted the scent of rose and lavender as they left the room.

Valere stared at his goblet, twisting the stem as if he were entranced by the ruby glow of the wine. His father and brother-in-law let the silence fill the room. He would not speak of Tansy. He would never speak of her to these people.

"It is apparent," Mr. Windsor spoke at last, "that Lucille's remark took on added meaning to you, Valcourt. Perhaps you would explain?"

Valere shifted in his chair so that he presented an upright profile. He looked his father -in-law in the eye. "There is nothing to explain."

"Father," Evan said, "Valcourt is a Creole — "

"I have been in Louisiana thirty years, young man. Do not presume to lecture me on Creole morality. Or the lack of it." He stabbed his finger toward Valere. "You did not marry some poor Creole woman who expects a sinner for a husband. You married my daughter."

Valere's jaw tightened. He had never seen the sense of firing guns or slashing sabers at one another, but if he were a dueling man, he would be contemplating which cousin would act as his second. He raised his head and met Mr. Windsor's glare.

"I believe Creole men make excellent husbands, sir," Valere said, his free hand fisted on his thigh.

Mr. Windsor nodded at the servant to bring the humidor, selected a cigar, and puffed as the man held a match. Once he had a glowing tip and an aromatic cloud of smoke, he pointed his cigar at Valere. "Damned well better."

Valere stood stiffly, made a slight bow to each gentleman, and left the room. His knees and ankles stiff, he crossed the hallway like a stick man. He'd not been dressed down since he'd left the nursery. Insufferable, smug, provincial, narrow-minded *Américains*. He would not forget their snide superiority.

When he found the ladies, Lucille was whispering in his wife's ear. His gut churned at the satisfied gleam in the harpy's eye. Never in his life had he thought to strike a woman, but he envisioned himself grasping Lucille's pinched face in his big hand and shoving her to the floor.

"Mrs. Valcourt, it's time to go."

"So soon?" Mrs. Windsor crooned.

"Yes, ma'am." He made her a bow and then looked to Abigail.

He held his breath. What if she refused to come? Her eyes were on her hands held tightly at her waist. Humiliation lapped at his boots, rose to his knees.

Without looking at him, Abigail crossed to Mrs. Windsor and kissed her cheek. "Good night, Mother."

Valere's throat eased. He offered Abigail his arm and led her from the room, from the house, from her horrible, hateful sister.

They walked the three blocks to the Valcourt townhouse. As soon as they were inside, Abigail lifted her hand from his arm and without a word or a glance, climbed the stairs to her rooms. Valere stayed behind to nurse a bottle of wine. He had a good head. He could drink the whole damn bottle and still climb upstairs with perfect equilibrium.

He was not given to introspection. He was not given to deep thought of any kind. He had no need of it. He was wealthy. He was established. He was young and healthy. Nevertheless, black thoughts weighed him down.

His father had kept a *placée* all the years his mother had been alive. Still did, in fact. Bridgette had a very fine house on Rampart, was a beauty even at her age. Maman had probably had no inkling of her existence. If she did, she certainly never complained. She had been a good wife to his father, and he had given her children, wealth, status, a home in the country and in the city. That was as it should be. Having a placée did not make a man less of a husband. Every Creole man knew that. What was the matter with these rod-up-the-butt Americans?

Valere grew sentimental as the wine flowed through his veins. Abigail was such a pretty little thing. He'd expected her to be as sweet as she was pretty. She would be sweet to him if it weren't for that scheming ... he searched for a word strong enough for his rancor ... that scheming, ugly sister. Why did Abigail listen to her? Had she no loyalty? He was her husband!

Valere picked the bottle up by the neck and rose to his feet. He walked quite steadily, extremely steadily, to the door and up the stairs, his aggrieved indignation growing the closer he came to Abigail's bedchamber. By God, she could squirm or lie motionless as a board under him as she chose, but she owed him a houseful of children. In his inebriation, Valere believed he adored children, that he craved a dozen. And they'd every one be sons, goddamn it.

Her door was locked. It was always locked. He tapped on it with the lip of the bottle. She did not respond. He pounded the door with the heel of his hand.

Abigail opened the door. She was in a white muslin nightdress with satin roses appliquéd around the neck. Her blond hair curled around her shoulders.

So pretty. He pushed his way into the room. She had three candelabra lit. Now he could see her face. Swollen red eyes, dark circles.

"You've been crying."

She turned away from him. "You're drunk, Mr. Valcourt."

"No. Not drunk. I'm never drunk." He spoke distinctly. He knew he did.

He placed his hand on her shoulder. She stiffened. He rubbed his thumb over the pretty muslin, feeling the delicate bones underneath. Too pretty to cry.

She shrugged his hand away. "I know."

His wine-soaked brain sensed nothing ominous in her words or tones. "You know what, sweetheart?"

He reached a hand to touch her cheek, but she slapped it away.

"I know about her."

Like the sun peeking through a cloud cover, an errant ray of understanding lit his mind. He considered denying it, but if she knew, she knew. And what of it?

"It's got nothing to do with you. Nothing to do with you and me."

"Nothing to do with me?" Abigail's blue eyes looked black, her voice hissed like an angry cottonmouth. "You spill your seed with her, how am I supposed to have my babies?"

Oh. Was that all? He smiled indulgently. "My dear, I have sufficient seed for a dozen women." He laughed softly to himself, it was such a good joke. "I have sufficient seed for two dozen women."

Before the pain registered, Valere was aware his head had been violently turned to the side. Then the stinging of his cheek explained that his wife, tiny little Abigail, had slapped him.

Surprised, though not offended, he said, "Don't do that."

Arms held tightly to her chest, her shoulders heaved. Poor Abigail. He'd comfort her. He'd take her to bed and show her how much he loved her, how much love he had to give. Plenty for everyone.

"I can make you happy, Abigail." He held his arms open to embrace her. "You've just been too tense. Now you're used to it, you just need to relax. You'll see."

She moved away from him. "I want my babies."

He smiled at her, a genuine, affectionate smile. He was an affectionate man. She'd see. He would make her very happy. "I'll give you babies. Come here."

She held her hand up, that pretty little hand not much bigger than a child's. He could see her throat moving, see her blinking away tears.

"I will allow you in my bed until I am with child. Then you will not touch me again until I am ready for the next child."

"Abigail." His voice carried all the reproach of an injured man.

She raised her chin. "Or."

He tilted his head, waiting for the or.

"Or you can give up your whore and have free access to my bed."

Abigail to this point had not been a willing nor compliant bed partner. It had not been particularly satisfying to bed her. A man likes the woman to at least move under him. Like Tansy. He was always happy in Tansy's bed. He passed a hand over his eyes. Damn, marriage pulled the guts out of a man. It was hard to think after so much wine. It was dim in the room. He was damned sleepy.

But Abigail was his wife. He was supposed to have her. Anytime he wanted to.

"All right."

She narrowed her eyes at him. "All right, you'll give her up?"

"Yes. I'll give her up."

She clapped her hands to her face and sobbed violently.

"Come here, my darling." He wrapped her in his arms. "Don't cry."

He led her to the four-poster piled high with pillows. He pulled the counterpane back, sat her on the mattress, and gently undressed her. He smoothed her hair off her shoulders so he could see her perfect, small breasts. She crossed an arm over her chest and scurried under the covers.

Valere was much quicker with his own clothes. He tore off his jacket, vest, cravat, shirt, excited that Abigail watched him with her big blue eyes. When he unbuttoned his pants, she turned her head and pressed a fist to her mouth.

He climbed into bed beside her and took her into his arms. She allowed him to caress her back, the nape of her neck. When his penis brushed against her thigh, she jerked and pulled away. "I won't hurt you, sweetheart. I never have, have I? Not since the first time?"

"It doesn't hurt much," she whispered.

"Relax, Abigail. I'll make you a baby."

But she didn't relax. After a few minutes of stroking and petting and kissing her, her body was as rigid as it had been on their wedding night. Throbbing with need, he saw no point in waiting. He nudged at her thighs, but she did not open for him. He raised himself and looked into her eyes. "Do you want a baby?"

She spread her legs, and he plunged into her. So smooth, hot, tight. He rocked in and out, he thrust and lunged, faster and faster until he spurted out all the seed any one baby could need. He collapsed on top of her, heedless for a moment how he smothered her.

She shoved at him. He rolled off and reached for her to come lie her head on his arm. She turned away and hunched on the far side of the bed. He stretched an arm toward her without quite reaching her. In moments, wine-dark sleep pulled him under.

## Chapter Fourteen

Monday morning, Christophe opened his classroom and set about preparing for the day, still in a stew over Tansy's failure to appear at the picnic. It had been her idea, after all. He had not imposed on her. She had imposed on him. He could have been ... he didn't know where he would have been instead, but he would have done something besides wait for her under some blasted tree like a schoolboy waiting for a pretty girl.

He emptied the chalk tray and coughed at the cloud of dust he raised. It was his own damned fault. He allowed himself this insane fantasy of Tansy shedding Valere like an old skin and declaring herself his, all his. But Tansy was not like his mother. Not like Musette. He doubted it had ever occurred to her she could be something other than a rich man's pet. Independence had never been her destiny.

He'd thought teaching at the school would suggest to her otherwise, but she still danced to Valcourt's tune. He scraped the boys' desks across the floor into orderly rows. Well, he was through with her. Let her borrow books from Denis Fournier. Let her take picnics with Valcourt.

He taught the morning lessons, smiling and attentive to his students. Underneath, he simmered. When he saw her, he'd be polite. That was all. If she spoke to him, he'd have to answer, but he'd show her that though she might be a pawn to her rich man, he had no intention of being her pawn.

At 11:30, he met Rosa and Denis in the faculty room. He hoped Tansy stayed away until her class started at noon so he could eat in peace, but as soon as he sat down, he heard her footsteps in the hallway. The muscles in his shoulders bunched up.

She walked in with a smile on her face. That was Tansy, always smiling, always eager to please. To please everyone but him. He accepted the decanter of wine from Denis and poured himself a glass.

"*Bonjour*," she said to all of them.

*Tansy*

Rosa and Denis answered her. Christophe did not.

"*Bonjour*, Christophe."

He raised his eyes to her, meaning to send her a freezing glare. In spite of himself, he responded with a quickening of the pulse, a certain extra-sensitivity of the skin. He clamped his teeth. She'd sent Martine in her stead as if he were a child to be mollified, as if it didn't matter whom he picnicked with. He did not return her smile.

Her gaze skittered away. She took the chair between Rosa and Denis. The three of them chatted about boys and recess and grade cards. Christophe's stomach closed. He couldn't swallow. He pushed his lunch away and shoved his chair back.

"Christophe?" He saw her throat move as she swallowed. Good. She looked guilty. "Christophe, wait a minute."

She pulled a book out of her bag and handed it across the table to him. "I came across this book and thought you'd like to have it."

He held her gaze, the book in her hand suspended between them. He let the seconds pass. He didn't want her damned book. Then her eyes teared.

Goddammit. He took the book. Without so much as looking at the title, he left the room.

Tansy trudged home. The center of her chest felt bruised, as if Christophe's cruelty had been a physical blow to the heart. When she'd given him the book, he looked at her as if he despised her, as if he would rather throw the book in her face than take it from her hand.

Once she was home, she would have curled up on the sofa and wept if she had not had Alain to tend to. She kept seeing the knot along Christophe's jaw line, the whitened lips. Most of all, the dark, depthless eyes. She tried to swallow the hurt. She had mending to do. She had supper to see about, Alain to occupy.

Sometime between bathing Alain and tucking him into bed, the complexion of her hurt changed from deep blue to the first pale tinges of red. Christophe had been rude, very rude. Looking at her as if she were a worm, so disdainful that her apology had died in her throat. For what? Because she missed a picnic in the park? She hadn't forgotten him, hadn't left him to dawdle waiting for her. He liked Martine, loved being with Alain. So what did he have to complain about?

She hadn't been rude to him. She hadn't glared at him. The tiny muscles at her hairline contracted and her teeth clamped together. How dare he leave her arm outstretched holding that heavy book? How dare he not even look at the title to see what she'd chosen for him? She tossed her mending aside. Damn him. She'd even made strawberry tarts just for him. He was mean, petty, and cruel. She'd never buy him another book. She'd never ask him to another picnic.

Her breath hitched, she gasped, and sobs shook her. Loneliness washed over her in overwhelming, purple waves. Her lovely parlor, dark in the corners, seemed empty and desolate.

She startled at the rap on her outer door. For one unreasoning moment, elation licked at her sore heart. Christophe had come to apologize! That momentary taste of relief and joy made the descent into disappointment all the darker. She opened the door to Valere.

He shoved his way in, took her in his arms and kissed her hard, pressing her lips against her teeth, covering her nose with his cheek. She drew back, but he grasped her all the tighter.

She struggled to free her head. "Valere, I can't breathe."

He loosened his grip, stepped back enough to look into her face. "But you're glad to see me?"

His eyes were too bright. Had he been drinking? "Of course I am."

He jerked her back into his embrace and growled into her neck. He pulled at her bodice, bent his head and consumed her, licking and sucking.

"Valere. Valere, slow down."

He lifted her into his arms, his face nuzzling her ear, and carried her into the bedroom. After the fervor in the parlor, Tansy thought he meant to throw her on the bed and ravish her like a wild animal, but he lay her down gently, kissed her sweetly, and then lay on his side next to her. "You are glad to see me, aren't you?" he whispered.

In the darkness she heard the note of loneliness in his voice. She cupped his face in her hands and kissed his eyes, his brow. "I am very glad to see you, Valere."

Slowly, she undressed him, petting and caressing as she eased his clothes off. Tenderly, she made love to him, pouring all she had into soothing him, to pleasing him. When he'd climaxed and his body relaxed, she cradled his head against her breast while he slept.

She'd never seen him like this. Certainly sometimes he came to her with a rabid appetite, but tonight he had not simply craved sex. He'd needed her. She kissed his hair. Something was very wrong between Valere and his wife. Perhaps she forbade him her bed. Whatever she did, she hurt him.

She tightened her arm around his shoulder. Valere nuzzled her breast and shifted so that he could slowly sweep his hand up her back in a silken stroke. He made love to her, this time, with gentle kisses on her mouth, her neck, her throat. His hand whispered over her body, tracing her contours, caressing her hip. When he entered her, she wrapped her legs around him and scraped her teeth against his shoulder. They came together in a long, shuddering climax.

As they lay together, their bodies limp, Tansy thought that if Valere made love to his wife like that, she would not, could not be unhappy with him. She wondered if she could teach him, if she should teach him, how to love a frightened girl.

Valere's regular breathing told her he was asleep. She was drifting away herself until a selfish thought roused her. If his wife began to please him in bed, would he still want her? What would she do if Valere left her? It would break her heart.

Wouldn't it? She would be sad. She would miss him. But would it break her heart? She clutched at him in his sleep, unwilling to probe for the answer.

## Chapter Fifteen

The boys in Tansy's class were dears, everyone one of them. Marcus often seemed like a great grown boy with his solemn, steady kindness, but now and then he'd giggle over some foolishness, or he'd slip into silliness himself, and she was glad he still had the heart of an eight year old. René had ceased obsessing over the size of his chalk pieces. Instead he wiped incessantly at his board, removing every trace of chalk residue before he would write the next problem.

David, the new boy, continued to be withdrawn. She coaxed him into looking at her when she spoke to him. She praised him, she encouraged him, but he still rocked when she sat too near. She tried placing her hand on his arm to still him, but he froze. She removed her hand and he resumed rocking.

Tuesday, David arrived at school with a bruise on his cheek. When Tansy came in, Rosa took her aside. "See if you can find out what happened to David. It doesn't look like a blow, but something is amiss with that child."

Once she had the boys stringing beans together to make their own abacuses, she took David to the back of the room. He situated his chair so that he was backed into the corner and began his rocking. Tansy carefully placed her chair so that they could talk quietly, but mindful not to sit too close or the rocking would intensify. She began with the complicated math problems he adored. "Sixty-three thousand four hundred and twelve take away eleven thousand twenty-two." She quickly scribbled the problem on her own slate to get the answer, but he beat her to it without benefit of chalk and slate.

"Fifty-two thousand three hundred ninety."

Tansy frowned at her slate. She erased the second two and corrected it to a three. "Right."

They worked companionably, and David's rocking almost stilled. "You have a bruise on your cheek," she said.

*Tansy*

He continued the rather slight movement to and fro. He evidently saw no reason to comment on her statement of fact.

"How did you get it, David?"

He glanced at her, all he was ever able to do before his eyes darted back to his slate or his lap or the window. He touched the bruise with a slight crease between his eyebrows as if he were trying to remember. "I stepped on a doll."

"You stepped on a doll? How did that hurt your cheek?"

"I tripped on the doll."

"And so you fell?"

He had nothing more to add. After Tansy's two hours, she went home and collected Alain from Mrs. O'Hare's. Then she went back to the Academy to speak to Rosa when school was out. "David says he tripped over a doll."

Rosa grimaced. "Maybe. Still, I think I'll stop by this afternoon."

"I'll go with you."

Rosa shook her head. "I don't want Alain along."

Christophe stood not five feet away, his arms crossed, watching the boys rushing out of the building on bursts of pent-up energy. Tansy raised her voice slightly. "Christophe?"

He turned a carefully blank face to her. He had hardly spoken to her in over a week. If he looked at her at all, his eyes froze her marrow. She curled her hand into her skirt to hide her nervous fingers. "I would like to meet David's parents, to go with Rosa to see them after school. Can I leave Alain with you for half an hour?"

"What about Mrs. O'Hare?"

Tansy swallowed hard, ashamed. She'd been trying to use Alain to bridge this rift between them.

"I'll keep him." He turned his attention back to the boys darting past in a dance of chaos.

Tansy found Alain at the back door pounding erasers, a fine dusting of chalk in his hair. "Come, sweetheart. I'm going to run an errand and leave you with Christophe." The main hallway was emptied and quiet now. She put on a bright smile and walked into Christophe's room. "Here is my treasure."

He did not look at her, did not acknowledge she had spoken. Alain walked over to where Christophe sat at the desk and leaned over his lap. Christophe ruffled his hair. "How would you like to walk down to the river to see the ships?"

"Steam ships?"

"Could be steam ships. I think I heard a whistle."

He rose to retrieve his hat. Tansy stood in front of the peg by the door. He stopped and shot a glance at her. She felt like curling into a small withered ball under that cold blast. She moved aside.

He put his hat on, took Alain's hand and left the room, not having granted her a single word. She tried to conjure up the righteous anger that had sustained her for the first days after he'd taken her book in such a scornful manner. But she'd run out of anger.

Rosa waited for her in the hallway. They walked the six blocks to David's home and knocked on the door. A pleasant looking woman of medium color answered, a little girl with bright black eyes on her hip. Mrs. Thomas wore a neat cotton day dress and a modestly tied tignon. She looked at them blankly.

"I'm Rosa LeFevre. This is Madame Bouvier. We are David's teachers."

Mrs. Thomas smiled uneasily. "David just came in. Is he in trouble?"

"Not at all. We try to know the families of all our students, and we hoped you would take time to visit with us."

"Of course." She opened the door wide and welcomed them to her parlor.

The room was comfortable, the furniture good if not expensive, the floor bare but polished. Several toys were strewn about. Mrs. Thomas gestured for them to sit down.

"Is David behaving at school?"

Tansy heard the anxiety in her voice. "He is no trouble, Mrs. Thomas," Tansy said. "In fact, he is a remarkable boy. His facility with numbers is extraordinary."

"Yes, it is."

"Did you or your husband teach him?" Rosa asked.

David's mother set her little girl down and she toddled over to pick up her set of wooden cups that nested one inside the other. Mrs. Thomas tucked a stray hank of hair into her tignon. "As I remember it, my husband spent an afternoon with him talking about multiplication when David was six. He already had picked up his numbers, I'm not sure how. My husband is an accountant. I suppose he watched Mr. Thomas with his figures."

"I've never seen a child so able."

Mrs. Thomas flashed a worried look at Rosa. "Is it so very peculiar?"

Rosa tilted her head. "Unusual, certainly."

Mrs. Thomas nodded again, her eyes focused on the near-distance. "My husband's brother is the same." She flushed in embarrassment. "The rocking. The numbers. You know."

"How very interesting," Rosa said. "Does David play with his sister? Romp and get into trouble here at home? Cause a ruckus?"

Mrs. Thomas looked at them blankly. "A ruckus?" A shadow darkened her face. "I wish he were a child to cause a ruckus."

"I see. I thought perhaps he'd run himself into a door jamb or failed to catch a ball. The bruise on his cheek."

Tansy watched Mrs. Thomas closely. She showed no discomfort at reference to David's bruise. "He tripped over Nancy's doll and fell against the stool." She seemed to be remembering the moment with some sadness. "He didn't even cry."

She looked from Tansy to Rosa, seeming to understand all at once. "You're worried that we hit David, that that's how he got the bruise." Mrs. Thomas smiled, the saddest smile Tansy had ever seen. "We don't hit David. We love him." She suddenly pressed the back of her hand to her mouth. "We do the best we can."

"I'm sure you do. I raised three myself, and there were days I wanted to dive into a pile of pillows and hide. Whatever the challenges, that's all any of us can do, Mrs. Thomas. Try, and hope for the best." Rosa turned to Tansy with a slight nod. She was satisfied, and so was Tansy.

Rosa stood. "We're happy to have David at our school, Mrs. Thomas. We'll work to keep him challenged, to help him develop his remarkable talent."

Mrs. Thomas's eyes glistened with tears. "Thank you. I'll tell my husband how kind you were to call."

Walking back to the school, Rosa said, "I suppose it's a difference like any other. Some of us can't sing and others are canaries. Some can't dance, some can."

"The rocking, though. That's strange."

"I once had a student who bit his nails until they bled. Maybe David will outgrow the rocking. Carlos grew out of the nail biting."

"I hope so. It's hard for the other children to like him."

They were at the entrance to the school. "Well. We'll do what we can for him. I'm going up to prop my feet on my big comfy ottoman."

Rosa climbed the outer stairs to her apartment. Tansy let herself into the main hallway. The building, empty of boys, was quiet and still. Her footsteps were loud on the cypress boards.

She found Christophe's room empty and sat down at his desk to wait for him and Alain. He didn't keep his room so tidy as Rosa did. The desks were awry, the chalk tray under the blackboard full of powder. His desk was cluttered with books and notepaper.

Tudor England lay atop a pile of folders with a bookmark halfway through the volume. She pressed a hand to her chest in relief. Things could not be so bad between them if he were reading her book. Idly, she straightened a few papers with one hand, hardly bothering to square the corners. Her eye caught on the letter head of a sheet of paper. Baton Rouge Academy in heavy, formal lettering. "Dear Mr. Desmarais, We are pleased to offer you the position, Instructor of History, to begin at your earliest convenience."

There was more, but Tansy's cold fingers dropped the page. He was leaving?

The front doors burst open, Alain's running footsteps echoing in the hallway. "Maman! We saw a steamship!" He careened into the room. "The man pulled a rope and made the boat whistle."

Christophe entered the room behind Alain, prepared to resume the frosty cloak he'd worn around Tansy the last ten days, but his stomach twisted when he saw her face. She was trying to respond to Alain, to exclaim about smokestacks and whistles, but her lashes were wet. His eyes fell on the open letter from Baton Rouge.

He'd meant to leave without telling her goodbye. It would be easier that way. When she'd missed the picnic, he felt as if a bell had gone off in his head. What was he doing looking forward to a picnic with another man's woman, another man's child? It was madness to wait for a happiness that would never come.

She looked at him over Alain's head, her eyes deep with hurt. He'd told Musette goodbye that very morning. She'd kissed him and cupped his cheek in her palm and wished him well. But saying goodbye to Tansy, how could he bear it?

"Alain." He opened a drawer in his desk and pulled out a ball. "You can roll this up and down the hallway. Don't throw it high, just roll it." Alain took the ball and scampered to the hall.

He stepped to the desk where Tansy sat. He could see each individual eye lash. He smelled the lavender water she wore.

"You're leaving?"

He nodded.

"You weren't going to tell me?"

He swallowed. He shook his head.

Tears spilled over her cheeks. "Why?"

Instantly, anger flared from the inside out, so hot it must surely consume them both. "Why? You can ask me why?"

The bewilderment on her face seared his heart. How could she not understand? What did she expect of him?

Frustration and need welling up, he grabbed her by both arms and took her mouth, not in the tender, sensual kiss he'd dreamed of. This was about pain and yearning and despair. His heart pounding, he dragged his lips over hers, he forced her to open her mouth to him. She trembled. She pulled against his arms, a small cry escaping from her throat. He didn't care. He was lost in the wanting, in the taking.

Then she wrapped her arms around his neck. Her tongue tasted his lip. He softened his kiss and fell into it. Cradling her face with his hands, he whispered his kiss over her lips. "Tansy."

Her breath shuddered against his mouth. "I don't want you to go."

His arms strained around her, enclosing her as if he could absorb her into his body. Her breath on his neck was a caress. "I want you," he said, his breath ragged. "I've always wanted you."

She leaned back to look at him as if she searched for meaning in his face. Did she still not understand how it hurt him, every day, to see her and not touch her, not love her? "Marry me, Tansy."

She blinked. She blinked again. "But he is Alain's father."

He dropped his arms. His heart turned to cinders. A dozen arguments he could give her. He'd presented them to her in his lonely, angry nights many times. But she had to choose this. She had to choose him. He would not coerce. He would not beg.

Their gazes locked. Sorrow and resentment warred in his chest, but her gaze held no hope, only resignation. Shaking his head, he stepped away from her.

"I can't do this any longer."

She reached her hand out. "Christophe, please."

He stiffened. "Will you marry me?"

She dropped her hand. With a raging impotence, he turned on his heel and strode from the room.

Tansy flinched when the outer door slammed. Alain's ball rolled down the hallway and bounced off the baseboard. Shadows crept from the corners, slid across the floor, and flowed over her and into her. Where there had been pain and longing a moment before, there were now only these shadows.

## Chapter Sixteen

Tansy didn't hear a word of Alain's chatter on the way home from school. She didn't see how she could breathe, her chest hurt so bad. How could he have thought she could take Alain from his father? She had never been free, not since Maman had sanded the ink of Valere's signature on that contract.

She'd been a fool. She'd told herself she and Christophe could be merely friends. After all, he had his seamstress. She had Valere. She hadn't let herself think about those moments Christophe's mask slipped, revealing feelings deeper than friendship. She hadn't let herself see there could be an us.

With trembling fingers, she touched her lips, remembering the burn of his mouth on hers. His heat had flashed through her, flaming through her body into her soul, burning away every illusion. She loved him. And she had lost him.

She picked up her pace, tugging at Alain's hand. She'd break down here on the street if she didn't get into her house, into her room. At her door, she searched frantically for the key in her bag.

"*Bonjour!*" Valere in his gleaming boots strolled along the walk, swinging his cane.

Tansy felt a murderous resentment. She could not take care of Valere now. She could not.

He lifted his hat in greeting and smiled as if he'd brought her a merry treat. "I'm free this afternoon."

"I saw a steamship, Papa," Alain told him.

"Did you? And did it blow its whistle?"

Tansy led them inside and fought to calm herself. In the dim light, she could rely on Valere's lack of perception to hide her feelings. If she concentrated on him, maybe she could shove the pain in Christophe's face from her mind.

Valere bent his knees to settle on her sofa, then stood again. He'd sat on an open book. He snapped it shut and tossed it to the floor. She gritted her teeth, resisting the urge to slap his face, and slap it again. He'd thrown her book. He'd lost her place!

Not trusting herself, Tansy backed away, her fingers curled. Valere lowered himself and stretched out one long leg. Alain climbed onto the sofa next to his father. The image of Alain draped over Christophe's lap, Christophe's casual, intimate mussing of Alain's hair came to her. But Valere hardly noticed his son. Instead, he was occupied with adjusting his waistband. He's getting fat, she thought with a dart of scorn.

"I could read to you, Papa," Alain said.

"So you can read now, eh?" Valere patted Alain's knee. "Good for you."

She was about to shout "Of course he can't read. He's four!" But she bit it back.

Alain scampered to his room and came back with his book of fables.

"Shall I make lemonade? Or squeeze you some orange juice?"

"Coffee, please."

Tansy left Valere with his head leaned back, eyes closed, as Alain began to run his finger swiftly over the lines of print. "It was a hot summer day."

At the kitchen table, Tansy closed her eyes and leaned into her fists on the table top. Hot tears rolled over her cheeks. She stopped her breath, holding in the gasping sobs that threatened to erupt.

"Tansy."

She startled and sucked in air.

"Are you all right? Did I scare you?"

She swiped at her cheeks and turned to Valere with a smile. "I'm fine."

The man really was dense. How could he not see the misery shrouding her?

"I'm taking Alain to the babysitter."

"Fine. Thank you." She hadn't known Valere even knew which cottage was Mrs. O'Hare's. "Wait." She gathered half dozen oranges in a napkin and handed them to Alain. "Be a good boy. I'll see you in the morning.'" She bent over to hug him and kiss him.

Leaving the cottage, Alain trailed behind his father. Tansy's heart twisted. Why had not Valere reached down for his son's hand? He would have.

She gave her head a quick shake. Get on with it. She had coffee to make. She had Valere to entertain. This was her life, not some fantasy Christophe had imagined.

She ground the roasted beans, added sweet water, and put the pot over the fire to brew. She sliced a loaf of bread and spread guava jam on each piece. Valere returned noisily through the house to the kitchen.

"Guava? My favorite." He wrapped his arm around her shoulder and popped a slice of bread in his mouth.

"You're in a fine mood," she said.

He grinned, a tiny smear of jam at the corner of his mouth. "My Arabian won the third race yesterday."

She curved her lips into a smile. "Congratulations."

He pulled her to him and gave her a smacking kiss, his mouth full of bread and jam. He plucked her tignon off and ran his fingers through her hair. "Let's go to bed."

He drained his cup of coffee and followed her to the bedroom. She took her dress off and hung it up with great deliberation. She placed her shoes in the armoire, heels exactly positioned at right angles to the cabinet shelf. If only in this small way, she controlled her life.

Valere pulled his boots and jacket off. She carefully untied his cravat and draped it over the valet. Then the vest, the shirt, his pants and drawers. He crawled into bed and she followed. He put his hands behind his head with a pleased look on his face. "With the winnings from the Arabian, I believe I'll buy St. Croix's bay. She'll be a winner, he says."

Tansy wondered if Valere were as undiscerning in business dealings as he was with the women in his life.

"And you shall have a new wardrobe. Do you need anything for the house? The roof, the cistern all right?"

"Thank you, Valere. The house is fine."

He rolled onto his side, ran his hand over her flank, squeezed her buttocks. "Give me a kiss."

As if her body belonged to someone else, she willed it to kiss Valere, her lover, her protector. Her lips brushed over his. He wrapped his arms about her and deepened the kiss. She felt nothing. No blinding flash of awareness or heat or desire. The memory of Christophe's kiss was keener than the actuality of Valere's mouth on hers. His erection prodded her thigh. She opened for him and they began the old ritual.

When he lapsed into a depleted doze, Tansy stared into the last shadows on the ceiling. Soon it would be dark. Valere would want to go to some dinner, some private gathering, and she could be alone. She closed her eyes. How desperately she wanted to be alone.

When he roused, she reheated his coffee while he dressed. At the door he said, "I can come early tomorrow," his tone implying this would please her.

"How early?"

"Maybe noon. Or one." He leaned down to kiss her. "*Au revoir.*"

She caught at his sleeve before he could leave. "Valere." He waited, his brows raised in question. "I won't be here mid-day tomorrow." She watched him, wondering she had dared to say she would not be available. Was it not her duty, her purpose, to be here when he wanted her?

"Oh." Briefly a shallow line appeared between his brows. "Another day then."

She closed the door behind him and let out her held breath. She didn't light a candle. She wanted the dark. She wanted silence. On the sofa, she curled her feet under her and pulled a satin pillow to her chest.

Her world had cracked. What would she tell Alain? He would miss Christophe, more than he'd miss his own father should Valere leave. Who were the people Alain loved, who loved him? She supposed she should count her mother, but Maman was a rather forbidding, unaffectionate grandparent. Really, just herself, Martine, and Christophe.

She pressed her palms against her eyes, struggling for control. Valere would set Alain up in business or send him all the way to the Sorbonne someday. However uninterested he seemed, Valere was generous. And perhaps there would be another child. Perhaps a little girl. Sometimes men lavished their affection on little girls. He might dote on her. Certainly a daughter of Valere's would never have to toil in a hot kitchen or ruin her fingers rolling cigars. But could her little girl marry? Maybe she would be lucky. Maybe she'd find a free black man, educated and prosperous, marry for love, raise babies, and be a wife. Tansy stared into the darkening room. More likely a daughter of Tansy's would attend her first quadroon ball at seventeen, as she had, and be contracted a few months later.

Tansy wiped the tears off her face. She didn't have a daughter. As for herself, she didn't need a husband. She had Valere. She had Alain. Her own cottage, clothes, a generous allowance. The life she'd been born to was a good life.

At least Alain was at Ms. O'Hare's. She didn't know if she could keep this awful pain from him. She buried her head in the pillow, despair choking her.

At midnight she woke, still huddled on the couch. For a moment, she remained still. Then she scrambled to her feet, her heart beating in a near-panic. She dressed hurriedly, winding her tignon carelessly. In the kitchen she rummaged in the cupboard for an old oil lantern. Once she had it lit, she let herself out onto the street.

She had never walked the streets alone this time of night. It was probably foolish. She didn't care. Her heart thumping hard, she stepped rapidly down her block, cut right, cut left, and walked four blocks more. Christophe's windows were dark. When did he mean to leave? How long ago had he planned this? Before the picnic, or only afterwards?

She pounded on the door and listened for his footsteps. She heard nothing. Fear threatened to buckle her knees. Maybe he'd already gone upriver. Maybe he was at the seamstress's house, in her bed. She lifted her fist to pound again when the door swung open. The lantern revealed Christophe in his trousers, bare footed, bare-chested. He stared at her, his face unreadable. Hot wire twisted in Tansy's chest. What if he sent her away?

She stepped inside and set her lantern on a table where it cast odd shafts of shadow and light. His eyes were dark hollows. His night beard shaded his cheeks. They stood there, in his foyer, the three feet between them a chasm, his face a mask of indifference.

"Christophe?" she whispered.

She saw in his eyes the moment he surrendered his anger. An instant of bleak hopelessness yielded to a flicker of warmth. "Why are you here?"

Nothing mattered now, nothing b… …phe. "Please." Don't go, she meant. Don't leave me, I c… …t if you leave. "Please," she said again.

He raised his arms. She threw herself into him, frantic to hold him, to possess him. She gripped his hair and opened her mouth over his, insistent, hot, and demanding. He was inert under her desperate kisses, and fear clawed at her that he would not forgive her. Then a shudder ran through his body.

He swept her up and carried her to his bed. He lay her down and for a moment only gazed at her. Then he cupped her jaw and kissed her tenderly, sweetly. She didn't want tenderness. For too long she'd buried this craving, this secret need to feel him, taste him, take him. She reached her mouth to his, tearing at his pants, wanting to suck him down with her into a frenzied whirlpool that would drown out every thought, every glimmer of reason.

"Tansy." He stopped her hands. "Not like this."

With a soft, slow, gentle touch, his fingers whispered over her eyes, trailed down her neck. His palms glided over her breasts while he kissed her slowly, gently. She tried to stroke him, to please him, but he pushed her hands to rest against the pillows above her head and moved on with his mouth, his teeth, his tongue, suckling and teasing and tasting.

She'd never been loved like this, as if she were precious. She closed her eyes and moaned as he played her body, his mouth drifting over her ribs, her belly. He nuzzled her between her legs, licked her open, probing, his tongue lapping with feathery touches. She gasped, surprised, overwhelmed. Valere had never... she had never. She dug her heels into the mattress, the aching, yearning hunger growing with every stroke of his tongue. Relentless, he soothed her with his hands on her hips and belly. He provoked her with his mouth until a helpless deep-throated cry tore from her, her hips bucking against him, her body erupting with heat.

He moved up to kiss her face, to wipe the sweaty lock of hair from her forehead. She still pulsed and throbbed as he pushed into her. She exploded again, the darkness suddenly yellow with the fire behind her eyes. He rocked deep into her body until he reared his head back, his neck straining, his breath tortured.

She clutched him while he pumped himself into her, every muscle strained and taut until he exploded in a massive shuddering groan. On a gulp of air, he fell to her side and pulled her close. He stroked her hair, her back, and then he was still. His breathing slowed and he was quiet.

She hadn't known it could be like this, this astounding need and torment and joy. Pressed against him, she felt the beat of his heart under her cheek. Hers. He was hers. She twined her fingers through his. This. This was completion. Total deliverance of oneself to another. She breathed in the scent of his skin. She was his.

But as she listened to the thrum in his chest, her contentment eroded, breath by breath. In its place, dread seeped into her heart. She was his as she had never been Valere's. But she couldn't have this. She couldn't have Christophe.

She shouldn't have come. She had crossed those darkened streets driven by the pulsing need to see him, to touch him. And she'd betrayed Valere. She'd betrayed herself. And Christophe.

She eased herself off the bed. Too much the coward to be here when he woke, she found her chemise and her dress.

Christophe wakened to a deep contentedness. This is happiness, he thought. He'd known it would be like this, a joyful singing in the blood, a total surrender to all that was Tansy. She was his now, only his. She'd needed him, she'd wanted him. He reached for her, his fingers aching to touch her hair, her skin.

She was across the room. "You're dressing?" He got up and lit the candle, yellow light playing on her black hair, casting shadows over her face. "You don't have to go."

She didn't look at him. He raised her face to him, forced her to look at him. "You don't have to go." He kissed her. He'd never tasted a kiss so sweet. His fingers tangled in her hair and he moved his kiss to her eyes.

She turned her head from him. "I shouldn't. I can't. Christophe, I shouldn't — "

A cold fog descended. He dropped his hands from her arms. With icy clarity, he understood. She had come to him, she had loved him. She had let him love her. And it hadn't changed anything.

"I thought you came because you would marry me." Bitterness choked his voice.

She shook her head, averting her face from him. The muscles in his arms twitched with anger. His voice tore out of his throat. "What did you think would happen here? Why did you come?"

She covered her face with her hands. He wanted to grab those hands, to crush those fingers until she hurt the way he hurt. He fisted his hands and turned his back on her. "Get out."

"Christophe."

"Do not tell me you are sorry."

"No," she whispered. "I'm not sorry. But I never ..."

"Leave." He hoped the word struck her like a fist of ice. There was no warmth, no tenderness left in him. She had taken that.

He heard her fumble with her lantern, the flame long dead, and heard the door latch close after her.

He stood in his bedroom, the night air chilling his naked body until the cold penetrated to his core. That was how he would feel from now on. Cold.

## Chapter Seventeen

Tansy felt light, as if her bones were hollow, when she closed Christophe's door behind her. She stumbled through the streets to her cottage and let herself in. She'd thought she would weep, but she only listened to the quiet house. She didn't sleep. By morning, a pounding throbbed behind her eyes. She brought Alain home and did her best to concentrate when he wanted her to watch him play.

Martine came in the back door and Alain called to her. "Watch this." He spun his top so that it traced circles on the floor for five, then six seconds before it toppled over. He grinned, very pleased with himself.

"Well done!" Martine pulled out a chair at the table and plopped down. "Frederick just left," she said, her smile lighting her whole face. She lost that light as soon as she actually looked in Tansy's face. "What on earth? Are you ill? Do you have a fever?"

She felt Tansy's forehead. Tansy waved her off. "I'm not sick."

"You not only look sick, you look like you've been sick for a week. What's wrong?"

Without having known she was even close to breaking down, Tansy clapped her hands over her face.

"Oh my dear," Martine said. "Alain, darling, would you get me a glass of water? You're a sweetheart."

She rubbed Tansy's shuddering back. Once Alain had left the room, she said, "Now tell me. What's happened?"

"Christophe's gone."

Martine's hand stilled. "He was here?"

"Gone. To Baton Rouge."

"Tell me what's happened."

"He's going to teach at Baton Rouge Academy."

"You didn't know? He didn't tell you?"

Tansy shook her head, wiping at her cheeks.

"Well," Martine sighed. "I don't guess he had to."

Tansy's face scrunched up again, a thin wail escaping the back of her throat. Martine held Tansy, letting her sob. Then she poured her a glass of wine.

"Drink that. Then tell me."

Tansy told her, but not everything. Not about last night.

Martine was not surprised Christophe wanted to marry her. "You, Tansy, were willfully blind."

"Yes. I was." Alain stood nearby, a glass of water in his hands, looking at her with big, solemn eyes. "Come here, darling. Maman's all right."

She cuddled him and patted his back. "Look," she said and managed a watery smile. "I'm all right. Just weepy this morning. Everything's fine."

His dark eyes accused her. "You said Christophe was gone."

She nodded.

"He wouldn't go without me."

"Oh, darling. He didn't want to leave you. But he had to. He had to go to another school, another city."

Alain stood very still for a moment. Then he set the water down, returned to his top, and spun it, and spun it again.

"He'll be fine," Martine said quietly. Tansy looked at his solemn face, his concentration on the spinning top. He loved Christophe. She didn't know how Alain could be all right, at least not today.

Martine put the water in front of her. "Drink all of it." She rifled through Tansy's kitchen and produced a plate of bread and cheese. Tansy shoved at it, but Martine shoved it right back. "Eat that or you'll be sick. Alain does not need a sick maman."

Tansy tore off a piece of bread and rolled it in her fingers.

"If you don't put that in your mouth, I'm going to force it down your throat. When did he leave?"

The bread tasted like old paper in her mouth. On a sudden thought, she got to her feet with such force her chair fell back to the floor. "Maybe he's still here, finishing up at the school." Tansy grabbed Martine's hand. "Will you take Alain home with you?"

"Of course, but what are you — ?"

"I have to talk to him. I have to go."

"Tansy, unless you've changed your mind — "

Tansy kissed Alain on the head and headed for the door.

"Wait! You don't have your tignon." Martine handed her the swath of cloth draped over the back of the sofa. Tansy wound it around her head as she walked, heedless of style or neatness.

She covered the blocks between home and school torn between fear he would be there and fear he wouldn't. How could she face him? But she had to see him, to explain.

As she approached Christophe's classroom, her breathing grew shallow and contracted. Light-headed, she steadied herself against the wall. The murmur of children's voices came through his open door. She gulped at air and stepped into the doorway. Mrs. Thatcher bent over a student's desk.

Tansy stepped back and flattened herself against the wall. He wasn't there. He wasn't there. Head down, she hurried to Rosa's room. She stopped in the doorway, wondering what she'd meant to do, what she could possibly say. Rosa looked up from her desk and immediately got to her feet. She left the children working at their tables and guided Tansy back into the hallway.

"He's gone," Tansy said.

"Yes. He's gone."

Tansy's hand writhed around the other one. "Is he ...?"

Rosa shook her head. "No. He isn't coming back."

"You knew he was going?"

"I thought he might. He woke me this morning to tell me."

"It's my fault."

Rosa drew a deep breath. "I don't know if it's your fault, but it is certainly because of you."

"What am I going to do?"

Rosa tilted her head to look at her. "Tansy, you've already done it. You made your choice."

A bitter sound almost like a laugh came from Tansy's throat. "Choice? I had no choice."

"No? Tansy, tell me something. Who was the last person in your family to be a slave?"

Tansy pulled her head back. "What does that — ?"

"Was it your grandmother, your great-grandmother? Go home, Tansy. I'll manage without you today, and tomorrow if you can't come back. It will be your choice."

Blind and numb, Tansy hardly knew how she got from the school to Martine's door. Martine let her in and nodded toward Alain.

"Has he been crying?" Tansy asked.

"No, but I wish he would." She looked over her shoulder where Alain arranged a deck of cards on the rug. "He hasn't said one word since you left."

Tansy lowered herself to the floor. He didn't acknowledge her, so she picked him up, put him in her lap and wrapped her arms around him. "Are you sad, Alain?"

When he didn't answer her, she turned him so she could see his face. He wouldn't look at her. "I'm sad, too. We'll miss Christophe." He wriggled free of her and resumed sorting his cards.

"See?" Martine said.

"It's going to be hard. Christophe was good to him."

"Christophe was a father to him," Martine amended. "He was. You couldn't see that?"

Tansy rubbed her hands over her face.

"Get some sleep," Martine said. "Alain is fine here with me."

At the back door, Tansy turned. "Last night, your first night with Monsieur DuMaine?"

"It was good, Tansy. Very good. I'll tell you another time. Go home."

Tansy walked across the connecting courtyards as if she waded through molasses. She let herself into her kitchen where the plate of bread and cheese still lay on the table. She sat down, pulled the plate to her and stared at the food a moment before she tore a piece of bread and put it in her mouth.

In the bedroom, she took off the dress she'd worn since yesterday. She kicked off her shoes and stared at them a moment, then picked them up and placed them precisely in their place. Her mind a gray haze, her blood flowing like sludge through her veins, she got under the covers.

A knocking cut painfully through the fog in her brain. Her head ached and her mouth tasted like dirty stockings. She opened her eyes to the light and shadows of late afternoon.

She answered the door and Valere stepped in smelling of sunshine and horse. "You were asleep?"

She nodded, pushing the hair off her face.

"It's five o'clock. Why were you sleeping?" He peered at her. "Are you ill?"

She thought a moment. "Yes. I'm sick."

"Oh."

He didn't seem to know what to do. He still held his hat in his hands. She'd make it easy for him. "You should go, Valere. You don't want to catch anything."

"I'm sure you'll feel fine tomorrow. You're never sick."

She drew a deep breath. "Yes, Valere. I'll be fine."

He brightened at that. "Go back to bed. I'll see you tomorrow."

She closed the door behind him. She smelled bad. She must look worse. She should take a bath before she went for Alain.

She drew water but couldn't be bothered to heat it. She washed and dressed. Why hadn't Valere asked where Alain was, who was taking care of him? She brushed her hair and wrapped it in a clean tignon. It didn't matter. Valere knew she had Mrs. O'Hare and Martine to keep Alain whenever she needed them. He just wasn't used to thinking about the responsibility of taking care of him. She thought enough about Alain for both of them.

When she went to Martine's to fetch him, Alain sat at the table eating his supper. Martine insisted she sit down and eat, too. When she'd drunk the lemonade and eaten the meat pie from the corner bakery, the ache between her eyes eased.

"Did you have a nice time with Martine?" she asked Alain.

He tore a grape in half before he ate it.

"Alain?" He swung his legs, as always. His face was clear of grief, but he did not look at her.

"He probably needs to go to bed early," Martine said. "It's been a hard day for him, too."

Tansy took him home, washed his face, and put him to bed. "Would you like a story?"

He rolled away from her and faced the wall. She stroked his hair. "It'll be all right, Alain. It will be."

When Estelle Bouvier strode into the cottage the next evening, Tansy girded herself to withstand whatever onslaught her mother planned for her. While Tansy poured her a glass of wine, she sat on the sofa and watched Alain's cavalry swarm over castle walls.

"Your horses are unique, Alain. I don't believe I've ever seen any others climbing vertical walls."

"Maman," Tansy murmured. She needn't have worried. Alain paid no attention to her.

Estelle shrugged a shoulder and tasted her wine. "Not bad," she said. "It has bottom."

"I bought it at Gallatin's."

Estelle set her glass down and made a show of turning her attention, and her scrutiny, on Tansy. "So Christophe has gone."

Tansy knew that's why she'd come. To see if she could perhaps pick at the wound. She deliberately shrugged exactly as her mother had.

"You are disturbed?" Estelle said.

"I'll miss him, I suppose."

Estelle studied her a moment, her shrewd eyes narrowed. "You suppose? Perhaps I misunderstood the attachment."

"There was no attachment, Maman. We were friends. I'm happy he has this opportunity. He's a scholar. He should be at an important academy."

Estelle picked up her wine. "For once, you have your feelings in line with your obligations. It's a wonder Valere never knew of your friendship with Christophe. I can't imagine any protector tolerating that close a friendship with another man."

"It never came up."

Estelle surprised her. She reached out and gently placed her hand on Tansy's arm. "It's for the best, Tansy. I'm proud of you for thinking things through, with your head, not your heart."

Tansy gulped back the sob threatening to erupt. Her mother's sharp tongue she was accustomed to. Her kindness she was not.

"You have Alain to think of, after all. It's not as if Valcourt were black-hearted. If he mistreated you or the boy, I would take steps to protect you. But your man is generous, he's gentle, he's good to you. This is where you belong." She took her hand from Tansy's arm and resumed her no-nonsense tone. "I'm pleased I did not have to berate you for foolishness."

She drained her wine. "I must go. Alain, come and kiss your grandmother."

For a moment, Alain seemed not to have heard. Then he stood up and kissed Estelle's cheek. Without waiting for a return kiss or a touch, without so much as a hint of recognition on his face, he settled back with his toys, his back to both mother and grandmother.

Estelle raised her eyebrows at Alain's uncharacteristic coldness. Tansy chose not to explain. "*Bonsoir*, Maman."

Estelle sailed into the evening, her world in order. As always.

Late into the night, Tansy sat in her parlor, rocking, her mind hazy, her feelings benumbed. She knew only that she hurt, somewhere, everywhere. She started when Martine let herself in the back door.

She spoke softly so as not to wake Alain. "I've brought a bottle of wine. Let's drink it down to the dregs."

Tansy got up to fetch the corkscrew and two glasses. She settled back in the rocker while Martine opened the bottle and poured.

Martine raised her glass. "To absent friends."

Tansy raised her glass and sipped.

Martine sat on the floor, her back against the sofa. She tapped Tansy's slipper. "How are you, my friend?"

Tansy leaned her head back and closed her eyes. When she opened them, she forced a smile. "I am waiting to hear all the details of your seduction. Or Frederick's seduction. Which was it?"

Blessedly, Martine did not press her but let out an enormous sigh. "I suppose we seduced each other. Tansy, he is the best lover I ever had. The best lover I ever dreamed of. He's ... " She winked and sipped her wine. "He's vigorous."

Tansy laughed. "Frederick DuMaine, vigorous. What else? Entertain me."

"He is experienced."

"Meaning what?"

"You know what I mean," Martine said with a sly grin. "He knows how to please a woman. All of a woman. Every part of a woman."

"I believe I take your meaning."

"And he can be gentle when ... we want to be gentle."

"I somehow did not imagine gentle is what you were looking for, Martine."

She grinned. "He is not always gentle. As I said, he's a vigorous man."

A pang of misery tore through Tansy at the sudden memory of Christophe, his hands, his mouth on her, his body in hers. Her skin still felt his touch, still felt his heat. She poured herself a second glass of wine.

"He brought roses," Martine said dreamily. "Three dozen red roses."

"So he's vigorous, experienced, gentle, not-so-gentle, and romantic. And this adds up to — a lovely first night together."

"Yes. A very lovely first night."

Tansy smiled, a genuine glad one this time. "I believe you're slipping from very great liking, Martine, to something a little more."

Martine's eyes were deep, dark and sober. "It isn't just the sex, Tansy. I think we really might make each other happy. And it feels wonderful."

"I'm glad. I like your Frederick."

They were quiet for a few moments. "Do you want to talk about Christophe?"

Tansy shook her head. "Alain and I are with Valere. Christophe is gone. There is nothing more to talk about."

## Chapter Eighteen

Valere swung his cane as he walked up his block. With his racetrack winnings in his pocket and a fine blue sky overhead, he decided to surprise Abigail by having mid-day dinner at home.

"What are you doing here?" she demanded.

He blinked. "May a man not come home for dinner?"

Abigail rang the bell with a vicious shake. When the servant arrived, she snapped out her order. "Set a place for Mr. Valcourt."

Feeling a little dampened, Valere nevertheless dug into his dinner with a hearty appetite. Abigail had little to say to him, but he was happy to focus on his soup, oysters, and beef. Over dessert, he smiled at his wife.

"You may have a new ball gown, Abigail."

Instead of smiling as she ought to do — what woman would not smile at having a new gown? — her pretty pink lips were whitened into a tight line. "Why?" she said.

He raised his eyebrows. "Why? Because I thought it would please you."

"Why now? The season is almost over."

He gave her a satisfied grin. "Because I've made a very tidy sum at the racetrack. My Arabian won!"

"I didn't know you had an Arabian."

"Oh, yes. Should you like to meet him? He's a fine horse."

"No, I would not like to meet him. How much?"

"I beg your pardon?"

"How much did you win?"

He frowned slightly. What a vulgar question.

"How much, Mr. Valcourt?"

"My finances are my responsibility, Mrs. Valcourt. You need not concern yourself."

"I thought they were our finances, Mr. Valcourt. I should like to know how large this windfall is so that I may spend accordingly."

"You may spend according to the cost of one very nice ball gown."

Abigail's narrow face took on a spiteful cast. "And what part of your winnings does one ball gown represent? Perhaps I should like more than one ball gown. Perhaps I should like three ball gowns. Or forty-three."

"That is a ridiculous statement, Mrs. Valcourt. I do not understand you. Your husband offers you a ball gown and you offer him a quarrel. What is the matter with you?"

The angry flush spreading up her neck all the way into her hairline made her eyes very blue, but the tight mouth seemed to sharpen her nose. Her looks were not improved. She flung her napkin across her plate, pushed her chair back, and with chin raised high, left the room in a regal march.

Valere stared at the remainder of his custard. He really had no more appetite. Such a surly young woman. Who would have expected it? All through the weeks of their courtship she had been only sweetness and amiability.

It really was very good custard. He picked up his spoon and finished the bowl.

He had the rest of the afternoon and evening to fill. He could go to Renault's and play cards, smoke a few cigars. He could see his man of business and discuss the distribution of his winnings among his investments. He could see about that bay of St. Croix's. Instead, he retired to his room and napped the afternoon away.

As evening fell he dressed and left the house without having seen Abigail again. He played a few rounds at Renault's and had a light supper. Then his friends persuaded him to go to the ball with them. The room was bright with candles and mirrors, and in the center, one of the new gas chandeliers. He had not arranged to have Tansy meet him here this evening, so he felt a little lost. He cast an eye over the fresh faces of girls hoping to attract a protector. Had Tansy been that young when he spoke for her? He supposed she had been.

He danced with Martine and with Madame Bouvier. He partnered with the placées of his friends. And then he'd had enough. He hired a hack to take him home, out of sorts and discontent. He'd looked forward to bedding Tansy this morning, which would have been a fine start to the day, but she'd looked damned awful. Dark circles under her eyes, no color in her face at all. He'd never seen her look so ill. Probably something she ate. She'd be fine tomorrow.

He undressed for bed, feeling restless and randy. He had a wife, for God's sake. And no matter how peevish she'd been earlier, she'd made a bargain. All the sex he wanted until she became pregnant. And she had made no announcement to that effect.

Wearing only a dressing robe, he took a candelabra to the connecting door between his dressing room and hers. He twisted the knob, but of course she'd locked it. He'd determined he would never again pound on a door in his own household. He took the key from his top shelf and unlocked it.

Only a patch of moonlight lit Abigail's room. She must be long asleep. It would be pleasant to wake her with kisses, to unplait her long braid and spread the silvery blonde hair on her pillow. Maybe she'd be more relaxed, more receptive if she were sleepy.

With a gasp, she rose from the bed like some specter rising from the grave. He raised the candelabra to show her it was only him, nothing to fear. She scrambled from the bed and backed half way across the room. She took her stand, feet wide apart, hands fisted at her sides.

"It didn't work."

Her tone was not simply her usual irritation. It was a harsh and venomous hiss. He was befuddled, by the venom and by the statement. "What?"

"It didn't work. You said you'd give me a baby but you did not." She actually bared her teeth at him. He swallowed, a little afraid of her. Was she mad?

"Look at this!" She raised her nightgown to show a spotted pad between her legs. He recoiled, shocked at such a crude display.

He averted his gaze. "For God's sake, Abigail. Lower your dress."

"Oh, it's all right for you to use me night after night, but not for you to have to see what you've done. You know what this means. There is no baby!"

He swallowed hard. Tansy never behaved like this, but he'd heard some women did seem a little distraught when they had their courses. He'd have to be patient.

"Young ladies know little about this, Abigail. You have misunderstood. It often takes months, sometimes many months, before the womb finally accepts the seed and quickens with child. It simply hasn't been long enough for you yet."

"You're saying this is my fault!" She hurled herself at him, her fists punching at his face, his chest, his belly. He tried to keep the candelabra out of her reach, keep it from falling to the floor and burning the house down. Enduring her blows, he grabbed one wrist with his free hand and forced her to the bed. With her knees against the mattress, he shoved her over. Panting, she curled her fingers into claws and launched herself at him. He managed to set the candelabra down and seize her arms. This time when he tossed her to the bed, he covered her body with his.

"Stop! Stop it, Abigail."

She erupted in terrifying, gulping sobs. Her entire body quaked. Then, suddenly boneless, she erupted in helpless sobs. He felt her breasts and nipples through her muslin nightdress and silk robe, and to his own dismay he developed a demanding erection.

He released one arm to wipe at her damp cheek. Poor thing. He'd never seen anyone cry like this. Had not imagined anyone ever crying like this. "Shh," he whispered. "You simply did not understand, sweetheart. Everything will be all right. You'll have your baby."

He rolled to his side and brought her with him. Her shoulders shook, her sobs hot and wet against his chest. He rubbed her back, kissed her ear. Slowly she quieted. For once, she didn't stiffen under his hands. He bent his knees a little to keep her from feeling his erection against her thighs, but the longer she let him stroke her back, the harder he became. He let his hand drift down to her buttocks briefly. She still didn't stiffen. Taking courage, driven by the need between his own legs, he ventured to caress and nuzzle, taking his time, alert to any sign she might turn flinty under his hands.

He'd made love to Tansy now and then when she was still in her monthly. He had found no objection to it. In fact, he'd thought her unusually responsive those times. Slowly, gently, he raised Abigail's nightgown in careful increments. He ran his lips across her neck, his kisses hotter and more urgent. He brushed his lips over her pretty pink ones, delicately, insistently thrusting his tongue against her closed mouth. "Open a little, honey," he said softly. She parted her lips the least bit and he kissed her top lip, gently, carefully drawing it slightly into his mouth.

One hand firm between her shoulder blades, the other palm slowly circling the curves of her bottom, he allowed his erection to touch her. She startled and he withdrew, caressing, stroking, kissing.

"I'll give you a baby, sweetheart," he murmured in her ear.

He slid his hand between them. Motionless, she allowed him to stroke and explore. When he pushed a finger inside, she jolted, then returned to an inanimate state. He loosened his robe, rolled her to her back and spread her legs. "Put your knees up, Abigail."

She complied. "Put your arms around me." She hesitated, then did as he asked. He shifted to kiss her breast through her thin nightgown. He coaxed and teased with his tongue, with little effect, and moved to the other breast. His erection lay between her legs, pressing against her. He clamped his teeth together, trying not to thrust and plunge into her in headlong abandon.

She was still comparatively malleable, her body softer under him than he'd ever known it. Gently, he slid into her, kissing her, caressing her. She accepted him, accepted his weight and his slow thrusts. And then his restraint broke. He plunged into her hard and fast until he pushed himself over the edge, into that painful ecstasy of emptying and pulsing.

He rolled off her and pulled her to rest against his chest. When he'd caught his breath, he stroked her hair.

"Did it work that time?" she whispered.

He breathed out a laugh. "I have no idea, Abigail. We'll have to wait — "

Abigail scrambled to her knees. "What do you mean you have no idea?" Her voice tightened into a high-pitched demand. "You're supposed to know! You stuck that thing in me again. Did it work?"

He reached for her. "There are other reasons to do what we just did," he said, making an effort to hide his growing impatience. "Do you realize that?"

She slapped him, scraping her nails across his cheek. She scurried off the bed and stood their trembling in the candlelight. "You get out," she breathed, her voice a low hiss. "Get out!"

He stared at her. His pretty bride, her mouth now twisted in an ugly bitter grimace, her vividly blue eyes crazed. A hint of fear tightened his throat. Perhaps she was mad.

Her breath a sibilant wheeze, she stretched out her finger in a trembling, straining point. Humiliation rolled over him. He closed his robe and walked stiff-legged into the deep darkness of the dressing room. He closed the door and leaned against it as waves of nausea rose from his stomach. What if Abigail was indeed a madwoman? And, God help him, he'd have to bed her again if he were to have an heir.

## Chapter Nineteen

Tansy sat on the edge of Alain's bed and stroked his forehead. "Time to wake up, sleepyhead." The thick lashes fluttered and he opened his eyes. Any other morning, he would crawl into her lap while he yawned and snuggled. This morning, he merely looked at her, his gray eyes dark as slate.

Tansy took his hand and kissed it. "You're still sad."

And angry with her, she guessed. How could his maman let this happen? Is that what he was thinking?

"You know, I think Christophe is waking up just now and he's thinking about Alain. What is Alain going to do today?"

Something flickered in his eyes. "He's probably yawning and stretching." She yawned and stretched. "He's probably going to climb out of bed," she tousled his hair, "and scratch his head. Then he's going to say, 'I bet Alain is getting ready for breakfast right now.'"

Tentatively, his lips curved into a small smile.

"Come on. I'll let you slice a banana all by yourself."

When she had him at the table, she placed a banana and a paring knife in front of him. Don't hover, she told herself. He's four years old. Still, she watched every finger as he sliced through the peel. She hadn't told him he should peel it first, after all.

He had not spoken since early yesterday. When he put the knife down and said, "I did it," she let out a long sigh. He was going to hurt for a long time. But at least he would talk to her, would try to … not forget, but adapt. He surely could not grieve so very long. He was only four.

At eleven o'clock, Martine came in through the courtyard door. She nodded at Alain playing on the floor. "Has he spoken?"

"Three words." Tansy told her about the banana.

"That's good. It's a start. Why don't I keep him instead of your taking him to Mrs. O'Hare?"

"Thank you. I think he needs the quiet time."

Tansy arrived at the school early to show Rosa that she could depend on her. However constrained her life was, she had this. She had this room full of boys waiting for her, eager to know what she would do with them, eager to learn. And she chose to be here.

She shoved awareness of her emotional bruises to a safe corner of her mind. They had no place here. She cheered herself up by beginning the lesson with a song and even managed to coax David into singing part of the chorus with the other children.

She prepared to leave as the boys filed out for their two o'clock recess. Denis Fournier called to her in the hallway, a book in his hand. "Tansy."

She waited for him. He was a sweet, kind man, his skin nearly as light as hers though his tightly curled gray hair, his full lips and broad nose gave strong indications of his ancestry. Of part of his ancestry. She wondered, as she waited for him to catch up to her, why no one ever considered that people like Denis, like her, ever thought of themselves as white with this much or that much African blood? Instead, they were colored, with a tad of white blood to ease the taint of their black skin.

"I hope I do not cause pain. I know you and Christophe, well, I know you are fond of reading, and so am I. It would please me if we could read the same books and then talk about them."

The dear man. He knew then, as well as Rosa, that she needed a friendly word. He handed her a volume bound in worn brown canvas.

She turned it over in her hands and opened it to the title page. "*The Life and Opinions of Tristram Shandy, Gentleman.*" She pulled up a smile for him. "Thank you, Denis. Thank you very much."

She let herself into her house still feeling light and hollow, like a dried-up corn husk. Like she was recovering from a high fever. The shutters were closed and she did not immediately see the figure sitting in her parlor. She jumped and pressed her hand to her chest. "Valere. You gave me a fright."

"Where have you been?"

She couldn't see his face, but his tone told her he was not in good humor. She set the book down on the table next to his chair. "I was borrowing a book."

"You're never here anymore."

She went very still.

"Where do you go in the middle of the day?"

"I have a friend who teaches school. I went to the school to borrow this book from him."

"Him?"

The hair on her neck pricked. He'd never used that tone with her before. She answered him lightly. "Yes. Monsieur Fournier. An elderly gentleman, a creole like me."

She unwound her tignon and tossed it on the sofa. "Have you waited long? Shall I make you some coffee?"

He turned his head toward the book. Then he looked at her. "You read too much."

She tried a soft laugh. "How can one read too much?"

Though she could not see his face clearly, his hands fisted. She'd made a mistake. She had no experience with Valere like this, sullen and angry. What was he angry about? He'd never minded before when he called and she was not at home.

Without warning, he picked up the book and hurled it across the room. "No more books! You hear me? No more books."

She swallowed hard but stood very still. "Valere?" she said softly. "What's wrong?"

"You will do as I say." He rose from his chair slowly. "You will please me. That is what you're here for."

She'd never been afraid of Valere, never. But with his height and bulk looming over her, she stepped back from him.

"Of course I want to please you, Valere. You know I do."

He grabbed her upper arms and yanked her to him. He pressed a ferocious kiss against her lips, demanding entrance into her mouth. Holding on to his sleeves to keep from falling, she jerked her head back, gasping for air, frightened.

Valere, her sweet, mild Valere, grabbed her hair and pulled her to the bedroom. He tossed her onto the bed and ripped at her skirts, tore her drawers, and opened his trousers. He took her.

Tansy lay numb beneath him, stunned. She could not respond. He didn't want her to respond. He wanted only to punish and take.

He came in a violent paroxysm, shuddering and gasping. He collapsed on top of her, his face buried in the thickness of her hair. Any other time, Tansy would have stroked his back and kissed his neck. She lay there, shaken, dazed.

He rolled over and covered his face with his hands. "Oh, God." He turned away from her. She could barely hear him. "Did I hurt you?"

"Yes." She hoped he could hear how cold she felt. How abused and degraded.

His shoulders heaved, shaking the bed. Tears flowed from between his fingers and great gasping sobs erupted from his chest. "I'm sorry, Tansy. I'm so sorry."

Grief welled up, for herself, for Christophe, and now for this wounded man. What had that woman done to him? Something truly awful to have turned him into the brute he'd been a moment before. This was not the Valere she knew.

She took him in her arms, made him rest his head on her breast. "Shh," she said. She ran her fingers through his hair and caressed his shoulders. "Shh." Whether it was contentment or sorrow, disappointment or pain, whatever Valere brought into this house, he was her life, and he needed her.

## Chapter Twenty

Weeks passed. Even though the soreness over her heart ached, regret sometimes coming over her in overwhelming waves, Tansy squared her shoulders determined to make the best of the day to come. She tied on an apron and attacked the dust and clutter she'd allowed to build up in her parlor. Among the books leaning untidily on her shelf she found Christophe's tome about the French Revolution. She'd never had the chance to talk to him about *égalité* and whether that ideal were practiced anywhere on the earth. She held the book to her chest and closed her eyes. This one thing she had of him.

In her mind, she composed long letters to Christophe. She imagined long letters from him, full of forgiveness, of love, of hope. But of course there were no letters, no forgiveness, and no hope.

She'd done everything right, hadn't she? She'd listened to her tutors, obeyed her mother, and honored her protector. How could life be like ashes in her mouth? What had she done that was so wrong? Yes, she'd used the façade of friendship to deny Christophe's feelings and hide her own, even from herself. But what else could she have done? Even if she'd allowed herself to think of Christophe as more than a friend, she could not take Alain from his father. She'd had no choice.

She placed the book back on the shelf, Rosa's remark flitting into her mind. Who was the last person in your family to be a slave?

Tansy's mouth tightened. That was simply unfair. Of course Valere didn't own her, but they had made a life together. They had a child together. She slapped at a spider web as if she fought a viper. Christophe asked too much. Couldn't he see she owed Valere everything — he had given her the house, he paid for clothes, food, everything.

As quickly as the anger had welled up, it abandoned her to aching, terrifying need. She covered her face with her hands. How could she live with this void in her chest? How could she ever be content again? She should hate Christophe for tearing away all comfort, all peace. How could she go on now that he had turned her world black and purple with bruising, crushing grief?

She pressed a hand to her mouth. She straightened her back and smoothed her apron. She drew one breath, then another, and another. That's how one went on, one breath at a time.

She took Alain to Mrs. O'Hare's and readied herself for the evening. By the time she met Valere in the ballroom, she wore a determined smile. Was not life lived moment by moment? She would make this moment happy. She had a new gown. Valere looked very fine. Why should she not have a wonderful evening? Since that brutal night, Valere had treated her as if she were a fragile bloom. She should enjoy his attention, not chafe at it as if he were smothering her.

As Valere danced her around the room, the music seeped into her pores like a healing balm. She need not look at the orchestra where another man sat in Christophe's chair. She need only feel the music and glide among the other ladies in their bright gowns, waltzing and twirling as though they were a garden of primroses stirred in a scented breeze.

Martine and Frederick danced by, gazing into each other's eyes. Instead of Martine's hand held lightly in his, their fingers were intertwined. Tansy swallowed at that glimpse of intimacy. Their connection encompassed the carnal, yes, but so much more. A sympathy of mind and an understanding of the other's heart bound them, too.

Valere squeezed her hand as they danced. "You're distracted tonight."

"I was only listening to the music."

Valere had sworn he would never hurt her again, that he would try always to please her. She would try, too. She smiled at him, vowing to put away heartache and live her life pleasing him. In spite of good intentions, however, her smile faltered into a bitter quirk. *Candide's* author was right to satirize fools like her who convinced themselves they lived in the best of all possible worlds. One could live blindly, stupidly, like Candide, as long as one's eyes had never seen truth behind the gauzy screen of complacency. Once that gauze was torn, no more peace.

DuMaine asked Tansy to dance. She smiled at him, too, but he seemed to see only the strain behind it for he did not smile back.

She knew the sleepless nights had robbed the luster from her complexion and her eyes, and Martine would surely have told Frederick about Christophe. She trained her gaze over Frederick's shoulder and concentrated on the music.

When Tansy and Martine took lemonade with Tansy's mother, Maman did not seem to notice Tansy was not in looks. Her attention was all for Monsieur Girard. She listened raptly when he spoke. She tapped his arm with her fan when he laughed at something he himself had said. So Maman wants another protector, Tansy thought. She had not expected her mother to ever ally herself with a man again. She had invested the inheritances from her former patrons and was comfortable. Perhaps she was simply tired of being alone. Perhaps even hardened characters like Estelle Bouvier could be lonely.

Monsieur Girard had a merry way about him, full of pleasure and fun. And somehow he found Estelle attractive. She watched her mother smile and flirt, her charm a masterful performance. Estelle's eyes sparkled, her complexion glowed, and she smiled and smiled and smiled. Maman made her own best world.

Martine leaned over to Tansy and whispered. "I believe your maman is in like with Monsieur Girard."

Valere interrupted. "I must go." He took Tansy's hand in both of his and kissed her cheek. "I shan't come tonight," he said as if it were an apology, "but perhaps tomorrow night." Tansy hoped her bright smile hid her relief to be free of him for the night.

In her determination to continue on as if life were worth living, Tansy and Alain met Denis Fournier at an outdoor café bordering the square. The sun shone, the breeze cooled, and the smell of jasmine, gardenia, and fresh growth scented the air. Denis greeted them formally, bowed, and pulled out a chair for Tansy. He shook Alain's hand and said, "I'm very glad to see you on a Sunday afternoon. Will you have a beignet with me?"

Tansy nudged him gently. "Yes, sir, thank you."

Fournier beckoned a waiter to bring them two coffees, lemonade, and beignets.

"You brought me another book?" Tansy said.

"If I'm not rushing you, yes, I did."

"You are not." She dug in her shopping bag and pulled out another volume. "I've finished this one."

"I believe it took me two months to read Tristram Shandy and you've managed it in one! What did you think of it?"

As Tansy and Denis talked over their favorite passages, especially those about poor Tristram's nose, Tansy relaxed. Alain happily swung his legs, powdered sugar all over his face and hands. She didn't fuss at him for licking his fingers. Instead, she sipped at her coffee, glad they sat outside on such a lovely day.

Tansy became aware of a shadow across the table. She looked up and there stood Valere, ashen, anger and hurt at war in his face. She moved as if to rise from her chair, but Valere stepped back, his eyes boring into hers.

Two ladies arrived at his side, one tall, thin, sour. The other dainty as a fairy cake, blonde and pretty. The wife. Both women stared at her openly, the pinch-faced one's expression an odd mixture of avid curiosity and loathing, Abigail's eyes wide, comprehension dawning slowly.

Tansy searched the baby-doll face for signs of cruelty. Behind the prettiness must be a vicious character to have hurt Valere so. How else to explain the turmoil he had been in these last weeks? Needy, demanding. Not like himself at all. At this moment, Tansy saw only shock and alarm on Abigail's face, drained so that she looked white and ill. She grasped for the other woman's arm.

Tansy's gaze shifted. The sister? Her eyes had lost their glint of disgust. It was a self-satisfied gleam of triumph now. With sudden insight, Tansy knew this woman was the source of much of Valere's unhappiness. She poisoned her sister, poisoned their marriage.

The sister boldly swept her gaze over Tansy, head to toes and back, lingering on the tignon with a sneer on her lips. Tansy felt nothing at such pointless malice. She returned her attention to Valere who seemed unable to move or even to look away. He'd waited too long, far too long, to be able to simply nod as if their gazes had locked by chance and walk on.

The tableau was shattered when Alain said, "Hello, Papa."

Abigail's hand flew to her mouth. She gagged and staggered. Her sister took her arm and hurried her away, murmuring in her ear.

"Valere?" Tansy said softly. In his hurt and confusion, she was sure he'd misunderstood what she did here with Denis. "Should you like to meet my friend, Monsieur Fournier?"

Fournier rose to his feet and bowed stiffly. Valere's cheeks colored, his fingers curled. Tansy had to forestall the eruption she sensed building under his flushed skin. She rose from her chair. Leaving the books on the table, hoping formality would indicate to Valere that there was no intimacy between her and Denis, she curtsied. "Good bye, Monsieur Fournier. Thank you for the coffee."

She took Alain's hand and led him away. Valere strode off in the other direction.

Tansy's fingers shook as she unlocked the door. She didn't know whether to expect Valere at any moment, or perhaps not for days. The poor man had looked shattered. He had looked betrayed. He'd seen Denis and assumed the worst. Even though they were in public, Alain between them, even though Denis was old enough to be her father.

A few months ago, before his marriage, Valere would have thought nothing of seeing her having coffee with an older gentleman. But now, he was bruised and raw from whatever troubles he was having in his marriage. He suspected the worst only because he was vulnerable and unsure of himself. But she had never betrayed him, never would.

Flames fanned her face. She had betrayed him. That night with Christophe, she had betrayed him. But she'd renewed her commitment to Valere, had let Christophe leave her for Alain's sake, and for honor's sake. She could make him see that he could trust her loyalty. Because, truly, he need not doubt her.

She settled Alain on the sofa and read to him until mercifully his eyes drooped and then closed. She carried him to his bed and closed the door. Then she sat in her rocker, hands in her lap, and waited.

Valere did not knock. He let himself in with his key, then stood at the door with his hat in his hands. Without a word, she led him to the sofa, poured him a glass of wine, and sat beside him.

He held the goblet loosely between his legs. "They wanted to see the steamships."

"Yes." She wondered if she should explain. Or should she wait? Surely after he'd had this time to think, he didn't misunderstand.

"Are you lovers?"

"What? No!"

"There were books on the table."

She straightened. "Yes. We like books, Denis and I."

"Denis?"

She touched her forehead where an ache was building. "Denis. Monsieur Fournier." She flicked her wrist in a dismissive gesture. "We are friends, Valere. Nothing more."

His manner was strangely subdued. She had no trouble imagining the gloom filling his mind. She had felt it herself these last weeks, the confusion and unbalance and disappointment.

"You said you would not read anymore." He spoke like a petulant child, but with the hint of a blade in his voice.

She had likely never contradicted Valere in all their years together, so she considered carefully before she answered him. "Valere, you said you did not want me to read anymore. I don't believe I agreed to give it up."

He set his wine aside untouched. His body tensed and he looked her directly in the eye. "But now you will." His voice had turned low and harsh. "You will leave off with the books. You will not see this man again."

"Valere, that is not reasonable. Why should I not — "

He rose abruptly and paced across the room. "Because you are my placée, that's why!"

Not long ago, Tansy would have simply agreed to his demands. He was her protector after all, her lover. She would have acquiesced to whatever he asked, then led him to her bedroom. That was her role in life. To serve him, to please him. She hadn't minded, before.

What she should do is simply make love to him. They wouldn't have to talk, just engage physically and sensually. But she didn't want to make love to him. She wanted him to understand that she had a right to be.

She shook her head. "Valere, you have my loyalty. You have my affection and my body. But I have a life when you are not with me. I ... I *am* when you are not here." Unwisely, perhaps, she added, "You have another life besides what we live together here in this cottage."

He snorted. "That's not the point. I pay all your bills. I buy you pretty clothes." Temper flared in his eyes. "You are supposed to be mine."

Her own temper ignited. "I am yours. But you can't expect me to be nothing, to do nothing, when you are living your other life!"

He stabbed a finger at her, his face red, his eyes narrowed. "You will read no more!"

Tansy glanced at Alain's door. She didn't want him to hear his father shouting at her. She would have to calm him down. "Valere, I will do this. From now on, you will not see me read."

His finger still suspended in the air between them, he blinked, then leaned back. All at once, as if the starch in his backbone dissolved, he slumped into a chair. "You never used to quarrel with me."

The thought leapt into her mind. I didn't used to know how stupid you are! She blinked it away. Valere was hurting. She went to him and took his hand. "Valere. Something is wrong. Do you want to tell me what it is?"

He turned his face from her, flushing. He shuddered. When he spoke, his voice was hardly more than a whisper. "She is unnatural."

"Unnatural?"

He wiped a hand over his face and looked at the ceiling to keep from showing her his eyes. "Her sister made her that way. Her sister hates me. And I don't know why."

"I saw the venom in her, Valere. I can believe she is poisonous."

He swallowed hard. "I don't know what to do."

Tansy didn't either. She held his hand and stroked his sleeve. "It will get better, Valere. Give it time." She had no idea if that were true.

"I made an ass of myself in front of both of them. I have to go ... set it right. Somehow."

"She knows about me?"

He nodded. "But she thinks I gave you up."

"And Alain called you Papa." Valere's hand in hers had gone clammy and the skin around his mouth was white. She couldn't apologize to him for Alain's revelation. He was Alain's father, he had never denied it, and a four year old could not be expected to be discreet.

"I don't want to go," he whispered.

Tansy squeezed his hand. "Valere, you're a good, kind man. You can fix this."

He drew a deeper breath and nodded his head. He picked up his hat. At the door, he looked back at her with as bleak an expression as she had ever seen. "You won't see him again?"

He had lied to his wife about giving her up. Maybe that was what she should do. Lie. I'll never see him again. I'll never read another book. She could say the words. And she'd despise herself.

"I will not betray you, Valere. You have what I promised you — my affection, my regard, my bed."

He had not heard the answer he wanted. Or expected. But she could see he hadn't the spirit to insist. He left to do what he could with the mess of his life.

Another Sunday afternoon. Tansy and Martine sat in Martine's parlor with their needlework while Alain played on the rug. When Martine heard the knock on her door, she snapped her head up. Then she burst into the radiance of a woman in love. "He's early," she whispered.

She let Frederick in, all handsome, urbane six feet of him. Before he could take his hat off, she had her arms around his neck and delivered a heated kiss. When he spied Tansy and Alain, he actually blushed. Gently he pulled Martine's arms down and made a sheepish smile. "*Bonjour*."

"*Bonjour*, Frederick." Tansy gathered up her threads and bobbins and nodded at Alain to put his toys away.

DuMaine raised a hand. "Please don't go. This must be Alain." He bent from the waist. Alain looked into his face, then soberly shook hands.

"So you've built a fort?" DuMaine squatted down to admire the fortifications.

Tansy raised her brows at Martine who smiled smugly. She knew what she had. She walked to her small kitchen for the pitcher of sangria she had waiting for him.

He lowered himself to the carpet and stretched his legs out. "You are general of the blue coats?" he asked, pointing to the line of soldiers closest to Alain's knees.

"We're going to send the British back all the way to France!"

DuMaine laughed. "And won't the French be surprised. Shall I be the redcoats, then, while you array your forces?"

Martine handed Tansy a glass of sangria and set DuMaine's on the floor next to him while he arranged the tin redcoats. When she sat in the chair behind him, he shifted slightly so he brushed against her knees. She rested the toe of her slipper against his thigh.

Tansy closed her eyes in a gray wash of loneliness. All the years with Valere, all the afternoons and nights in her bed together, she had never felt this simple intimacy she saw between Martine and Frederick. Their need to touch, as casual as it seemed, was more than sexual. Affection, tenderness, comfort. And connection. A knowledge each of the other.

Valere didn't know her at all. Had Christophe understood her? She swallowed hard. He had, hadn't he? He'd known her better than she'd known herself. He'd seen the blinders she wore and had hated her for them. As if she'd been willfully blind to the constrictions in her life. A needle of resentment stung her. How could he blame her? She'd been leading the life meant for her. She had Valere and Alain, security — she'd been satisfied.

And while she'd been satisfied with her life, Martine had been restless and lonely. Now their fates were reversed, but Martine was more than satisfied. She was happy. Tansy caught Frederick's glance at Martine, the quick, small smile they shared over Alain's head. Did the two of them talk? What did they talk about? Martine had said he read poetry to her. "Ode to the West Wind," she'd said. Christophe had given her "Tintern Abbey" to read once. How would it have been to hear him read it to her, his voice, his tone, his inflections added to the words on the page? She blinked away that painful glimpse of what might have been.

Frederick's hand soared down swiftly, a cannonball whistling toward the troops, and the battle commenced. At the last minute, the ball missed its target and plowed down a row of his own redcoats. Alain whooped and led his legions into the gap made by the cannon burst.

This man wants children, Tansy thought. She looked at Martine who gazed on the two males with a doting love. Martine does too. She said a short silent prayer to Mary Mother of God that they would be so blessed.

Tansy finished her wine. "Time to go home, Alain." She bent to put his soldiers in their box and then glanced at him when he did not help her. His lower lip trembled, his eyes focused on the floor.

DuMaine touched Alain's knee. "We'll play again."

Alain's eyes brightened. His smile widened with hope. "Will we?"

"Yes. We will."

"Thank you, Frederick," Tansy said softly.

He got to his feet, towering over her. "It was my pleasure."

Martine wove her arm through Frederick's. Comfortable, and more, Tansy thought.

Back at home, she fixed supper and had to laugh at Alain gulping down the food on his plate. It'd been too long since he'd shown any appetite. "Slow down. That drumstick isn't going to walk off and leave you."

Alain had been happy today because a kind man had played with him. Maybe she hadn't tried hard enough to engage Valere with his son. He was not a cold man. Only thoughtless and careless. She hated to think it of him, she had never thought it before, but she had to add, selfish.

## Chapter Twenty-One

When next Valere arrived, his spirits were improved. Tansy fed him a modest supper and decided this was an opportunity for Valere to give his son some attention. "Will you entertain Alain while I clean up the kitchen? I'll take him to Mrs. O'Hare in a little while."

With the prospect of satisfaction only slightly delayed, Valere sat himself on the sofa, put his hands on his knees, and contemplated his son. "Well. What would you like to do?"

Tansy saw Alain eye his box of soldiers in the corner, but he'd never seen his father on the floor. "I could bring you a book," Alain said.

Alain climbed onto the sofa, handed his father a book, and leaned in close to watch him read the words. Tansy lingered in the parlor door, a cloth and dish in hand, to watch and listen. Valere cleared his throat before he began. In only moments, she understood that Valere could barely read. He formed the words, stumbling only now and then, but there was no fluidity to it. No expression. And, she thought, no true understanding. Her eyes teared. How awful, to have all the riches to be found in books closed off to you. Perhaps that's why he didn't like to see her reading, because it made him feel left behind.

She walked into the room to rescue him. "Would the two of you like to play a hand of cards with me? I believe Alain could play if I helped him."

A sheen of sweat glowed on Valere's forehead. He wiped his hand across his mouth and drew in a breath of relief. Instead of accepting her offer of cards, though, he raised his brows at her. "Isn't the Irish woman expecting him?"

Her compassion for Valere evaporated. Instead, she ached for Alain that his own father had no interest in him. As for Valere, she was tired of making excuses for him. He was simply the man who had seeded her womb. He was not a father.

As she walked Alain to Mrs. O'Hare, Tansy reminded herself to be fair. Was it so unusual for a white father to be uninterested in his colored children? Her father had teased her and told her how pretty she was, he'd hugged her and kissed her. She knew other mixed-blood children, though, who'd grown up with indifferent fathers. Martine, for instance. Valere? Perhaps he was simply ordinary. Or worse, his heart no deeper than a puddle.

Mrs. O'Hare opened her door, narrowed her eyes, and said, "And who is this come to my door? Is it the King of Ireland, then?"

Alain laughed. "No!"

"Is it the Dauphin of France?"

"No! It's me, Mattie!"

Mrs. O'Hare raised her brows in surprise. "It's Alain?" She opened her arms to him and he rushed in for a hug.

"You go along, love," she said to Tansy. "My prince and I have peas to shell and stories to tell."

Tansy touched his hair. "Good night, sweetheart."

"Good night, Maman."

At her own door, Tansy paused. Her protector waited inside. He expected more than acquiescence. He expected a lover. He expected to be loved. When had loving Valere become a task? When had it become something she had to work at?

She heard her mother's voice scolding. You treat him right. He's a good man, he's generous, he's faithful. Tansy's lip curled in bitterness. Faithful. She supposed in her world, Valere's having a wife was not unfaithful. She straightened her shoulders. Valere kept the agreements laid out in their contract, and more. She had nothing to complain about. She went inside to fulfill her own side of their agreement.

Every day offered beauty and joy, Tansy reminded herself, if she would keep herself open to it. Yielding to dark thoughts had become too easy. Even now, with the scent of honeysuckle perfuming the air as she walked home from school, she had to stave off dread of the next three months. Five more school days, then Rosa would close the Academy for the summer.

What would she do with herself for three months? In past years, Valere had rented a cottage at the prosperous coloreds' resort on Lake Maurepas, and for the month of July she and Alain escaped the sweltering heat and the ever-present fear of yellow fever in New Orleans. At the lake, Valere took her to card parties and picnics. He rowed them on the lake, her with her parasol, Alain with his fingers trailing in the water. At the hotel, along with other white men who left their wives and children elsewhere, he dined with her openly.

Ahead of her, a tired-eyed woman hovered in the doorway of Nicolas Augustine's establishment. Memory flashed back to the day Maman had dragged her into the brothel and upstairs to see the faded woman lying in dirty sheets. Automatically, she crossed the street, glad Alain was with Mrs. O'Hare today and wouldn't see the sad-eyed woman in the soiled red dress.

She forced her mind to turn away from the scent of despair emanating from the brothel door. She and Alain might have to spend the summer in town. Valere had a wife, now. She no doubt expected him to take her to the family plantation on the Cane River for the summer. Tansy plucked a sprig of honeysuckle to take home and wondered where Christophe would spend the summer. He might travel. He had plenty of money. He could go to New York or even Paris. No reason he had to stay in Louisiana.

She found her door already unlocked, Valere standing in the middle of the parlor.

"Again, you were not here."

She stilled at the menace in his voice.

She set down the sprig of honeysuckle and unwrapped her tignon. "Have you been waiting long?"

"Where were you?"

She swallowed hard at the uncharacteristic scowl and the glint of anger in his eyes. If she'd been to the market, she would have a shopping bag in her hands. If she'd been to Maman's she would have Alain with her. If she'd been at Martine's, she would have come in from the courtyard. Then this day, at last, she would tell him where she went in the afternoons.

"You've been with that old man. That ... book man." He said the word book with explosive spite.

"Denis? No, I have not, Valere. Sit down. Let me open the back doors and get some air in here. Here, give me your coat."

One of his large hands fisted. No, he would not hit her. Not Valere. She went to him and touched his cheek. "Valere, sit down."

"Where were you?"

"Sit down," she said gently. "I'll tell you where I was."

She pulled his coat off his shoulders and opened his cravat. She was about to sit on the stool at his knee, then thought better of it. She was not a child, not a small creature to sit in a submissive posture. She sat in the chair across from him.

"You were overheated, I think."

"Don't try to change the subject, Madame."

Madame? When had he ever called her Madame? "I was at Rosa LeFevre's Academy for Boys, Valere. I teach there two hours every day."

He stared at her. She chased away the image of a fish gazing stupidly though shallow water.

"You have a job?"

"Yes."

His scowl held fast. "You had only to tell me that you didn't have enough money."

"Valere, I don't need more money. I do it because I want to."

The line between his eyes deepened. "Why?"

She looked at him. What would he think when she told him? He'd always been mild and accommodating. But his marriage had gone sour, he was hurt, he was not himself.

"Because I'm bored."

His head jerked back. "You're bored?"

"Yes. I'm bored."

Valere leapt to his feet and towered over her. For the first time, Tansy felt intimidated by his size, by his strength.

"You mean I bore you. After all this time, you've decided I bore you."

"Valere, that's not what I meant. I'm simply bored all the hours of the day I spend here with only my own thoughts for company. I like teaching. I like being with the other teachers and with my students. I feel useful, Valere. And for the first time in my life, I'm good at something."

"You're good at being my placée. That's what you're good at. That's what you're good for. That's who you are. My placée."

Tansy wanted to stand, to meet him on her feet as he was on his, but Valere stood so close his knees brushed her skirts. She gripped the arms of her chair.

"I am your placée, but that is not all I am. I am a teacher, Valere."

He leaned over, his hands painfully pressing hers into the chair arms. "I signed a contract. Your mother signed a contract. You are my placée. You are not a teacher."

Tansy heard the tremor in his voice. "Valere, sit down, please."

Abruptly, he swiped his arm across the side table, knocking the lamp to the floor, spattering whale oil across the boards. Thank God it had not been lit.

He drew himself up. "You will be here in this house when I want you. Anytime, day or night. You will not go to the Academy again. You will be here for me!"

Immobilized, Tansy stared at his hard eyes, at his clenched jaw. A trembling started at her knees, moved through her body, down her arms, into her fingers. He was telling her she had to be nothing. She was nothing. Only a body for his convenience.

What if she just said *no. I won't*. She searched his face. He'd never asked for much. Just that she be kind to him, receptive, available. And now, his eyes were red-rimmed, his cheeks flushed.

But what if she said no?

If he had railed at her, perhaps she would have tried it. But he stepped back, his hand plowing through his hair. "You need me, Tansy. Don't forget that. You and Alain. I take care of you. I protect you."

She pressed her palm against her mouth and closed her eyes. Yes, he did. He did take care of them. She didn't have to stand on the street in front of a brothel, hoping to earn a few coins with a stranger. More important, Valere ensured Alain had enough to eat, that he was safe, that he would have a future.

She dropped her hand into her lap and gazed at Valere's polished boots. "One more week," she said quietly. "I have to go one more week, to finish."

She heard his intake of breath. He had won. "One more week then."

He took his hat and paused at the door. "It's only the marriage that has you upset," he said. "I have neglected you, Tansy. I won't anymore."

The door closed. She listened to the house for a long time. A cricket had got into the kitchen again. A mockingbird sang in the courtyard. And all the world was gray.

But she had done the right thing. The necessary thing.

## Chapter Twenty-Two

Christophe rented a room in one of the smaller hotels at Lake Maurepas. He stretched his legs along the walking paths and chatted with old friends from New Orleans and new friends from Baton Rouge. Late afternoon, he met the coach and smiled when Musette disembarked.

She turned her cheek up for a quick kiss. Her hand on his arm, their strides comfortably matched, they strolled along the lakeshore in the shade of tall pines.

"I've missed you," she said.

He squeezed her arm. "I've missed you, too."

They walked to the end of the pier and watched a water bug glide over the surface, a turtle stick its nose out of the water for a breath of air. A pelican splashed down and skied to a stop to float and look pensive.

"I love it here," Musette said. "Thank you for asking me."

"I don't know why we didn't do this last year, or the year before."

"Because we got to see each other any time we wanted last year and the year before. Are you happy in Baton Rouge?"

He leaned on the pier railing. "It's a challenge every day, learning the curriculum, staying ahead of the students. They're quite a different kettle of fish compared to ten year olds. Like every other healthy sixteen year old boy, their minds are on girls, short, tall, fat, thin."

Musette laughed. "But you like it."

"I do."

She asked him another question, her tone somber. "Then you're not coming back?"

He took her hand. "No, I'm not coming back."

She leaned against him, her arm around his waist. They watched the sun go down, then retired to their room.

Christophe had told the truth when he said he'd missed Musette. He hadn't tried to find anyone else to bed in Baton Rouge. He was too raw. Too disappointed and hurt and ... furious. Tansy refusing to marry him had torn him open, but he hadn't been surprised. He knew her. He knew she needed — he knew she thought she needed — a protector. As if Valcourt's money could keep her cocooned from all the uncertainties and fluctuations in life. He might almost forgive her timidity. She had been raised to be timid. When he was angriest, though, he called it cowardice.

What he did not forgive was her coming to him in the night. Her loving him, letting him love her. Her body had been as hungry and demanding as his own. She had wanted him. She had loved him. And then she'd said no. Again. He hated her for it.

But this was Musette. He pulled off her tignon and ran his fingers through her long hair. Slowly, he undressed her, revealing all her glorious length of limb and heaviness of breast. He ran his hands along her arms, over her hips. She drew him to the bed. Yes, he had missed Musette.

The fourth day of their vacation, Musette chose to nap while Christophe took a rented pole and a bucket of bait to the shore. He lay back on the grass and occasionally thought to watch his line. He didn't care whether he caught anything. He just liked the excuse for sitting idle next to a body of water, enjoying the sun and the breeze and the birdsong, a straw hat pulled over his eyes. Eventually he lost his shade. He put his shoes on and gathered up his pole and what was left of the bait.

Coming from the lake and entering the main pathway back to the hotel, he nearly collided with a well-dressed woman with a parasol. She startled. She stepped back. And she rooted into the ground, her eyes fixed on him.

He couldn't speak. Why had he not thought she might be here? Why had he taken the chance?

He saw only her eyes, wide, shocked, pained. He hated her. He hated the yearning he saw in her face.

"Christophe," she whispered.

She smelled of jasmine, her flawless skin as pale as moon glow, her eyes darker than night. A flood of heartache swept over him, drowning him. She had loved him. And then she'd let him go.

She raised her hand as if to touch him.

He turned away. "Don't."

"Christophe, please."

He froze her, burned her, punished her with his gaze. He wanted her to hurt. To be sorry. He wanted to grab her to him, to take her mouth, kiss her eyes, her neck. He craved her with a desperation stronger than the night she'd left his bed.

"I ... " she said.

She what? She'd changed her mind? She had had only to pick up a pen and paper to tell him so. And she had not.

He brushed past her, leaving her on the path, his heart pounding with bitter pain.

Tansy couldn't breathe. She couldn't see. Her arm and shoulder burned where he'd brushed against her. She groped for the bench across the path. Nearly concealed amid azalea bushes she lowered herself and dropped her head. She fisted her hands to stop their trembling and gulped air into her lungs.

He hated her. It was in his eyes. He hated her and he would not forgive her. Ever. She tried to benumb herself. This was an old hurt. She had no reason to grieve afresh. It was over.

Yet suddenly her lungs expelled a long hard sob, and then another and another. She shook with desperate gasping shudders. The rush of tears flowed down her face and neck and into her bodice. She fought to control herself before Valere looked for her on the path.

She heard his steps crunching on the oyster shell walk. She bit her lip and stretched her hands open. She must stop this. With a ragged breath, she wiped her cheeks and stood up.

"Here you are. Hiding in the bushes."

She swallowed to clear her throat. "Azaleas," she said. "They must have been gorgeous in the spring."

He peered at her. "Your face is red."

Tansy waved vaguely toward a patch of wildflowers across the path. Perhaps there was ragweed among the daisies and buttercups. She didn't know. Valere wouldn't know either. "Ragweed. Did you hear me sneezing? Let's move away."

She took his arm and together they strolled back toward the cottage where Maman sat with Alain.

"I believe I will have trout for supper. And perhaps quail."

"That sounds good, Valere."

Christophe crossed the grounds in long, hard strides to the other side of the parkland where a stream flowed toward the lake. He tossed his pole and bait bucket to the ground and splashed into the water without removing his shoes. The cool water came up to his calves and then over his knees. He pushed and splashed upstream, his heartbeat too loud in his ears to think. He couldn't let himself think. He didn't dare feel. He pushed on, shoving at dangling willow branches, stumbling through mud and muck.

When his mind cleared, he slowed his wild plunge against the creek's current. He had no idea how far he'd come. Probably half way to Bayou Manchac. He put his fist on a cypress tree and pressed his forehead against it, his breath still harsh. He could have stayed in New Orleans. He could have seen her every day at the Academy. He could have seen Alain. God how he missed Alain. He hadn't even asked about him.

Things could have gone on as they always had. Until there would have been nothing left of him but an aching shell.

Wet to the waist from stepping in holes and tripping over sunken logs, he dragged himself up the bank onto a grassy spot. Elbows on his knees, head bent, he thought of all the platitudes people used to soothe themselves. Life is no flower garden. There was ever only one Eden. You can't always have what you want. Suffering makes you stronger. God never sends more trouble than you can bear. He raised his face to the sky and laughed. All true. And none of it did anything to ease the ache.

It would get better, he told himself. Even broken hearts healed.

Somewhere along the way, he'd lost his hat. He ran his fingers through his hair and eyed the thick growth along the banks. He'd have to return the way he'd come, in the creek.

He slogged back to the hotel in his ruined shoes, his heart heavy and bruised. Musette would wonder where he was. He'd have to tell her he couldn't stay.

# Chapter Twenty-Three

Tansy worked hard at being pleasant the rest of their time at Lake Maurepas. Didn't Valere make himself agreeable to her mother and hold Alain's hand when they walked along the lakeshore? Hadn't he been particularly kind since she'd agreed to give up teaching — since she'd agreed to give up any sort of life beyond tending to him?

She schooled her countenance to show nothing but good cheer. That was the bargain, wasn't it? Yet the harder she tried to be light-hearted, the more she felt her true self retreating deeper behind the façade of happy smiles. She resisted the rising poison of resentment, but in unguarded moments, it bubbled up from her core, and she wondered how long she could pretend all was well.

When Valere left them to join his wife at the family plantation for the rest of the month, Tansy's tension headaches eased off. Frederick rented a cottage for Martine and himself, which made Alain very happy. He fished with Frederick and played with the stray kitten Martine adopted. Even Estelle seemed happy with her Monsieur Girard, who'd taken a set of rooms at the hotel.

Tansy reached for the mantra that once had kept her focused on the happiness to be found in any present moment. There is only now, she'd so often told herself. She found no comfort in it anymore. Yes, the lake breezes full of summer scents charmed her. Alain's laugh, his delight in being alive restored after weeks of grieving for Christophe, relieved her. Yet contentment remained as remote as happiness.

Alone at night, she punished herself with memories of Christophe. That day when she was still a girl, hidden in the jasmine vine, the scent sweet and heavy — her first kiss. It had not been Christophe's first kiss. He'd flickered his tongue over her lips and she was ready to give him everything he asked of her. Then Maman had screeched at them from the French doors. The next night, Maman had put her on the market. Tansy passed a hand over her eyes. Such an ugly phrase. Slave women were put on the market. She'd seen them through the open archways at the Maspero Exchange standing on a block. Before Maman had gripped her arm and rushed her away, a well-dressed gentleman had lifted a woman's skirt with his cane, another had pinched her behind. Tansy had avoided that corner all the years since.

Abruptly, she sat up in bed, tense and angry with herself. She was no slave. Put on the market was just a turn of phrase. She struck a match and lit the lamp. She would read until she slept. No more memories. No more brooding. She had made the right decision to placate Valere. He was Alain's father. He held Alain's future in his hands.

At the end of the month, she and Alain returned to New Orleans. Musty air and a family of mice who'd taken up residence welcomed them home. She opened the windows and doors, set traps for the mice, and hoped she didn't catch any. After supper as Tansy read to Alain, he had a sudden fit of coughing. She stroked his back as the cough wracked his small frame. Within minutes, sweat plastered hair to his forehead. She placed her hand at the back of his neck. Fever. Well, fevers were common in childhood. She fetched a damp cloth and wiped his forehead and chest. He'd be fine in the morning.

With no warning at all, his supper erupted from his mouth, sour and pungent. She kissed his face and held him close. "Poor baby." She cleaned him up and put fresh sheets on his bed. Then she gave him water with a little wine in it to help him sleep.

Valere came in about ten o'clock that night. She didn't greet him at the door as she usually did but called him to the back of the house. She sat on the side of Alain's bed, a basin at her feet, a cloth in her hand. "He has fever."

Valere put a hand on either side of the doorway. "He seems to be sleeping all right."

She smoothed the hair off Alain's forehead. "He is, isn't he? I thought you were at Havenwood."

He heaved a great sigh. "I was there. For a few days."

So what was he doing here? Hardly anyone remained in New Orleans in the summer. With whom would he play cards, smoke, drink?

"Will you sit with him while I change clothes?"

Valere seemed suspended in the doorway.

"Valere?"

"Yes. All right. Go and change."

Tansy slipped out of her shoes and put her soiled dress in a basin to soak. She brushed out her hair with quick strokes, put on her wrapper and slippers, and returned to find Valere had not moved from the doorway. Still, she was glad he was here. Valere didn't let his imagination run away with him. She took his arm and leaned her head on his shoulder. She knew children had fevers all the time, but it scared her nonetheless. It could be anything. Yellow fever, diphtheria, cholera, pneumonia. "It will probably amount to nothing," she said.

Valere patted her hand. "He'll be fine." He paused a moment, uncharacteristically embarrassed. "Are you coming to bed?"

She looked at him, wondering if she had heard him right. "And leave Alain alone?"

"No, of course not. I was concerned you might overtire yourself."

She knew better. How could he think of the bedroom with his son lying sick?

"Well, I'll be off. Just stopped in to say good night."

"Can't you sit with me a while?"

"No, no. I'll go on." He pecked her cheek and was gone. He had not even stepped over to the bed to feel Alain's cheek.

In the early hours of the morning, Alain woke in a coughing fit. His nose ran, and he cried when he coughed. Tansy made a tea with honey and lemon and helped him sip it. "Honey is the very best thing for a sore throat, sweetheart. Drink it all."

He slept again, and Tansy dozed in her chair. By daylight, Alain's ear throbbed and his cough scraped at his throat. She gathered him in her arms and carried him to Martine's back door. When Martine finally arrived, sleep rumpled and heavy-eyed, she took one look at Tansy's face, then at Alain's glazed eyes.

"I'll send Frederick for the doctor." She hurried back into the house to rouse him and tell him where the doctor lived. Then she followed Tansy back to Alain's bedroom.

"I'm out of honey," Tansy said.

"I am, too. I'll get some from Mrs. O'Hare."

When Martine returned with the honey, she said, "Two other children Mrs. O'Hare keeps are sick. Fever and cough and sore throat."

Tansy made a concoction of lime water, Mrs. O'Hare's honey, and orange juice. She coaxed Alain to sip at it every few minutes until it seemed to settle his cough.

Frederick came in a short time later. "The doctor is on a call. I left word for him to come as soon as he gets in." He knelt beside Alain's bed. "Feeling rough, are we?" He looked at the glass of juice on the table. "Think you can drink a little more of this?"

Frederick helped Alain sit up and held the glass steady as Alain brought it to his mouth.

"Did you come to play with me?"

Frederick laughed softly. "Not today, my friend. When you feel better, we'll line up all your soldiers and have a grand battle." Frederick looked at Tansy. "What do you need? Shall I make a run to the market?"

Tansy's breath hitched. "Thank you, Frederick. Would you bring lemons? And a cone of sugar."

"And something for us, Frederick. Some bread. Ham? Meat pies? We would rather not leave the house until the fever breaks."

"Leave it to me."

Dr. Benoit arrived mid-morning and took note of Alain's red-rimmed eyes, the cough and runny nose, the ear ache and sore throat. He placed his fingertips at the pulse point in Alain's throat and counted the beats.

"His pulse is good. Strong and steady." He palmed Alain's forehead, closed his eyes, and gauged the heat in his blood. "It's high, but not alarmingly so."

Tansy swallowed hard. "Is it the yellow jack?"

Dr. Benoit pulled down Alain's lower lid and then his lower lip. "I don't believe so."

Tansy pressed a hand to her breast and closed her eyes. Not the yellow jack.

"Just a childhood fever?" Martine asked.

"Let us hope it is no more than a passing contagion." He dug into his satchel and handed her a paper packet. "Willow bark. Brew it in a tea and get it into him. It'll bring the fever down. He may sip at a spoonful of orange-flower water or champagne. Otherwise, only the fever tea. He doesn't need to be drinking any more than necessary." He rose and packed up his satchel. "Keep the doors and windows closed. Chill is a very real danger. I'll stop by this evening if Mrs. Dugan isn't delivering her eleventh child."

Dr. Benoit did not return until the following morning. He sat on the edge of Alain's bed, pulled him into a sitting position, and pressed a wooden cylinder against his chest.

For a mad moment, Tansy's sleep-deprived brain thought he was going to poke the cylinder into Alain's little body. "What are you doing!"

Dr. Benoit raised his brows at her. "It's a stethoscope. The latest thing from Paris." He put his ear at the other end of the cylinder and listened.

Tansy gripped her hands together when she saw the frown line between his brows. "What is it?"

He smiled at her. "Nothing a mild bloodletting won't take care of."

"Bloodletting? But he's only four."

"Don't worry, Madame. I shall take only a small amount. May I have a bowl of hot water, please?"

The doctor pressed a hot compress to the tender flesh of Alain's inner elbow. When the skin was rosy red, he withdrew his brass scarificator from his satchel. Tansy blanched. A doctor had applied one to her own arm when she'd had a sprained ankle. Martine squeezed her hand and whispered, "Don't frighten him."

Alain scooted away from Dr. Benoit, his eyes wide. "It's all right, lad. I do this all the time, and big lads like you hold their arms very still and it's over before you know it."

Tansy nodded. "It'll be all right, Alain. It hurts very little, less than a scrape on the knee. Isn't that right, Doctor?"

"That is exactly right." Dr. Benoit applied his brass scarificator to create four shallow cuts in the skin. He encouraged the blood to flow by placing Alain's elbow in the pan of warm water.

Tansy's heart flip flopped at Alain's whimper. She held his hand and promised him it would only be another minute. She caught Dr. Benoit's eyes and told him silently that it would be only another minute.

"I'm not one of those, Madame, who would take half a man's blood to cure him of fever." He wrapped a tight bandage around Alain's wounds. "I'll leave you more of the willow bark. Keep him cool. He'll come around."

By mid-day, small red spots erupted on Alain's face, then behind his ears and in his hairline. The fever spiked, though Tansy labored to keep it subdued. Alain winced when she let in the sunshine and she shuttered the window again. When the fever held off and Alain shivered, Martine brought her new kitten over to curl up at his side.

The raised spots spread down Alain's arms and erupted in the folds under his arms. When the fever spiked again, he scratched at the spots, hardly knowing what he did.

"Measles." Dr. Benoit stood over Alain's over-heated form with his arms crossed. He turned to her. "You had the measles as a child, Madame? And you, Madame?" he asked, looking next at Martine.

"I don't know," Tansy said.

Martine passed a hand over her tired eyes. "You did. The same year I did."

"Very good. Can't have the nurses coming down sick. I'll return to my surgery to concoct a remedy for the itching and another for pain and fever. I'll send them to you."

The next day, the spots clustered on Alain's trunk, down his thighs and calves to his feet. His ears were swollen with masses of red welts. Tansy pulled down his lip and with horror saw the bumps had invaded his mouth.

Estelle relieved both Tansy and Martine so they could rest. Martine moved in with her, Frederick continuing to bring food and comfort. Valere appeared a second time and again stood at Alain's bedroom door. "How is the little fellow?"

Tansy threw her arms around his neck and sobbed. "I'm so scared, Valere. I've never seen anyone so sick." He held her close and patted her back. When Tansy's sobs subsided, he stepped back into the parlor.

Martine looked at him coldly from Alain's bedside. "Have you not had measles, Monsieur Valcourt?"

"I did. The itching was quite memorable."

"Then it is perfectly safe for you to come say hello to your son." Martine held her hand out for him to approach.

Alain lay awake, but listless, removed from everything but the vagaries of fever and ear ache. His face and chest shone white with ointment, making his dark eyes luminous and large with a yellow crust over the bumps at his lower lids.

Tansy heard Valere's hard swallow. He made no move from the doorway and in fact held her a little closer. "I can see he is in a bad way. How do you feel, son?"

Alain glanced at his father with indifference. He closed his eyes.

"Well, I must go." He squeezed Tansy's upper arms and put her aside, then showed himself out.

Tansy stood staring after him. He had not even approached the bed. Could not even sit with her and she so scared. She put a hand to her forehead and leaned against the doorjamb.

"I am growing to hate Monsieur Valere Valcourt," Martine hissed.

Tansy, who always defended him to Martine, had nothing to say.

When Frederick came in, Alain's eyes brightened. Frederick stooped down next to the bed and pressed a hand to Alain's forehead. "Shall I give him some more of the tea?" Tansy handed him a cooled cup of Dr. Benoit's blend of willow bark, crushed lobelia seeds, and a drop of turpentine.

"Go lie down, Tansy. You, too, Martine. I'll sit here a while."

With leaden steps, Tansy walked as far as the sofa and lay propped against the arm.

"I'm going out for a few minutes," Martine said. She stepped outside for the first time in three days and squinted against the bright sun. Then she strode toward the Academy, climbed the outer stairs, and knocked.

Rosa looked at her curiously when she answered the door.

"I'm Tansy's friend."

"Come in then."

"I don't have time. Alain is very sick. It's the measles." Martine pressed fingers to her mouth before she spoke again. "You know how to send word to Christophe?"

Rosa stared at her a moment, then glanced at the clock over the mantle. "If I hurry, I can make the last mail boat."

Back at Tansy's, Martine let herself in. She didn't speak of where she'd been and Tansy didn't think to ask. Estelle sat with Alain, tempting him with a strawberry red candy. He allowed her to place it on his tongue, then lay down again.

"Have you eaten?" Estelle said. "When did you last sleep?"

Tansy waved a hand vaguely. She had no idea when she'd eaten or slept.

Estelle poured her a glass of wine. "Drink this. Eat something. Go to bed."

Tansy shook her head. "I don't want to leave him, Maman."

"Fine. Then lie down on the floor. But sleep."

Alain's fever rose, plunged into violent chills, then rose yet again. His breathing became labored and shallow. His ribs showed now, and his face looked thin and drawn.

Tansy went on her knees to pray. She paced and she hovered, resisting the fear that threatened to overwhelm her. All through the night, neither Maman nor Martine could persuade her to leave the room.

Tansy sat on the floor next to Alain's bed, her forehead against the mattress, his foot clutched in her hand. Alain had finished a dose of sedative and was sleeping, propped up on the pillows. She closed her eyes and fell into a gray half sleep. As if from a long distance, she heard a knock at the door, then the murmur of voices. She felt no curiosity. She was too tired, too frightened to care who had come.

Someone entered the darkened room. She heard the rustle of fabric and the slight creak of leather boots, then a warm hand on the back of her neck. "Tansy."

She couldn't open her eyes. It wasn't Christophe, anyway. Just a dream.

Then she was wrapped in his arms, his body behind her, cradling her. And she slept.

# Chapter Twenty-Four

With no hint of a breeze coming through his window, Christophe stripped off his clothes and went to bed, prepared for another sweaty, uncomfortable night. He was still awake an hour later when someone knocked on his door. He pulled on a pair of pants and opened up to a messenger standing there with a letter.

He gave the boy a coin, then lit the lamp with a sense of dread. A letter from Rosa. What could be so urgent that she'd sent it special delivery?

He scanned the contents, an icicle of fear chilling his core. He tossed a few things in a bag and strode for the door until common sense prevailed. Only a mad man of a captain ran his ships on a moonless night, the threat of snags and collisions too great now the river had receded to its late-summer levels. Renting a horse to take himself downriver was pointless. In the dark, following a moonless road, he'd be so slow it would be quicker to wait for morning and take a steam boat. So he paced, anxiety for Alain eating at him. And for Tansy. If anything happened to Alain, she would be destroyed. He covered his face with his hands. If anything happened to Alain, he would be destroyed.

Sleepless and unshaved, he was at the docks before dawn and boarded the first south bound ship leaving town. He stood on deck, his hands behind his back, his throat taut, and let the mist from the paddle wheels bathe his face. The miles passed by, miles of forest and fields. He paced, he gripped the railing, willing the paddle wheel to churn faster. If he'd thought it would help, he would have jumped in with a tow rope and swum. Ten miles an hour going downstream, he'd heard. He calculated they'd be in New Orleans well before dark.

On both banks, he saw slaves at work reinforcing the levee. Building fences. Chopping wood. His mother's brothers, if they still lived, toiled like these men. Probably he had cousins on one of these plantations. He hoped they fared well, as well as possible for slaves. When his mother had been sixteen, she'd bargained for her freedom with her body and had never looked back. And so Christophe's hands were soft, his back unmarred by the whip. He could read and write and travel from Baton Rouge to New Orleans with no man's by-your-leave. With what bitterness would those cousins look at him if they knew how he wallowed in his misery because he could not have the woman he loved. They would surely mock him, and he would deserve it.

In New Orleans at last, he disembarked and strode through the crowds on the levee, bumping shoulders and side-stepping dogs and children. Rosa had written that if he had never had the measles, he must not come. He had had the measles, but it wouldn't have mattered if he had not. His gait long and quick, he made his way to Tansy's cottage and knocked.

Estelle Bouvier let him in. He tried to read her face, to know if he was too late. Her eyes revealed a moment's surprise, and then she'd murmured, "Of course." She drew him in and patted his arm with a half smile, and he heaved out a breath.

She told him how the illness had progressed, then let him in to Alain's bedroom. He slept fitfully, his chest straining with the effort to breathe. Tansy sat on the floor, her eyes closed, her head resting on the mattress. One slim hand encompassed Alain's foot.

Iron bands squeezed Christophe's chest. His throat swelled. Alain, his boy, fiery spots all over him, so frail a breeze could blow him away. And Tansy — his anger with her meant nothing now. She needed him.

He caressed the back of her neck. "Tansy."

She breathed out a great sigh without opening her eyes. He lowered himself to the floor behind her, straddled her with his knees, and wrapped his arms around her. He pressed his forehead into the hair piled on the back of her head and tightened his arms around her.

When Alain awoke, Christophe unfolded himself gently so as not to wake Tansy. He passed a hand over Alain's head, looking into the eyes bleary with fever. Alain raised his arms to him. Christophe gathered him up and hugged him gently. He sat him in the rocker for a moment, then lifted Tansy onto the bed.

When Tansy woke, Maman was erecting another steam tent to relieve Alain's breathing. He was in Frederick's lap, she saw by the trousers emerging from the bottom of the covering sheet. How kind he was. Martine had chosen a good man.

She had no memory of having climbed into the bed, but her mind was clearer now she had slept. She watched Maman renew the steam, pouring boiling water from the copper kettle, both Alain and Frederick shrouded under the tent. She listened to Alain's wheezing breath ease until she could barely hear him. Maman sat beside her and together they listened to the clock ticking in the next room. Fifteen minutes, the doctor had said.

Maman stuck her fingers in the pan under the tent. "It's cool." She folded back the sheet and Tansy stretched out her arms to take Alain. Her mind froze for a moment. Not Frederick? Christophe rose, his eyes fixed on her. A guttural exhalation moaned from her chest. She gripped Christophe's sleeves and rested her forehead on Alain's shoulder. Her body shuddered, struggling for breath. She felt Christophe's kiss on her hair.

Estelle took her by the shoulders and moved her to the bed. "Sit down, Tansy."

Christophe lay her boy across her lap. Alain's breathing still rasped. "Christophe came to see me, Maman," he said, and closed his eyes.

"Yes, yes, he did," she said, her voice harsh from the tightness in her throat.

Christophe sat beside her, one hand on Alain's thigh. He reached for her hand and gripped it. They sat together silently, the three of them.

When Alain's lungs strained again, Christophe held him against his shoulder like a small child and walked the floor with him. Night fell. Alain's fever rose.

They lay him on his bed and fanned him and cooled him with wet cloths. Martine came in with a bucket of ice just off the steamship. They packed it under his arms, around his neck, over his chest. When the fever plummeted, he shivered. They wrapped him up and held him close.

The fever spiked again while Dr. Benoit was there. He forced Alain to swallow a strong fever brew he'd made from roots and herbs, including quinine and a double measure of willow bark, then took the chair nearby to wait. Martine and Frederick sat in the parlor, her head on his shoulder, his arms around her. Estelle paced the floor. Christophe and Tansy sat on either side of Alain's bed, fanning him, murmuring to him.

At two o'clock in the morning, as suddenly as a spring rain, Alain broke into a heavy sweat. Beads of it rolled off his forehead, dripped from his neck into the hollow at the base of his throat. In only minutes, the sheet under his body was damp, then soaked.

"Is this it?" Tansy whispered. "This is the break?"

Dr. Benoit wiped a hand over his weary face. "This is it. The crisis is past."

Tansy clutched Alain to her and erupted with wrenching sobs. Christophe reached across Alain's body to clasp her neck and bowed his head.

By morning, Alain's eyes were clear. He was weak, his drying spots itched, and he said his eyes ached. But he was better. So much better. Tansy lay down next to him on the bed and slept, his arm cradled against her breast.

When she woke, she was in the bed alone. A breeze gently lifted the sheer curtains. A murmur of voices came from the other room. She combed her fingers through her hair and sat up. Feeling light and dried-out, she went to find her son. And Christophe. Her loves.

Christophe looked haggard, bags under his eyes, his linen wrinkled and limp, yet he seemed at peace sitting at the table with Alain in his lap. She stood in the doorway a moment, watching them. How right they looked together, Alain leaning back against Christophe's chest, Christophe's arm wrapped across his body, loose, but secure. How could it be right that Valere never had, never would, hold his son the way Christophe did?

Martine looked up from urging Alain to eat a slice of pineapple. "Here, Tansy, come sit down." She pulled out a chair and set a plate of grapes and cheese in front of her. "Eat."

Tansy shook her head. "I'm not hungry."

"Eat, I said." Martine poured her a tall glass of water from the jug. "And drink that. Then you can have a cup of coffee."

Tansy laughed weakly. "Who knew you were such a mother hen?"

"Well, I guess I didn't know it myself." She held out her hands for Alain. "Come here, sweetheart. Let's get you cleaned up and have a nap."

Alone with Christophe, Tansy had nothing to say. She rolled a grape around on her plate. Sunlight from the open courtyard doors lit his face, calm and self-contained, though shadows under his eyes showed he hadn't slept.

"How did you know?"

"Rosa sent word."

She nodded and tore the grape in two. It had meant everything to have him here, to help her bear the fear and the waiting. To know he didn't hate her totally and completely after all.

"Thank you. For being here."

"I love him."

"Yes. I know you do." She hesitated. "He's missed you."

A blade-sharp flicker lit his eyes. A muscle jumped in his jaw. So he was angry still. She could imagine what ran through his head just then. So Alain had missed him? Whose fault was that?

How she wanted to crawl into his arms. He loved Alain. He loved her. If he would only come back, they could see each other at the Academy.

Christophe had made it clear that was not enough for him. And for herself? Could she be satisfied to see him at school, only as colleagues, never as friends? Never another stroll on the levee with Alain between them, never another chance meeting in the park? Could she be satisfied with that? She shook her head. She couldn't lie to herself anymore. She couldn't see Christophe, yearn for him, and be true to Valere. And she had to be true to Valere, didn't she? She had signed a contract. She had made a commitment. He took care of her and Alain. He would give Alain a future.

"Are we still friends, Christophe?" Without moving her arm, she stretched her fingers as if she could reach him across the table.

For an instant, his gaze softened. Then that same muscle in his jaw bunched into a knot.

"Where is Alain's father?"

She looked at the shredded grape on her plate and shook her head, her throat too tight to speak.

Christophe pushed his chair back. "Eat that. Tell Alain I'll see him this afternoon."

Christophe picked up his hat and let himself into the street. With every step he took, his anger grew hotter. Friends? She wanted friendship, after what they'd meant to each other the night she'd come to his bed? Blind stupid fool. She didn't know who the hell she was. She thought she could be a child forever, cocooned in a paper contract. How could a woman of imagination and wit be so unable to see beyond the ink on a piece of paper?

The August sun beat down, defeating the breeze, baking the pavement. Leaves on the trees and vines hung still and limp. His cravat nearly choking him in the heat, he strode past his own cottage, let to tenants now, to Musette's house.

She registered surprise and then pleasure as she let him in. She hugged him and stepped back to look at his pale face and heavy eyelids. "You're exhausted. What's happened?"

She made coffee and he told her about Alain. "This is the woman from Lake Maurepas — her son?"

Christophe nodded and twisted his coffee cup in its saucer.

"Is he yours?"

"No." He stood up. "Can you let me sleep here today?"

"Of course. I have two fittings this afternoon, but we won't make much noise. You can rest."

In Musette's shuttered bedroom, Christophe undressed, climbed into the familiar bed, and lay with his forearm over his eyes. He tried to let the tension ease out of his body, but frustration still roiled in him. Tansy wanted to be friends? Damnation. If all he wanted was friendship, by God, he and Musette could have married long ago. Musette had loved her husband deeply; she knew what marriage could be. She didn't pretend what she had with Christophe was only friendship. It was only friendship.

Christophe fisted his hands in the sheets. Musette had her memories, her business, her independence. Tansy pretended to have a life with the man who paid the bills. Tansy hadn't as much courage as Musette had in her little finger.

He couldn't sleep, not now. He got up and tried to force Tansy from his mind. He leaned into the window overlooking the courtyard and pressed his forehead against the glass pane. Alain had looked nearly gone when he'd arrived yesterday. Wasted. His skin dry, thin, and pale, his eyes sunken. Alain hadn't even recognized him for several moments and when he did, he'd managed a little half-smile before he closed his eyes again. Fear had knifed through him. He'd wanted to crush Alain's small body to his and hold on to him so he couldn't slip away.

Christophe rubbed at his face and returned to the bed. He had to sleep or he'd never make it back to say good bye.

As weary and hollowed out as she felt, Martine imagined Tansy felt much worse for the strain of the last days. "Go. Take a bath. Sleep. I'll sit with Alain."

Martine changed Alain's sheets and his clothes, then lay down beside him. When the front door opened, she got up.

"*Bonjour*, Martine," Valere said as he let himself in. His hair was freshly barbered, his shave immaculate. He seemed quite jovial, a smile on his simple face. No shadows of fear around his eyes.

Martine crossed her arms. Valere half offered her his hat, but she merely glanced at it.

You loathsome worm, she thought. He squirmed under her gaze. She smiled the kind of smile she imagined on a nasty boy's face as he pulled the wings off a fly.

"Hot day," he said, and set his hat on the table all by himself. Maybe she should congratulate him.

"But then it's August," he added. "Of course it's hot."

She said nothing while he babbled on. "I'm usually on the Cane this time of year. Much more pleasant than New Orleans. I'm not sure why it's so deucedly much hotter here."

"Your son nearly died last night."

His eyes widened. "Alain?"

"Yes, Alain," she snapped. "You knew he was sick. You knew he had the measles. Yet you did not come by to see how he was."

She saw his Adam's apple shift under the linen of his cravat. "He's better now?"

"Do you have any idea how frightened Tansy has been? Did it never occur to you that she might need you?"

The idiot looked at her blankly. Clearly the thought of being needed was new to him.

"You know Frederick DuMaine." It was not a question. "He has been here, hours on end. He fetched the doctor. He brought in groceries. He took care of us."

Valere flushed deeply. "No one told — "

"Tansy is sleeping. They both are. You can't see them."

She watched the blood flooding his face and neck. Probably no one in his life had ever spoken to him with such disrespect. Unless it was his wife and sister-in-law, she thought with some satisfaction. She hoped that, mixed with the indignation, shame pumped through his veins. She hoped it burned like acid.

She picked up his hat and handed it to him. He managed to scrape some dignity and fled from the house. Tansy would be better off if the fool never came back, not that Tansy had figured that out yet.

Martine peeked in on Alain. Already his color was better. His breathing was almost easy. She closed the door and made the sign of the cross over her breast, saying a short prayer of thanksgiving.

She was tired, and it would be just as well she weren't here when Christophe returned. He would be leaving again, she thought, and it would be painful for all of them. As soon as Tansy got up, she'd go home and to bed.

---

Christophe knocked on Tansy's door, his heart knocking against his ribs. For a moment, they stood in her doorway plumbing the depths in each other's eyes. In her ashen complexion and sunken eyes he saw the toll fatigue and fear had extracted from her. Behind that, he sensed the chasm that still gaped between them. Even his being here for Alain did not seem bridge enough between what he wanted and what Tansy thought she had to have.

She let him in. "Maman brought a basket of food. Are you hungry?"

He shook his head. "How is he?"

Her smile, so full of relief and hope, pierced him. He ached to touch her, but he willed his hands to remain at his sides. If she had thrown herself into his arms when she answered the door, he'd never have been able to leave her, and he'd have been lost. Better this way, that he make his own life, that he not waste his years yearning for another man's woman.

"He's much better. He's just eaten a little broth and half a peach."

"I'll see him then. To tell him goodbye."

He saw the joy in her eyes fade out. Saw the hurt darken them. His gaze flickered over the mahogany humidor she kept for Valcourt. He hardened himself against her. If she were unhappy, it was entirely her own choices that made her so.

He stepped into Alain's room. Sleepy-eyed, he lay peacefully in his bed. The spots swelling his tender ears were shrinking and drying. The puffiness under his eyes looked better. Christophe sat on the side of the bed and ran his fingers through Alain's freshly washed hair.

"You've had quite a time of it, haven't you?"

Alain nodded, his face very grave. "I won't die now, will I?"

Christophe kissed his forehead. "No. You won't die. In a few days, you'll be chasing Martine's kitten. You'll be knocking over castle walls and tearing through the house and driving your maman to distraction."

Christophe swallowed at the brightening in Alain's eyes, at the smile on his lips.

"I make her crazy. She likes it though."

"I know she does. Alain, are you awake enough to talk to me?"

He nodded that he was.

"Between here and Baton Rouge, the river wiggles and twists so that we're about a hundred miles apart, you and I. It's a long way, but I want you to remember, no matter how many miles separate us, I still belong to you."

"Do I belong to you, too?"

Christophe hesitated. Of course Alain did not belong to him. Never had, never would. He had a father. But if Alain owned a piece of his heart, then he surely owned a piece of Alain's, too. He flattened Alain's palm against his starched shirt. "Yes. You belong to me in here."

He kissed the small hand. "I don't want you to be sad that I'm leaving, Alain. We'll always be friends. I will see you again. And as soon as you're old enough, you and I will write letters to each other. All the time. As many as you like."

"But you'll come back?"

"Can you name the months? How long is it till Christmas?"

Alain held up his fingers and counted off the months.

"That's right. I'll come see you at Christmas." He lifted Alain and hugged him gently. When he lay him down again, he said, "You have a job to do now. You have to eat and rest and get well so that when I come back we can go the park and to the levee, and maybe we'll go to a horse race."

"I've always wanted, my whole life, to see a horse race."

"Then we'll go, first chance we get. You sleep now. I'm going to leave, but remember, we belong to each other."

*Tansy*

Christophe closed the bedroom door behind him. Tansy stood in the center of the parlor, her hands at her sides, her eyes depthless. He had not seen Valcourt here in the twenty-four hours since he'd arrived. No one had mentioned him. Did she still think he was a father to Alain? Did she still think she owed him her loyalty? Her life?

He wanted to fold her into his arms, to hug her close. He wanted to kiss the shadows away. He wanted to love her. That had not changed. But she did not ask him to stay. That had not changed either.

"It meant everything to me that you were here. Even when Alain was sickest, I think he knew you were here, and that he had to get well for you. Thank you, Christophe."

He blinked at the sheen blurring his vision. For the thousandth time, he let an if only slip into his mind. No. If she were not his, he didn't want to see her.

"He'll be all right now. You don't have to be afraid anymore."

There seemed to be nothing more to say. With a little shake of the head, Christophe picked up his bag, found his hat, and left her once again.

## Chapter Twenty-Five

The day after Christophe left, Tansy greeted Valere without a smile, without a welcoming kiss. She put his bouquet of ox-eye daisies and cornflowers in a vase and set them on the parlor table. Then she sat with her hands in her lap and said something about the weather.

She would not go to bed with him, the memory of Christophe in this house too vivid, too raw.

She looked at Valere dispassionately. He sat with his knees separated, his waistcoat straining against his belly, a suggestion of softness along his jaw line. The air of happy contentment that had characterized him, that she had found attractive and comfortable, had dissipated. Signs of stress around his eyes and an air of discomfort indicated he had lost his hold on the predictable, biddable life he'd once led. Marriage had not enriched his life.

"How is Alain today?"

"He's improving."

Valere nodded his head toward Alain's door. "I could look in on him."

"That's not necessary. He's sleeping."

He attempted a laugh, though it came out wrong. "Martine tell you she laid into me?"

"Yes, she mentioned it."

"Here's the thing, Tansy. No one told me Alain was so very ill. In fact, I am quite cross with you that you did not send for me."

Cross with her? If he had been in a towering rage to have been excluded from this dreadful crisis, she would have respected that. But cross with her? She tilted her head to study him. Had he convinced himself he was an injured party? Or was he merely embarrassed?

Perhaps she should be angry with him, but she was not. What she felt for him at this moment was simply pity. He didn't love Alain, a child of sunshine and laughter who would have adored him if Valere had involved himself at all. Did he love anyone? He cared for her, she thought, but not enough to have been with her through these last hellish days. Frederick, a man with only a tenuous connection to her and Alain, had been a better friend.

Maybe she would rediscover a measure of affection for him in time. For now, just below the pity, she felt ... indifferent.

"Would you like a cup of coffee?"

He licked his lips, clearly uncomfortable. Poor Valere. This house had always been a happy, welcoming place for him, and recently had become a refuge from the troubles at his home.

He sat forward and rubbed his hands across the fabric stretched over his knees. "Well. I suppose you're too tired to make coffee today." He looked at her hopefully. He wanted her to exclaim and say of course she wanted to make him a pot of coffee. She lived to make him coffee, to soothe his woes, to satisfy his lust. In fact, that was exactly what she had lived for.

"Perhaps another day," she said.

At the door he turned back to her. "I'll come tomorrow, then, shall I? To see how Alain does?"

"If you wish."

She closed the door behind him and returned to sit with Alain while he slept.

In the following days, Tansy felt as if she lived in a large multi-storied house, drifting from floor to floor. On top the windows were open to sunshine and fresh air and here she rejoiced in her son's recovery. No more fears hid in the shadows as Alain slept less, ate more, and began to be restless in his still-weakened body. He was improving with every day.

On the middle floor Tansy entertained Valere, kept house, and shopped at the market, going through her daily tasks as if this normalcy ensured a good life. Busy with mundane tasks, she did not have to think or to feel.

In the lowest level of this house, a low-lying miasma curled from dark corners where she hid her disappointed hopes. When she could bear to look into those shadows, she saw herself as Christophe must see her. Weak and aimless, only half the woman his seamstress had made herself into.

Dutiful. That's what she was. Maman said smile, she smiled. Maman said sign on the black line, she signed. Valere said be in this house waiting, and she waited. She'd given up school, given up those two hours of being someone, of finding more inside herself than Maman or Valere had any use for. But when Christophe had asked more of her, she'd said no. Her own heart and body cried out for Christophe, and she'd still said no. She'd done it for honor and for Alain. Hadn't she?

Avoiding further introspection, avoiding pain, Tansy cleaned every nook and corner of the house. Re-ordering her drawers, she found her burgundy apron emblazoned with RLAB for Rosa LeFevre's Academy for Boys. She pressed it to her face, imagining she could still smell the scent of wax and chalk and dozens of sweaty little boys. She closed her eyes for one more inhalation, then resolutely put the apron away, under the linen handkerchiefs.

She rearranged her wardrobe, every hanger precisely four inches from the next, every shoe aligned, every shawl carefully draped. Then she sat and looked at her perfect house. All these tiny victories over chaos and disorder, they did nothing against measles or loneliness or this nagging feeling of worthlessness. Who else kept her shoes lined up like soldiers on parade? Did Christophe's woman fight the uncertainties of life with tidiness?

She'd invested in carefully folded linen and precisely stacked books the same way she'd invested in Valere, as shields against life. He protected her and Alain against hunger and want, of course, but somehow, she'd given him the power to control the future. Carriage accidents, exploding steam ships, yellow fever, measles — as if Valere had become God and could prevent pain and fear in this life.

She could hear Alain playing in the next room. "Here, kitty, here kitty." He'd begged Martine to let Jezebel visit for the morning. Tansy moved to see if Alain remembered to be gentle with her when a furious gray blur tore into the room, Alain chasing with a piercing shriek. Jezebel skidded under the bed. Alain fell to his belly to crawl after her. The cat scooted out the other side and leapt for safety in the wardrobe, scattering Tansy's shoes, knocking a dress from its hanger, then raced out of the room. Alain, breathless with excitement, scrambled after her.

In under ten seconds, Alain and Jezebel had obliterated her pitiful, careful attempts to control her world. A slow smile tickled her mouth as she looked at a rose satin shoe tossed on top of her black kid boots. Her smile growing, she reached for the wardrobe door, and in a leap of faith that catastrophe would not ensue from jumbled shoes and skewed hangers, she slowly closed it.

Every moment, every now could not be perfect. She didn't need perfect. She needed possibilities. She needed courage, not certainty.

The week before school was to start, Tansy left Alain curled up on the sofa with Maman. She had hardly left the house for three weeks and stretched her legs in a long stride. Rosa had called twice, bringing grapes for Alain, a book for her. Today she meant to return the visit.

Rosa's apartment above the classrooms was light, airy, and cluttered. Books, papers and pens lay haphazardly on tables; three shoes peeked from under the sofa at odd angles. Yet which of them, Rosa with her disorder or Tansy with her books precisely aligned, controlled her own life? Certainly not Tansy. She had ceded control to Valere. She meant to change that.

When Tansy felt they'd had enough polite discourse, she drew a deep breath and put aside her coffee cup. "Rosa."

Rosa smiled at her. "Yes, Tansy?"

"Rosa, I want to teach full time."

Rosa set her cup down. "All day, every day?"

"I know you have a teacher for every classroom, that Mrs. Thatcher has taken Christophe's class. But there's the room at the end of the hall. It's full of old desks and chairs and flags and dusty boxes. I could clean it out. I could have a class in there."

Rosa steepled her fingers under her chin.

"You could expand the school. You could accept a class of younger boys, six and seven year olds. And the new students would offset my salary."

"And what about your protector? He would allow you to be unavailable from eight o'clock until four?"

A dart of anxiety in her breast, Tansy sat quite still for a moment. She drew in a steadying breath. "I do not intend to ask him if I may. I intend to tell him that I will."

Rosa rubbed the inner corners of her eyes. Tansy tensed. She had thought, she had hoped, that Rosa would immediately, enthusiastically accept her proposal.

"I've never had a class that young. I have no lessons prepared for that age group."

"I will make lesson plans."

She met Rosa's level gaze. She could do this.

"The thing is, Tansy. If I open the school to a new class, it is essential that it continue through the term. It would be disastrous if after a few weeks, you had to abandon them because your protector insisted you must. Your life is not your own, is it? You have accepted a protector. You must answer to Monsieur Valcourt."

Tansy got up and walked to the window. Two half-grown cats slept in the shade of a banana tree. She had denied Alain a kitten, knowing how badly he wanted one, simply because Valere might not want a cat in the house. "Are those kittens downstairs yours, Rosa? Are they part of Ophelia's litter?"

"Yes."

"Is it too late to take one home? May I have one for Alain?"

Rosa raised a brow. "If you're doing this for Christophe — "

Tansy closed her eyes tightly against the squeezing in her chest. She drew a slow, shallow breath until the pang eased. "I've lost him, Rosa. He isn't coming back, not for me."

The humid air of the room thinned, the clarity of the light intensified. She felt as if every moment of her life had led to this one inescapable, inevitable decision. "Rosa, I will not quit mid-term. If Valere will not accept this, I will put an end to our contract."

Rosa's brows rose nearly to her hairline. "You've thought this through? You've always been taken care of, first your mother, then your Valcourt. You've always had security and protection."

Tansy shook her head. "I've clung to Valere, Rosa, as if he had God's ear and no harm could come to Alain and me as long as he took care of us. I'm not quite such a fool now. There is no true security in life. Valere's protection did not prevent Alain from nearly dying."

"You will be alone in the world."

"No more alone than you. No less secure than you."

"But my children are grown. Your child will have no father."

"He has a poor one now. I don't think he will notice when he has none."

Rosa got up and came back with a bottle of wine and two glasses. "This will require some thought. I'm not ready to say yes, or no." She poured for them both and sat down again. "Explain to me why you would sacrifice Alain's future prospects for ... " She waved her hand vaguely toward the school rooms below. "For this. You will make a living, but it will be a poor one compared to what Monsieur Valcourt gives you each month."

Tansy took her time formulating an answer. Some of the thinking she had done about this had been in the back of her mind, as if it had hid from consciousness and then emerged into the light when she was ready for it.

"When Alain was so sick, Rosa, I didn't care whether he would grow up to be a doctor, or a businessman, or have a big house and a carriage. I just wanted him to grow up." She looked out the window as if finding new truth in the treetops and clouds. "Alain does not need wealth to have a good life, Rosa, to become a good man. What he needs is to discover what he can do for himself."

"That is the way of strong men, yes."

Tansy cleared her throat. "Denis came from a humble family, I believe. He worked hard and put himself through school here in New Orleans. He's a scholar and a teacher. I'm sure his mother is proud of him."

"He is her darling."

"And look at Christophe. When his father died, he was just a boy, yet his mother made a life for herself and her son. She raised Christophe to make his own way, and look what he's accomplished."

She couldn't sit still with her life opening up before her. She paced to the window and back. "I want Alain to have courage and grit, like Christophe. He won't learn that from Valere, and he couldn't learn it from me, not the way I handed my life over to someone else. But I can change, and not just for Alain, Rosa. I want to discover what I can do for myself, too. I want more, to do more, to be more."

"Denis and Christophe, you understand they struggled to get themselves an education, to survive. Without your Valcourt, life for you and Alain will not be easy."

"I'm tired of easy, Rosa. I'm tired of all of it."

Tansy met Rosa's shrewd eye as Rosa focused on her, taking her time, thinking. "All right. This is what I'm going to do." She tore a piece of paper from a tablet and wrote a figure on it. She folded the paper into a tight square and handed it to Tansy.

"Go home. Make a budget, a careful budget, and decide what you absolutely must have to live. Then you may open that paper. That is what you will earn at the Academy. But only September through the first week of June. I believe you will find managing on that little amount of money would be a greater challenge than you imagine."

Tansy strode home with chest lifted high. Whatever the number Rosa wrote on that slip of paper, Tansy meant to make this work. She would not cut Alain off from his father, not if Valere cooperated with her, but she and Alain, from now on they would direct their own lives.

Tansy told Maman that she had simply been visiting her friend Rosa. She did not share her plans. Maman would not approve.

When Valere came, she had not yet worked on the budget Rosa required. She still thought Valere might be persuaded; perhaps he cared about her enough to give her these hours of freedom during the day. Ah, no. The word "give," again. Being given freedom — that's the wrong avenue to what she wanted. She meant to seize those hours.

She hoped, then, that she could take what she wanted without hurting Valere or pushing him away. He was Alain's father. He had to understand, though, that she needed more out of life. And if he couldn't understand, the budget would not matter. She was going to do it anyway.

After they made love, she poured him a glass of wine and together they sat up in bed, leaning against the headboard. "Valere, I want to talk to you."

He put one hand beneath his head, his bare arm pale in the candlelight. He closed his eyes. "Talk away, my dear."

"Valere, I have loved you, and you have been good to me. But I'm not the girl you took under your protection five years ago. You're not the same young man. You have a wife. I have Alain. It's time for us to make adjustments to our understanding."

He opened his eyes and cast a wary glance at her. "What kind of adjustments?"

*Tansy*

She swallowed hard. "I am going to teach at Rosa's Academy for Boys. Every day. Eight till four."

His jaw tightened. He shifted to face her. She held up her hand. "Let me finish, Valere. I will still be here for you in the evenings and every weekend. Alain will still be your son. And because I am making these changes, you will reduce my allowance accordingly."

Valere set his glass on the table, sloshing the wine over the lip "You aren't a teacher. You don't know anything about teaching. Are you bored again? Is that what this is about?"

"Yes, Valere, I'm bored. I'm more than bored. I want to grow and learn and do something useful. I want a life."

"You have a life. You're already grown. You have a child. You have me."

She shook her head, gazing into his eyes. He would never understand. "It's not enough. It's not, Valere."

"You need another child. That's what you need." He reached his arm across the bed and touched her breast. "I'll give you another baby. You'll be content. Remember how happy you were when Alain was a baby?"

Another baby? She'd be trapped. She'd be stuck. She'd never be anything but Valere's woman, the mother of his bastard children.

"No, Valere. I don't want another baby. I want you to agree to this."

He snorted. His mouth curled in disgust. He swung his legs off the bed and pulled on his clothes with such haste he misbuttoned his shirt. He didn't even bother to tie his cravat.

"Valere?"

He left her without a backward glance.

## Chapter Twenty-Six

Proudly wearing the apron embroidered with the bold letters RLAB, Tansy waded into the store room cluttered with boxes and chairs and tables. Inside the boxes were everything from tattered text books to brittle-paged student essays.

Alain amused himself with the old picture books, running his finger along the lines as he pretended to read to Ophelia, who'd been a lonely cat all summer with no little boys to pester her.

Tansy moved everything to the hallway, then raised a cloud of dust with her broom.

"I thought I heard sneezing," Denis Fournier said.

"Denis! You're here today?"

"Getting ready for the invasion of all the little princes next week. Would you like some help?"

"I'm going to need buckets and buckets of water to scrub this floor."

"Done."

They worked till noon and sat down together with their bagged lunches. Alain, still recuperative, lay down on the blanket Tansy had brought and quickly fell asleep.

"Christophe came," Tansy said.

"Yes. Rosa told me. He has a special attachment to your boy. And to you."

Tansy met his eyes. "Alain is not his son. That's what you're wondering?"

"Forgive me, my dear. It is none of my business. I only saw how sad you were in the spring when he went away."

"Well. No more moping about for me." She gestured at the disorder around them and smiled. "Too much to do."

"I miss him, too," Denis said.

Tansy let out a slow breath. "Yes. Well, he's gone." She stood up and squared her shoulders. "And I'm going to turn this store room into a class room."

Later, she and Alain walked home hand in hand, both of them dusty and tired. She found her door unlocked and paused at the stoop. She had not seen Valere in more than a week. Had he relented? Or was there to be a renewal of the battle she had begun?

She found Valere half-asleep on the sofa, his legs stretched out, the wine decanter at his side.

"Hello, Papa," Alain said.

Valere sat up and ran his hands over his sleepy eyes. "Hello, young man. Look at you. One would never know you were ill. Scared your mother, you did."

Tansy thought Alain still looked like a child who'd come close to the end not so many days ago. His face was pale and the suggestion of those faded spots still remained. He'd lost weight, and hollows still shaded his cheeks.

"Yes, sir." Alain picked up his half-grown kitten curled on a chair. "This is General Ney," he told his father.

"General Ney? What a strange name for a cat."

"He helped Napoleon beat the Prussians. That's what Monsieur told me."

Valere looked at Tansy with narrowed eyes.

"Frederick DuMaine," Tansy said. "Martine's protector."

Valere nodded. He knew DuMaine. "Before Waterloo, then?" He looked at Tansy. "You see, I know my history."

Of course he had heard of Waterloo. New Orleans had been inflamed ten years before with the news that Napoleon was truly finished this time. She had been twelve years old. Valere must have been almost a young man. He'd remember the bands playing dirges in the street, the sermonizing from the pulpit, the speeches condemning the British. Even though he apparently did not remember who had won that battle.

Valere rose from the sofa and sauntered over to Tansy. "Have you missed me?" He took her by the upper arms and kissed her with a hard persistence.

"Alain," she said, stepping away, "let's see if Martine is home. You can bring General Ney."

When Tansy returned from Martine's, Valere took her to the bedroom and undressed himself. She stood at her mirror to remove her tignon and let her hair down. There was a distinct smudge across her forehead from cleaning the classroom. Dust-streaks smeared her bodice. Valere didn't seem to have noticed.

An hour later, Valere looked into her mirror to tie his cravat. "I am very glad that little fancy of yours is over, Tansy. I'll come again tomorrow at the same time, around two."

She stood in her shift, bare-footed, her brush in her hand. "No, Valere," she said softly. "At two, I shall be at the Academy getting ready for school to start on Monday."

"I've been thinking about that," he said as he untied the knot and tried again. "You're restless. Summer can be dull in the city, can't it? We'll go to the balls again when the season starts. And I'll take you to the races. You liked that, didn't you?"

"Yes. I liked the races."

"And you love to dance."

His eyes were on the intricacy of the knot he attempted in his cravat.

"Thank you, Valere. I enjoy the balls and the races. But I will not be here at two o'clock tomorrow."

"And doubtless," he continued, as if she hadn't spoken, "you need an increase in your allowance. A little more money in your pocket should keep you busy buying tignons and dresses and slippers. And Alain must have outgrown everything over the summer. You will enjoy outfitting him from top to bottom."

She stepped in front of him and stilled his hands. "Valere. I'm not trying to push you away, and it's not more money I want." She took one of his hands and held it in both of hers. "I hope you will come perhaps at five or six. Or later. But I won't be here at two o'clock tomorrow afternoon."

The corners of his mouth whitened, and his eyes darkened into black ice. He lightly wrapped his fingers around her throat. She felt the latent force in his fingertips as he tightened his grip on her neck. She ignored the tremor of fear and held his gaze, insisting he look at her and remember who they were together.

He rubbed his thumb over the hollow at the base of her throat. "You will say no more about this school. You will be here at two o'clock tomorrow. Or eleven, or whenever I say."

She palmed his cheek. "No, Valere. I will be home a little after four."

He pressed his thumb into her throat. "Your mother signed a contract." His voice cracked. "You signed it."

She swallowed hard against the pressure of his thumb. "And I, just as you, have the right to end it. I haven't asked for that, Valere. Only for an amendment. You may adjust my allowance. You may come to me at any other time. That's all I ask."

With no warning, he shoved her away with such force she bounced off the bed. "You straighten up or you'll find yourself without a protector at all. I will cut you off. No more dresses. No more French wine and plumes for your hair. You may starve for all I care!"

He fled the room, his cravat half tied. The outer door slammed behind him. Slowly she rose from the bed. Starve, he'd said. The old threat: smile at the gentlemen — or starve. Learn to please — or starve. Or — join Collette Augustine at her brother's brothel. She ran trembling fingers over her bruised throat. She didn't believe it, not any more. She had a strong back, a readiness to work. There were other possibilities in life.

Two hours later Tansy's mother marched in with all the energy and ferocity of a tropical storm. She halted in the middle of the room and pointed a finger at Tansy. "You are a fool!"

Alain, propped up on the sofa with his kitty, gazed at his grandmother with somber eyes. He showed no distress at the outrage in her voice and stance, but General Ney tensed, the hair at the back of his neck rising.

"Maman, would you like to sit down? A glass of wine? Or I could make coffee for you."

"Don't you dare change the subject. I know exactly what you've done, you stupid stupid girl."

Tansy moved Alain's foot and sat down on the sofa next to him. She smoothed her skirt over her thighs, then folded her hands in her lap.

"You look at me, my girl! I don't know where you got this ridiculous notion that you will abandon your protector and set yourself up as a teacher." She said the last word as if it were a great insult. As if she'd said 'set yourself up as a slops collector.' "You will write Valere. You will grovel if that's what it takes. You will beg him to take you back. Now. This instant."

"No, Maman."

Estelle's voice rose half an octave. "No? You tell me no? After all the work I put into writing a contract that every girl in New Orleans envies? After bringing him to the point, extracting every advantage from him — for you — you will not throw that away."

"It is my decision, Maman."

"You will do as I say!" Estelle strode two steps and slapped Tansy across the face.

The cat leapt from the sofa and ran to the other room. "Maman!" Alain cried. He wrapped his arms around Tansy's neck, inserting himself between her and his grandmother.

Tansy held him tight. "I'm all right, darling. It's all right."

Estelle whirled away and paced the floor, her heels a rapid tap across the floor boards. She halted in front of Tansy and leaned in. "Where is the paper? Where is the ink? You will write Valcourt at once and beg his forgiveness."

Tansy got to her feet, Alain in her arms, his legs wrapped around her waist. "I'd like you to leave, Maman. I don't want you here now."

Estelle reared back as if she'd been struck. "Leave? You tell your own mother to leave?"

Tansy stiffened her legs so her knees would hold steady. "Until you are calm, until you accept that I am a woman grown, yes, Maman, I want you to leave."

Estelle's lips tightened till they were white. Her eyes sparked with fury.

"You'll be sorry for this — " She swept her arm out to encompass Tansy's dreams, her ambitions, her outrageous foolishness. Her voice shaking and furious, Estelle finished, " — this madness."

She banged the door behind her, the cottage suddenly quiet, calm, normal.

Alain clung to her neck, his face buried against her shoulder. As she rocked him, waiting for their hearts to slow down, a lightness came over her. She'd done it. She'd stood up to Valere. She'd even stood up to Maman. Tansy had taken back her life.

## Chapter Twenty-Seven

In her sparkling converted storage room, Tansy breathed in the smell of wax and polish. She opened the window for air, then stood at the front of the room, her hands clasped in front of her. Seven chairs at seven small desks. That's how many boys she would have. This would be the first day of the first year of school for them. She knew exactly what she wanted to do to introduce them to their new lives.

Denis leaned into her door. "If this were the theatre, I'd say break a leg."

Tansy smiled. "Then we'll pretend I am Lady Macbeth about to go on stage."

"Oh, no. Not that horrible woman. Perhaps you are Portia in all her wisdom and compassion."

Rosa stopped beside him. "You have everything you need?"

Tansy nodded toward the tables, each with a slate, each slate with a child's name printed on it. She wished Christophe were here to see her new classroom. "I have everything. We'll have a wonderful time."

"They are fortunate children, Tansy, to be with you. We'll see you at lunch."

A minute later, the bell rang, the front doors opened, and the sounds of dozens of feet filled the hallway. After much laughter and shuffling, the boys lined up in two rows facing each other and waited. Rosa said a few words of welcome, then called her ten students by name to follow her.

Denis did the same, then Mrs. Thatcher. That left seven very small boys looking a little frightened, awaiting their fate. Smiling, Tansy drew them into a circle. She read her list of names and said how do you do to each of them, then marched them into their classroom.

All day long, she encouraged and demonstrated, loving every minute. When the day was over, tired as she was, she walked home feeling tall and proud. She had broken her contract with Valere. She would still have her cottage, that was part of Maman's initial bargaining, but she would have no more allowance, no more support for herself and Alain. There would surely be difficulties ahead, but these students were hers. She would regiment their days and their studies, guiding and nudging and cheering them on. She would teach them all their letters and later in the year, she would teach them how to read, every one of them. What a glorious new life.

In October, scudding clouds, gusty winds, and that characteristic, hard-to-describe light in the sky promised a tropical storm. Rosa dismissed the students an hour early so that everyone could scurry home before the storm hit. Tansy held on to her tignon against the growing wind and collected Alain from Mrs. O'Hare's. Together they checked all the windows and latched all the shutters.

Tansy liked storms, the energy blustering outside, the sense of safety inside, the heightened awareness. Thunder and lightning, however, terrified Martine. Tansy tapped on her back door. "You better come over now before the rain starts."

Martine answered the door with a big grin. "Frederick is here. He says he will single-handedly keep the lightning away, and he'll personally see to it I'm too busy to notice the thunder."

"I'll stay with you, then," Alain said, taking a step to move inside.

Martine passed her fingers over her mouth to hide a smile. Tansy put her hand on his shoulder. "Then I would be alone, Alain. Please, will you stay with me?"

"Frederick will miss you, Alain, but I'll keep him company and you take care of your maman."

By five o'clock, it was dark. Rain drummed against the roof and wind bent the lemon tree in the courtyard. Tansy and Alain ate a picnic supper on the floor by lamplight, General Ney curled up between them. They played a game of cards. They wondered where the birds were taking shelter. They hoped all the dogs on the streets had found a dry haven away from the wind.

The wind intensified, and the sporadic bursts of rain developed into a steady onslaught. Alain climbed into her lap, uneasy, so Tansy gathered blankets and together they constructed a tent between the sofa and the chair. They added a pallet and pillows and settled into their snug refuge, the lamp still lit and casting a rosy glow through the sheltering blanket.

The last big blow that roared upriver from the Gulf had been when Alain was just a baby. Valere had stayed with them, worried she might be frightened or that the roof might tear away. They'd huddled and cuddled in her bed and listened to the wind howling with Alain between them. She'd loved him then, those first two years, hadn't she? She'd made herself forget the searing heat, the all-encompassing thrill of that first stolen kiss with Christophe.

Somehow, she'd molded herself into a woman content with Valere's attentions. She'd called it love, and she supposed it had been. A tepid, dutiful love. When had that conviction she loved Valere turned to affection, then to tolerance? Why had it happened? Had she simply grown up? His lack of humor had not bothered her those first years. His stolid nature had seemed to promise security. Then those same qualities became stifling, like a damp gray blanket growing heavier with every proof that she could not admire Valere.

Who said admiration was necessary between a placée and her protector? No one, of course. Certainly not Maman. She remembered how Evangeline Ebert cried when her mother had negotiated a contract with a bald man twice her age with bad teeth, over-long fingernails, and a morose nature. Attraction, much less admiration, did not figure into the transactions that governed Tansy's world. She'd been fortunate, compared to Evangeline. Valere was a handsome man. Always clean. Of an even temperament until his world had tilted — first a disagreeable wife, and then Tansy's own demands. Whatever else, though, they'd had Alain together.

Her dissatisfaction had not been born the night she'd gone to Christophe, the night she'd felt her whole being afire, encompassed, and complete with Christophe's body atop hers, in hers, possessing hers. Even after that, she'd gone back to Valere. Even then she'd been willing to suppress her own wants, her own larger self, for the protection Valere offered.

And now, she had no protector. Instead, she would protect herself. She would protect Alain.

Once Alain was asleep, Tansy crawled out of the tent and stood at the French doors to watch the storm. Lightning splintered the dark in near-continuous display. The willow tree in the Thompsons' courtyard beyond her back wall lashed furiously in the wind. A piece of roof tile hurtled past. She really should have had someone put planks across these back doors with their many panes of glass.

Eventually, too tired to watch anymore, she settled in with Alain, spooning his warm body beneath the tent. A thudding, shattering crash woke her. She climbed over Alain and lit the lamp. Some missile had knocked the shutter off and splintered the window in Alain's bedroom. She put a hand to her stomach at the glass shards glittering where his body would have lain. The wind pushed in, twisting the curtain, driving the rain. She tried to pull the shutter to, but it was impossible. She dragged the bed away from the window hoping the rain would not drench the mattress, but the fierce wind drove her out. Chilled and wet, she retreated into the parlor and pushed a table and then another against the door to keep the wind from bursting through.

She dried off and returned to hold Alain against her, to keep him safe. She couldn't go back to sleep with the violence of the storm swirling into the next room.

She could clean and dry the floors, the bed, the furnishings, but how much would it cost to replace the shutter and the window pane? She recalculated how much money she had for the month. She'd feel the pinch, now Valere had cut off her allowance.

Rosa had warned her it wouldn't be easy. No matter. She could do the laundry herself from now on and she need not buy the best wine Gallatin's had to offer. She'd manage.

A few blocks over, Valere sipped a last glass of wine and watched the gutters overflowing, water runneling down the center of the street in a swift stream. He remembered the last time a hurricane had hit New Orleans. Alain had been just a tiny baby, and Tansy had snuggled with him as the wind shook the cottage. She'd been happy with him then. Maybe she wouldn't be so irritable once this storm sucked the last of the heat out of Louisiana. She'd had more than a month to settle down, to realize she needed him. She'd certainly be over this nonsense of working. Tansy didn't need to work.

He heard Abigail stirring in her bedroom. She'd been glowingly pretty when she announced to her parents, her brother and sister, and him, all at the same time, that she was to have a baby. Not "we," but "I am to have a child," she'd said. He would have liked for her to tell him privately first. Wasn't that what wives did? Tell their husbands first, blushing, proud, and maybe a little anxious that he'd be pleased? That's what Tansy had done. Abigail had not given him the chance to take her into his arms and assure her he was the happiest of men. He would have kissed her. He would have reminded her that she was cared for, both as wife and mother of his child, but he could not in front of her starched-lace family.

Still, he was pleased. He'd promised her a child, and he'd delivered. He'd enjoy having a little girl, maybe with her mother's fair hair and blue eyes. A little girl he could spoil and show off and buy presents for. Now, before Abigail went to sleep, he'd tell her how happy he was. They could cuddle in her warm bed and listen to the thunder and the howling wind.

He tapped on her door and entered, eager to pet her and fuss over her. She met him in the center of the room, her feet planted, her arms crossed.

"You are not needed here, Mr. Valcourt."

For a moment, he stood there in his dressing gown, befuddled. Not needed here? He glanced toward the windows, safely shuttered. She wasn't afraid of the storm, is that what she meant?

"I didn't think you were afraid, Abi — "

"You have accomplished your purpose in this room. You have no business in my bed hereafter."

Then he understood her. He had impregnated her; his efforts were no longer required. Anger and shame blended in a hot flush. "I think you misunderstand, Madame. I have come as your husband. I have come because it is my right to come."

Abigail snorted through her small nose. "You have had your rights. You have a child growing in me at last."

"That does not necessitate our suspending marital relations, madam." He took a step closer. "Not at this early date."

Imperiously, Abigail held her palm out to stop him. "Oh, but it does. They are suspended. And if the child I bear is a boy, an heir to the great Valcourt estates, they will be suspended ever more."

A blaze of lightening outlined her small form in the flowing white nightgown. She stood with her chin high, her mouth a prim, smug line. He'd tried all these months, he really had tried. He'd been patient and kind. He'd thought perhaps she had come to accept, if not welcome, his attentions to her body. He never hurt her. Tansy seemed to like to be held for a time when he was finished, and he'd remembered to do that with Abigail, too. And still she scorned him. The look on her face was pure loathing.

He hated her. At that moment he would gladly have wished her to the devil, her and her sister and their endless carping, their endless discontent. Her face, so pretty he'd once thought, was only hard and mean. She would never be happy with him. He would never have a peaceful home with her.

Thunder shook the house. His hands fisted. He could overpower her, take her, punish her for making him feel dirty and useless and unwanted. The law allowed a man to rule his wife, to master her. He'd heard other men speak of taking their reluctant wives, of forcing their needs on their women. He'd heard them boast, proud of what they'd done to prove themselves masters in their homes.

Valere wiped his hand over his eyes. He couldn't do it. He'd forced himself on Tansy, and he'd hated himself for it. He'd never do that again, to any woman.

Feeling like a whipped dog, he retreated to his own room. His life was in a shambles, his dream of wife and children and happiness shredded. Even Tansy, his own dear Tansy who had always made him feel loved and welcome, had turned him away. He went to bed and wrapped his arms around a pillow and hugged it to him while the rain lashed the roof and the thunder rattled the windows.

The next day, Valere crept around his too-quiet house. He heard Abigail and her hatchet-faced sister murmuring in the parlor. Perhaps he'd have a word, show his wife her little tantrum meant nothing to him. He shoved the door open. There she sat with her embroidery, a beam of sunshine gilding her hair. How could a woman this pretty be filled with so much ugly spite? His eyes flickered over Lucille, the hateful bitch, the source of all the poison in his marriage.

"Ladies," Valere said.

Abigail stopped speaking mid-sentence, her needle poised in the air, and looked at him with cold eyes. "Mr. Valcourt?"

Valere licked his lips and glanced at his wife's sister. Lucille for once did not glare hot darts at him. Worse, she smirked.

Humiliation roiled through him with the certain knowledge she knew Abigail had dismissed him like a dog who'd peed on the floor.

He turned on his heel, his ears hot with shame. He would go out, play cards, have a drink with his friends. That's what he'd do. And then what? Go home to dinner with Abigail, her sitting prim and silent at one end of the table, he sitting glum and silent at the other end? And after supper? He'd find no peace in this house. Even the servants no longer made any great effort to please him.

Through the afternoon, he played cards, discussed the storm, drank too much. Several of the men made off-hand comments about their wives, without fondness or even respect. This was the way of it, then. Men did not look for comfort at home. He'd known that. He'd only forgotten when Abigail had bewitched him with her pretty face and false smiles. He didn't need her anyway. He had Tansy.

By now, she'd know how foolish she'd been. She had missed a second month's allowance. She would be sorry she'd made him do that. It was time he insisted things go back to the way they were. Whether he came in the early afternoons or at midnight, Tansy would be glad to see him, just like she used to be.

He stopped at the store and had the clerk wrap up a set of wooden blocks for Alain. That would please Tansy. He wanted to please her, he always had. He tapped on her door with his cane.

When she took his hat from him, he swept her into his arms for a kiss, feeling very gallant. Then he turned to his son, playing on the floor with the ever-present soldiers. "How are you, Alain?"

Alain only glanced up and returned to his lines of attack. "Hello, Papa." Valere felt a little deflated, but, well, the boy was involved with his Brits and French.

"Will you make coffee for me?" he asked Tansy. She'd turned her head when he kissed her, but she seemed all right now. His pretty, sweet Tansy.

"Of course I will. Sit down. You can help Alain with his battle plans."

Valere sat with his feet straddling the approximate contours of the battlefield. "So who's going to win, this time?"

"I don't know yet."

The children today. Shouldn't Alain look at him when he'd been asked a question? Valere gestured at the arrangement of the

French forces. "Your line there is broken in the middle. You almost have a V instead of a straight line."

Now Alain looked at him, but Valere did not like the expression on his face. "The V is so that more of them will survive the first charge."

"Well, see here. I've brought you a new toy so that you don't have to be everlastingly playing soldiers." Valere handed him the package wrapped in green paper.

Alain hopped to his feet and hugged the package to him. "Thank you, Papa! What is it?"

"Open it and see." Valere smiled as Alain tore at the paper, his eagerness making up for the earlier lack of enthusiasm.

"More blocks!"

"Yes. Every boy should have a set of blocks. You can build towers and walls, and see here, they're not all the same size."

Alain nodded knowingly. "I know how to play with them." He put his hand on Valere's knee. "Thank you, Papa. They're very nice blocks. You want me to show you how to build a bridge?"

"That's all right. Maybe next time."

Alain put his new blocks to use building a redoubt for the French to defend. Valere watched him absent-mindedly. He smelled the rich Cuban beans brewing and hoped Tansy had some rolls to go with it.

When she came in with the tray, she did indeed have a plate of small poppy seed rolls and butter.

He winked at her and accepted his cup. "Just like old times, isn't it?"

He blew on his coffee to cool it and dipped his roll. He felt the tension melting away like the butter in his hot coffee. In this house, he was the master. Tansy understood that. He eased back in his seat and smiled at his pretty Tansy sitting across from him with her hands in her lap. Prettier than Abigail. Nicer than Abigail. He squelched the quick image of Abigail's sneering face. Tansy never ever sneered or snapped at him. He smiled again. "Good coffee."

"Valere, you know I'll be at the Academy every school day. Your being here — does it mean you have accepted my conditions?"

Quick as lightening, heat flashed from his chest, rose into his throat and flamed behind his eyes. "Your conditions, madam?" He stood up and deliberately intimidated her with his body, so much stronger and larger than hers. He saw her quail. Let her, by God. "You are my woman. You do not propose conditions."

"Valere, sit down, please."

"You will do as you always have done. You will be here waiting for me, whether it is ten o'clock at night or ten o'clock in the morning. I bought you with that contract, and don't forget for one minute that I have paid the bills here all these years. You can't afford to throw me over." He stepped closer, his hands fisted.

She stared at him with wide eyes, her lips parted. She touched her throat, and he remembered he had bruised her there with his thumb. When she looked down at his fists, he blanched. She feared he would hit her? His Tansy? The flood of heat turned into a rush of nausea. He wiped a hand across his eyes. What was he doing?

He swallowed hard and blinked. He would never hit her, but she had to listen to him. "I want you here," he said stabbing his finger toward the floor. "You'll be waiting for me, here." She had to understand. She had to take him back. If he didn't have Tansy to love him, he had nothing. He swallowed the panic threatening to disgrace him with quivering need.

Tansy placed her hands on his sleeves. "Valere." She stood up and kissed his jaw.

Oh, God. Yes, she did love him. "Tansy," he breathed. He wrapped his hands around her waist, dipped his head to forgive her with his kiss.

"My darling Valere." She cupped his cheek with her hand. "Please understand. I can't go back to the way we were, me waiting here as if my only purpose in life was to be your bedmate. I'm more than a bedmate, Valere. I am."

To his shame, tears spurted from his eyes. With long quick strides, he reached the doorway and escaped before he disgraced himself by begging her to love him.

## Chapter Twenty-Eight

Tansy looked back at her earlier life and marveled she had once been content with dull, slow days. From early morning until she fell into bed exhausted, she reveled in the teaching, the planning, the fun of being with her seven boys. At home, she found ingenious ways to economize. On Sunday afternoons, she met with Denis to talk about their books. If she cried into her pillow at night, yearning for Christophe, well that was the price she paid for having been a fool. The blame for Christophe's leaving lay entirely with her. If she had trusted herself ... but she hadn't. What might have been, the most bitter words in any language. And so she ached for what she could not have, then rose to face the new day, determined to focus on what remained: purpose.

In November, a rousing rain storm lashed New Orleans. Tansy dashed home through streets flooded almost to her ankles. By the time she picked up Alain and shoved the door against a gust of wind, water ran in rivulets off her hem and sleeves, her tignon and her nose. Alain crouched on all fours and shook himself like a dog. "Come on, Maman. Try it."

"I, Alain, am not a dog. I'm a cat." She daintily licked at her wet paw and grinned at his giggles.

She made a fire and got them out of their wet clothes before she discovered the puddle behind the sofa. She mopped it up and Alain placed a pan under the drip. Keeping the smile on her face, Tansy searched the cottage for any other leaks and let out a long breath when she found none. During the evening, she watched the stain spread across the ceiling. Another drip developed three feet from the first one.

After Alain went to bed, she counted out her money. Two more weeks until her next paycheck from Rosa.

The next morning she stopped off at the contractor she knew Valere had hired once before. She walked into the shop where a man bent over a lathe and another honed a set of chisels. Mr. McCall looked up from his desk, a pencil behind his ear and scowled at her like she was in the wrong place. She raised her chin. Why shouldn't a woman contract to have her roof fixed? Musette Vipont surely took care of such details herself.

When McCall gave her the estimate, she blinked. So much? Too much. She nodded at him. The roof had to be fixed. At home, she opened the wardrobe and surveyed her ball gowns. Valere had paid a great deal for each of them, and here they hung, like money in the bank. She fingered the fine needlework on last year's favorite, a cream and gold gown with sprigs of green embroidery at the neck and hemline. She'd loved this gown, but she'd love a patched roof even more.

She left Alain with Martine and carried the gown to Madame Celeste. A bell tinkled as she entered the consignment shop which was, like Madame herself, perfumed and elegant. Tansy had never needed to buy second hand shoes and gowns, but she knew the proprietor by reputation. Madame Celeste, a tall, slender woman with a sharp face, glided over to her.

Tansy unwrapped the dress and held it out. Madame held it to her face and sniffed. Tansy set her mouth, insulted at the implication she would have offered a soiled dress. Next Madame laid the dress out on her worktable under the back window. She examined every satin rosette, every fold of silk. "A snag here," she said, pointing at a minute imperfection at knee level. She turned the gown over and peered at the hem where Tansy herself had mended the stitching. Madame raised an eyebrow.

"A fine gown, at one time. A bit worn, of course."

"You can sell it?"

Madame Celeste shrugged. She wrote a sum on a tag and pinned it to the sleeve. Tansy calculated the likely discount a buyer would negotiate plus Madame's percentage and bit her lip. Repairing the roof would take every dollar she could expect.

"How long might it take?" Tansy asked.

"For someone just your size to come in?" Madame Celeste eyed her as if she'd sneezed into her hand. "I sell dresses, not prophecies."

When Tansy had walked into the shop and the formidable sharp-faced woman had looked down her nose at her, Tansy had inwardly trembled. But the imperious sniff, and then the sneer, evaporated the intimidation she'd felt. "Perhaps you could buy the gown outright?"

With the impatience of the put-upon, Madame Celeste marched to her cash drawer. She counted out a small pile of bills, Tansy counting along with her. And so the roof was fixed. The following weeks, Tansy thought, were sent by some evil god to test her resolve. The next disaster occurred on another blustery, rainy day. Alain eagerly met her at the door when she picked him up from Mrs. O'Hare's. "Look, Maman." He sat down on the floor and flapped his loose shoe sole for her.

"We were to the park this day," Mrs. O'Hare explained, "and whilst I saw to Marie's skinned knee, this one and that one," she said, nodding toward Alain and Jean Pierre, "ran into a monstrous puddle and stomped and splashed before I could chase them out. Rascals, both of them."

Tansy eyed Alain's ruined shoes, the last pair that didn't pinch his feet. Where was she to find the money for new shoes? "These things happen, Mrs. O'Hare. What little boy could resist a puddle?"

Tansy bought no wine, no coffee, and no beignets. A body required neither wine nor coffee, after all. She amused herself thinking of all the people in the world who'd never had a cup of coffee. All those people in China? The Indians in South America? She'd survive, though she thought doing so without a morning cup of coffee would be hell on earth.

Alain, fully recovered now, suddenly shot up like a magic bean stalk. Tansy eyed him in all his Sunday finery. His wrists extended beyond his sleeves, his ankles protruded beyond his pants legs. She counted her coins. She added up her expenses. The water man who delivered fresh water from the bayou north of town had to be paid. Food. Fuel. Lamp oil. There was nothing left for shoes. She fingered her lovely mauve ball gown, admired the delicate silk roses across one shoulder. Well. Nobody needed eight ball gowns, after all.

The next day, Madame Celeste greeted her with a snide smile. "Another gown so soon?"

Tansy swallowed her pride. She could no longer afford it. "Yes, Madame. As you see."

She conducted her negotiations with a tight smile, then stepped next door to Carlyle's Children's Store. What an extravagance it had been, taking a four year old to Mr. White's for tailor-made trousers and jackets. No more of that. From the sale table, she bought Alain two pairs of broadcloth pants and two shirts. If she washed every day, they would see him through the winter.

She waited at the corner for a pause in the traffic. Out of nowhere, a pair of ragamuffins ran at her, brushed by on either side, and darted into the street between two wagons, right under the horses' noses. The shouting red-faced butcher tore out of his shop after them. Shaking his fist, he brought himself up short at the curb and yelled after the fleeing boys.

"Damned kids," he roared, then turned his indignation on Tansy. "Stole a sausage long as my hand, right out from under my nose." He stomped back toward his shop.

Tansy looked for the boys after she crossed the street, but they'd vanished. Their arms and legs had been stick-thin, their faces pinched with hunger. The younger boy, barefoot and raggedy, had not been much older than Alain. She clutched her bundle close, anxiety nipping at her. That child's mother wanted him to be rosy-cheeked and well-shod, too. What if Tansy couldn't do it, couldn't keep Alain from becoming so hungry he dared steal a sausage out from under the butcher's angry fists?

She pulled her shoulders back. This was no way to go home to Alain, timid and afraid. She had a closet full of ball gowns, like money in the bank. She could read and write. And she had a job. They'd be fine.

The weekend came and Tansy settled in for a quiet evening with Alain. Martine had other ideas. "Come to the ball with us," she said.

Frederick seconded the invitation. "I'll wait with feigned patience while you change if you'll come with us." When his gaze lit on Alain, his face lit up. "In fact, it won't be feigned. Alain and I need an hour at least to defeat Wellington."

Alain scrambled off the sofa to fetch his soldiers. Tansy hated to disappoint him, but balls were no longer in her budget. Valere had not sent her the season's ticket, and she really couldn't spare the money for Alain to stay overnight with Mrs. O'Hare either.

"Not for me, thank you. I've retired my dancing slippers. You can tell me all about it tomorrow."

Martine opened her mouth, then hesitated. Tansy had not mentioned being short of money, but Martine could figure it out for herself. Martine took Frederick's arm. "You can play soldiers tomorrow," she said to her lover as if he were her petulant three year old.

Frederick rolled his eyes. "Tomorrow, Alain, while Martine tells your maman who wore yellow ribbons on purple satin, we'll teach Napoleon what he should have done at Waterloo."

The disappointment on Alain's face tore at Tansy. He had no man in his life now. Not Christophe. Not Valere. Was she foolish to have pushed his father away? Was she too selfish? But did Alain truly miss Valere? He'd not gone silent at his loss the way he had when Christophe left New Orleans. No, like Tansy herself, Alain missed Christophe, and it pained her that such a small boy carried such a weight of loneliness.

Late the next morning, Martine and Frederick arrived for brunch at Tansy's table with a bottle of wine. Instead of hello, Alain declared, "You can be Wellington this time."

"Oh, no. Not unless you give me a rainstorm. The General's troops do love a muddy field."

Alain and Frederick both rushed through dinner and adjourned to the parlor floor for the great battle. Martine poured another glass of wine for herself and Tansy. "Now," she said, "for what really matters in this world — gossip."

"Do tell. Who was there?"

Martine, adjusting her skirt to lean back in the sofa, found a piece of paper behind her. She gazed at Christophe's likeness, her expression unreadable. "You've made the nose too long," she said quietly.

Embarrassed, Tansy held her hand out for the crude drawing. Like some lovesick school girl, she'd been trying all week to get his likeness, but she was no artist.

Martine looked at her, and Tansy cringed at the pity she saw before Martine managed to make her expression casual.

"Shall I fix it?"

Tansy shrugged. "It's nothing. As you please." But she handed Martine the pencil.

Martine sketched. Without looking at Tansy, she said, "You're having a hard time of it. Surely Valere will continue to support Alain, at least."

Tansy waved her hand in the air as if it were nothing. "Maybe someday. When he isn't so angry. For now though, I don't need him." When Martine looked skeptical, she added, "Yes, there are days I feel like I'm drowning. But there are good days, too, when I could fly straight into the clouds and sing like the nightingale all the way down."

"You must let me know if you get into difficulties."

"Oh, no. I can do this. I only need to pay more attention to where the money goes. Don't worry about us." She wondered if Martine had noticed the patch on her shoe, or the lack of coffee in her house. "Now, then, who was at the ball?"

"Adrienne, looking dreadful in, guess what, yellow and purple. Frederick must be prescient. Annabelle and her Monsieur Duval. I swear she's gained another ten pounds, but they were all smiles."

"Maman there?"

"Ah, yes, Estelle." Martine wet her finger and smudged the pencil marks to smooth Christophe's hair. "Your maman and Monsieur Girard smiled and held hands during the intervals. They smiled and held hands when they danced. I believe the Estelle I've known all my life has been whisked away and replaced by this besotted woman. Or maybe she's only pretending. I can never tell with her."

"I don't suppose she asked after me," Tansy said. "Or Alain."

Martine shook her head. "She did not. And I did not accommodate her by volunteering any information about you either. Let her swallow some venom and get herself over here if she wants to know how her daughter does."

It hurt, that Maman had cut her out of her life. Why couldn't she understand this feeling of being sidelined from her own life, of having no joy or ... juice left in her? If Maman would only let her, she'd try to explain. Those last months with Valere, she'd felt as if she were an orange left too long in the bowl, the rind thinning and withering. She simply could not let the life be sucked out of her anymore, sitting, waiting, simply existing. But to Maman, money and security were everything.

Martine glanced at her and then away. "Do you miss Valere?"

Tansy ran her hand through her loosened hair. "Sometimes."

"Do you miss him or just the sex?"

"Martine!" Tansy laughed, but Martine was right. Missing sex was a greater pang than missing Valere's company. Even now, she felt disloyal thinking such a thing, for the truth of it was, it was not Valere's arms she missed. But she would not tell Martine how many hours of every day she yearned for Christophe. She'd driven him away, and she had to live with that.

"Well, I see no reason to deny it if you miss the other. And now that I think of it, I'm surprised he hasn't been by to see if you've changed your mind."

"He did come by. I found a bouquet of asters on my stoop when I came home from school last week. They looked like they'd been stomped on."

"Hmm. Not a subtle man, is he?" Martine fingered the stem of her wineglass. "He was there, at the ball. He danced with the Frognard girl twice. And once with Jessica Arceneau."

Tansy knew both girls. Gillianne Frognard came out two months ago. Jessica about the same time. Seventeen years old, on the market for their first protector. So Valere truly had left her. She wrinkled her nose and swallowed. She would not cry. She had chosen to let him go. The nose wrinkling didn't help, though. Maybe she'd had too much wine. She swiped at a tear, hoping Martine didn't see.

"Well," Martine said. "He's just a man. There are others."

Tansy laughed. "You can say that when the love of your life is on his knees playing soldiers."

"Some men are special, I concede. But Valere, he's not special, Tansy." She handed Tansy Christophe's portrait.

Somehow Martine had captured him, the sensual mouth, the intelligent eyes, the hint of daring, the humor. It was Christophe. Tansy swallowed the longing. "Thank you," she whispered.

The string of catastrophes continued. On a Wednesday morning, Tansy went in to wake Alain and found his forehead hot and his eyes fever-dulled. In a panic she grabbed him up and ran to Martine's back door.

"Send for Dr. Benoit," she told her and dashed back to her house. She bathed Alain with a cool cloth for an hour until at last Dr. Benoit came, Martine hovering at his elbow. Dr. Benoit pulled Alain's eyelid down, had him stick his tongue out, and examined his skin all over.

"What is it? Can the measles come back? You won't bleed him, will you?"

"Settle down, my dear. This is the sixth or seventh child I've seen this week. They seem to pop right out of it in two or three days."

*Tansy*

"And then they're fine?"

"And then they're fine. I'm pleased how your boy has put back his weight. He will be himself again by the weekend."

Just as the doctor said, Alain felt fine by Friday afternoon. Then it dawned on Tansy she hadn't the money to send Dr. Benoit his fee. She'd missed three days' work while Alain was sick and her pay went to the substitute teacher Rosa had to hire.

If she didn't buy coal or firewood, she could send Dr. Benoit what she owed him. But Alain might catch a chill in an unheated house. She put Alain to sleep and sat with paper and pen, figuring her accounts. She gnawed at her thumbnail, something she hadn't done since she was twelve. She'd never known this constant thrum of anxiety. Rosa was right. She didn't know how to be poor.

During the night, she woke in a sweat, the sheet balled in her fists. Images of those hungry little boys' desperate pale faces as they ran from the butcher shop lingered in her mind, as vivid on waking as they had been in her dream. How was she to sustain her courage with images like that in her mind? Fear lurked like the shadows in the corners, under the bed, sliding down from the ceiling and seeping into her skin. What would she do when all her ball gowns were sold and still Alain outgrew his clothes? What would she do if she herself were sick and couldn't work?

She hugged her pillow to her, her stomach in knots. When she finally drifted off, it was with thoughts of oranges, buttered bread, and big fat sausages for Alain's breakfast.

She woke with dread pressing on her chest. She sat at the kitchen table, her forehead pressed into her hand. She'd let herself believe she could do this, be a teacher, be an independent woman. She felt queasy and gray and heartsick. She was going to have to ask Valere to take her back. If it wasn't too late.

She took out a sheet of writing paper. She sharpened a quill and opened the ink pot. She stared at the blank page, her hands in her lap. Nausea swirled in her belly and rose into her throat.

Just do it, she told herself. She closed her eyes and tried to compose the words. Dear Valere, she would write. I have been a fool. I thought I didn't need you anymore, and now I can't ... I can't afford coffee or tea or wine. I can't afford to buy Alain new clothes without selling my ball gowns. I'm a failure. A nothing. Just as you thought. Come back to me and I will ... continue to be a nothing. She fisted her hands. Not a teacher. A nothing.

She dipped the quill in the ink pot. In her elegant script, she wrote Dear Valere. Her grip on the quill tightened. She pressed the nib into the paper. Then, as if the quill had grown red hot, she dropped it on her desk and stood up. She didn't have to do this now. Tonight, when she had prepared herself, she would write to him.

She put the kettle on. A cup of hot lemon water would at least warm her. She held her hands over the fire as the water heated and felt as low as she had ever felt in her life. Now and then, she had allowed herself to think that Christophe must be proud of her. Rosa would have written him that Tansy taught full time now, that she was like his Musette Vipont, self-supporting and independent. How he would despise her when he heard she'd gone back to Valere. But she had to do it, for Alain.

She heard her boy in the other room talking to General Ney, safe and happy and well fed. He'd never be like those children stealing food, racing away, their hearts thundering with fear. She'd do what she had to to make sure of that, even if it meant — God, she could hardly say the words to herself — even if it meant going back to being merely a rich man's toy.

She fed Alain his breakfast, unable to swallow anything herself. She felt as though she might faint, but of course she would not. No reason to faint. She was simply being reasonable. Admitting the truth of who she was, a placée who wanted what was best for her child. There was no shame in that.

After school, instead of picking Alain up at Mrs. O'Hare's, Tansy wrapped her blue velvet gown and trudged the avenue to Madame Celeste's. The woman no doubt made herself a tidy profit off Tansy's need, but that did not make her pleasant. She did her usual close examination by the light of the window, sniffed, and twitched her sharp nose.

"How much?" Tansy asked, humiliation gripping her by the throat.

Madame Celeste performed the ritual of scratching a figure on a price tag. Tansy grit her teeth and agreed. She would stop at Dr. Benoit's and pay his fee on the way home. That at least should bring her some ease for the night. She'd write to Valere, and it would be done. No more worrying. No more dreaming ... No more dreams.

Tansy pressed a hand to her stomach. She felt she might be sick, sick of herself, of feeling helpless and scared. And how would she feel with Valere back in her life? Surely this awful fear would be gone.

She stepped onto the sidewalk. A tall well-made man leaned against a hitching rail with his arms crossed. Nicolas Augustine. He gave her a lazy smile, his gaze raking her from toe to tignon.

"Tansy Marie Bouvier."

A cold chill swept through her. Like a toothed predator targeting the weakest gazelle in the herd, Nicolas Augustine had found her at the lowest moment of her life. She fisted her hands to hide her trembling fingers, tilted her chin up, and swept past him. When he fell into step next to her, she picked up the pace, but his long legs easily kept him at her side.

"You don't have to avoid me, *ma chère*. I only want to spend a few minutes with a pretty lady."

"I don't desire your company, monsieur."

He showed no offense. "You don't know me, Tansy. But I know you. I've had my eye on you ever since you were a girl. A beauty like you, how could I not lose my heart?"

Tansy stopped abruptly in the middle of the sidewalk. "You think I am some green girl to swallow such tripe? We have nothing to say to each other."

His hand lightly traced the length of her arm, his eyes burned through her bodice and scorched her skin. She knew who he was, what he was, and still her pulse leapt at his touch.

"Then we don't have to talk," he murmured, his voice suggesting more fleshy communion. His gaze painted her neck, her lips, her breasts. "Your Monsieur Valcourt is looking for a fresh face — you see, I know all about you." His voice flowed over her, into her, smooth and warm and dangerous. He touched a long finger to her cheek. "Are you lonely in the night, *ma chère*? Do you miss a man in your bed?"

Tansy jerked back and strode away from him, her heart racing. He strolled beside her with perfect ease. "I know you have brought Madame Celeste three gowns. I know you have expenses and other ... needs. I want to help you, Tansy. You know I can help you. A woman like you, you shouldn't be alone, and you shouldn't have to do without."

He took her elbow and made her face him. "Tansy, I want you." His voice, low and seductive, created a sense of intimacy even though they stood together on a busy street. "I've always wanted you."

The man was a furnace of sexuality. She felt his heat through her sleeve, penetrating fabric and skin and muscle. The planes of his face, the carved plush lips, the lingering gaze — Tansy had never seen, never felt, such a raw sensual force. For a moment, the man lay a film of neediness, of lonely yearning — for her, only for her — over the confident, captivating manner. "Let me love you, just a little. Give me a chance to show you how good we can be together."

Acid rose in her throat. The old threat, plaçage or prostitution, safety or degradation. She gazed into the eyes of ruin, beautiful brown eyes, long lashed, full of sincerity and promise. Girls like her, Maman had said, quadroon, beautiful, helpless — they required a patron. The only alternative in her world was an alliance with a man like Nicolas Augustine who would exploit her youth and her looks until she was used up.

The image of the greasy-haired woman sleeping in a shabby room on dirty sheets came to her as vividly as the day Maman had dragged her into the brothel. Tansy pulled her arm away. "Is this what you say to the women who live in your house? That you love them?"

He flashed her a grin. "I do love them, *chèrie*."

She looked with contempt into his seductive eyes. "Do not speak to me again, monsieur."

The man's easy charm turned to ice. He gripped her arm again, this time without tenderness. "I see you selling off your gowns. You buy that boy of yours used clothes, you walk in patched shoes. Soon you won't be able to keep food on the table." He leaned in close, his clove-scented breath nauseating. "You'll see it soon enough — you need me." The low purr turned to a contemptuous snarl. "You'll come to me. But, darling, don't wait till your tits dry up and your skin's yellow with hunger. I'll have no use for you then."

He released her arm and resumed his mask of charm and good will. "You know where to find me. *Au revoir*, my beauty."

She watched him saunter away, loose-limbed and lithe as a tiger, sinuous as a reptile. A shudder of cold dread ran down her back. She reached for the awning post to keep herself on her feet. Valere, or Nicolas Augustine. The trembling moved into her shoulders, and then up her neck. Bile threatened to choke her. Valere or Nicolas Augustine.

Tansy picked up her hemline and ran all the way home as if she were chased by dogs. She slammed the door behind her, then bent over and gasped for air, waves of panic stealing her breath. She gulped at the sobs wracking her body and sank to the floor. As abruptly as they had begun, the sobs shifted into belly-deep bursts of laughter.

Helpless hysteria seized her as maddened guffaws and weeping drained all sense and strength. When at last the crazed spasms degenerated into pants and hiccups, she sprawled where she'd dropped to the floor. A strange calm flowed through her, leaving her languid and oddly passive. The hard floor welcomed her, the quiet house promised her peace. She closed her eyes.

When she raised herself from the floor, she felt depleted but strangely tranquil. The most dreadful fate of her imagination, becoming one of the poor creatures in Nicolas Augustine's brothel, stared her in the face. But it didn't have to happen. She knew what to do. She washed her face and went to fetch Alain from Mrs. O'Hare's.

Through the evening, as Alain played, as she washed and dressed him for bed, the page on her desk seemed to glow in her peripheral vision. Dear Valere. She would write the letter. Valere would shield her forever from want and worry, from Nicolas Augustine and hunger and fear.

Once Alain was asleep, she sat at her desk and stared at the page, inert. She waited, for some inner signal, some impulse to drive her to pick up the pen. A moth flirted with the candle flame. The clock ticked on.

A knock on the door startled her out of her reverie. Valere stood at her door for the first time in weeks. "Hello," he said, standing uncertainly, his hat in his hands. Numbly, her first thought was that she wouldn't have to write the letter after all.

She could almost see Fate in the shadows, mocking her, forcing her choice between Valere and Nicolas Augustine. She took his hat. "Come in, Valere."

He looked around the room, obviously uncomfortable. "Alain gone to bed?"

"Yes. Would you like to look in on him?"

"I think I would."

She opened Alain's door quietly and Valere walked into the room. He stood over the bed a moment, just looking at his son. "He's bigger, I think," he whispered.

"Yes. He's been growing."

He walked back to the parlor and sat in his favorite chair. She had no wine in the house to offer him. She couldn't even make him a pot of coffee.

"How are you, Valere?" He didn't look well. Beautifully groomed, as always, but there were circles under his eyes and he'd added a few pounds.

"Well, thank you. How are you, Tansy?"

She hoped her earlier emotional maelstrom didn't show. She still felt light-headed, in fact, but she said, "Alain and I are well, thank you."

The silent moments stretched out. "My Arabian won two races this fall," he said.

"How very exciting. And did you buy the gray you spoke of?"

"Yes, I did. He's coming along. Took third at Metairie last week."

"Congratulations."

He took a breath. "See here, Tansy, I don't want to talk about horses. I've come to give you another chance. I'll take you back if you're ready to see reason."

A singular coolness washed over her, a cooling of the nerves throughout her body. "If I'm ready to see reason?" Her old mantra came to her. There is only now. She hadn't said that to herself in months. She hadn't needed it because she'd had more than simply now. She'd had hopes and expectations for tomorrow.

"Mac told me he'd been out to patch the roof. I know about the broken window. And, look, Tansy, even I recognized that gown of yours, the blue one, in the shop window. You've been selling off your ball gowns."

She made herself unclench her hands. "Yes, there have been expenses."

Valere came to her on the sofa. He took her hand and smoothed out her fingers. "You're not meant to struggle over money, sweetheart." He kissed her forehead.

A tide of loneliness and need flooded her. She leaned into him as he kissed her eyes. Was it so hard to accept him, along with the condescension, the "seeing reason"? Was that such a high price to pay for safety and comfort and affection? She could let him take her to bed and hold her and make love to her. And she'd never have to lie awake worrying again.

"I've missed you," he said and took her into his arms. His kiss was sweet and gentle. Tears welled in her eyes. It had been so long since she'd been held, and after the leering heat in Nicolas Augustine's eyes, she felt safe in Valere's embrace. This was, if not love, affection. Permanency. Security.

She stroked his cheek. "Valere."

He cradled her other hand against his chest and smiled at her. "Yes, my love?"

Her hand stilled. My love? Valere had never called her his love, had never said he loved her in all their years together. In fact, he didn't love her. He simply wanted her, the convenience and comfort of her. And she didn't love him. But plaçage had never been about love, had it?

What would it cost her, what would she lose in exchange for Valere's protection? Tomorrow morning, her seven little boys were to have a Day of Rhymes. They were going to make long lists of rhymed words on the big chalk board at the front of the room. They were going to make up rhyming lines of poetry and conjure up a rhyme for every bite of food on their plates or objects in their pockets. She was looking forward to reaching into her own pocket and producing an orange for them to try to rhyme. They were going to have such fun.

And Valere would take her back only if she narrowed her world to this cottage, to waiting for him and tending to him. He didn't even want her to read.

He kissed her and ran his hand down her back. She did want him. She wanted him so much at that moment. She cupped his face in her hands and kissed him with all the affection she'd ever felt for him. She blinked at the tears spilling over. "Valere. I did so want to love you."

He kissed her wet cheeks and smiled at her. "We'll be happy again, you and me and Alain."

Slowly, she shook her head. "No, Valere. I can't."

His body jolted. His hand at the back of her neck tightened. Tansy stepped away from him.

"You need me," he said. "You need my allowance. You need my name to keep the likes of that Augustine fellow from following you around."

"You know about him?"

"The Quarter is a small town, Tansy. You were seen this afternoon. Without me, men like that lowlife will be after you all the time."

"And so you came to me tonight to save me from him? Oh, Valere, thank you. You don't know what it means to me that you would do that."

"You're my good girl, Tansy. Of course I'll protect you."

"But you don't understand. I don't think I understood either." She lay her palm against his heart. "Dearest Valere, it's not like you think. Not like Maman has always said. Just because Nicolas Augustine says come, I don't have to go."

"Of course not, but you're vulnerable. And you have Alain. And expenses. We'll go back to the way we were, forget all this ever happened."

She gathered his hand in both of hers. It was all so clear now. "No, my sweet Valere. No."

He stared at her open-mouthed. "You'd send me away?"

"Yes. I must send you away."

"I'll take the Frognard girl," he said, his voice harsh. "I won't give you another chance."

She swallowed. This was the moment. Valere ... or patched clothes and worry and counting pennies. And it meant pride and accomplishment and becoming.

"I'll always care for you, Valere. But I don't need you."

She studied his face. He was hurt, angry, and confused. He didn't understand, and that was reason enough to send him away.

She walked over to his hat and held it out to him. His face red, his eyes wet, he swallowed. Then he straightened. He took his hat with one last searching look at her face.

She closed the door behind him and leaned her back against it. It was done. She had cut her last tie to Valere and all he had to offer. She truly was on her own now.

## Chapter Twenty-Nine

Tansy put on her slippers and robe and padded into the parlor where the letter she'd begun to Valere only yesterday morning still lay. Dear Valere it said. She had used him, she supposed, as he had used her. He had kept her from want and worry and, just as importantly, from the fear of want and worry. She'd changed her mind about what she feared, however.

There lay the parchment that would have condemned her to a diminished life once and for all. She reached for the paper to crumple it into a ball, to throw it into the cook fire, but she paused. She had to be canny, thrifty, and smart. She scissored off the writing and slipped the rest of the page into the drawer. The strip that bore the humiliation of her doubts and fears she folded and folded until it was a small tight square. This she threw into the fire and watched it flame brightly before it was consumed.

She got Alain up and fed him a big breakfast. He swung his legs as he ate his sausage and rice. Happy, healthy, trusting his maman to keep him safe. And she would. As other women did, women like Christophe's mother, or his Musette, or Rosa. They had survived without a Valere or a Nicolas. So would she.

"What rhymes with book, Alain?"

He licked a finger. "Cook, took, shook, mook, sook, look."

She smoothed his hair. "You are a great rhymester, Alain Valcourt. You ready to see Mrs. O'Hare?"

He was. She dropped him off and walked on to school. Later in the morning, when her boys had covered the board with cat hat sat mat flat and free tea sea glee, she pulled the orange out of her apron pocket. The boys looked at her blankly for a moment and she smiled at them in challenge.

Theodor, a little boy whose father had a cigar shop, raised his arm and waved it madly.

"Yes, Theodor?"

"Torange!"

She grinned at the glint of mischief in his eye. "Orange, torange. Sounds like a rhyme to me. What exactly is a torange, Theodor?"

He looked stricken for a moment, but he rallied. "A torange is a big orange cigar."

Tansy laughed, so very pleased with his ingenuity. So very pleased to be his teacher.

On the way home, she dropped by Dr. Benoit and paid him the small fee she owed him. After supper, she felt too happy to settle down. "Let's go to the levee, Alain. Let's see which ships came all the way from India."

They swung hands and sang Alouette as loudly as they pleased. Lanterns flickered along the levee while stevedores continued loading and unloading cargo. The ships, anchored five and six deep from the dock shifted gently in the current, the lanterns in the mast tops twinkling like fairy stars.

They imagined that in one of these ships a fabulously rich raja wearing a purple silk turban and a ruby bigger than a hen's egg sat in splendor amid gold and silver and jewels. "Which ship, Maman?"

Tansy chose a ship with fresh paint and a proud up-turned bow. "That very one. If you close your eyes and breathe, you'll smell the spices he brought with him from India."

Alain closed his eyes and took in a deep breath. He opened his eyes and frowned. "Maman," he whispered, "it smells bad."

Tansy laughed. The river did smell bad, like sewer and tar and mud. "We're pretending, Alain. I'm going to pretend it smells like cinnamon." She breathed in deeply through her nose. "Hmm, cinnamon."

Alain tried again. He closed his eyes and breathed in. "Hmm, cinnamon."

Tansy grabbed him into a hug. "Let's go home and get you into bed. It's not your time to sail away to China or India or even Mobile."

That night Tansy slept deeper, more peacefully, than she had in weeks. Saturday she woke early and got her cook fire started. She fried three dozen fruit tarts and let Alain sprinkle them with sugar. She packed them up in a basket and together they carried them to the open market at Bayou St. John north of the Quarter. Within an hour, she had an empty basket and a pocket full of coins.

The next Saturday she took five dozen tarts, and in another basket, paper, quill, and ink. Once the tarts were all sold, she set out a hand-lettered sign: Letters written, 25 cents. She wrote only one letter, but the one-eyed sailor who had her write his mother back in Massachusetts promised to tell his mates about her.

Very pleased with her success, Tansy sat next to her oil lamp that evening after Alain had gone to sleep. She picked up her bobbins to work on the lace collar she had been tatting for months. Madame Celeste had had a lace display in her shop, and Tansy had noticed she asked the world for a three inch wide yard of lace no finer than the collar Tansy worked. She could sell this collar. She could make lace ribbon in the evenings and sell that. And she could buy coffee, thank heavens.

Christophe would be pleased with her.

The thought had come to her unbidden. She worked hard not to tantalize herself imagining Christophe sitting across the parlor, his nose in a book while she sewed or read or simply watched him in the lamplight. Some choices could not be undone. He had made a new life for himself, a hundred miles up the Mississippi. It didn't matter to him anymore what she did.

But he'd promised to come see Alain at Christmas time. He would see she'd shed the life he'd always despised. She was as enterprising as his seamstress, as purposeful as Rosa. He should be proud of her. More important, she was proud of herself.

Christophe refolded Rosa's letter and tapped it against the edge of his desk. They exchanged letters regularly, hers generally full of news about the school and the people they both knew. News of everyone except Tansy. This letter, however, had been all about Tansy.

She wrote about Augustine, the brothel owner, about Tansy's selling gowns and fruit tarts, yet she wrote nothing about Valcourt. Would Tansy have to sell her ball gowns if she were still the man's placée? It's what he'd ached for, her turning Valcourt out of her life.

And if she had, would she marry him now? She could have written him she'd detached herself from Valcourt. She could have written him that she was teaching, and told him about her students. She should have written him about Alain and his recovery, whether he was growing and learning and if he missed him. It had been months, and she had not bothered to write.

He leaned his face into his hands. He'd moved to Baton Rouge for the chance to build a new life. Maybe to find someone else and forget Tansy. But it wasn't going to happen. He knew that now.

So many times he'd been tempted to present her with a list of his assets. His earnings as a musician and as a teacher. The houses he owned in the Quarter, the half interest in the bakery on Decatur. His bank account. But he'd always held back out of pride. He didn't want her to come to him because of his damned assets. He wanted her to want him.

Images, scents, tastes of the night she'd come to his bed washed over him. He tried to never think of that night, but at moments of weakness, he was overcome with searing memory and burning humiliation. That she could love him like that, and then leave him. He welcomed the anger that knotted his jaw. Damn her, anyway. He shoved back from the desk and picked up his valise. The steamship left for New Orleans in half an hour. But he was not going in order to see Tansy. He was going to see Alain. And Musette and Rosa and Denis. Not Tansy. She'd made her choice.

He arrived in New Orleans on Christmas Eve and took a room at a hotel near Rampart overlooking Congo Square. Tomorrow the slaves would have a few hours off to dance to the drums and sing and celebrate. Maybe Musette would like to come down with him. They could drink rough rum and dance and forget for a while the white blood in their veins, the taint that removed them from their African ancestors and turned them into solid citizens.

No, what he hoped for was an afternoon with Alain.

He unpacked his valise. In the bottom, wrapped in his shirts, was the boat he'd carved from a block of balsa wood for Alain's Christmas present. After he'd proved it would float, he'd painted it red and blue with yellow port holes. Tomorrow, if the weather was good, he and Alain would launch it in the stream the other side of Congo Square.

Rosa had invited him to her Christmas Eve party, but Tansy might be there. He knocked on Musette's door instead to join her and their old friends in telling stories and playing music and dancing in her small parlor. After too many cups of rum punch, he said goodnight. A cold front had come through. The night was cold and clear. He decided to walk off the buzz in his head before he retired to his hotel room.

He could have stayed the night with Musette, he supposed. She'd kissed him goodnight with enough warmth to let him know he'd be welcome, but he'd seen the way Charles Mansard had watched her through the evening. Charles was a good man, widowed more than a year now. If Musette had a chance to be happy with Charles, Christophe should get out of the way.

He walked across the Quarter till he was in front of Rosa's Academy. A single candle burned in Rosa's upstairs window. The party was over, then. He thought about climbing the stairs. Rosa would give him a glass of wine and tell him to put his feet up. He'd had enough wine and he wasn't fit company. He'd see Rosa tomorrow when he could bring the book of John Donne's poems he'd found for her.

He walked past taverns whose yellow light and raucous celebrations spilled onto the pavement. Cats scurried in the shadows after rats; otherwise, the streets were quiet. He paused across from Tansy's cottage. Candlelight seeped through the shutter at her bedroom window. Was she alone? It was late. Surely on Christmas Eve Valcourt would be home with his wife, would have to get up early for Mass. But what if she shared her bed with someone else? Bile rose in his throat at the thought. All those years she'd been with Valcourt, if she should now betray him with yet another man. His step faltered. Betrayal? Yes, it would be betrayal. He had not imagined that she cared for him. She had branded him with the heat of her body and the need in her heart the night she came to him. If she could do that to him, then take another man, he would — what would he do? He would have to leave Louisiana. He would go to France. Paris, or Lyon. Or maybe he'd sail to Indonesia or North Africa.

He returned to the hotel, suspicion gnawing at him. She was a changed woman, Rosa had written. Maybe she wasn't Tansy anymore. Maybe she'd turned hard, having to fend for herself. Maybe she did what so many former placées did, taking lovers as they pleased.

He wiped his hand over his face. He'd conjured up this phantom lover from nothing. He had no evidence, no reason to think she had taken up with a new man. It shocked him, how painful the thought was. He really didn't think he could bear it.

"Stop it." He'd said it aloud, he realized, his voice harsh and desperate. He lit the candle by the bed and opened up Rosa's volume of poems. He'd read John Donne until he could sleep.

Christmas morning, Alain bounced onto her bed. "Get up, Maman. Christophe is coming today!"

"Today?" She pushed the hair out of her face.

"He promised. How many months until Christmas, he said, and I counted August, September, October, November, Christmas!"

"But he may not mean Christmas day, darling. He might mean tomorrow or the next day." Why couldn't he have written her when he was coming? He must know Alain would be waiting for him. And why couldn't he have written her anyway? She could hardly write to him first. If he'd just sent her a few lines, inquiring about Alain, for instance, she could have written back. She could have told him about school, maybe hinted that she was no longer tied to Valere. Would she be so brazen? He'd think she was telling him to come get her.

Well, that's what it would mean, wouldn't it? Valere is gone. No man here. Come get me. Impossible. He'd think she just wanted a man, any man, to take care of her like Valere had done. She certainly did not mean any such thing. If that's what he thought, he could just keep himself in Baton Rouge. She didn't need Valere or him, either. And how was she supposed to plan the day with Alain expecting him to appear at any moment?

When Alain heard a knock at the door, he flew off the bed. Tansy heard him unlatch the front door and fling it open. Lord, what if it really were Christophe and she not yet dressed, her hair a fright? No glad shout came from the front room. She let out a breath of relief.

"Good morning, Grand-mère." Maman had come by? She had not seen her since they quarreled over Valere. Well, Christmas Day was a good time for reconciliation. She hurriedly put her wrapper on and tied her hair back. Estelle appeared at the bedroom door.

"I thought we'd go to Mass together."

Tansy took in the stiff shoulders and carefully blank face. Maman was unsure of her welcome for the first time in her life? She walked over and kissed her mother's cheek and was rewarded with a quick, hard hug.

At the hint of wetness in her mother's eye, Tansy kissed her again. "That would be lovely. If you'll help Alain dress, I'll put myself together. Do we have time for coffee?"

"I'll make it." Estelle cleared her throat. "Dress for a cold day."

They walked to the St. Louis Cathedral, the bells calling everyone to mass. After a half hour of elbow to elbow, knee to knee worship, they emerged into the sunshine.

"Martine and Frederick are having us to lunch, Maman. Won't you come with us? You'll be welcome."

"No, I can't. Monsieur Girard is taking me to Antoine's for a champagne brunch." She hesitated, and Tansy wondered if she saw a slight blush in her mother's cheek. "We're celebrating our ... understanding."

"He's spoken for you?"

"Yes. I must admit, I made him a good deal. I'm not so young, after all, and I rather like him."

Tansy laughed. "So you made him 'a good deal'? You must like him very much indeed." She kissed her cheek. "I'm happy for you, Maman. And for Monsieur Girard."

Estelle glanced at Alain whose attention was fixed on a puppy squirming in a little girl's arms. "Part of our agreement, Tansy, was about you. He will pay for your subscription to the balls for as long as you remain in need of a protector."

Tansy's shoulders dropped. She let out a long breath. "Maman. Do you not see? I am not in need of a protector."

Estelle briskly rearranged the strings of the reticule hanging from her arm. "Yes, well. For as long as you like, then." She pecked Alain on the top of his head. "Good morning to you. I shall come by later in the week."

Tansy watched her mother walk quickly through the crowd exiting the cathedral, on to her new patron. Maman did not understand, not yet, but at least she had reentered her life. For that she would say an extra rosary of thanks.

They had a festive lunch with Tansy and Frederick. Cuban coffee, coconut cakes, ham, sweet potato pie, and fresh asparagus. Alain had opened Frederick's present first and ate with his six new cannon arrayed around his plate, three for the British, three for the French.

 Martine sat close enough to hold Frederick's hand while she sipped her coffee. Tansy had never seen her look lovelier. "This afternoon," Martine said, "we're going — " She took a sharp breath. "Oh." She turned rounded eyes on Frederick. "Oh, I felt it again."

She took Frederick's hand and placed it over her abdomen. "Feel it?"

Frederick grinned like a boy. "I feel it."

"Alain," Martine called, "come here." She held his hand against her belly and waited. "There. Did you feel it?"

Alain frowned. "What's wrong with you?"

Martine smiled at him. "There's a baby growing inside me. A girl or a boy for you to play with someday."

"Well, if it's a boy, we can play. But I don't play with girls."

Frederick mussed his hair. "We'll see about that. Come on, let's blow up some hillsides with those cannon."

After an hour of sitting like a coiled spring, Tansy wished Martine and Frederick a happy Christmas and took Alain home. She checked whether Christophe had left a note on the front door. He had not. Determinedly, she set out her bobbins and worked at lace making. Alain played happily with his cannon, interrupting the quiet with eruptions and explosions and loud shrieks of missiles flying through the air. Under the sounds of war, the clock ticked on.

When the knock came, Alain instantly stilled. He looked at Tansy, then rushed for the door and threw it open. "I knew you'd come!" He threw himself in Christophe's arms and buried his face in his chest.

Tansy blinked her eyes dry and rose with all the control she possessed. If she didn't keep herself in check, she'd throw herself into his arms just as Alain had. Her face wooden, she forced a smile and welcomed Christophe into her home.

Christophe dropped the package and caught Alain up, hugging him and laughing with him. "Of course I've come. I promised you I would, didn't I?"

"Happy Christmas, Christophe." Tansy stood six feet away, still as a statue except for hands twisting around each other. "It's been a lovely day, hasn't it? Cold, but sunny. A good day for Christmas. It should be cold for Christmas, after all. December should be cold."

He scooped up the package, carried Alain inside and closed the door. Then he turned to Tansy. She did not reach out her hand in greeting nor take a step closer. "Happy Christmas to you," he answered.

She had lost weight, her face thinner, her gown looser. But her skin still suggested rich cream, and her gaze was still direct from dark, luminous eyes. She clasped her hands before her in a tight wad. She was tense. He tried to swallow the disappointment rising in his throat. She wasn't glad to see him.

"Come sit down," she said. "I have wine punch. Oh, you need a glass. I'll get you a glass. For the punch."

He'd never seen her like this, unnerved and babbling. "Thank you." Uncomfortable at her discomfort, he carried Alain with him to the sofa and eased down. Tansy left them, to get the punch, and he shifted Alain in his lap.

"Let's have a look. I've heard of boys growing a foot in a few months." He ran his fingers through Alain's hair. "But I don't see any sign of another foot."

Alain grinned and held his thumb and forefinger an inch apart. "I grew this much."

Christophe squeezed Alain's biceps. "And you're twice as strong as the last time I saw you. How tall do you plan to grow?" He noticed a neatly sewn patch on Christophe's knee. Never before had he seen Alain in anything but well-tailored, pristine clothes. Tansy had indeed changed.

"Tall as you!" Alain threw his arm up as high as he could reach, knocking the humidor at his elbow. His father's humidor, Christophe knew. Filled now not with cigars but overflowing with thread and bobbins and a pair of scissors. Valcourt truly did not come here anymore. Then why was she so ill at ease?

He glanced up to see her standing in the doorway, the glass of punch in her hand, staring at him. She advanced to him quickly, her hand outstretched to give him the glass. He held his hand out, she moved to set the glass on the table, then as he dropped his hand she held it out again for him to take it.

She sat across from him, heels together, hands in her lap. She hadn't brought a glass for herself. "Did you have a good trip down?"

"Yes. A cold wind on deck, but sunny. Look, Tansy, if you're expecting someone, I can come back later."

She looked up at him, startled. "No. No, I'm not expecting anyone."

He nodded. "All right." He handed Alain his present. "What do you think I've brought you?"

Alain eyed the package, then hefted it in his hands. "It's not a book."

"No, not a book."

"It's not blocks. Or soldiers. It's not a ball. What is it?"

"Open it."

Alain tore at the paper and then drew in a sharp breath. "A boat! Look, Maman, a real boat."

"If your mother says it's okay, we'll take her down to the stream and see how she floats."

"Can we, Maman?"

"Of course."

"You'll need your coat and a hat, Alain." Christophe said.

Alain went for his things, and they were alone together. Her eyes were wide, unblinking. What was she thinking behind that blank stare?

"I walked by last night. I saw your candlelight through the window."

"You didn't stop in."

"It was late. I thought you might — I thought you might be entertaining."

She drew her brows together. "Rosa didn't tell you? Valere doesn't come here anymore."

"You're free then."

Her breath hitched. "Yes. I am free."

He swallowed once. "You haven't taken a new lover?"

As if he'd thrown warm water on her icy coating, she felt her face crack. "A new lover?" The tension drained right out of her and in flowed white hot indignation. "All these nights I've sat in this very room, wondering what you're doing, who you're with, and you ask if I have a lover?"

She paced away, then whirled back to face him. She wanted to slap him. She wanted to grab him and shake him. "Well, what if I do have a lover? I can do as I please, can't I? I make my own way, just as much as your seamstress ever did." She faced him with her hands on her hips. "Maybe I will take a new lover."

In slow increments, his lips turned up, his eyes lit.

"What are you grinning at?"

Slowly he rose from the sofa. He stepped toward her, towering over her, that damned grin on his face.

"You wondered what I was doing, who I was with?"

She effected an elaborate shrug. "Maybe it crossed my mind. Once."

"I wondered what you were doing, who you were with, every day. Every night."

She breathed out, trying to manage a shrug and an indifferent tilt of the head at the same time.

He stepped so close her skirt touched the toe of his boots. His hands stroked up her arms to rest on her shoulders.

She crossed her arms. "I am very mad," she managed.

Soothingly, he crooned into her ear. "I can see you are. Very mad." His lips drifted over her neck.

She held herself still. She didn't know whether to grab him or run, whether to cry or laugh.

"I'm sorry I made you mad." He whispered his lips across hers. "Will you forgive me?"

Suddenly it was too much. She grabbed him around the neck and held on. He enveloped her in his arms, one hand gently pressing her face into his neck. How she'd yearned for this man, missed him, dreamed of him. Regret had nearly swallowed her whole, and now he held her close, his breath on her neck, his lips brushing her ear.

"I buttoned my coat by myself. Let's go," Alain said.

"Just a minute," Christophe said. "I need to hug your maman a little longer."

She shuddered, getting her breath under control. Alain plopped himself on the sofa and examined his boat. "The lanterns are lit inside. That's why the windows are yellow."

"Uh huh." Christophe thumbed the tears off Tansy's face. She placed her hands on his wrist and tried to smile at him. He kissed her softly, briefly. "Let's go sail that boat."

Tansy packed extra pants for Alain in her shopping bag. They were going to a stream, after all. He would surely get wet. She added a shirt and sweater to the bag, all the while a silly grin on her face, the feeling of floating on clouds just beneath the ordinariness of packing extra socks.

They walked on either side of Alain, holding his hands, listening to him chatter, very little to say themselves. Once they were at the stream, Tansy sat on a blanket in a spot of sunshine while Christophe and Alain launched the boat into the current and then cheered. It floated like a cork. They raced it against a floating leaf, then a floating twig. They rescued it from a stand of cattails and tugged it along by its string.

Christophe joined Tansy on the blanket. He took her hand in his. His thumb was calloused, his fingers warm. She gripped his hand and held on tight. Nothing ever had felt so right, the two of them connected, wordless, as they watched Alain play.

They dried Alain off and headed home. Christophe bought them cones of fresh boiled shrimp to take home for supper. She hadn't asked him to stay, he didn't need her to.

As dark fell, they ate their shrimp. When Alain introduced Christophe to General Ney, Tansy watched Christophe's hands as he stroked the cat. Every move he'd made all afternoon had captured her, every expression on his face had captivated. She wanted him, and she could have him. No more obstacles, no more mistaken loyalties to keep them apart.

Alain fell asleep on the sofa and Christophe put him to bed, gently pulling the covers up to his chin. Tansy stood in the doorway watching as Christophe smoothed the hair from Alain's face and kissed him.

He rose and followed her from the room, quietly closing Alain's door. There were only the two of them now. No need to talk of cats and sailing boats.

"Do you want coffee?"

He shook his head. "What do you want, Tansy?"

Her breath quickened at the look in his eye. She wanted him to love her the way he had that night at his cottage. She looked into his eyes. "I want you."

She kissed him. When he didn't respond, she tipped her head back.

"How? How do you want me?"

She nibbled his bottom lip, teasing him. "On the bed. Under the bed. In the kitchen."

He took her arms and held her away. "Tansy. What do you want from me?"

"What do you mean?"

He stepped back, his face darkening. "I don't want a Christmas fuck."

She cringed at the hardness in his eyes. "Christophe? I don't … What do you want?"

"You. Alain. The three of us belonging to each other. I want it all."

She put a hand to her throat. "I don't need a man to take care of me, Christophe."

The skin creased around his mouth and between his eyes. She saw him take a hard breath, trying to hold his anger in. "Did you ever think that marriage is more than a financial contract? I'm not one of your mother's clients, for God's sake."

She stared at him, terrified he would storm out and leave her alone, aching for him, twisting herself in knots wondering what she should have done. "I know that. It's just that, for so long, I was only Valere's woman. I am my own now, Christophe." She took a step toward him, her arms raised. "Christophe, I … " She reached for him, but he grabbed her wrists.

His voice was very quiet. "You don't know the difference between belonging and possession, Tansy. I would no more own you than you would own me."

He kissed her then, hard and urgent. She gripped his lapel with one hand to hold herself upright and grasped his hair with the other. His hand was at the back of her neck, the other pressing her waist against him. She leaned into him, her bones liquid and warm.

Abruptly, he broke the kiss and stepped back. "Figure it out, Tansy."

Stunned, she watched him find his hat and let himself out.

# Chapter Thirty

Between New Years and the middle of January, Tansy wrote three letters to Christophe. The first was angry and indignant, accusing him of being thick-headed, stubborn, and hateful. The second one was reasoned, calm, and logical. The third was abject pleading. She tore each of them into shreds and fed them to the fire. And then a letter came from him. He wrote about the book he'd just read and would send to her separately. He wrote about a student who had hilariously gotten into trouble with a pail of manure and a handful of matches. He wrote about the weather.

He had written nothing about his feelings for her, but she clutched it to her breast as if he had declared himself in a sonnet worthy of Shakespeare.

Winter rain, gloomy afternoons, none of it dispelled the joy that letter brought. It didn't matter what he wrote. The fact he'd written at all was the great gift. Hope added color to all the hours of the day. She answered, he wrote again. She collected little details of her day to write to him in the evenings. She never mentioned the penny counting, but proudly told him how she had herself climbed to the roof and pounded down a lose shingle with a borrowed hammer. Alain now knew how to draw all twenty-six letters, so she spelled out a short message for him to add to the bottom of her pages. Christophe included a note for him in his next letters.

For three months, he wooed her from a hundred miles upriver. For three months, she taught, she sold fruit tarts, she made lace, and she wrote letters on the levee for a quarter a piece. She accumulated a stash of extra coins in her velvet bag. She had more than only *now*. She had plans, expectations, and anticipations.

Inevitably, Nicolas Augustine accosted her on the street again. Leering, he purred at her. "Looking good, *ma petite*. You ready to taste my candy? I been saving it just for you." He leaned close and murmured in her ear. "We'll be so good together, Tansy Marie."

Her pulse did not race. Her heart did not flutter in fear. "You do not interest me, monsieur." She walked on past him, no urge to run or to barricade herself against the threat of what he offered. Within twenty paces, her mind moved on to other things.

And then in late March, Tansy received a very short note from Christophe. "I will arrive on Good Friday. I will want an answer then."

Five days he'd given her. As always when she was anxious, she scoured the cottage. Everything in its place, except that since the cat had rampaged through her closet, she deliberately let her shoes sit awry on their shelf. Good Friday, she dressed in her green velvet gown with her matching silk tignon. She dressed Alain in his best clothes, mended though they were, and spit polished his shoes one last time before she led him out the door. Two steamships were arriving from upriver today, one at two o'clock and another at four. They would meet the first, and if he were not on that one, then the second.

The wind was blustery, but warm. Flags waved from sailing masts, and sun glinted on the waves of the Mississippi. Stevedores called out to each other in an almost unintelligible creole. Alain hopped from foot to foot, excited at all the bustle, eager for Christophe's steam ship to paddle into town.

Christophe was not on the two o'clock boat. Tansy took Alain home for a tense hour and a half. Neither of them could concentrate on anything, not soldiers or lace making or books. What if she presumed too much? Maybe he wasn't ready for this? What if she'd waited too long? He might be coming to see them, but he might also be coming to — Oh she didn't know what. She'd planned this, she'd put the day's events in motion. She'd just have to believe in hope.

By three-thirty they were back on the levee watching the ships. Finally, at five minutes after four o'clock, a gaily painted ship in white with red trim blew its whistle, backed its paddlewheel, and eased into the dock. Passengers disembarked single file.

Christophe descended the plank, his eyes on his feet. By the time he reached the pier, Tansy and Alain were waiting at the end of the roped corridor. He grinned and held his arms out for Alain, who rushed under the rope and leapt on him.

Tansy scooted under the rope too to get at him so that they made a three-way hug. "Let's get out of this crowd," Christophe said and led them off the levee.

"We don't have much time," she said. "Let's cut up Toulouse Street."

Tansy took Christophe's valise so he could carry Alain, though his skinny legs had grown so long his feet dangled almost to Christophe's knees. Alain had many things he'd saved up to tell Christophe, starting with the squirrel General Ney had caught this morning. He kept Christophe so busy that when Tansy led them to the side of the cathedral, he stopped, surprised.

"What are we doing here?"

She smiled at him. "Come inside and you'll see."

The side door led into a dim corridor, quiet and cool. Tansy knocked on the door at the far end, paused for a moment, then opened it. Christophe followed her into Father McDougal's inner sanctum and stopped, open-mouthed. Tansy took his arm and squeezed it.

"You know everyone, of course."

Christophe's mother kissed his cheek. Tansy's mother kissed his cheek. Rosa followed with her own kiss. Denis shook his hand.

Martine said, "Give me the imp, Christophe," and reached for Alain. "You know Frederick DuMaine?"

Christophe and Frederick exchanged friendly nods. "How do you do?"

Musette stepped up to him and she too kissed his cheek. She winked at Tansy as her new husband Charles shook his hand.

Father McDougal emerged from the anteroom. "Ah, the bridegroom has arrived. Excellent."

Christophe looked hardly less stunned than when he'd entered the room. Tansy leaned into him and stood on tip-toe to whisper in his ear. "Will you marry me, Christophe?"

His beautiful eyes focused on her, only on her. The whole world was in those eyes. "I will," he said, and his smile lit every dark corner of doubt left in her.

Father McDougal led the party into the nave. Tansy and Christophe took their places at the altar, Alain between them, and the priest began the ceremony with all the reverence and holiness of sacred matrimony.

"In the eyes of God, I now pronounce you man and wife."

Tansy turned her face up to Christophe for his kiss. He first brushed her eyes with his lips and then lingered on her mouth.

"I love you," he murmured.

"And I love you."

They walked as if on parade down Royal Street and then up St. Phillip to Martine's cottage where a lavish supper awaited them. Tansy managed an oyster and a mouthful of cake, but she was too excited to eat. As soon as it was decent to leave the party, she kissed Alain good night and took Christophe home.

"Are you tired?" she asked. She fingered the knot of his cravat.

"Not a bit."

"You want to go to bed anyway?" She untied the knot.

"I could be persuaded."

"Ah. That's what I thought. I had to marry you to get you into bed." She crooked a finger at him. "Come this way."

Quietly, slowly, they undressed each other. They climbed into bed and for a moment, they simply held each other. Tansy broke first. "That's enough of the serious lovey stuff. Come here."

Christophe laughed and began the not so serious lovey stuff that went beyond soulful looks to the serious exercise of lips and hands and heat.

An hour later, the sheets damp and snarled at their feet, Tansy's hair tangled in his hands, Christophe rolled her on top of him. "Mrs. Desmarais. Do you feel owned?"

"No. Not owned. Just loved." And she kissed him.

## The End

# Bonus Section:
## Sample Chapters from Gretchen Craig's *Crimson Sky*

*With Gretchen Craig's meticulous attention to historical detail, Crimson Sky documents the clash of the two great civilizations. In 1598 when the Spanish come into the land, the puebloans fight for their faith, their culture, and their lives.*

Zia's world has been shattered by her husband's loss, by murderous marauders, and by drought. To save her child from starvation, she accepts the protection of a Spanish conquistador, but is the security he provides worth abandoning her religion, her culture, and her identity?

Diego Ortiz has yearned for a home and a family in this strange new land. When he meets a beautiful woman of the pueblos, he offers her not only protection for her child and herself, but also his everlasting love.

TapanAshka, left for dead after an ambush in the forest, challenges death itself to achieve his two heart's desires, returning to Zia, and exacting revenge against his greatest enemy, the Spaniard Diego Ortiz.

~ ~ ~

What **reviewers** are saying about *Crimson Sky*:

"Craig's historical research is excellent, but I'm more impressed with how quickly and thoroughly this author immerses the reader in an ancient culture. Not since Clan of the Cave Bear have I seen this happened as masterfully as it does in Crimson Sky."

- - KB, the storiologist

"It has been years since I've read historical fiction this good. Margaret George, eat your heart out. If powerful storytelling is your thing, if factual research is your thing, if three dimensional characters, both primary and secondary is your thing, if great story structure with interwoven sub-plots and few if any holes is your thing, then Crimson Sky is certainly worth your time. Ms. Craig shows such an in-depth portrayal of this culture, that I feel like I've been living with them this past week. My heart has been torn out, put back, torn out again. She portrayed both the Native Americans and the Spaniards as humans, inherently weak, yet with an inner strength to survive."

-- **Anne Conley**

# CRIMSON SKY

## Chapter One

### The Attack

    Zia cuddled her baby close against the autumn chill, his sweet breath warming her cheek. In the dark, she curled his tiny hand around her finger and nuzzled his soft black hair. With the men of the village following the elk, the bear, and the deer to replenish the scant stores of food for the winter, TyoPe comforted her in the long nights when she worried about her husband.

    Even as a very young hunter, TapanAshka had killed bear and mountain lion and had said the prayers to their spirits, yet it could be the next bear he hunted might turn on him with claws and teeth, or the mountain lion he tracked might circle round and come on him from behind.

    Sleepless, Zia gazed at the stars visible through the open hatch in her ceiling. So many, and Zia took comfort that each star was perhaps a spirit who watched over her from on high. Surely those same star spirits protected TapanAshka at his campsite, in his sleeping robe so many days journey from home.

    Out in the night, a dog yelped furiously, and then — silence. A tingle of unease crept up Zia's spine. Fastening her gaze on the night sky through the hatchway, she strained to hear, to see.

    Overhead, a faint scraping, then footsteps. She sat up, every muscle tensed. With the men away on the hunt, no one should be out this late. She concealed TyoPe in the blankets and lit a torch, the blood thrumming in her ears.

    As she stepped toward the ladder, a black-streaked face thrust through the hatchway, grinning and leering at her. Fear surging through her, Zia lunged for the ladder to shove it aside, but already hard brown feet slid down its sides.

Snarling, Zia dropped the torch and launched her weight onto the intruder's back. She clamped her teeth on his ear, she clawed her nails over his bare skin. With a great howl, the man whirled, but she held on, tasting his blood in her mouth, feeling it well up under her fingers. He thrashed around the room, trying to shake her off, turning over baskets and jars, casting grotesque shadows against the wall. In a wild attempt to free himself, the marauder rammed Zia against the ladder.

The air knocked out of her, she lost her grip and fell to the floor. Though starved for breath, her only thought was to save TyoPe. If she could reach the torch, she could thrust it into the devil's face, chase him up the ladder. Struggling to breathe, she stretched her arm toward the fallen torch. Her fingers only inches from the prize, the raider grabbed her by the hair, hauled her upright, and smashed his fist into her jaw.

Zia awoke with a cool cloth pressed against her swollen face. By morning's first light, her glazed eyes took in the upturned baskets, the broken pottery. She jolted up, pain searing through her jaw. "TyoPe!"

"Rest easy," Grandmother said and pressed her back down. "You see, he is well."

Zia opened her arms for her swaddled babe and pressed her face against his soft hair. TyoPe was safe. Nothing else mattered. In a moment, she would say the prayers of thanksgiving to Sanatyaya, but for now she wanted only to breathe in the sweet scent of her little one.

Zia remembered her sister. "HaNah, the boys?"

"Your sister and her babies are unharmed. How badly are you hurt?"

Zia touched her swollen jaw, throbbing yet strangely numb. "I will be well, Grandmother. What of the others?"

"Bring the child. You will see."

As she rose, Zia's head spun from nausea and pain. She steadied herself, then tied TyoPe in a sling around her neck to climb the ladder.

In the open air, broken pottery littered the terraces. Splashes of blood stained the adobe where a grandfather or a daughter had defied the raiders' knives.

Zia followed Grandmother across the roofs and down the ladders. At her sister's doorway, HaNah's dog lay dead. Zia's throat tightened. Yesterday, Ring Eye had chased sticks, yipping in joy. Today ants dined on his blood.

At the sound of HaNah's whimpering, Zia hurried inside. Her sister held Little Cricket to her breast, nursing him. Little Turtle, the toddler, leaned against her shoulder. None of them showed a mark nor a bruise.

"HaNah, you are well. Your boys are well. Why do you cry?"

HaNah's shrill voice arrowed through the pain in Zia's head. "They took everything. We'll starve!"

Zia tamped down her impatience. "We will not starve. The men will return. We will have meat."

Zia's thoughts were on her friends now that she saw HaNah and the children were safe. She turned to go, but HaNah grabbed for the hem of her skirt.

"Don't leave me," HaNah cried.

Zia clamped her teeth together and blanched at the pain that shot through her jaw. She had no time for HaNah's moaning. For once, HaNah must comfort herself.

Zia crossed the terraces while all around her women wept. TyoPe's small weight over her heart anchored her as she paced over the roofs of the second level to her friend ChoTaye's room.

At the open hatchway, Zia's nostrils flared at the strong blood smell. She climbed down the ladder into the smoky dimness. ChoTaye rocked on her knees, her eyes closed, her scalp bleeding where she'd torn her hair. Her oldest son lay dead on the floor.

Zia's gaze tracked the blood that had flowed from the gaping wound in Long Arm's chest, down his arm, to the club beside his hand. Only in the last days, his voice had begun to crack, but he had died a man.

Zia sat beside her friend and wept with her. When others came to grieve with ChoTaye, Zia climbed from the dim chamber to see what had happened in the rest of the village. Women and children gathered in the square with their dead. The older boys and the grandfathers who'd stayed behind from the hunt had fought hard, but the Keres people of Kotyit were farmers, and neither their strength nor their skill had been equal to the raiders'.

The fallen were laid out on the stones. Zia sank to her knees. So many lost. How could it be the mockingbird sang in the pinon tree when grief lay like smoke over the village? Her gaze swept over Sees Far, who told funny stories, Big Nose, who made toys for the children. And here lay T'sina's daughter. All summer, the boys had followed her around the village, had dreamed of touching her shining hair, her full lips. She would have chosen her mate this winter. Zia felt each loss and for the moment forgot her own joy that TyoPe lived and raised her voice to keen with the other women.

When she could wail no more, Zia sought out Mitsa, the friend dearest to her heart. She was not near her grandfather who lay on the cold stones with the other fallen men. She was not among the mourners in the square.

"Where is Mitsa?"

"I haven't seen her."

Others looked over the bent heads gathered in the square. "I have not seen her all day," another said.

A fist grabbed Zia's heart. She called out, "Mitsa!" She searched through the village, her fear infecting the others. No one found Mitsa.

"They've taken her!" HaNah cried.

"You know what they'll do to her," Oneefa said quietly.

Zia's head dropped, weighed down. Mitsa in pain, defiled, frightened, and there was nothing she could do to save her.

The women sat in silent clusters, their faces slack, their senses numbed in defeat and fatigue. The Kotyits had expected no trouble. They'd had peace with the Tewas to the north for many years. The nomadic people of the plains had come to them in friendship to trade, to form ties. And so the hunters had left the village confident the grandfathers and a few stout men they left behind would protect their families from any stray wanderers. But someone had come in force, come to murder and thieve.

"They were Querechos," Oneefa said. "Did you see? Those wide, sharp cheekbones? Querechos."

"No," T'sina said. "When they came in the summer, they were friendly. I gave three gourds for their sunflower seeds."

"Sashue traded arrowheads for a buffalo hide," HaNah said. "They were good people."

Oneefa pointed a shaking finger toward the bodies they would soon bury. "They did this."

"But not the same Querechos who came to us when the crops were green and high. Maybe these were outcasts."

"Those Querechos knew we had food."

"No matter," Grandmother interrupted. "No matter now. Put your quarrel away."

For a time, no one spoke. They thought of what the raiders had taken with them. Food. All of Kotyit's food. Because of the drought, this year had brought another meager harvest. In the storerooms, where reserves of corn, squash, beans and nuts should have been, there were only the footprints of the thieves.

Zia pressed a hand to her forehead. She had not eaten this day, and her head ached, her jaw ached, her belly ached. What were they to do? Sees Far had been their leader while Hoshkanyi Nahia was away with the hunters, but his withered body lay on the stones. Someone, Zia thought, would have to organize them, to tell them what to do.

ShoHona! Zia thought. He would know what they should do next. Her second thought brought fresh pain. ShoHona must have been felled along with the other sentries or the raiders would not have been able to sneak into the village.

She raised herself and shifted TyoPe in her arms. "We must see to the sentries."

Grandmother stared at her from a face weathered into deep wrinkles, her eyes nearly hidden by their lids. "Wherever the Querechos left them, the crows are at work on their eyes."

"Grandmother, don't say it." Zia bent to hand TyoPe to Grandmother. The pain in her jaw shot down into her neck and shoulder, but she made no sign of it.

Oneefa touched her son's arm to rise. "Yako and I will come with you."

Kotyit lay on flat land along the river. Close by, the western mountains cast long shadows over the village. To the east, the plain stretched to purple and brown hills. The sentries had placed themselves where they could see across the valley, up the river, into the slopes, but last night, in the narrow moon's faint light, the raiders had gotten past them.

A trio of circling buzzards led them to Bear Foot and Two Fists. An undulating blanket of blue-black crows covered their bodies. Yako rushed at them, scattering them in a black squawking mass.

Though her gorge rose, Zia knelt to sprinkle sacred corn meal from the pouch at her waist and say a short prayer for their spirits' swift journey to Shipapu. Then, eyes averted, she and Oneefa covered the ravaged faces with their cloaks to spare them from the birds.

ShoHona, too, must be dead, his sightless eyes taken by the crows. Zia didn't want to see him that way, but his body must be tended, and his spirit needed their prayers.

They found him near the path leading from the river. The crows had not discovered him, but black flies buzzed over his body. In life, ShoHona had thrown a spear the farthest and shot an arrow the quickest. Now blackened, congealed blood covered the top of his head where once heavy black hair had grown. Zia put a hand to her mouth and swallowed bile.

Nearby, two marauders lay dead. Zia felt no pity that the ants crawled over their faces, into their mouths and noses.

"Look," Oneefa said, pointing to the tracks in the dirt.

Zia read the signs. "Four of them."

"It took four men to bring him down?" Yako said, reverence in his voice.

As before, Zia knelt to sprinkle the corn meal and say the first prayers to speed ShoHona's spirit on its way. She touched his chest and closed her eyes to say a silent good-bye.

Hope flared at the faintest rising under her hand. She put her cheek to his mouth and felt the stir of air.

"Oneefa, he's alive!"

She spoke his name and touched his lips to waken him, but not even his eyelid flickered in response.

"We'll take him to Grandmother," Zia said. "She'll know what to do."

They staggered into the village dragging ShoHona's heels in the dirt. The women circled and gawped at the terrible wound on his head.

HaNah, surprising all who knew her, said, "I have a fire. Bring him to me."

Her doorway was in the lower wall instead of the roof, and her rooms faced the morning sun. They stretched ShoHona's length in front of the hearth.

Zia looked for other wounds. Surely men did not lie deathlike from being scalped. When she washed the blood from his face and head, she discovered a purple knot where the murderer's club had smashed into his skull.

Under Grandmother's eye, she cleaned the massive wound and applied a poultice of pounded yarrow root and ash. She wet his lips with cool water, then squeezed drops onto his tongue. He was unconscious, but he swallowed.

"You have corn meal for the spirits?" Zia asked her sister.

"My children have cried all day from empty bellies, but I have not fed them the holy meal."

Grandmother nodded. "You did right, HaNah."

Zia sat back on her heels. "We should do the healing ceremony for ShoHona."

HaNah turned swollen, distrustful eyes on her sister. "We should wait for the shaman to come home."

"ShoHona needs the spirits' help now."

"We are not shamans, Zia. What if we anger Payatyama?"

Grandmother spoke, and it was final. "We are Keres women. The spirits will hear us."

Zia brought two eagle feathers from the kiva. Grandmother brushed them down ShoHona's body and up again. Gently, she whispered them across his great wound. HaNah leaned in to speak in Zia's ear. "What if she does it wrong?"

"She won't do it wrong."

Grandmother held the feathers firmly in her right hand and then struck them into her left palm, dislodging the evil she'd extracted from ShoHona's body. She shook the feathers to the north, west, south, east, above and below, scattering evil until its strength had no direction.

Zia held a corn-ear blessed by their great shaman Tyame Tihua before he left on the hunt. She breathed on it and passed it to HaNah and then to Grandmother to do the same.

"Our Mother sends you breath," Grandmother intoned. "She sends you life. She sends you health. The Mother has breathed through us. Now we give her breath to you."

Grandmother held the corn to ShoHona's mouth. "Take this breath, ShoHona. Know that the Mother of Us All holds you in her heart."

ShoHona yet lay as if dead. Not a finger twitched, not an eyelid quivered. But his mighty chest rose and fell with the Mother's breath.

Murmuring the prayers four times, Zia, HaNah, and Grandmother sprinkled corn meal in each direction, then over

ShoHona's body. Each of them made a new prayer cross of two sticks and tied turkey feathers to it. They placed the crosses on the floor, braced with pebbles to keep them upright.

They'd done all they could do. They left him by the fire to attend the burials of their friends.

The women had dug graves in the soil down river from Kotyit. They had opened the slack jaws of the dead and placed a pinch of sacred corn meal in each mouth. Zia helped fold the lifeless bodies into a sitting position in their graves. The women then placed pots and baskets and treasured pieces around the dead. They sprinkled meal and four times recited the prayers for departed spirits. And it was done.

Zia's empty belly clenched. Her jaw throbbed. The drone of the chanted prayers and the smell of fresh-dug earth, of blood and death, made her dizzy. TyoPe in one arm, she helped Grandmother walk back into the village.

The sun sank below the hills. TyoPe held tight in her shawl, Zia climbed down the ladder into her own room.

She hadn't returned to her home since the early morning. Exhaustion weighing her down, she looked at the bedding where she should have lain down with TapanAshka. She yearned to wrap her arms around him and bury her face against his chest.

Her gaze roamed over the broken baskets and pottery. For comfort, her fingers sought the turquoise stone TapanAshka had tied around her neck before he left. Gone. She hadn't realized. She wept as if the lost stone were the keenest of all her griefs.

TyoPe nuzzled her breast, and she opened her dress to him. "Don't fret," she whispered. "Your father will come. All will be well."

She sat with her babe near the smoky fire and watched the flames cast shadows on the floor. She ignored her hunger and the pain in her jaw. Instead she worried about tomorrow.

Zia had nursed her son during the day, but she'd had only water herself. How long could she feed TyoPe if she didn't eat?

# Chapter Two

## Hunger

Zia woke to the familiar whistle of a quail. *Ka-loi-kee, ka-loi-kee*. She was instantly alert, and hungry. Not like the hunger after a day working in the fields. Not like the hunger that spiced a stew of venison and squash. She felt hollow and her head ached.

After she nestled TyoPe into the blankets to finish his sleep, she collected a handful of pot shards and kissed them, asking the spirits for a true aim. Then she climbed the ladder.

*Ka-loi-kee, ka-loi-kee.* She crept across the terrace to peer over the edge. She watched the brush where she'd seen quail only a few days before. She had ignored them then, her belly full of corn and beans.

The dry leaves of the creosote bush rustled. A quail waddled out from under the bush — a clear shot. She hurled the shard. Missed.

Startled, the quail bobbled down the path. She threw another chunk. The bird took flight and was gone.

"Any other morning, I would have laughed to see you trying to kill a bird with a piece of pottery." Oneefa shook her head. "What are we to do?"

The father spirit Payatyama cast his warm rays over the land, the brown hills to the west rose sharp against the cloudless blue sky, and the autumn air smelled of pine and smoke. Zia breathed in, breathed out. Though she was hungry and her jaw ached, she was alive. TyoPe was unharmed. Grandmother was well. Youth, strength, and hope ran through her veins. Today she would find food for herself and her family.

"We can fish. We can lay rabbit traps. We'll rake through the dead stalks. Are your boys awake?"

"It's hard to sleep when you're hungry. They'll come."

Zia fastened her hair to keep it out of the way. She fingered the hem of her dress, stiff with the blood of Two Fists. Washing it would have to wait. Food first. She tightened the knot of her dress at one shoulder, leaving the other bare, then tossed on her short cape, slung TyoPe in a shawl from her back, and she was ready.

Most of the fields were in lower ground where rain run-off could be channeled into irrigation ditches. Zia surveyed the sun-shriveled remains of the harvest. It didn't look promising. They would have fish, and meat when the men returned, wild greens and cacti, but corn is what kept their bodies warm through the long winter months.

With Oneefa and her boys, she covered the first field before the sun was high. Zia used a forked stick to sift through the dried corn stalks, hoping there would be ears, even loose kernels, on the ground beneath the dead leaves.

At the square they emptied their sacks onto the ground cover where others had brought their finds. The women gazed at the meager gleanings. Perhaps a bushel of beans and two of dwarfed corn, some gnawed by mice and rats.

"It'll never be enough," HaNah said.

"It's a start."

HaNah and Grandmother stayed behind to shuck the corn and shear the kernels from the cobs. Zia and the others made their way back to the fields where each corn stalk supported brittle bean vines and yellowed squash leaves.

Yako worked with Zia. A boy his age, she thought, ready for his first growth into manhood, he'd ache with the hunger in his gut. That he did not speak of it showed he already had stepped away from childhood.

They found a few overlooked pumpkins, misshapen and small. The vines hid late bean pods, and they gathered every one, no matter how stunted.

At home, Zia joined HaNah and Grandmother making corn meal. HaNah sat on her knees, leaning into the grinding stone and crushing the kernels against the stone basin. Grandmother took the coarse meal from HaNah to refine in her own basin. Though Grandmother had spent all the years of her long life grinding meal four or five hours a day, the effort taxed her. Zia knew from her pale face she must be as light-headed as she was.

HaNah scowled, her lip drooping in pout at the monotony of her labor. "If Sashue were here, at least the time would go faster."

Grandmother cocked an eyebrow at Zia, mischief in her eyes. "I too miss the company of Sashue's drum and flute," she said. "Your husband is worthless, but he amuses us."

"Sashue is not worthless," HaNah answered hotly. "No one appreciates how hard he works."

Zia shot of gleam of fun at Grandmother, knowing her sister would miss the double meaning of her words. "You're right, HaNah. No one appreciates Sashue as a man who works hard."

Zia had never liked Sashue, but he was TapanAshka's cousin, her sister's husband. He was part of the family, and so she hid her smile from HaNah.

The sun sinking behind the mountains, at last every household had enough ground corn to feed themselves the first meal of the day. Zia's headache disappeared as she ate a flat corn cake and a watery bowl of rabbit stew flavored with wild green onion and bittersweet juniper berries.

HaNah poked at her stew. "I hate juniper berries."

For Grandmother's sake, Zia spoke with a cheer she didn't feel. "If the birds and bears haven't eaten them all, we'll find blackberries tomorrow."

In dry years like this, the vines were stingy with fruit. They would find enough to feed them for a week, maybe two. But through the whole winter? Zia didn't see how the parched land would feed so many with so little in the store rooms. How long would it be before TapanAshka and the other hunters returned with meat?

From her own gourd, HaNah sopped up bits of rabbit with a flat corn cake and put the bread in Little Turtle's hand.

"No, HaNah. Your body feeds the baby." Grandmother put her own bowl between her grandson's folded legs. "I am old. I don't need so much."

HaNah bent over Grandmother's hand and breathed on it. "Grandmother, thank you for feeding my son."

Zia held her tongue. Perhaps, if Little Turtle were hers, she would have done the same. But she would not see Grandmother go hungry while there was food in her own bowl. She poured meat and broth into the old woman's dish.

"Eat, Grandmother. We will have enough for everyone. I promise."

Grandmother shook her head. "Zia, you make an empty promise. Have you not heard your elders tell of hungry years? Sometimes, there is not enough."

"Please, Grandmother. Eat."

Grandmother took a bite, then handed the bowl back to Zia.

The fall wind whistled through the cracks of the hatchway that night. Zia woke chilled and achy. She thought of

Grandmother's feather blanket the raiders had taken. It had belonged to Grandmother's own mother, and many children had snuggled under it in winters past. Grandmother must have had a cold night in HaNah's rooms. Tonight, she would wrap her in her own cotton blanket.

With TyoPe on her back, Zia emerged into the new day. She closed her eyes, tilted her face to the sun, and said a silent prayer. For the Keres people, the days were full of communion with the spirits, with comfort and gratitude for their favor. Despite her hunger, Zia smiled as she repeated the prayer the fourth time. Perhaps, somewhere under this same sky, at this very moment, TapanAshka raised his face to the sun and prayed to Payatyama to lead him safely home.

Zia followed the southern path, a digging stick in her hand, intent on finding tubers that, dry and tasteless though they were, would feed them. Yako caught up to her and showed her his bow. "In case the raiders are still around."

She shifted TyoPe on her back and spoke with the respect a man deserves, even if he was a very young, very skinny man. "Thank you, Yako. I feel safer when you're with me."

Both of them hungry, they listed all the foods they might find this late in the season, if they were lucky. They knew the plants the people had eaten in past famines, plants that were left alone when food was plentiful, some so bitter they could be tolerated only by rolling them in white clay.

Zia and Yako had better fortune than that. They found six golden tomatillas still on the bush and a bramble of blackberries the bears had missed. With her digging stick, Zia harvested a patch of hard little wild tubers. She cut the thorns off prickly pears turned purple by the cold nights. Yako, to show his gratitude to the spirits, danced all around a yucca before he picked its half a dozen fruit.

Half a day's walk from the village, they climbed a low rise to gather pine nuts. In the lee of a boulder, they rested. Zia nursed

TyoPe, meeting his black, solemn gaze, letting his hand grip her finger. Once he was full and asleep, Zia stretched her weakened legs out. Already, she felt the lack of food. Already her knees ached.

She said yet another prayer to the spirits, hoping for rain, for the return of the hunters, for a lazy rabbit to come her way. On the next mesa Zia spotted a column of dust kicked up by the wind. Above, a hawk rode the currents, gliding effortlessly in the clear air. When she shifted her gaze back across the valley, the dusty spiral still smudged the sky.

Smoke.

Her heart thumping, Zia kept her voice steady. "Yako, what do you see?"

He followed her pointed finger. "Someone has made a fire with green wood."

"But who? The Tewa village is over there." She pointed far to the right of the smoke plume.

Yako leapt up. "It's my father. It's the hunters."

"No, Yako." Zia pulled him down beside her. "Our hunters will come from the south and west, and that is north."

"So whose fire is it?"

Zia watched understanding grow in Yako's eyes.

"It might be them. The Querechos. With our food!"

For the first time in days, Zia felt Payatyama's rays penetrate her chest and chase away the darkness around her heart. "And maybe Mitsa is with them, alive."

"What if it is them?" Yako asked, the joy drained from his voice. "Will they come back again?"

Zia shook her head. "There's nothing left for them here. Unless they want prisoners to trade to the Navahos. But prisoners have to be fed."

She watched the smoke spiraling over the mesa. She forgot the pain in her knees, the ache in her belly. She guessed it was little more than a half day's hike from the village to the smoky campfire. If you were strong, and fast. They were less strong every day.

"Quick as the fox, Yako. Let's tell the others."

Back in the village, they told what they'd seen.

"It's only the Tewas, out on a hunt," T'sina said.

"Or the cursed Querechos, cooking our beans over their fire."

"I hope the beans swell in their bellies until they burst."

"Well, what if it is them?" HaNah said. "Even if Zia did see the raiders, we're just as hungry now as we were before we knew they were so close. And we'll be just as hungry tomorrow."

HaNah pointed her finger at Zia as if she were the cause of their troubles. "And if it is the raiders, they'll come back." With every word, her voice rose in pitch until it was a thin piping. "They'll kill the children and take the women."

Many women heard HaNah and took up the same lament.

Moaning would not help them. Zia raised her voice to be heard. "The snows will come soon, and it will be too difficult to travel with captives. Nor will they have extra food for slaves."

As usual, HaNah wouldn't listen. She wept and held her young ones to her breast. Zia sensed a few of the other women were close to panic as well, their mouths turned down, their eyes rounded with fear.

Zia's headache pounded, her jaw throbbed, and her stomach felt as though it churned on gravel. What little the women had fished or scavenged so far was enough for one small meal a day, but there would be less and less to find as they searched farther and more thoroughly.

She could stand the hunger. But if she didn't have enough to eat, her milk would dry up, and TyoPe would go hungry. That Zia would not allow. They had to get their food stores back.

The sun was going down. The wind dropped. Zia stood on the low wall around the square, her face showing little of the fear curling in her belly.

"Our husbands will not be back before the moon is full." She looked into the eyes of every mother. "Our children must have food now."

The women spoke among themselves. She waited, knowing the answer to their problem was going to frighten them.

"We have to go after our corn," she said.

HaNah's shrill voice was the loudest. "We're women, not warriors!"

"They'll kill us!"

"No men. No weapons. How can we fight the marauders?"

Zia reminded them, "They have our corn. Our beans. Our squash. The fields are bare. Winter is coming."

Again she looked at her neighbors and spoke quietly. "Mitsa may still be alive."

T'sina shook her head. "No. By now, she's dead."

"The men will bring back deer, elk, even a bear," ChoTaye argued. "We'll have meat, fat meat, for the winter."

But not soon enough. Zia imagined TyoPe crying, his belly empty, and herself helpless as he grew weaker and weaker. It must not happen.

"The hunters will not return in time," she said. Her calm certainty swayed some of the women.

Oneefa stood. "Zia is right. The children, our grandmothers — they can't wait for the men."

HaNah jumped to her feet. "We are not warriors!" In a voice quavering with panic, she shouted, "We are not men! If we go after them, they'll kill us."

No one missed her husband at that moment more than Zia did, but she straightened her back to project a confidence she didn't feel.

"If our husbands were here, they would sharpen their knives, harden their arrow shafts in the fire, and paint their faces. The shaman would lead them in the dance to please the spirits, to ask them for protection and courage." Zia looked into dark, frightened eyes. "We women could stay safe at home, tending to our babies. The men would go after the thieving renegades. The men would bring the food back.

"But our husbands are far away. We cannot wait."

Some of the women kept their eyes on their laps, timid and afraid. Yet a few met her gaze, their eyes shining with the same determination coursing through her veins. They would not see their children starve.

Deep in her chest, Zia felt the fear thumping and jumping. But she would do this thing. For TyoPe.

"We'll leave at first light."

*You have been reading the first chapters of Gretchen Craig's novel,* Crimson Sky. *Available on Amazon in paperback and Kindle.*

# ABOUT THE AUTHOR

Gretchen Craig's award-winning novels, rich in memorable characters and historical detail, are profiled on her website at **www.gretchencraig.com**.

Further details are available at her Amazon Author Page at **amazon.com/author/gretchencraig**. Gretchen also invites you to visit her blog at **glcraig.wordpress.com**.

Made in the USA
Columbia, SC
20 July 2020